"WHERE IS THE STONE?"

"Gone," Herrak moaned from behind his rotting fingers. "The mirror took it."

"What mirror?" Darvish rubbed his face. It was very hot in Herrak's hidey-hole.

Aaron pointed to a three-foot oval that was almost hidden by Herrak's bulk. It was a black mirror, its surface absolutely nonreflecting.

With the edge of his sword at Herrak's throat, Darvish breathed the question onto the fat man's face. "Where. Is. The. Stone?"

"The wizard has it. He came to the mirror, said he would trade me a thousand precious things for The Stone of Ischia. A thousand for one! He sent the thief through the mirror last night." Herrak gasped from the pain in his magic-rotted body. "I had The Stone just before dawn. I passed it through the mirror. I held it." Herrak's fingers were black to the second joint now.

The Stone, the heart of Ischia, was gone.

"The wizard," Darvish grabbed Herrak and shook him viciously, "where is he?"

"In the mirror!"

"Where is the other end of the mirror?"

"I don't know!" Herrak wailed.

His anger suddenly drained, Darvish let the fat man go. That was the end of it then—Ischia was doomed. . . .

THE
FIRE'S STONE

TANYA HUFF

DAW BOOKS, INC.
DONALD A. WOLLHEIM, PUBLISHER

375 Hudson Street, New York, NY 10014

First Printing, October 1990

1 2 3 4 5 6 7 8 9

PRINTED IN THE U.S.A.

For Uncle Albert, who knows what family means.

One

When the procession reached the edge of the volcano, the thief abandoned all dignity and began to scream. The priests ignored her, allowing her terror to bury the droning of prayers. The crowd, packed onto the platforms that hung over the crater, murmured in satisfaction; it was, after all, her terror they had come to hear.

"They say she actually got her hands on The Stone." The pudgy merchant dabbed at his ruddy forehead with a scented cloth. The heat of the sun above, combined with the rising waves of heat from the molten rock below, had driven the temperature in the viewing areas distressingly high. "They say she came closer than anyone has in the last twenty years."

"They say," repeated the young man, forced into proximity, and thus conversation, by the press of the crowd. His voice hovered between scorn and indifference. His gaze stayed on the stone. Red-gold, as large as a child's head, it sat enthroned on a golden spire that rose up out of the seething lava some thirty feet beneath the platforms. A captured fire burned in its heart, the dancing light promising mystery and power. The Stone kept Ischia, the royal city of Cisali, from vanishing under a flood of fire and ash, from choking in the sulfuric breath of a live volcano. *And they say the thief actually got her hands on it.* He applauded her skill if not her good sense.

The prayers ended.

The priests of the Fourth, their dull red robes like bloodstains against the rock, stepped back and two massive acolytes lifted the bound and writhing body into the cage.

A collective almost-moan rose from many of the spectators on the public platforms and the young man wondered if this execution was intended to be a religious occasion. The religion of the region, not only of Cisali but of the surrounding countries, operated on a number of complex levels involving both priests and wizards, secular and nonsecular rituals. The One Below—a type of mother goddess as near as the young man could determine—had borne nine sons, the Nine Above, and the Fourth—none of them had names—was the god of justice.

The screams took on a new intensity.

The young man's gaze flickered to the royal platform. Only the twins were present. The descent would be feet first, then, and slow. It was said in the city that the twins were also bound to the Fourth although they had never entered the priesthood and were certainly not wizards.

Justice. His lips twisted up off his teeth.

"You're, uh, not from the city." The merchant was definitely more interested in his neighbor now than in the day's event.

Ginger hair, cropped shorter than was currently fashionable, pale skin, sharp features, and a slight build marked said neighbor as an outlander. Amid the placid and pleasure loving city dwellers, his scowl and brittle intensity marked him just as surely. There were few outlanders in Ischia, certain policies of the king had been set up to discourage them from staying.

"Is this your first time watching The Lady?"

The young man merely grunted. He thought the local name for the volcano—or more specifically for the crater—ridiculous.

"Perhaps," the merchant wet his lips and reached out a tentative hand, "you would let me buy you a drink?"

"No." The hand was avoided; the young man radiating disgust.

The merchant shrugged, disappointed but philosophical—outlanders, who could fathom them—and again turned his attention to the crater.

Smoke rose from the thief's soft leather shoes.

Making his way down the terraces, slipping deftly between merrymakers, the young man considered the fate of thieves in the royal city. He hefted the weight of the merchant's purse, lifted almost without thinking as he'd left, and the corners of his narrow mouth quirked upward in what served him for a smile. Well, the man *had* offered to buy him a drink.

* * *

"Aaron!"

The outlander looked up. Pale fingers stopped playing in the contents of the merchant's purse. Brows, a lighter ginger than his hair, tufting thickly over the center of silver-gray eyes, rose.

"Don't waggle those demon wings at me, boy. That was the third time I called you. What keeps you so enthralled you ignore me in my own house?"

"I went up the mountain today. To see the drop."

The old woman on the couch snorted. "Disappointed you, did it?"

Aaron scowled, animation returning to his sharp features. "You don't know what you're talking about, Faharra." He shoved the purse deep in the pocket of his loose trousers.

"Oh, don't I?" Clawlike fingers plucked peevishly at the fringes of her silk shawl. "I still have my wits about me, boy. More wits than even you give me credit for." She tried a knowing laugh, but it turned to a fit of coughing that left her gasping for breath and glaring fiercely. "I see more than you suspect. Get me some wine." As Aaron moved to the small table by her couch, she snared the edge of his tunic. "Not that crap. My granddaughter has it so watered, I could wash with it. There's a flask of the good stuff in the trunk."

The trunk, a massive ebony box entirely too covered in ivory inlay, was locked. It took Aaron less than five heartbeats to deal with it.

"You'll kill yourself with this stuff one day," he remarked conversationally, handing her a full goblet.

"And who has more right?" Faharra drank deeply and licked withered lips. Although her hands shook with the tremors of age, she didn't spill a single drop of the wine. "For sixty-two years I was the best gem cutter in Ishchia." She took another swallow. "I cut the emerald that sits atop the royal staff. One huge stone it is and emeralds aren't easy to cut, let me tell you."

"You've told me," Aaron broke in, bored. He refilled her goblet until the deep red wine trembled just below the metal edge.

"And if you behave yourself, I'll tell you again."

She drank in silence for a moment while Aaron replaced the now empty flask and relocked the trunk. Let the granddaughter wonder. He wiped away the barely perceptible smudges his fingers had left on the ebony, then went and sat on the wide marble window ledge, gazing out over the tiny garden at the city beyond.

"You got sunburned," Faharra said at last. "Good thing you usually work at night."

Pale fingers touched a high cheekbone. He winced and his eyes rose to the red-gold light just barely visible over the rooftops of the upper city.

"Don't worry, lad." The old woman's voice was almost kind. "You'll get your flogging. They only drop those who try for The Stone."

Aaron's gaze snapped down from the mountain. Although his night vision was very good, the shifting shadows of dusk defeated him and he could barely see the ruin of the gem cutter amidst her shawls and blankets and pillows. His voice when it came was hardly his own. "What?"

"You think I don't know why you settled here, boy, after all your years of wandering?" Faharra rolled the rich summer taste of the wine around her mouth and decided. She was too old to continue dancing around Aaron's pain; her time was fast running out and unless he listened to her, she feared Aaron's was as well. She could see him very clearly, outlined against the evening sky. But then, she had always been able to see him clearly. "We flog our thieves to death. Flog them to death in the market square." Her mind wandered briefly back to the days in the market when her hands had been steady, her eye true, and her skill sought by kings. "Flog our thieves to death," she repeated, sliding back to the present. "But we have to catch them first."

The thief at the window might have been carved in stone, so still he sat.

"You're too good a thief, Aaron my lad. If you truly want your cousin's death, you're not going about it very well."

Faharra watched his face tighten and his jaw set and knew what ran through his mind. Only the memory of his cousin's death closed him up that tightly, shut him even further within himself than he usually was—and that was far indeed. She wanted . . . oh, she wanted many things: her youth, her skill, her patience, time. She saw Aaron as the last jewel she would ever cut. No, recut, for he was already a diamond, hard and brilliant but with a flaw deep in the many faceted heart of him.

Soon, someone or something would strike that flaw and

the young thief would shatter into a million tiny shards. Faharra intended to prevent that and she thanked the Nine Above and the One Below every day for the accident that had brought Aaron into her life; had brought meaning into her life just when she thought meaning had degenerated to bowel movements and watered wine.

The thief, who had slipped shadow silent over her window ledge, had no way of knowing she had fallen from her couch and rather than call her granddaughter—the patronizing bitch—had decided to spend the night on the floor. As comfortable a place as any, old bones ached on down as much as on tile.

Sidling along the couch, reaching for the tiny gold hourglass that stood on the table beside it, the thief had stepped on her.

"Watch where you step, you clumsy ox," she'd snapped. *"I didn't live this long to be a carpet for such as you."* Remembering, she smiled. Aaron's jaw had dropped and those wondrous eyebrows had risen, the perfect picture of surprise. And when she had refused to call the watch, surprise became, just for an instant, something else entirely—another emotion that passed too quickly for Faharra to define.

"I get few enough visitors as it is, boy. I'm not of a mind to have those I do get arrested."

He had lifted her back into bed, then sat on the window ledge while she talked at him—she in the darkness, he silhouetted against the night sky.

That first night, she recalled suddenly, was the first of the many times she had told him of the emerald. Well, nothing wrong with pride in a job well done.

As he finally readied to leave, she'd tossed him the hourglass.

"Take it, boy. I've no need to watch the sands of time run out."

He'd smiled then—a real smile, not the twisted expression that usually served—and as he disappeared she'd called out, "Come back!" She'd just realized the emotion that had followed surprise. Disappointment.

A thief disappointed that she hadn't called the watch?

That was the first question.

He came back. Not that night, but a week later she had

roused in the darkness to find him sitting on the window ledge.

Why had he returned?

That was the second question.

Faharra had soon found that her midnight visitor was more questions than answers. He clung to their developing friendship with an intensity that astonished her. He was young. He was passably attractive, in a sharp, outland sort of way. Why was he so desperate for companionship? Even thieves had friends. What made her safe when the rest of the world was kept at a distance.

Aaron had saved her from boredom, from loneliness, from lying alone and forgotten in the darkness. She would save him from himself. She chipped away at his shell of stone and night by night uncovered bits and pieces of his past, enough so she could ask further questions.

He had left home at barely fourteen. Why? He had chosen to become a thief, a profession he excelled at, true, but not one destined to provide a steady income, peace of mind, or a ripe old age. Why? She might be safe, but young women terrified him and young men were fiercely taboo. Why?

Actually, it took little digging to find that the taboo against young men was strictly cultural. In Aaron's homeland the soil was poor, the growing season short, and the neighbors likely to torch the crops at any real or imagined slight. Every child was another pair of hands and every pair of hands was desperately needed. Same sex pairs produced no children and same sex love went from being impractical, to being a crime, to blasphemy against god—a god Faharra felt held asinine ideas of what constituted blasphemy, and who in their right mind could believe there was only one god anyway?

Blasphemy was punished by fire.

Unfortunately, Aaron's religious instruction had been intense.

"*I was Clan Heir,*" Aaron had explained with a shrug, "*and Clan Chief rules both people and priests.*"

Perhaps. But Faharra watched him watching the crowds that passed outside her garden and wondered if, maybe, the priests thought they were saving him from the fire.

From Clan Heir to thief. Quite the fall. And more than just a thief. . . . Where others plodded, Aaron danced. Where others fell, he soared. How better to deny a father whose word was absolute law. Faharra had been pleased to run into that answer at last. Her own father had been the worst kind of horse's ass and she had been overjoyed when her strong-minded mother had finally divorced him. Her personal theory said that one father could do more to mess up a child's life than every mother in existence put together. She realized she was not entirely without bias on this matter, but that was all right; she blamed it on her father. What had Aaron's father done to turn his son so far from him and what he stood for?

Aaron's mother had died in childbirth.

Aaron felt—had been made to feel—responsible for her death. Was that what made Faharra safe as a friend? That she was too old to bear children? And Faharra added a hearty thank the Nine and One for that.

It took her ten months of poking and prodding and sifting tales to get to the one question that led to all the rest.

"Aaron, what happened to your cousin? What happened to Ruth?"

Aaron grew so still Faharra could almost see the stone she had spent long months chipping away reforming around him. He grew so still he might have become stone himself. When he finally spoke, his voice, in painful contrast, was almost matter-of-fact.

"My father had her flogged to death."

And then he disappeared; slid off the window ledge and into the night, carrying his own darkness with him.

In the tedious hours between Aaron's visits, Faharra had held his past up to the light, turned it, studied it, and knew she had all the answers but one. What had happened up in the northlands so many years ago that the pain still ruled Aaron's life?

"My father had her flogged to death."

That was the easy answer. It explained nothing more than why he'd finally settled in Ischia where thieves died under the lash. Looking for his cousin's death, he'd someday make the mistake that would guarantee it.

When he came back, the walls were thicker than ever.

Faharra knew the weak spot now, knew where to place her chisel and strike the blow, but she was afraid. *I'm all he has,* she told herself. *Can I destroy the walls without destroying him, too?* And in back of that . . . *He's all I have. I can't risk driving him away.*

"Selfish, selfish, old woman!"

"Crazy old woman," Aaron muttered.

Faharra started and realized she had spoke aloud. While she had lain, wrapped in memories, Aaron hadn't moved. It was full dark now, with no moon or stars to break the blackness, but she could still see him on the window ledge, a shadow against the shadow of the night. He swung his leg over the sill, balanced half in and half out of the room.

"Aaron." She grubbed among the things she had to say to him but couldn't hold one long enough to bring it clear. "Come tomorrow," she managed at last.

She felt his eyes on her; studying, weighing, knowing, she was sure, what she wanted to say. It was, after all, the only thing unsaid between them.

"All right." A long pause, as though he were examining his words. "Tomorrow." Then he was gone.

Faharra drank the last dregs of wine in the goblet and sighed. If he returned tomorrow then maybe, just maybe, he was ready to admit to the pain that made his choices for him. And maybe, just maybe, she would have time to cut this last gem, her greatest work, before she died.

Aaron moved across the rooftops of Ischia, almost happy although he wasn't sure why. He leapt lightly from a marble corner, clung for an instant around the scaled neck of a gargoyle, and dropped to a balcony railing ten feet below. His soft leather shoes whispered along the ornate iron, then he launched himself across an alley to land cat-quiet on the flat root of the building one story down. He paused, checked that he remained unobserved, sped across the width of the roof, and swarmed up the intricate carvings on the adjoining building until he was once again three stories above the street.

Let other thieves slink in alleys, he would take the high roads of the city.

Two buildings and a heart-stopping swing from a flagpole later, he dropped onto the wall around Faharra's garden. He patted his pocket; the gaudy cluster of gems had survived the trip. He looked forward to hearing Faharra heap abuse on the jeweler who had created the ugly brooch.

"More good stones are ruined by the setting some asshole

*jeweler puts them into than by a hundred gem cutters with
bad eyes and drinking problems.''*

She'd said it before.

He paused and remembered what else she was likely to
say tonight. His stomach twisted. He stared ahead at the
black rectangle of her window. His brows lowered until they
met in a deep vee above his nose, looking more like demon
wings than ever. Then he shook his head and went on. His
teeth were clenched and his shoulders had knotted with tension, but he went on.

I'll humor the old lady. She deserves that much at least.
More, he could not admit to, not yet, although the thought—
the hope—of putting his burden down had become almost
too strong to ignore.

He stepped gingerly onto the branches of a slender fig
tree, then swung one leg over the wide marble sill of Faharra's room.

The room was very quiet.

Aaron's stomach twisted tighter.

The couch was a shadow against the far wall. Even with
eyes adapted to the night, Aaron could not pierce the smaller
shadows piled on it.

He slid into the room and padded silently across the tile
floor. The old woman slept so seldom now, he didn't want
to wake her. He'd just make sure she was comfortable and
leave.

By the end of the couch his foot touched something.
Something that rocked and sang metal against stone. He
bent. Faharra's goblet. Not quite dry so someone, probably
a servant, had poured her a drink before she slept.

He could see the wasted body of the gem cutter now,
lying amidst the pillows and shawls and blankets. Another
step and he could see her face.

She looked very annoyed.

Her eyes were open.

He touched her hand. The fingers were just beginning to
stiffen.

"How did you know," he asked the god of his father, in
a language he had not spoken for five years, "that I loved
her?"

Two

Scented smoke curled about the mausoleum and the finger bells of the mourners broke the evening into a thousand tiny pieces of sound. Perched high on one of the more ornate tombs, safely out of sight, Aaron blocked his ears against the noise which threatened to shatter him as well.

Faharra's granddaughter had spared no expense and the procession from the house to the temple crematorium and then out into the necropolis had been a spectacle worthy of the best gem cutter Ischia had known.

"And yet while she lived," Aaron growled softly from his vantage point, "you couldn't spare an hour to sit with her, nor any kindness to lighten her day."

Her thickening figure nearly hidden beneath her funeral draperies, the granddaughter appeared the picture of bereavement as hired dancers carried the brass urn into the squat marble building that held fifteen generations of her family's remains. When they emerged, when the wailers had sent a last chorus to the gods, she turned and, tenderly supported by two of her closest friends, led the procession back to the city.

Aaron watched the tottering figure leave and his lip curled. If that fat sow felt anything at all, it was pleasure at being the center of attention. Not for a moment did he believe that the red and yellow veils hid sorrow.

When he could no longer hear the maddening chimes of the finger bells and the heavy *scent* of sandalwood had been swept clean by the evening breeze, he dropped silently to the ground.

The door to the mausoleum was locked and the lock wound tightly about with red and yellow ribbons.

A violent twist tore the ribbons loose and a heartbeat later Aaron dropped the lock on the ground beside them. The door, well oiled, swung silently open. He stepped inside.

He worked and lived in shadow, but this darkness felt different, a part of the mausoleum like the brass fittings or the carved friezes. It etched a boundary about the light spilling in through the open door, cutting it into a rectangle of gray on the floor and barely allowing it to spread beyond. At the edge of the dim illumination, almost in the center of the tomb, stood an altar; the Nine Above grouped about the One Below who cradled a brass urn in marble arms. Faharra. She would stay in the deity's embrace until another of her family died and then her urn would be moved back to the shelves that lined the walls.

Aaron couldn't see the shelves—behind the altar the darkness thickened into a solid black wall—but he could feel the weight of the dead and was thankful he had no need to pierce their sanctuary. He had come for what lay with the One Below. The gods of Ischia held no terror for him, for without belief a god is nothing and Aaron believed only in death.

At the edge of the rectangle of light, he paused and stretched an arm out into shadow. *No, not quite.* His hand groped at air. He would have to take one, maybe two steps past the boundary.

He suppressed a shudder. Crossing into the darkness, even the less well defined darkness by the altar, felt like crossing into the realm of the dead, into their world not just their resting place, and the demons of his childhood flickered for an instant around the perimeter of his sight. Then his hands lay on the urn and he could ignore the darkness and the dead now that he held what he wanted.

Quickly working the stopper free, he dipped a tiny gold vial into the coarse ash. Until this morning it had held Faharra's favorite perfume and the smell of jasmine still lingered. He'd stolen it while the funeral director worked not twenty feet away. Once filled and sealed with a bit of wax, he hung the vial about his neck on a piece of silk cord, tucking it safely under his shirt. As he pushed the stopper back into place, he frowned. The granddaughter had been true to the end; the urn was plain brass, embossed but not jeweled. An insult to the greatest gem cutter Ischia had known.

The greatest gem cutter Ischia had known. . . .

An idea crept into the back of his mind.

He straightened and raised one foot to turn and leave.

Without really knowing why, he put it down again. Just barely visible, the face of the One Below gazed out at him with serene compassion.

"She hated to be left alone in the dark," he whispered, the voice barely recognized as his own. He pressed the vial against his chest. "Now she won't be. Not entirely." He tried to stop the cry of anguish that was rising up from the place where it had lain hidden for the last two days, but it proved too strong. It rose and built and when it crested it caught him up and dashed him down and he was lost within it.

A shriek of horror brought Aaron back to himself and he gazed stupidly about, wondering where he was. The white blob of the fleeing, and still shrieking, acolyte told him only that he remained on temple grounds. Vague memories of a run through darkness, slamming into stone, falling and rising and running again, were of little help. The fig tree beside him said more for the number of tombs had long since crowded any trees out of the necropolis. He looked up to see a hawk-nosed woman glaring down at him and after a moment of terror realized she was stone.

The Nobles' Garden.

The bodies of the nobility were given to the volcano, their likenesses then carved in anything from granite to obsidian and placed in the section of the temple grounds reserved for such monuments.

The acolyte, walking alone among life-sized statues of the dead, had seen coming at him out of the darkness a face apparently unsupported, for Aaron's clothes were dark. Assuming the obvious, he screamed and ran.

With a brief bow to the lady's memorial, Aaron headed for the temple wall at a quick trot. He strongly suspected the acolyte's report would be investigated by a less impressionable mind and he had no wish to tangle with the temple guards.

A broad scrape across the back of one hand oozed blood, but his wild flight seemed to have done no more damage than that. Although his throat was dry and sore, he felt calm, almost serene. During the remaining hours of the night he would repay the friendship of the best gem cutter Ischia had known.

Her final resting place deserved to hold a sample of her art.

He would return to her the emerald from the top of the royal staff.

"Although I hesitate to ask and you may tell me it's none of my business . . ." The fat man ran stained fingers lightly down the heavy gold chain until they rested on the medallion that hung from it. ". . . how did you come to acquire this?"

"You're right, Herrak. It's none of your business." Aaron stood motionless in the shadow of a heavily overladen bookcase, blending with the clutter of the room, his eyes never leaving the enormous man behind the desk. "Will it pay for what I need?"

"A man in your line of work should learn more patience," Herrak chided, the smoke-stick bobbing on his lower lip. He hefted the chain in his left hand and with the right dusted ash from the protruding shelf of his stomach. Almost nonexistent brows drew down in concentration and a slow chuckle escaped with the next lungful of smoke. "However you managed it," he said at last, "His Grace is not going to be pleased to find it missing."

"Forget His Grace," Aaron growled. "Get on with it." He'd stolen the chain just after leaving the Nobles' Garden; to get to the royal staff he would have to get onto the palace grounds, but only Herrak had the means for that and Herrak's price was high. The fat man had no need for further wealth, he desired the different, the dangerous, the unique to shuffle into the rat's nest of his townhouse never to be seen again by any eyes but his. Aaron had not dealt with Herrak before but knew he was the only man in Ischia who had what he needed tonight.

And if the chain and its medallion were too little? Aaron beat the thought back. They couldn't be. Not enough night remained for him to find something else and get the emerald as well. His Grace's security system had already cost him too much valuable time.

"The charm you need, my friend, is costly," the fat man murmured more to himself than to the young thief. He hefted the chain once more and smiled, his eyes almost lost behind the bulges of his cheeks. "But I think this will meet my price. The irritation its loss will cause His Grace is almost worth the price alone. Almost,'' he repeated hurriedly in case Aaron should get ideas. "Yes, this will get you your charm.''

"And a grappling iron.''

Herrak's nearly buried eyes beamed with anticipation. Almost as much as the treasures it brought, he loved the bargaining, the give and take, the jockeying for position, the power of words. He spoke the first phrase of the ritual; "Do you haggle with me, then?''

Aaron's lips thinned and the demon wings of his brows drew down over his eyes. "No. The charm is useless alone. I get both, or no deal. I can put the chain back as easily as I took it.''

For a moment there was no sound except the soft beat of a moth's wings against the glass chimney of the lamp. Herrak couldn't believe his ears. An ultimatum? Had this, this thief just given *him* an ultimatum?

"Make your choice,'' the thief continued. "I haven't much time.''

It could be a bluff, but Herrak didn't like the young man's tone. He fingered the medallion, and chose. "And a grappling iron,'' he agreed. Stretching out an arm, he snagged a small wooden box off a pile of precariously balanced bric-a-brac, opened it and plucked out a tiny twist of silver. "This will not stop magical attacks, but it will get you through the wards.''

Leaning out of the shadows, Aaron snatched it from him. "And the iron.''

A pudgy finger pointed.

Both the charm and the folded hooks disappeared within one voluminous trouser leg, and the young thief jerked his head once in Herrak's direction.

"You're welcome,'' Herrak said dryly to the space where Aaron had been. He stroked the chain and imagined His Grace's expression when he awoke and found it missing. Rumor had it that the chief magistrate slept with his chain of office draped over his bedpost; the only time he took it off. A pretty bit of thievery that.

Spitting the wet end of the smoke-stick from his mouth, Herrak settled the chain about his neck. Definitely worth what he'd paid for it. He almost wished he could see the young thief's face as the weakened hook broke free and he plummeted to the ground. "Never mind," he comforted himself for missing the treat, "if he survives the fall, I shall enjoy hearing about his execution."

The stone of the gargoyle he clung to began to warm under Aaron's body heat and of the two, the gargoyle looked more likely to move. Behind him, Ischia lay as quiet as it ever got. Before him, the palace sprawled to the very lip of the volcano, a counterbalance to the massive bulk of the temple that loomed out of the darkness on the far side, the reflected fire from the crater staining its walls. The wall around the palace rose no more than seven feet high, a symbol rather than an active deterrent. Stretching above it, invisible and easily forgotten, were twined the wards of the court wizards.

Aaron had studied the stories of those thieves who had attempted the palace as an artisan would study his craft. One of two things always happened. Either the charm they had purchased failed, in which case the wards destroyed them, or the beasts that watched the grounds at night tore them apart. There were legends, of course, of thieves who had blithely walked in and blithely walked out with treasure enough to build palaces of their own, but the truth lay with the broken bodies hanging lifeless on the gate at dawn, a grisly reminder to others who might try their luck.

For the wards, Aaron had to rely on the charm Herrak had sold him. He didn't like it, it gave the control to another, but he had no choice. If he was to get Faharra's emerald, he had to go over the wall. As for the beasts, Aaron preferred to take his chances with the two-legged kind, for their senses were easier to manipulate.

An errant breeze wandered up from the town, bringing a scent of baked fish and apricots. Aaron's stomach tightened. He couldn't remember the last time he'd eaten. Time enough for food when he had the emerald.

"You don't take care of yourself, boy. You're too skinny by far."

Too well trained to start, his hands tightened involuntarily around the stone throat of the gargoyle. The voice of memory had been growing louder since he'd left the fat man's.

"Be quiet, old woman," he told it. *"I'm doing this for you."*

He dropped his gaze to the sentry post almost directly across from his perch on the top of the single storied addition to the Duce of Lourence's townhouse. By royal decree no residence might look out upon the palace, but the Duce who had built the addition had been an ambitious man and attempted to bend the rule by cutting no windows in the wall on the palace side while leaving the flat roof as a terraced patio with a direct line of sight. The Duce had not survived his first garden party. His successors were less ambitious and longer lived. Aaron was the first creature larger than a gull to walk the terrace in three generations.

As Aaron watched, the sentry's jaw tensed, stifling a yawn, and she shifted the crossbow slightly in the crook of her arm.

Soon.

He began to work his muscles, readying himself for the run on the palace wall.

The heavy slap of leather soled sandals against the cobblestones jerked him to full awareness and he leaned slightly forward, the pale gray of his eyes gleaming between narrowed lids.

Now.

As the sentry stepped out to greet her relief, Aaron moved. Shadow silent, he swarmed down the ornate stonework of the Duce's Folly, sped across the cobblestones and leapt for the top of the palace wall. The soft toes of his boots found an easy purchase against the rough stone and he propelled himself up and over, dropping lightly on the balls of his feet into a small courtyard. The whole thing had taken under a minute, just less than the time it took for the sentry to be relieved, the only time when all attention was not on the wall.

He listened for the alarm, but all he could hear was the sound of his own blood pounding in his ears.

Crouched in shadow, he stripped the leather bindings from below his knees and replaced his boots with sandals. He rearranged his small pack so that the straps were hidden and made his way cautiously along the courtyard wall to the covered walk running the length of one side. Following the faint indentation worn in the marble by other, more legitimate feet, he came to an open arch that led to the main courtyard just inside the palace gates, checked the position of the inner sentry, then stepped boldly out into the light.

"Half the trick of thieving," he'd told Faharra, *"is to*

behave as though you have every right to do what you're doing.''

"And the other half,'' Faharra had snorted, ''is having more balls than the Nine Above.''

The demon wings had flown in broad astonishment. ''All Nine?'' he'd asked and been rewarded by the old woman's laughter.

He wore the dark green livery of the chief magistrate, liberated earlier in the evening when he'd taken the chain. It would blend with the shadows as well as the black he normally wore but better still, it would hide him in the light. Even at this time of night, it would not be unusual for messages to move between the chief magistrate and the palace.

The sentry at the inner arch watched Aaron approach with a minimum of interest. Anyone who came by him had already passed the gate, had already been recognized, had already been declared safe. His time could be better spent burying his face between the soft mountains of his Lia's breasts. As Aaron came closer, into the light of the torches that flanked the sentry post, he did wonder briefly why the chief magistrate had taken an outlander into his employ but it was none of his concern after all. . . .

"State your business," he droned, dropping the point of his pike.

"Package for their Royal Highnesses."

The twins were always referred to thus, as a single unit. Aaron had no idea why he had chosen them as his silent accomplices, but he remembered the thief inching feet first into the volcano. . . .

The pike snapped up, the guard's fingers moving restlessly along the haft, itching to make the sign of the Nine and One. To come between the twins and their toys was never healthy. "Straight ahead to the first cross corridor, make a left, pass four corridors, make a right, give it to the guard at the end of the long gallery."

A nod, the barest bending of his neck, and Aaron passed into the palace.

The sentry shivered as the outlander went by. The eyes in the pale-skinned face had been flat and dead and empty of all emotion, like chips of silver-gray stone. He'd seen corpses with more life in their eyes.

May he and their Royal Highnesses have the joy of each

other, he thought and tried to lose the chill in the memory of Lia's flesh.

The corridors, built wide and high to catch the breezes, were, for the most part, empty. The few who moved about at this hour—servants tending the lamps that broke the palace into bars of light and shadow, a drunken noble on her way to the Nobles' Quarters, a pair of yawning ink-stained clerks scurrying home to bed—paid him no mind for the livery of the chief magistrate was well known and if he walked in the palace, he'd passed the gate.

The dim and the quiet settled over Aaron like a cloak, wrapping him in a feeling of safety both false and dangerous. Aaron recognized it, but didn't seem to have the energy to deal with it. He felt as though he were dreaming and the further he walked, the stronger the feeling grew. At the end of the long gallery, he almost trusted the dream enough to let it carry him forward into the sight of the guards.

And then he remembered that trust meant betrayal.

He faded into the darkness caught in the deep bay of a shuttered window and froze. The louvers had been left open to allow the air to circulate, but fortunately they had been angled in such a way he would not be seen from the gardens. The livery would not carry him past the two guards at the door leading to the royal apartments and that one small door was the only exit deeper into the palace.

"He keeps it in an anteroom off his bedchamber."

Aaron rested his forehead against the polished wood and waited for Faharra to finish. He couldn't work when she was so close.

"Perhaps he fondles it before he sleeps. There's more life in a well cut gem than in many a well born woman."

His eyes on the distant guards and his other senses spread about the gallery, he slipped the latch from the shutters and opened one just enough to ease through. The hinges sighed faintly. He froze and listened to the silence, then risked an alarm once more as he pushed the shutter closed and secured it with a bit of wax.

"You're too good a thief, Aaron my lad."

"Yes," he agreed silently, watching his hands as though they belonged to someone else. *"I am."*

Moving quickly, for the air smelled of dawn and the servants would be stirring soon, he changed back to his boots and resecured the baggy bottoms of his trousers, working by touch while his eyes grew reaccustomed to the dark and his ears sifted the night for any sound of an alarm.

If the dogs were close. . . .

Halfway down the length of the gallery there was a wall; the barrier to the private gardens of the royal family.

Aaron had no idea if it was warded.

If it was, he didn't know if Herrak's charm would work again.

"It isn't easy to cut an emerald that big, let me tell you."

"You've told me, Faharra," he responded softly, and leapt for the top of the wall.

He crouched there for a heartbeat, balanced against the night, weighing his next move, then he flung himself through the air a body length and more and into the arms of a honey locust. He'd take the high road when he could.

The snap of a broken branch.

A low grunt of pain.

The royal garden stirred as the hunters came to see what had made the sound.

Aaron, his back tight against the slender trunk of the tree, pressed his hand against his hip and breathed shallowly through his nose. The smell of jasmine was almost overpowering, but keeping his teeth clenched prevented the pain from escaping. The branch he'd snagged had not been able to bear his weight and as he'd fallen the broken end of another had slammed into his hip. His fingers were sticky.

He shifted, precariously balanced on a branch not much larger than the one that had broken, and shrugged out of his pack. He didn't have time to give in to pain. The blood would bring the hunters and he had to be ready.

"The Clan Heir fights through pain!"

"Shut up, Father," he spat. "I'm not doing this for you."

From around the dark bulk of a hedge, belly low to the ground and tail lashing, came the first of the hunters. The other two quickly followed, drawn by the blood scent. They were larger than the mountain cats of Aaron's childhood, bulkier, less sleekly muscled. They grouped around his tree and one reared, claws spread wider than Aaron's hand, ripping deep gouges in the bark.

While other thieves had made the sign of the Nine and avoided their comrades hung on the palace gates in fear that the luck of the dead would rub off on them, Aaron had learned the lessons they offered. The great cats had declared their presence on more than one of the bodies. He broke the seal on the package he carried, careful not to touch any of the pungent herb with his hands.

The blood scent became suddenly of secondary importance. Rounded ears snapped forward and slitted eyes opened wide. Curiosity joined forces with this new and enticing smell and together they won. When the herb package crashed down behind a hedge, the hunters followed.

Aaron slid to the ground, keeping his weight on his arms as long as possible, then he hurried along the garden paths toward the bulk of the palace. He didn't know how long the herb would hold the hunters so he moved as quickly as he could, ignoring the pain because he had to, ignoring the warm wetness that slowly molded the thin cotton trousers to his leg. For the same reason he had gone over the wall at the sentry post, he now headed toward the one rectangle of light looking down onto the garden; an enemy seen could be avoided. Bypassing the windows on the lower floor—they would lead only to confrontations with guards patrolling the corridors—he pulled free the grappling iron and a soft length of silk rope.

In all of Ischia, only the temple and the palace were free of the ornate stonework that provided ladders for the city's thieves.

The thin metal hooks of the grapple were padded, but when it struck the tiled edge of the roof it rang dangerously loud. Aaron paused, sagging against the cool stone, but no new lamps were lit and no one appeared against the light on the balcony his rope ran so close beside. Stretching until his hip blossomed freshly with blood and pain, he grabbed the rope, braced his feet, and forced his body up the wall.

Just past the balcony, where he carefully kept his eyes from the spill of light lest he lose the dark, Aaron felt the rope tremble in his hands. Then it jerked. Then he slid sideways a few feet. Then he fell.

If the slide had moved him another hand's span. . . .

If his injured leg had obeyed his will for a few heartbeats more. . . .

The edge of the balcony railing caught the back of his calves. It spun him round, clipping his forehead against the stone, and slammed him down on his back on the balcony tiles.

He thought for a moment that the green lights exploding

in his head were the emerald he sought, shattered now beyond retrieval, shattered beyond even Faharra's ability to repair.

The emerald. . . .

He had to get the emerald for Faharra.

He tried to rise.

The face bending over him drew back, and tossed an obstructing shock of deep black hair away from pale blue eyes.

Aaron forgot how to breathe, forgot how to move . . .

Ruth. His cousin had tossed her black hair so and often teased him to cut it for her, short like a man's, so it would no longer fall in front of her eyes. Her pale, winter blue eyes.

. . . forgot the pain of the present as the pain of the past tightened its grip. And, lost in the past, he didn't see the sword descending.

Three

The forged steel struck the balcony railing with enough force to mark the softer iron, the noise of the blow echoing through the garden and frightening a pair of night roosting birds up into the air with a wild flurry of wings. His Royal Highness Prince Darvish Shayrif Hakem, third son of the king, slid his gaze along his scimitar's blade to where it rested some four feet above the pale throat it had been intended to hit.

He frowned and drank deeply from the large gold goblet in his right hand.

"I miss'd. I nev'r miss." Something had distracted him. He peered down at the sharp featured face. Something. . . . Recognition danced just beyond his grasp although he *knew* he'd held it an instant before.

"Bugger the Nine!"

Frustration turned to anger and the anger, riding the crest of the night's wine, poured down on the body at his feet.

Eyes narrowed in concentration, he pulled the weapon back, ignoring the shriek of protest as the tip hit the marble of the balcony floor and dragged across it. The creature— The boy? The man? The thief! —had not moved since he had fallen so unexpectedly out of the night.

"Just hold still for a little . . . bit . . . longer. . . ." His sword seemed to have gotten heavier, but he managed to heave it up into the air where it dipped through dangerous figure eights a hand's span above his bare shoulder. The thief merely continued to stare, although Darvish, drunk as he was, would have willingly bet the contents of the treasury that those strange silver eyes were not focused on what was in front of them.

Which is me. Darvish took another drink, the muscles of his sword arm bunching as he kept the weapon precariously aloft. *The rude little prick; staring at me without even seeing me.* The sword swung down again.

The song of steel striking stone a finger's span from his ear snapped Aaron up out of the past. He jerked, and blinked, shattering the memory that held him immobile, and the blue and black spun about until they returned to the face of the young man standing splay-legged above him. It wasn't his cousin. His cousin was dead.

"Shit!" Darvish tossed back half the remaining wine. "Miss'd ag'in! I cannot poss'bly be *that* drunk." At least the thief now looked aware, an improvement of sorts even if it would make him harder to hit. Scrubbing his forearm across the dribbles of ruby liquid running down his chest, Darvish yawned, swayed, and lost his grip on his anger. He waited to see what would happen next. It was only fair, after all, to offer his visitor a move.

The emerald. Through the pounding in his head, Aaron remembered. He had to get to the royal staff and steal the emerald that crowned it. He'd failed Ruth and she'd died. He wouldn't fail Faharra even though she was already dead. He would get her the emerald, her finest work, to adorn her tomb. He had to get her the emerald. Fear and pain and hunger and grief lashed his thoughts into chaos, but through it all the great green stone shone like a beacon. He clutched desperately at its light, using it as an anchor and a lifeline, allowing the darkness to take the rest. Nothing else mattered.

Rolling to his knees, away from the distorted image of his face on the curved blade of the sword, he swayed and retched, his empty stomach clenching and unclenching like an angry fist. The pattern in the marble blurred and ran an inch from his nose and he fought the seductive urge to lay his head on the cool stone and surrender. But no. Not this time. He wouldn't surrender and he wouldn't run away. Gasping for air, barely clinging to sanity, he forced himself to his feet.

"Mov'ng," Darvish observed appreciatively, draining the goblet and tossing it with drunken aplomb over the balcony railing.

The muted sound of metal bouncing on grass was lost in Aaron's labored breathing. One step, two, moving blindly, his eyes fixed on Faharra's emerald, he put out a hand to brush a barely perceived obstacle out of his way.

The icy fingers of the intruder, splayed against the prince's chest penetrated even through seven hours of steady drinking. This was *not* the way a thief caught by an armed man should act. Indifference caught Darvish's wandering attention the way fight or flight would not have. He was so taken by surprise that the blow, weak as it was, pushed him to one side.

"Hey!" He lunged forward, his sword clattering forgotten to the floor. The sudden movement shifted the load of wine he carried and twisted the room on its axis.

With one of the prince's arms about the younger man's waist and the other flailing for balance, the two staggered forward together in a caricature of friendship until the edge of the bed caught them just under the knees and they fell. The warm flesh struggling under him decided Darvish on a new course of action and he fumbled for the ties to his captive's trousers.

Vaguely aware of silk and softness below him, Aaron began to fight against the unseen force holding him from above. Nothing would—nothing could—stop him from getting to the emerald and placing it in Faharra's tomb where it belonged. And then the weight lay still against his back. With a desperate squirm, he was free.

As he careened off the wall, groping for the door, the body on the bed began to snore.

Light first, hot and bright; lying across him like a blanket of molten rock drawn up boiling from the volcano. Then sound, a scream that drove barbed points into his ears again and again, pieces breaking off to work their way in deeper still. Gradually, he became aware of self. His skull felt too small for what it had to contain and arms and legs refused to respond. There were lead weights on his lids and a fire had lodged below his breastbone and was eating its way out.

Darvish moaned.

The sound, quiet as it was, brought bare feet padding toward the bed.

He wet his lips with a tongue barely less dry and croaked, "Close. The. Shutters." On the second attempt, he made himself understood and seconds later sighed in relief as the burning bands across his chest and face faded away.

He wanted nothing more than to lie there forever, unmoving, but his bladder insisted otherwise. Slowly, carefully, eyes still closed, he sat up, took two shaky breaths, and spewed the contents of his stomach all over the bed. Gentle hands eased him back against the pillows and a cool cloth wiped his face clean. He felt the soiled, stinking bedding stripped away and knew what he had to do. Teeth clenched, he raised a trembling hand into the air. Those same gentle hands spread his fingers and placed a clay cup within their curve. With help, he got the cup to his lips where it clattered against his teeth, but he managed to swallow the entire contents.

As always, it tasted worse than he remembered and for a moment he was sure he was going to die. Fires ran up and down the length of his body. He arched, spasmed, and collapsed covered in sweat. He'd complained once to a Wizard of the Third that the cure was almost worse than the affliction it cured. The wizard hadn't smiled as he'd replied, "It's supposed to be."

Feeling almost human, Darvish opened his eyes.

Oham, whose large, almost painfully ugly presence had been a solid constant in the prince's life for nearly ten years, slipped the now empty cup from lax fingers and said, face and voice carefully expressionless, "Highness, your bath is prepared."

"Of course it is." Darvish held out his arms and the dresser pulled him carefully to his feet, stripping off the red silk trousers he'd slept in the moment he was standing. "But first I have to . . ."

The youngest dresser approached with the waste pot, his knuckles white around the curve of pale green ceramic.

Darvish smiled and with much of his weight resting on Oham's thick shoulder, thankfully relieved himself.

"You're new," he said when he finished, reaching out and lightly pinching the boy's chin.

"Yes, Highness." The boy blushed and backed respectfully away with the brimming pot.

"Have you a name?"

Thick lashes lowered over velvet brown eyes. "Fadi, if it please, your Highness."

"Whether it pleases me or not. . . ." And it did please him. Darvish ran an appreciative look down the slim figure and sighed; it would please him more in a couple of years when the boy was bedable. Except by then he'd be gone. They always were.

"And now, Oham, the bath."

"Yes, Highness."

It amused Darvish how carefully the large dresser walked as together they made their way to the small tiled room off his bedchamber. The wizard's potion had overcome much of the damage done by too much wine, but his head still felt precariously balanced on his neck as if the slightest jar would topple it off. Oham knew that, of course, this was not the first such walk they had taken.

The water in the deep copper tub steamed invitingly, scenting the room with a faint odor of sandalwood. Darvish slid into it with a satisfied sigh and lay back, eyes half closed with pleasure.

He moved obediently to the pressure of Oham's hands, giving himself over to both their gentleness and their strength. Not until he was being dried did he remember and stiffen.

"Bugger the Nine!"

"Highness?" Oham stopped moving the combed cotton towel over the broad muscles of the prince's back and stepped away, unsure of how he had erred.

"No, not you!" An imperious hand indicated the dresser should continue. "My most exalted father has informed me I am to be married."

"I had heard, Highness." Oham offered nothing more.

"To a chit of a girl, barely sixteen, who I've never met, for the sole purpose of tying this country to hers."

"Your pardon, Highness, but is that not the reason that all princes marry?" He knelt to dry the prince's legs, his gaze fixed on the blue-green tiles in the floor.

"Yes," Darvish spat out the word and closed his teeth on the ones that tried to follow; the real reason he'd drunk himself into unconsciousness after the interview with his most exalted father.

The third dresser, who stood by the door waiting to serve, the perfect ubiquitous servant, reported to the lord chancellor, who reported to the king. He was a nondescript man of indeterminate age fitting neatly between Oham and the boy, and only the latest in a series sent to keep an eye on the third son, who, having no real power of his own, might be tempted to try for someone else's. Darvish made certain they had plenty to report as he filled his life with wine and his bed with every willing body he stumbled across and he had the lord chancellor's spies beaten as often as they gave him any kind of an excuse.

With a vicious mental shove, he pushed back the words and the feelings that went with them. For the first time in twenty-three years his father had had a use for him. Except he hadn't been asked, hadn't even been allowed to regard it as a service to the country. It had been a command; with no room in it for the one commanded. *You will marry this girl. Consider yourself betrothed and act accordingly.* Although Darvish had no wish to be married, that hadn't driven him to the night's excesses.

"I need a drink."

"Highness." The lord chancellor's eyes and ears presented a goblet, filled and waiting.

And that was the other thing; they made sure, these dressers who owed their loyalty to another, that he stayed on the path he'd chosen when he'd been old enough to understand—had been made to understand—his position at court.

Bugger them all. He drained the goblet, his throat working against the barely watered wine, two streams of red running down from the corners of his mouth. When he finished, he belched, yawned, and smiled. *Could be worse, I suppose. They could've slapped me into the priesthood.*

He stretched, working the kinks out, then obediently followed Oham back to the bedroom and stepped into the blue and silver trousers held out for him. He shifted his shoulders as a white silk shirt settled over them, enjoying the touch of the smooth fabric against his skin. Then he shifted them again, and had to admit he was, as he'd suspected, losing muscle tone. While Oham wound a silver sash about his waist, he tried to work out how long it had been since he'd gone to the training yard. One week at least, maybe as much as two; it was hard to say, the days all blurred with a wine-sodden sameness. He accepted his refilled goblet, then tipped back his head to drink as the chancellor's man began to pull an ivory comb through the wet mass of his hair. The tines caught against the movement and the comb dug sharply into his skull.

Darvish jerked, swore, smiled, and said, "Ten lashes."

"I will see to it, Highness." Oham's voice almost showed satisfaction.

Still smiling, Darvish stepped into his sandals and ran his

fingers absently through Fadi's hair as the boy knelt to lace them.

Out in the garden, the scream that had wakened him sounded once more.

"What the One was that?"

"Peacocks, Highness," Oham told him placidly, deftly replacing the goblet with a piece of bread. "The Most Blessed Yasimina received them as a gift and loosed them in the gardens this morning."

"Pea what?"

"Cocks, Highness."

"That's what I thought you said." He took a bite of the bread, thickly spread with chopped dates in honey, and headed for the balcony. "What the One is a peacock?"

"A bird, Highness."

"Right." Throwing back the shutters, Darvish stepped outside and squinted down into the garden just in time to see a large blue bird trailing a tail even larger disappear behind a bush. Of all the changes that had occurred since his eldest brother had married the Princess Yasimina, this looked to be the noisiest.

"Peacocks," Darvish repeated to himself. "I suppose she *always* had peacocks back home in Ytaili. I suppose her-brother-the-king had a hundred or so roaming about *his* garden." He rubbed at his temples as a high-pitched shriek bounced jagged edges off the inside of his skull. "I *suppose* I'm not permitted to shoot them," he sighed.

"No, Highness."

"Perhaps the city won't agree with them and we can ship them off to Ramdan. . . ." No fair that his second brother should miss all the fun just because he'd run from court to raise his family.

"They were sent to lift the Most Blessed Yasimina's homesickness, Highness."

"Well," Darvish aimed an imaginary crossbow at a scuttling bird, "if they get her to stop wailing they can scream under my window all they like." Her homesickness had driven half the court to distraction, none more so than her husband. It amazed Darvish that the crown prince had developed such strong feelings for a bride he'd known barely a year and had wed only to prevent a war. Strong enough feelings to allow this intrusion into the previously restful gardens.

I'll bet you asked Shahin, *Father. Didn't just tell him he was to be married. I'd have wed gladly if you'd only asked.* Not that his wedding would carry the weight that Shahin's had. His brother had married a Princess of Ytaili, wiping out centuries of conflict between the two countries. He would marry a child with no political importance at all.

He squinted up at the sun burning yellow-white in a cloudless sky, mid-afternoon by the angle. More or less his usual time for rising. Leaning on the balcony railing, his eyes half closed against the light, he finished the bread.

"I had the strangest dream last night, Oham. I dreamed a thief fell into my room. A quite attractive . . ." His palm, caressing the iron rail, found a mark that shouldn't exist, cutting off both the motion and the words.

"It was no dream, Highness. The guards found this thief you speak of staggering about the halls near dawn."

"So he's real." The prince ran a finger up and down the scar his sword had left and grinned, remembering how his dream had almost ended. "Where is he now?"

"Their Royal Highnesses have him in the Chamber of the Fourth, Highness." Oham's hand rose in the sign of the Nine and One.

"What!" Darvish whirled about to face the dresser who regarded him placidly.

"It is, Highness, where thieves and such are taken."

"Not this thief, by the Nine." In memory, pale eyes devoured his face once more. His heart began to pound painfully in his chest and fury burned the morning's wine away. "This thief's mine! Not theirs, mine!" He had always found the twins' diversions repellent, but the thought of them taking pleasure from the pain of something he considered his own drew his lips back off his teeth and curved his hands into fists.

Fadi scrambled out of the way as Darvish stormed by and then looked wide-eyed to the older dresser for guidance. Oham merely shrugged. What happened outside the prince's suite was not his concern. Inside, he did what he could.

Somewhere out of sight, the peacock screamed again.

As the guards snapped to attention and the heavy door swung open, a ripple of anticipation moved through the crowd of courtiers waiting in the long gallery outside the royal apartments. Fans were set aside, silks were patted smooth, and expressions ranging from polite interest to rapt adoration were fixed firmly in place. When they saw which royal emerged, the languid posturing, suitable for the heat of the afternoon, resumed. His Royal Highness Prince Darvish, while undeniably the life of any party, was useless as a purveyor of royal favor. Either he forgot the request entirely, the wine driving it from his mind, or he did something which so enraged his most exalted father that he was not permitted to approach the throne for an indefinite period of time.

Those closest bowed as he passed and wondered where he could be off to in such a scowling hurry. Neither the hurrying nor the scowl was like the prince.

"Well, I hope he's not going all dark and brooding," sighed one elderly noble to no one in particular. "We've quite enough of that going on now."

Out in the corridors of the palace, Darvish picked up his pace. If the thief had been with the twins since early morning there might not be much left to save. He fought to keep the full extent of his fury from showing; the last thing he needed was an interrogation from one of the lord chancellor's . . .

"Good afternoon, Highness."

. . . agents. Or worse yet, the lord chancellor himself. As a member of the royal family, Darvish held the higher rank but the lord chancellor held the trust of the king. The prince would be expected to pause, to converse, to place his concerns in a position of secondary importance, to recognize the lord chancellor's power. Darvish came to a decision between one step and the next.

"Give it to the Lady," he said pleasantly, without breaking stride.

"Highness!"

The prince quickly left the plump and elderly lord chancellor behind, blowing protests into an empty corridor. Later, when his thief was safe, he'd take the time to enjoy the shocked disbelief in the old man's voice. And he'd pay for it, later, when his father heard, but that didn't matter now.

The Chamber of the Fourth was deep in the oldest section of the palace, carved out of volcanic rock and close enough to the crater so the heat of the lava and the smell of the sulfur permeated the entire area. As Darvish crossed from

frescoed walls and tiled floors to chiseled stone, the marks
of the tools still raw generations after they'd been made, he
began to seethe, dwelling on the injustice that brought *his*
thief down to *this* place. By the time he reached the chamber, he'd worked his rage up to a fever pitch and had half
convinced himself that the twins had stolen a prized pos-
session.

As his palm touched the door, someone screamed behind
it. A hoarse hopeless scream, from a throat that had almost
no screaming left.

It rooted Darvish to the spot as it climbed and peaked
and died. Not until silence ruled again did it release him.
He kicked open the door, sending it slamming back against
the wall.

The room was not large and the stench from a dozen
kinds of smoke and as many kinds of pain was almost overpowering. He gagged, recovered, and sucked his next breath
through his teeth. Two slim figures in unrelieved black,
bracketing a table like pillars of night, looked up at the
sound. Identical hair and clothing, chosen to minimize sex-
ual characteristics, made it nearly impossible to tell them
apart even in the bright light of the half dozen hanging lamps
that illuminated their work. Heavy kohl, outlining eyes almost amber, distracted from minor facial differences. But
Darvish had known them all their lives and knew without
question who held the red coal poised at the end of long
pincers and who only watched.

"Shakana!" he bellowed at his younger sister. "Drop
it!"

She smiled, graciously inclined her head, and let the
smoking coal fall to rest on the blistered chest bound before
her on the table.

The scream pulled Darvish the length of the room and he
used the momentum to throw his brother aside. With the
calluses of his sword hand, he swept the coal onto the floor.

Shakana danced back, flicking the skirts of her robe away
from the sparks, her sandals making sucking noises as they
left the floor.

"You have no right," she began, but at Darvish's wordless
growl, reconsidered and held her tongue. Eyes locked on
her brother, she rounded the table to help her twin rise.

The thief's arms and legs had been manacled to lengths
of chain, then pulled tight; not yet to dislocate only to hold

immobile at the extreme limit of their stretch. His head had
been enclosed in a steel vise, the band across his eyes
grooved to hold heated iron pellets. Thankfully it was still
cold and empty. Three deep gouges ran the width of each
thigh; wizard marks, for flesh and blood were necessary to
trace the thief's trail through the palace. His genitals were
swollen but intact. On his chest . . .

. . . obscenely red against skin almost white, blisters
bubbling up from the most recent burn even as Darvish
watched, the marks of four live coals dropped and allowed
to cool while the flesh below cooked. The two oldest had
broken and split, blood and other fluids still oozing from
their angry centers.

The twins had barely gotten started.

With hands that wanted to tremble, Darvish fought the
bolts out of the head vise and as gently as possible eased it
free. The thief began to toss his head back and forth, whimpering softly.

"Don't!" Darvish snapped, reaching for the manacles.
"Stay still."

The tossing stopped. The whimpering continued.

His twin still gripping his elbow, Kasil stepped forward,
hands stained from contact with the floor. "You can't do
this, Darvish," he whined as the iron bands fell clear, exposing torn and abraded wrists. "He's ours."

"The One he is," the older prince snarled, struggling
with the last fastener. "He came into the palace through my
room, that makes him mine."

"But he's in *our* room now," Shakana pointed out coldly.

"Your room?" Blood had dried around the bolt, nearly
welding it to the band. "I thought this was the Chamber of
the Fourth. . . ."

She glared. "We serve the Fourth."

"You serve your own perverted appetites." He twisted
viciously and inch by inch forced the bolt clear. With the
thief lying unbound on the table he turned and faced the
twins, a crazy light having nothing to do with the lamps
burning in the depths of his eyes. "I'll fight you for him,"
he offered.

"Don't be . . ." Kasil tried to take another step forward
but Shakana stopped him.

"He means it, Kasil."

Darvish smiled grimly, the thief momentarily forgotten

in the anticipation of beating both pointy little faces into an unrecognizable pulp. It was his turn to step forward. The twins stepped back.

"Highnesses?" Two guards stood in the doorway, a third hanging limply between them. He was conscious, but terror had quite obviously sapped the strength from his legs and made it impossible for him to stand.

The guard on the left bowed as well as he was able. "Highnesses, this is the man who let the thief past the inner gate."

Shakana's face wore the expression a farmer's might while examining a bullock in the market. "He looks strong."

"Strong," Kasil agreed.

Darvish's bark of laughter brought a moan from the new prisoner and worried frowns from the twins. He ignored both—he had the thief, but the guard would die; nothing he did changed anything, he found it bitterly amusing. Carefully, he lifted the thief from the table. "You've got something new to play with," he said as he settled the suddenly dead weight. The barely visible rise and fall of the tortured chest became the only indication he carried a living man. "I'll take what's mine and go." The copper head lolled against his shoulder and fell back, exposing the long pale line of throat.

"Darvish . . ."

He had to pause anyway, so the guards could move clear of the door, their burden beginning to babble incoherent prayers as they moved further into the room.

". . . what are *you* going to do with him?"

Darvish threw a dangerous smile back at the twins, careful not to let the strain of carrying what was after all a full grown man, show. "Whatever I please," he said.

Four

Pain. Old pain, constant pain, and for that Aaron was grateful. The body could get used to anything in time, even, given a chance, the searing agony that existed where he thought his chest should be. It hurt to breathe. It hurt to think about breathing. Blind instinct tried to move him out from under the hurting. Training told him to be still. It was always better to be still, until you knew.

"He's conscious, I'm sure of that."

"He looks the same to me."

"You're not a healer, Highness." The middle-aged woman sat back on her heels beside the pallet and stretched. Formidable brows drawn down, she studied the work already done, then reached into the wicker basket resting on the floor by her right knee.

The prince peered over her shoulder. The thief had been under the healer's care for almost an hour but, Darvish had to admit, he still looked like shit. Between the twins and the wizards and the guards who had found him originally, there was hardly an inch of his pale body that wasn't coming up in purple and green bruises. His wrists and ankles wore bracelets of raw meat where he'd tried to twist free of the manacles and his chest was a bubbling mass of blisters and destroyed flesh.

"Can you fix him, Karida?" he asked.

The healer snorted as she eased the cork out of a squat clay pot. "He's not a toy, Highness, that careless playing has broken and a glue brush and a steady hand can fix. He's a man. A young one, but a man. I wonder if you realize that."

"Of course I do," Darvish replied, mildly indignant.

"Then what do you plan on doing with him?" Karida set

the cork to one side and dipped the first three fingers of her right hand into the pot.

"You mean after you've finished gluing him back together?"

The tone was so guileless, she had to sternly suppress a smile. "Yes."

"I'm not entirely certain."

She glanced up, although her hand continued to gently spread the salve over the thief's burned chest. "You're not?"

Darvish smiled his fecklessly charming smile. "Why worry about it now."

The pain was cooling. Dulling. Drawing back its edges until it no longer was all that Aaron was. Groping like a blind man in new territory, he tried to find the rest of himself. Something firm but yielding cradled his back and head. A bed? Perhaps. It didn't fit where he felt he should be, but it seemed most likely. He began to distinguish separate pains in his arms and legs, but next to the great pain, they were nothing, so he ignored them.

Then he remembered.

He had failed. Again. And he hadn't died. Again.

And now it seemed he wasn't likely to.

The physical pain no longer seemed so great.

The moan escaped before he could stop it.

"He moaned!"

"You sound, Highness, as if you've taught him a new trick." Karida restoppered the jug and replaced it in the basket, then rose lithely to her feet in a single, fluid motion. "He is very ill. I will be staying."

"You don't have to," Darvish began, but she cut him off.

"I know I don't." The healers enjoyed relative autonomy within the palace hierarchy.

His smile softened for a second into an expression few were permitted to see. "Thank you for coming."

"You're welcome." She looked him up and down with a critical eye and added, her tone dry, "Besides, it makes a nice change from the lover's complaints you usually call me to take care of. How is that by the way?"

"All better." Darvish spread his arms as if inviting her to see for herself.

She declined the invitation. "And if you'd keep away from

those cheap whores, you'd stay better. If you must visit the marketplace, why can't you stick to the expensive establishments? The One knows you can afford it."

"Because high-class whores," Darvish told her with a wink, "are too little different from the ladies of the court. I'm looking for a change of pace after all."

"Highness." Oham bowed when the prince acknowledged him and continued, holding out an armload of red silk. "It is time to dress for evening court."

"And for my most exalted father. . . ." An eyebrow quirked at the healer. "Maybe it's a good thing you're staying."

"Darvish."

"Shahin. What a pleasant surprise." Darvish smiled at his eldest brother and extended the smile to include the guard that followed the heir even into the royal wing. The guard returned the smile. The heir did not. The heir merely looked down his hawklike nose with the expression of disgust he always wore in Darvish's presence.

"Are you drunk yet?"

"Please, at this hour? Give me credit for an ability to pace myself, at least."

"I heard about what you did today."

"Of course you did." Darvish kept the bright smile pasted in place, but behind it he tried frantically to figure out his brother's interest. Years ago, before the wine, they had been friends—as much friends as the difference in age and the heir's position had allowed. Was there enough of that friendship left for Darvish to appeal to it? For him to ask Shahin to intercede with their father for his thief's life?

He forced his eyes to meet Shahin's for a heartbeat and then he allowed his gaze to drop. The older prince's face showed no indication he remembered anything but the wine.

"Why did you do it?"

The tone and the expression reminded Darvish so much of their father that his palms grew damp. "Save a man's life?" The laugh sounded false, but it was the best he could do at the moment. "Oh, I don't know. You've got Yasimina, she's got her peacocks, maybe I wanted a pet of my own."

Shahin's lip curled up, teeth very white against the black of his beard. "You're a disgusting . . ." Words failed him and with a final withering glare, he strode into his own apartments.

Darvish shrugged as the door slammed shut and the guard took up position outside it. "Nobody understands me," he sighed melodramatically, and, with his heart curiously heavy, continued down the corridor. He needed a drink.

From his position at the far end of the long audience hall, Darvish could barely see the great black throne let alone the man sitting upon it, but even through the milling crowds of courtiers he could feel the king's presence. He snagged a drink off a passing tray and let the familiar taste of the wine soothe him while he contemplated strategy. Sooner or later, one of his most exalted father's pages would find him and request that he approach the throne. Darvish harbored no illusions that the king remained long ignorant of anything that happened within the palace and his actions of the afternoon had probably been reported by several different people, those watching him, those watching the twins, the lord chancellor himself. Given that Shahin knew, the king certainly did. The question became, did he stay as far from the throne as possible, assuming out of sight out of mind, thus putting off the confrontation? Or did he begin now to work his way through the crowds so that when the summons came he had less far to walk under the eyes of the court.

He exchanged his empty goblet for a full one and decided on the latter; he had no objection to being talked about but he preferred to have more choice over the subject.

"Highness."

The low, throaty voice drew his head around in an almost involuntary action.

"Lady Harithah." He caught up the dimpled hand she held out and brushed his lips across its back. She tasted of some rare spice that set his pulses racing.

Eyes that sparkled like amethyst in sunlight looked up into his for an instant with unmistakable desire, then curved lids stained violet were quickly, and demurely, lowered. "I trust this evening finds you well, Highness."

"It does now," Darvish murmured, watching the almost sheer silk rise and fall across her breasts. He'd been admiring the lady from afar since she'd arrived at court, her much older and very protective husband in tow. Up close, she was unbelievable, with deep curves a lover could get lost in. He had smiled at her but nothing more, for even a royal prince does not cuckold one of the First Lords of the Navy. Except that now the lady seemed to be offering.

"I have heard your Highness has an interest in antique weapons. I have a sword of my husband's in my suite, if you would care to see it after court."

It still wasn't a good idea. "And your husband?"

The tip of her tongue lightly touched the full center of one moist lip. "My husband is at sea, Highness."

And when the Nine drop paradise in your lap it is not a mere mortal's place to say it's a bad idea. "I would be honored, Lady Harithah. Your room," he kissed the back of her hand again and turned it over and laid his lips gently against the palm, "after court."

As she walked away, each rounded buttock imprinted the silk of her full trousers for one warm second. Downing the wine remaining in the second goblet, Darvish reached for a third. And then he remembered.

The thief. When court ended, he should return to his injured thief. *Why?* He tapped the nails of his free hand against the embossed bowl of the goblet. *He's unconscious, he won't even know you're there. And Lady Harithah most certainly will.* His stomach growled and he headed for the nearest of the small circular tables piled high with delicacies. *Besides, Karida's with him.* Picking up a pastry, he shrugged off the memory of silver-gray eyes. *He doesn't need me.*

The evening had advanced well into night by the time Darvish felt the light touch on his elbow and the murmured "Highness" that meant a summons from the throne. He finished reciting the bawdy verse he had just composed for a limpid-eyed young lady, who blushed at the attention while her friends shrieked with laughter. He bowed theatrically at their applause, red silk sleeves billowing with the motion, and, when he straightened, took a kiss in payment. Then he turned—calmly, as if his heart had not begun to pound painfully behind his ribs—and acknowledged the page.

She inclined her head, fingers properly laced against the pale gray tunic, body positioned the requisite two paces away—close enough for privacy, far enough for movement. "My lord would see you now, Highness."

He bowed again, a gesture just on the verge of mocking. Composure unruffled, she turned and walked away, knowing that whatever he felt, however he acted, the prince would follow.

The throne had been carved many, many years before from a single block of obsidian and as he approached, Darvish kept his gaze on the gleaming black stone rather than the man sitting upon it. It was supposed to be a symbol of how the king controlled the volcano, and it impressed most people as it had been designed to. Darvish, however, had sat upon it. He had been very young and had been beaten for it afterward, but he remembered how cold and hard it had been and at that moment he gave up any desire to ever sit upon it again.

Of course, I'll never convince our most cautious lord chancellor of that. . . .

The lord chancellor stood to the left of the throne, his plump hands tucked into the full green sleeves of his robe, his round face serene. The serene face, Darvish well knew, was the most dangerous. The serene face meant his mind was already made up and only an act of the One Below could change it.

To the right of the throne, one hand resting lightly upon the stone, the other folded behind his back, stood Shahin, Crown Prince and Heir, Light of his Father. His expression had not changed since their earlier meeting.

I have not had enough to drink. I thought I had, but I was wrong. Too close to the throne for serving tables or servants, Darvish slipped a nearly full goblet of wine from the surprised fingers of an elderly lord and tossed it back. It was sweet and cloying, not the light mountain wine he preferred. *Still, princes can't be choosers. And anything's better than no wine at all.* He winked at the lord as he returned the goblet.

Then nothing stood between him and the throne. Even the page had faded away.

Heart beginning to pound, he continued forward, eyes on the tiles in the floor. When he caught the gleam of gold, the outermost edge of the royal crest that marked the actual boundary of the throne, he dropped to one knee and rested his head for an instant on the other. As a member of the royal family, he did not have to wait on the king's grace to rise, but the timing was delicate—too short a time and he was accused of being disrespectful, too long and they accused him of sarcasm. Either charge was usually true. Of-

ten, both were. Tonight though, for some reason, he felt
tired—nothing more, nothing less—so he stayed down a little longer and figured they could make of it what they would.

He lurched slightly as he rose, the most recent wine shifting queasily in his stomach, but his voice was steady as he
spoke the ritual words.

"You requested my presence, Most Exalted?"

Darvish couldn't remember the last time he'd called the
man father to his face. Tradition called for him to keep his
eyes lowered until the king spoke. He didn't. He never did.

The king's eyes were as obsidian black as the throne he
sat on and showed as much warmth as he looked down at
his third son. "You took something from the Chamber of
the Fourth this afternoon," he said without preamble and
without emotion. "Why?"

"Not something, Most Exalted. Some*one*."

Long fingers stirred on the broad arm of the throne. "Do
not make me repeat my question."

As if I could, Darvish thought and barely stopped the
wine from voicing the thought aloud. He drew breath to tell
the story he had concocted over the course of the evening's
drinking and dallying, paused, and said instead, "I didn't
like what was being done to him."

"It was no more, Most Exalted, than what is done in the
Chamber of the Fourth," the lord chancellor interjected
smoothly.

"I didn't like what was being done to *him*," Darvish
insisted.

"Is he your lover?" The question was asked without curiosity or caring; only because it was inevitable the question
be asked.

"No, Most Exalted, just a thief who fell from the night
onto my balcony."

"Why, then, did you take him from the Chamber of the
Fourth? Merely because you could?" The lord chancellor
leaned a little forward, his position challenging.

He wants me to say yes, Darvish realized, *so that they
can come and take the thief away. Merely because they can.*
And out of the blurry memories of the night before came
the sight of the thief's face, just after he'd opened those
amazing silver-gray eyes. Something. . . . Darvish raised
his head and looked the king full in the face, speaking slowly
as he sorted his feelings into words.

"There was already so much pain, I couldn't let them add any more. . . ."

"So you took it upon yourself," and the tone asked, *who are you,* "to stop it."

"Yes, Most Exalted." It was the only honest conversation he'd had with his father in years, and Darvish could see the man was not impressed. *What do you want from me?* he wanted to ask. But he didn't. He knew the answer. Nothing.

"Let him keep the thief, Father."

"What?" The king echoed Darvish's thought. He turned to stare in puzzlement at his eldest son.

Just for an instant, Darvish saw a speculative look in Shahin's eyes he'd never seen before, then it passed, replaced by the scorn he recognized only too well.

"If nothing else, it will teach him he must accept responsibility for his actions."

"But my prince," the lord chancellor protested. "A thief. Loose in the palace. An *outland* thief."

The emphasis drew the king's brows down, as it had been intended to, Darvish was sure.

"What of it?" Shahin's hawk gaze crossed the throne and pinned the older man. "It is not as if he will ever be unobserved."

Darvish wondered if he heard another meaning beneath his brother's words, if the "he" Shahin referred to was not the thief but Darvish himself. He turned the words over, but the wine frustrated his search.

"I have thought on this matter."

The ritual words jerked Darvish back to the question at hand.

"The thief should have died had you not saved him. He therefore has no life save what you give him. If . . ."

The tone said, *When.*

". . . you tire of him, he dies."

"As easy as that to dispose of a life, Most Exalted?"

Even the background babble of the court seemed to fade as Darvish watched his father's brows draw in. He wanted to say something to cancel the comment, but anything he could think of would only make matters worse.

The crown prince gave a snort of disgust before the king could speak. "You should know," and his voice cut like a scimitar's edge, "you've disposed of your own."

The danger passed and the king nodded slowly, acknowledging the wisdom of his heir's remark. This third son was not worth wasting anger upon. "I have finished with you," was all he said and he would have said the same to anyone as he dismissed them from his presence.

Darvish dropped to his knee again, then stood and backed the nine and one paces away. With the suggestion of a nonchalant smile carefully pasted on his face, he turned and plunged into the crowd of courtiers.

Frowning thoughtfully, Shahin watched him go. For years he had been convinced that Darvish was nothing more than he seemed; a wastrel, a buffoon, an embarrassment. Tonight—earlier in the corridor, and here—he thought he saw something more, that perhaps there was still a prince left inside the fool.

"You look worried, Highness."

"Do I?" While Shahin recognized that the man excelled at his job, that he had guided the king and therefore the kingdom on a prosperous course for years, he couldn't warm to him. Back when Darvish had first begun to drink, Shahin had asked the lord chancellor if something worthwhile could not be found for the younger prince to do.

"You'd trust something worthwhile to that?" the chancellor had replied as they watched a giggling Darvish being hoisted out of a fountain.

"No," Shahin had answered, and turned his back.

But now he wondered if perhaps he should have said yes.

"You're worried about something, Highness."

"Nothing," the heir lied and, warned by his tone, the lord chancellor backed away. Shahin watched his brother accept a goblet of wine and drain it. Was it too late?

Once they knew he was not likely to bring down the king's wrath upon them, Darvish was quickly surrounded by laughing young men and women who pressed food, drink, and themselves into his hands. He lost himself in their circle for a time and then danced his way to the Nobles' Quarters where the Lady Harithah kept the promises of her smile.

Darvish responded with enthusiasm—a dead man would've responded with enthusiasm—but somehow, his heart wasn't in it.

* * *

"Highness, the thief is awake."

Darvish stretched his toes out over the edge of the bath and regarded them sleepily. "Thank you, Fadi," he said when Oham had moved the razor far enough from his throat for speech. "I'll see him when I'm bathed. Has he spoken?"

"No, Highness. He just lies and stares at the ceiling."

"Go back to watching him," Darvish yawned. "Tell me if there's any change."

"Yes, Highness." The boy bowed, his gaze dropping from the rim of the tub where he'd anchored it to the prince's body shimmering under the water. He flushed, turned quickly, and began to hurry out of the room.

"Fadi."

He turned back slightly more slowly than he'd turned away.

Darvish grinned. He wished he had the energy to tease the boy, who was curious, obviously, but who was still considerably too young. *And I am too exhausted to live up to the expectations of a thirteen year old.* He'd gotten even less sleep than usual the night before. *Nine Above, it's no wonder her husband spends so much time at sea.* "Is Karida still with him?"

"No, Highness. She left this morning. Just after you . . ." Fadi paused, unsure of how to describe his prince being all but carried in by two grinning guards wearing only his shirt and his sandals. Squirming a little under Oham's gaze, he settled finally on, ". . . returned."

"And I'll bet she had a few things to say about my return, too."

The young dresser opened and closed his mouth. He couldn't repeat what the healer had said. Not to his prince. He squirmed a little more.

"Go." Darvish took pity on the boy and, with a wave of his hand that arced a spray of scented water through the air, dismissed him. "I can pretty much guess what she said anyway. Watch my thief for me."

Thankfully, Fadi sped out of the bathing room.

The ceiling was stucco. Aaron knew stucco. It crumbled under probing fingers and left its mark on hands and boots and clothing. A good thief stayed away from stucco. And Aaron was a good thief.

"You're too good a thief, Aaron, my lad."

"Not too good, Faharra," he told the memory. *"Or I wouldn't be where I am."* He was in the palace although he didn't know where and he still lived although he didn't know why. The angle of the wall told him he was low, on a pallet, not a bed. The pain that rose and fell with each breath advised against movement, but he tried to rise anyway, to see more of his failure. Teeth clenched, fighting the agony, he got his head up, but it did him no good as his vision blurred into jagged slashes of red and yellow and they became all he could see.

"Hey." A gentle hand pushed him down. "You're not supposed to do that. Karida'll have my butt if you undo all her hours of work."

Aaron struggled to focus on the speaker suddenly perched beside him. The large block of cream was a robe. The black above it, a tangle of damp hair. The blue—the winter blue—eyes. He closed his own.

"Are you in pain? I can call the healer."

It was a man's voice. Ruth was dead. He opened his eyes again.

"That's better."

The brilliant white smile that accompanied the words drove the image—no, the man—further from Aaron's memory of his cousin. She had never smiled like that in her entire too brief life.

"Look, have you got a name? I can't go on referring to you as the-thief-that-fell-onto-my-balcony indefinitely."

He swallowed, once, twice, before he pulled a voice up out of the knife edges in his throat. "Aaron." It didn't matter what he told them. Not any more.

"You sound worse than that One abandoned peacock, Aaron. Here."

One large hand slid behind his back and the other held a metal rim against his lips. The pain of being moved was nothing against the feel of the chilled water in his mouth, cooling and soothing the abraded tissue.

"In case you're curious . . ."

He wasn't.

". . . my name is Darvish, these are my rooms, and I pulled you out of the Chamber of the Fourth. You owe me your life."

Why didn't you let me die!

Something of the thought must have shown on his face, for the voice hardened slightly.

"If you want to die, just say so. You aren't that far from it."

One word would bring him the death he craved, but Aaron couldn't speak it. Had never been able to speak it. He'd lived with the knowledge of his cowardice eating away at him for years. Not even this close to death could he just give up and slide past the barrier. He would have to live. Again.

Darvish hadn't quite known what to expect from his thief, gratitude maybe but certainly not such bleak and utter despair. He'd seen men and women go to the volcano with more joy. It made him profoundly uncomfortable. He stood and frowned down at the young man on the pallet. "The healer says you can have as much fluid as you can handle. . . ."

There was no response. No reaction at all, as if the inner misery left no space for anything else.

Darvish suddenly didn't want to be in the same room with all that pain. It made him feel guilty, although he didn't understand why. He had nothing to feel guilty about. He'd saved Aaron's life.

"Oham!"

"Yes, Highness."

With the robe billowing out behind him, he strode back into the bedroom, heels slamming down into the brightly patterned rugs. "Get me my leathers. I'm going to the training yard."

Three hours later, winded, bruised, and aching, he felt a little better.

Nothing like getting your ass kicked, Darvish thought as Oham spread liniment over a battered section of ribs, *to get rid of guilt. You're in pain. I'm in pain. So stop looking at me like that.*

Aaron actually seldom looked at Darvish at all. Over the next few days he lay quietly, wrapped in almost tangible despair. He remained stoic while Karida treated him. He almost never spoke. Fadi brought him the waste pot periodically and if he needed to, he used it. He never asked for it. He never asked for anything.

Standing motionless and unseen in the shadow of a building, Shahin watched the arms master criticize Darvish's last session.

". . . and much too slow," he finished as the panting prince held out his hands to help the defeated pair of guards to their feet.

It hadn't looked too slow to Shahin, he'd been impressed by his younger brother's skill. For too long, he'd lumped Darvish in with the twins as unsalvageable, cursed by the wine as the youngest members of the royal family had been cursed by their birth—his hand sketched the sign of the Nine and One—but that would have to change.

Darvish, strangely unwilling to put up with the pointed questions and snide comments of his friends, spent a lot of time at the training yard.

"Looking at the bright side," he grunted as Oham wound a dressing about his throbbing knee, "if this keeps up I'll soon be back in shape. Or in pieces," he added, sighing, sticking a skinned knuckle in his mouth.

Even the wine held less allure than usual.

And then his most exalted father met him one afternoon in the corridor, ran cold eyes over the grimy and sweat-stained leathers and said with no discernible emotion at all, "It appears that thief will be the making of you."

Darvish made no reply, but that night he put on his gaudiest silks and he didn't sober up for three days.

"You look like shit."

Darvish belched, handed the cup now empty of wizard's brew to Oham, and squinted in the direction of the voice. For reasons he could no longer remember, although he assumed they'd made perfect sense at the time, he'd had Aaron, pallet and all, brought from the sitting room to the bedroom. It must have been a good idea, the thief was talking.

"You don't look so terrific yourself," he pointed out, balancing precariously on one leg as Oham stripped off his filthy trousers.

Aaron, reclining against a massive mound of pillows Fadi had piled at one end of his pallet, dropped a shoulder slightly, the closest he could come to a shrug. Any greater movement pulled at his healing chest and threatened to send him back into darkness. His lip curled as he watched the activity by the bed. "You're one of the royal princes," he said.

."Right first time," Darvish agreed, scraping at something he couldn't identify that was caked on the back of his left hand.

Aaron's brows drew down as he tried to remember. "Darvish. . . ."

Oham whirled about, the chains that held his sleeveless vest in place straining against his indignant breath. "You will call him Highness."

"Why?" Aaron asked dryly, lids falling to hood his eyes. "What will he do to me if I don't?"

"You can die!" Oham snapped.

"Yes. I can." *But I won't,* he thought, *my father's god isn't done with me yet.* The thought didn't bother him. Nothing bothered him any longer. He had no feelings, he had no life. He'd spent the last few days cutting all that loose. Let the hand of his father's god fall where it would. It didn't matter.

"He can call me what he wants," Darvish said, weaving his way to the bath. "Stop glaring at him, Oham, and come here. I'm likely to drown this morning without help." *And besides,* leaning heavily on the dresser the prince managed to get first one leg then the other over the edge of the tub, *I think I'd like to be called by my name for a change. And it looks like that black cloud he had himself wrapped in is finally gone, thank the One.* The cloud had been replaced by nothing at all, but Darvish was used to that.

Bath over, and feeling if not better at least as if death was no longer imminent, Darvish sat quietly watching the thief while Oham tried to work the tangles out of his hair. "So," he said at last, more because he wasn't up to silence than because he wanted to know, "what were you after that night you fell at my feet?"

Aaron dropped his gaze from the patterns of sunlight and shadow playing across the ceiling to Darvish's face. Why not tell him?

"I was after the emerald on top of the royal staff."

Oham made a choking noise and across the room, Fadi almost let a platter of bread and fruit drop to the floor. From where he was cleaning the bathing room, the lord chancellor's man strained not to miss any further confessions. Darvish only grinned.

"I figured you couldn't be after The Stone, being as how

you don't strike me as a complete idiot. The emerald, huh?''
He shook his head admiringly. "Why?''

Aaron's lips thinned. "Personal reasons,'' he grunted.
Faharra was his; her memory only the second thing worth
keeping in a life of failure.

"Suit yourself.'' Darvish took a peach from the offered
platter and began to peel it fastidiously. "I'd ask you to join
me,'' he said as Fadi gathered up the fallen peel, "but Karida says you're on fluids for a while yet. I think she's expecting you to regain your color.'' A drop of juice splashed
against the wall over Aaron's head as Darvish gestured with
the dripping fruit. "Of course, you being an outlander, this
is probably as much color as you'll get.''

It could have been an insult. Guided by their king, the
people of Ischia tended to think outlanders were little better
than barbarians and at best they treated them with patronizing tolerance. The attitude had made much of Aaron's
thievery easier. "Your eyes are blue,'' he said mildly.

Darvish wiped his chin. "My grandmother was from the
north. Fairly far north. A treaty bride.''

"The king is half an outlander?''

"I suppose that is what it means, yes.'' The peach pit
sailed over the balcony railing. "But never mention it to my
most exalted father.''

Aaron shrugged his minimal shrug once again. He
doubted he'd be mentioning anything to the king. And if the
king's third son, his blue-eyed son, failed to see that his
very existence reminded the king he was only half of the
land he ruled, a land he had tried to empty of other remind-
ers, well, it wasn't Aaron's business to point it out if said
third son was too blind to see it on his own. And frankly,
he could care less. The insecurities of the king were not his
problem.

"What are you going to do with me?'' he asked instead.
Not that he cared anything about that either—although his
heart, apparently unaware of his feelings, beat faster while
he waited for an answer.

"You mean when you get better?''

"Yes.''

Darvish studied the way the sunlight turned Aaron's hair
to burnished copper, the way the slightly lighter brows rose
at the outer edges then tufted thickly over the center of those

amazing gray eyes. It was a pity about the scarring but even so the lithely muscled body had appeal. He grinned, his meaning very evident. "I'll think of something."

Aaron's lips drew back off his teeth. "I'll see you in the Lady first."

Oh, so it's like that, is it? Pity. Darvish stretched and reached for another peach. He'd never taken an unwilling lover, and he had no intention of starting now. Enough men and women threw themselves in his path that he had no need to exhaust himself seducing one skinny thief. "Well, as long as we understand each other," he said.

Five

"Chandra? Chandra!" The piercing call echoed up the tower stairs, followed by a rustle of fabric and a heavy wheezing that suggested the person climbing could call or climb but not both.

The slim bronze figure sitting at the exact center of the tower roof gave no indication that she'd heard anything at all. Her long dark hair streaming out behind her like a pennant, she sat motionless, staring into the setting sun.

"Chandra!" The cry rose in volume; closer now, less muffled by stone and distance. "Chandra!" A head, wrapped in yards of purple veiling, popped up through the open trapdoor. The small black eyes, all that were visible of the face, widened as they saw the girl. "So there you are, Chandra. I might have known you'd be up here."

The sun having finally dropped below the horizon, Chandra turned from her contemplation of the rapidly purpling sky. "Yes, you might have," she said, "as I'm *always* up here at sunset."

"But not tonight!" Two plump hands beginning to show the marks of age, waved in the air like hysterical pigeons. "The messenger has come from King Jaffar."

"I know, Aba. I saw the arrival from my window. What with the banners and the horns and all it was hard to miss." She began to smoothly braid the heavy fall of chestnut hair. "The message has little relevance, however, as regardless of King Jaffar's answer I will continue to refuse to marry anyone."

"Oh-ho, big words." The older woman clucked her tongue at Chandra's glare. The young became outraged so easily. "You may say that now, poppet. . . ."

"I have been saying it all along, Aba, so it's hardly my fault if my father doesn't listen." Chandra's father, to her disgust, had made a long habit of only hearing what he wanted to. "And you needn't put it down to maidenly modesty," she added emphatically, "for I haven't any."

"Modesty indeed!" The black currant eyes widened, suddenly aware of her poppet's state of undress. "For pity's sake, Chandra, put a robe on before someone sees you!"

"How?" Chandra waved a graceful hand around. The tower was the tallest building on their country estate and from where she sat all she could see was sky and the cradling circle of mountains that made up the horizon.

"You *know* what nasty boys are like!"

Actually, she didn't—she never associated with people her own age, they were so *young*—but as her old nurse seemed to be working herself into a foaming fit, Chandra unfolded from the full lotus she'd been in for the last two hours, touching her forehead briefly against each knee as she straightened the leg. "My robe is in my rooms," she pointed out when she was standing, her tone just bordering on smugness, "and you're blocking the stairs."

Chandra watched her father paring an apple and wondered if she should speak first. Her position was, after all, a simple one; she was not going to marry Prince Darvish. Or anyone else for that matter. Ever. But so far marriage had not been mentioned—although the weather, trade, the olive crop, and the new bay stallion had all been trivialized—and Chandra was hesitant about bringing the subject up herself. *"When battle can no longer be avoided,"* Rajeet, her teacher, had told her, *"it is always wisest to discover your enemy's strengths and weaknesses and use those against him."* Of course, her father's only strength was weakness and that made it more difficult. Rajeet, being a Wizard of the First, and the First the god of war, never seemed to take that into account.

She watched the peel spiral to the table in one long strand and remembered how much that had impressed her when she'd been small, how whenever a crate of the imported fruit had arrived she'd begged him to peel one for her immediately. Many things had impressed her about her father then; he'd been a giant among men, everything a lord should be. They'd ridden together, walked together, read together. He'd shown her how to treat the people she would one day rule with wisdom and compassion. And then her mother had died, leaving an aching void where there had once been gentle laughter and warm arms, a void made larger because something in her father had died as well. Chandra had been ten. She'd tried to comfort him, but he would not be comforted, alternately raging and weeping, calling for the One Below to take him, too. Chandra, the child, couldn't understand what she'd done wrong. Her mother's death had not been her fault, she knew that even then, but somehow she had failed her father.

Even now, six years later, Chandra could not think back on that time without shuddering. Her potential as a wizard only just recognized, she had thrown herself into her studies, hiding from what her father had become and from her inability to help, piling up texts and tracts and her new knowledge between them. If he had no room in his heart for her, then she would make no room in her heart for him. Her power replaced her father's love and all the attention she'd given to him, she now gave to it.

Eventually, her father had found enough of himself to be a competent administrator, nothing more.

He reached for the scented linen napkin by his plate and rubbed at the apple juice on his fingers. Chandra resisted the urge to drum her own fingers against the lacquer tabletop. Would he never get to the point? Finally, he set the napkin carefully aside and the server moved forward to remove the low tables and bring in the cups of sweet coffee. Chandra let the first sip roll slowly across her tongue. A passion for the thick, rich drink was the only remaining activity she shared with her father and, although she knew it was foolish—a wizard should remain aloof from such ties—she could not bring herself to break that last link.

Lord Atman Balin settled back against the cushions and gazed at his daughter over the edge of the thin porcelain cup. He watched her swallow, saw the expression of pleasure spread across her face, and wondered if it was too late to find the little girl he had lost. Things had been so simple before the One Below had taken his beloved Matrika. When the three of them had lived in that perfect world, Chandra had been a laughing, happy child, open and accepting; he didn't recognize the silent, closed young woman she had become who seemed to watch everything he did with distant disapproval. She hadn't understood how he'd felt when his Matrika had been torn from him. And when he finally was able to explain, she hadn't wanted to hear. He sighed, his breath sending mahogany ripples across the surface of the coffee. It hurt that his daughter refused to understand him.

He could only hope that she understood what was expected of her as the only daughter of the ruling house; he feared, however, she did not. Thus tonight they dined alone.

"The messenger has returned from King Jaffar."

Chandra remained silent, waiting.

"He approves of the marriage alliance between you and his third son, Darvish."

Chandra had expected as much. The island her father ruled, while not large, was in a strategic trade position between the mainland and Cisali, King Jaffar's much larger island. Since her great-grandfather's time, they had been loosely allied with Cisali and it made sense that her father had sought a husband for her among Jaffar's sons, strengthening the alliance. There was only one problem.

"I am *not* going to marry this Darvish, Father. I told you that when you sent the proposal. It would have been better for all concerned had you believed me then."

"It's a good match."

"I know that, Father." Chandra had never argued that point. The facts were undeniable; the alliance held benefits for both countries and on a personal level the prince was by all reports, even allowing for the bias of marriage brokers, neither unattractive nor halfway to the One Below. "I am a Wizard of the Nine and I am not going to marry *at all*. Ever." She'd seen what marriage had done for her father: a few years of happiness, then almost total destruction. That wasn't going to happen to her.

"Then you wish your cousin Kesin to inherit. . . ."

"No, I do not wish my cousin Kesin to inherit." She hated it when her father's voice picked up that self-pitying whine. "Kesin is an ignorant lout without the brains the Nine gave pigs." *And you only bring him up to manipulate me into this marriage. Well, it's a dirty trick and it won't work!*

"Kesin inherits if my line does not continue," her father pointed out, smugly, she thought, sure he had outmaneuvered her. "As he has issue already, *you* must have a husband and an heir before I die." He spread his hands triumphantly, the red and yellow sleeves of the mourning robes he still wore fluttering ominously. "You are my only child."

"That's not *my* fault," Chandra snapped, setting her cup aside and rising to her feet. "You're not an old man. You are fully capable of siring more children."

"More children. . . ."

The pain on his face drove a knife into Chandra's heart, but she ignored it. He had to learn to face reality. He had to become strong, as she had.

"You don't understand," he said softly.

Chandra matched this man against the memories of her father and wondered how he could have become so weak. She didn't understand his pain nor why he insisted in wallowing in it. Her ears grew hot. It was embarrassing to see him like this.

"Chandra," his voice turned suddenly pleading, "you are all I have left of your mother. I want all this to be yours. You mustn't let Kesin destroy everything."

"*I* mustn't let Kesin destroy everything?" The rest of what she wanted to say caught in her throat and threatened to choke her. *I am not the one who spent years weeping and wailing! I am not the one doing just barely enough to get by!* But there was no point in saying it; her father never listened to facts, he just got emotional and started wringing his hands.

She bowed, her own emotions under rigid control, tossed her braid back over her shoulder, and left the room.

And the worst of it is, she thought as she returned to her tower, *I can't let Kesin inherit because he* will *destroy everything.* The thought of Kesin living in her house, riding her horses, attempting to rule her people made her feel almost physically ill. It wasn't that her cousin was a bad man, but he hadn't been raised to rule. Chandra knew her father had taken her final silence as assent rather than the denial of his emotions it actually was. He hadn't actually seen *her* for years. Ignoring her wishes, he would go ahead with the marriage plans. She would have to find another solution.

". . . always a solution, Chandra." Rajeet's image in the basin of water wavered and shook, her voice fading in and out. To actually communicate in this way took the combined concentration of both wizards involved and Rajeet's mind was obviously not on the conversation. ". . . don't wish your cousin to inherit and your father refuses to have more children . . . duty to the land, however, as . . . barely six-teen, ask your father . . . can be postponed a few years.''

"Rejeet, you don't understand." Rajeet's brother had certainly picked a fine time to demand Rajeet come home and help him win a war—right when Chandra needed her most. She drew herself up as well as she was able, given her position over the bowl, and declared, "I am a Wizard of the Nine. I will never marry.''

The image stopped wavering for a moment as the older woman smiled. "Never is a very long time at your age."

"You don't believe me?"

". . . believe in this instance it does not matter, Chandra. I assume . . . told your father?"

"Yes. But he doesn't listen." Chandra had long since given up believing there was a way to make him listen.

"Then . . . your intended."

"How?"

Rajeet's nostrils flared, a sure sign she had reached the end of her somewhat limited patience. ". . . a Wizard of the Nine; think of something!"

The image flickered and once again the bowl held nothing more than clear water.

"Very well," Chandra told her reflection now mirrored on the water's surface, "I shall. I don't need her any more than I need Father."

A sound in the courtyard drew her to the window and she peered down at King Jaffar's messenger, horns and banners and all, riding out. Her father had given him an answer. Well, she would give the whole lot of them another.

He can't even run his own life, she thought, pulling her head in, *I don't know what makes him think he can run mine.*

She flipped at the multifaceted crystal hanging down from the mobile in the window and, brow furrowed, watched the tiny rainbows that danced around the room. Rajeet had hung the mobile the day she'd arrived at the estate.

"Most people," she'd said, holding up a clay disk, *"are opaque to power, like this clay, but every now and then a child is born with the ability to act as a focus. Most of these children,"* here she started to hang nine curved ovals of colored glass from the disk, *"can focus only a small amount of the power available. They become Wizards of the First to Ninth, concentrating that small ability to focus on the*

single disciplines of the Nine Above." She'd lifted the disk
into the sunlight and each piece of dangling glass threw its
signature into the room.

"Every once in a great while," she'd continued, *"a child
is born who can focus more than just a part of the power."*
Then she'd hung up the crystal. It caught the sunlight and
divided it and its signature held not one but all colors.
*"These children are very rare and they become Wizards of
the Nine."*

"You have the potential to be a Wizard of the Nine,"
she'd said. *"If you study hard, there is very little you will
not be able to do."*

Rajeet, Chandra decided, for all she'd been only a Wizard
of the First trained in the discipline of the god of the sword,
had been right. She stilled the wildly swinging crystal. "I
am a Wizard of the Nine and I *will not* marry Prince Darvish."

"I *know* he's supposed to be handsome and young, Aba,
that's all anyone will tell me about him. There must be
more."

"Well. . . ." The old nurse drew the word out as she
drew the ivory comb through her charge's damp hair, pleased
the girl was taking an interest at last. "He's a third son and
that can't have been easy on him." A fair woman, she was
willing to make excuses for some of the things she'd heard.
"The heir has a place and a role to play, and a second son
is always welcome in case, the Nine and One forbid, something should happen to the heir. But a third son," she sighed
gustily, "a third son can never be certain of where he belongs. Don't wrinkle your forehead like that, poppet, you'll
make lines. I feel quite sorry for your Prince Darvish."

"He's not *my* Prince Darvish." Chandra frowned.

Aba smiled, her eyes almost disappearing behind the
curves of her cheeks. "As you wish, poppet." She continued to work the comb through the heavy mass of hair.

"What about his family? His brothers?" Rajeet had
taught her an object could often be defined by its surroundings.

"Shahin, the heir, is much like his father. Kinder, they
say, and less proud but as alike in appearance as if he'd
been crafted out of wizardry. He made a treaty marriage

last year, with a princess of Ytaili yet. Everyone hopes their marriage will stop the fighting. . . ."

"They aren't exactly fighting, Aba," Chandra protested.

"And they aren't exactly at peace either," Aba told her firmly. "Now, Ramdan, the second son, lives in the country. The heir and heir apparent are often separated thus, so that if some disaster befalls one, the other is safe. He married very young and has six, no, seven children. His marriage is his chief happiness, they say."

"You needn't keep dwelling on marriage, Aba."

"Not if you don't wish it, poppet." She paused while she worked out a tangle. "Then there's your Prince Darvish."

Chandra gritted her teeth but decided to let the possessive stand. It just wasn't worth the effort.

"They say he's an excellent swordsman." Most of the other things they said about Prince Darvish, Aba was not going to repeat. "They say his father never looked favorably on him from the moment of his birth."

"Why not?"

"He has blue eyes, poppet, and reminds King Jaffar that his own mother was not of Ischia."

"So?"

"The king is fiercely proud."

"Well, it was hardly the baby's fault he got blue eyes." For the first time Chandra felt something other than distaste for the prince.

Aba, sensing sympathy, intoned mournfully, "No, but it's been the burden he has to bear."

Chandra snorted, refusing to be manipulated by her nurse's tone. "Is he the youngest, then?"

"No. When Prince Darvish was nine, the twins were born."

Aba's voice sounded so peculiar that Chandra swiveled around to face her. "You're afraid of them? Why? You've never even met them. You've never even been to Ischia."

One plump hand made the sign of the Nine and One. "Their Royal Highnesses were cursed at birth."

"Cursed?"

Aba nodded. "Both were born with their faces covered, hiding from the gods even in the womb. The midwives wished to have them put to death immediately, bad enough to be a twin with only half a soul but to be cursed as well . . . but the king did not give his permission. They say he was too proud to acknowledge his seed could be cursed. He ignored them completely.''

''Their mother . . .''

''She agreed with the midwives, and never saw them from the moment of their birth. Servants raised them as royal children are raised.''

''Do they know that everyone wanted them dead?''

''They were cursed. . . .''

''Cursed?'' Chandra leapt to her feet and paced an agitated length of her room. ''I am a Wizard of the Nine, I don't believe in curses. What happened to them?''

''They were given intense religious instruction in the hope that the curse could be lifted.''

''And,'' Chandra prodded.

Aba sighed. ''They found a place with one of the Nine.''

''Which one?''

''The Fourth.''

''Hah!'' Chandra slapped her fist into her palm. ''I just bet they did, it gave them a chance to get their own back. I can't *believe* their mother wanted them dead. I don't like her, I don't like King Jaffar, and I'm glad I'm not marrying their stupid son.'' She took a deep breath. ''What happened to the queen? No one ever mentions her.''

Aba's eyes filled with tears. ''She died in the last wave of fevers. The fevers that killed your blessed mother.''

Chandra threw herself down on a pile of cushions and began picking at a silk fringe. Aba was almost as bad as her father about it. ''At least King Jaffar didn't fall to pieces.''

''Chandra!''

''Well, he didn't!''

Aba drew herself up to her full height, looking like an indignant purple pigeon. ''Queen Cizard was a cold woman. They say she placed her duty to the realm above all else, above her husband, above her children. They say her death caused barely a ripple in her family. Your father loved your mother. . . .''

''More than he loved anything else. I know, Aba. More than he loved himself. More than he loved his country. More than he loved me.''

Tears trickling down her face, Aba took a tentative step forward, and then stopped as Chandra's gaze pinned her where she was.

''I didn't put my father up on that pedestal, Aba. He

climbed up by himself. He had no right to fall.'' She would have helped him, but he wouldn't let her so he had only himself to blame for the distance between them. He chose to be weak. She never would.

"When you're married yourself, perhaps you'll understand,'' Aba offered. An unresponsive child could be held until the hurting eased. But a wizard—the old nurse sighed— she had no idea of how to deal with a wizard.

"I will never marry.''

"They say Prince Darvish has an—*How to phrase it?*— independent outlook. He will surely not expect you to give up yours.''

Chandra's eyes narrowed. "He won't get the chance.''

Aba shook her head in surrender, veils fluttering. She didn't understand. For a short while things had been going so well. Leaving Chandra on the cushions, she went to turn down the bed.

"Aba? Who do you refer to when you say, *they say?*''

"Why the servants, of course, poppet.'' She turned and waggled a finger wisely. "If you wish to find out about someone, question the servants. They're always around, but people seem to forget they have eyes and ears and tongues. I've been questioning every servant that has arrived from Ischia since this marriage was first proposed. I wouldn't let my poppet marry a stranger.''

Chandra nodded thoughtfully. "Thank you, Aba.''

The old nurse preened.

Shoulder muscles protesting, Chandra dumped the basket of earth out onto the roof of her tower and gave thanks that the oblong pile was finally large enough. She wanted nothing more at the moment than to take a long rest—she was a wizard not a laborer—but the stars of the Nine were too far along in their dance for her to risk losing the time. Tucking her sleeveless robe up between her knees and murmuring words of power as she worked, she began to shape the damp soil, following the instructions on the ancient scroll exactly and trying not to think of all the ways it had listed that things could go wrong.

It was harder than she'd anticipated. Theoretically, it was nothing she couldn't manage, but over the last few years, as her reach had at times exceeded her grasp, she'd learned that the distance between theory and practice was often greater than it appeared. This night's work, she felt, would be worth the risk although it didn't help that she had to work by starlight alone. Expending power to create any illumination would change the configuration of what she built. It hadn't occurred to her to bring a lamp.

Finally, although the murmured words became muttered at the end, a rough but definitely female form lay staring sightlessly up at the night. Chandra sat back on her heels and studied it critically. It didn't look much like her, she had to admit. It looked, well, ominous.

Don't be ridiculous. She turned aside to retrieve the rest of her supplies. *You're a Wizard of the Nine. That's a pile of dirt. It's nothing unless you choose to make it.*

Out of the corner of one eye, she saw movement and her mouth went suddenly dry. It wasn't supposed to move. It *couldn't* move.

It can't be going wrong already!

How do you know? asked a little voice in the back of her mind. *You've never done this before.*

Biting her lip to contain the unwizardly whimper that tried to escape, Chandra slowly looked down at her golem, straining to see details in the darkness. Maybe this wasn't the great idea she'd originally thought it. A night wind, heavy with the scent of damp earth, crossed the tower and dislodged a small ball of dirt, rolling it down off the stubby fingers to break into nothing against the stone.

Chandra remembered how to breathe. "Idiot," she said softly.

Hurrying now, having wasted enough time on stupid fears, she pushed two oval agates into the dark on dark indentations left for eyes and, moistening the dirt with a bit of saliva, stuck nine of her own hairs to the top of the head.

Keeping a close watch on the dance of the Nine, she readied the vellum strip and her ivory dagger, checking once more the words she'd inscribed on both. As little as she looked forward to marriage, she looked forward to being ripped to pieces by her own creation even less. Drawing the cool night air slowly in through her nose and out through her mouth, she sought the calm that was going to be very necessary in a few short seconds.

She couldn't find it. Her heart began to pound painfully hard. She needed the calm to guide the power down the paths she'd chosen. It wasn't there. In its place was the knowledge of what the golem would do to her if she failed. Of what the power would do to her without the calm to guide it. She wasn't ready for this. She should never have tried it without Rajeet, who, while not a Wizard of the Nine, was still a very powerful Wizard of the First.

She should stop. Now. Before things went that one step too far. Give up. Let the ship with the first installment of her dowry sail tomorrow without her. Think of something else.

Or marry the prince. Anything was better than what could happen here if things went wrong.

No! This is ridiculous. I know what I'm doing. She grabbed at the rising panic and held it, breathing deeply.

You're acting like your father, she berated herself, beads of sweat chilling the skin between her breasts. *Emotional. Hysterical. Stupid. If something goes wrong, it's those emotions that will have destroyed you just like they destroyed him. You are not like your father!* No, she wasn't. Not any more. Familiar anger took the place of fear and as the stars wheeled into position, Chandra slid into the calm and drove the point of the knife into the heel of her thumb.

Nine drops of blood struck the hollow in the center of the sculpted breast. When the ninth drop hit the earth, glistening almost black in the starlight, Chandra placed the rolled vellum in the lipless slash that was the golem's mouth.

Then she closed her teeth on a scream as the power of the Nine—more power than she'd ever channeled before—roared through the focus she had created.

"All on board?" The second mate's cry cut easily through the noise at the docks to the sailor at the head of the gangway.

"Aye, sir. Two nobles, six servants and a whole heap o'geegads finally loaded."

"Six? They told me five."

The sailor looked confused. Wasn't that what she'd said? "Aye, sir. Two nobles, five servants."

"Five?"

"Aye, sir."

The mate drew breath to bellow, then abruptly changed his mind. Five, six, what did one landsman more or less matter.

So it went the whole three days of the voyage. Five servants. Six. And no one seemed to think it mattered.

Chandra enjoyed herself hugely. She ate with the servants—themselves unsure if they were five or six—and slept hardly at all. She had worried, at first, about the nobles her father would send to accompany the dowry—if they knew her well, she doubted she'd be able to hold the spell—but the two lords had seen her at court maybe twice in the last five years and so wouldn't be a problem. Unnoticed, or at least unremarked, she spent her days investigating this new world of wood and water and hemp and tar and her nights marking the subtle variations in the dance of the stars.

This is not an adventure, she told herself sternly as the ship plunged over a wave and the salt spray beaded her hair. *If I can get the prince to back out, then I've gained the time I need to deal with Kesin and the inheritance.* Given time, she was confident that she'd come up with a final solution. A seabird skimmed past the sail and Chandra grinned, feeling a momentary pang of sympathy for her poor golem stuck supposedly sulking back in her tower; and thank the One she never went to court at this season, for the intricacies of that would have been far beyond the golem's limited abilities. At the thought of the golem, she sobered briefly, rubbing her hands over the sudden gooseflesh on her arms. She hadn't realized that focusing the necessary power to animate her double would hurt so much. *So I might as well enjoy any new experience that comes my way.* Even now, she could feel a faint echo of the pain sizzling through channels still raw and abraded. *I've paid for it.*

Late the third evening, when there were only clouds to be seen hanging dark and brooding over the ship and the waves were nothing more than rolling black shadows, Chandra settled in a sheltered cranny, the small silver bowl she scryed with between her knees. From under her plain, brown servant's tunic, she pulled out the locket that had arrived with the messenger from King Jaffar.

"My prince begs you to accept this," had said the letter, *a letter because she'd refused to see him. "It moves directly from his hand to yours."*

Chandra doubted that very much, but the portrait and lock of black hair the locket contained would be enough for her needs if, of course, the hair came from the prince. She rolled the soft strand between her fingers. If it had come from Prince Darvish, they were very careless about wizardry in Ischia. Perhaps she'd set them straight on that as well, while she was there.

With the locket propped to use for reference, she cast a hair down on the water in the bowl, drew the focus tight and fed power through it. Tensing a little at remembered pain, she was relieved to feel only the old familiar tingle. Rajeet disapproved of this sort of wizardly eavesdropping, but she also said that knowledge was strength. At this point Chandra figured forewarned was forearmed and anything new she could learn about her unintended betrothed could only help.

The water grew dark, then light, then a face began to form. It seemed to be the face in the portrait, at least as far as Chandra could tell through the contortions.

At first she thought the twists and grimaces meant torture, for her line of sight was limited to the face alone, but as she carefully pulled back, stretching the bounds of the focus, she understood.

Then the hair dissolved and the bowl was empty of vision and water both.

And for that, they want me to give up the power of the Nine? Chandra asked herself, putting the remaining hair safely back in the locket. She grabbed for her bowl as the ship rolled and it slid toward the rail. If the prince was as independent as Aba had said, it shouldn't be too hard to talk him out of the proposed marriage. Forehead creased, she reviewed what she'd been able to see of the prince's partner. It could only help her arguments that he obviously preferred his women more . . . fat.

Early the next morning, Chandra leaned her arms on the smooth wood of the railing and mourned the end of the voyage. They'd been at sea just long enough to show her a whole new world to learn, new lines of power, new focuses, new ways of thought. And now she had to leave it all to convince a prince that he didn't want to marry her. Life, she decided after a careful weighing of the facts, was on occasion most unfair.

She watched dawn brush the white terraces of Ischia with delicate highlights but was not impressed, her gaze drawn instead to the thin line of smoke rising above the top of the city. She assumed it came from the volcano, although she couldn't be certain as from her angle the crater was completely surrounded by buildings. *That* impressed her. That wizardry could protect an entire city built right to the edge of an active volcano.

The Stone of Ischia had taken nine Wizards of the Nine nine years to create. Chandra sighed. After she had dealt with Prince Darvish, she'd spend some time with it before she started for home. She focused a tendril of power toward the heights, then quickly snatched it back; something felt very wrong. Frowning, she wondered if she had breached one of the city's defenses. Surely The Stone would not repulse a Wizard of the Nine?

"Here now." The second mate dropped a weatherworn hand onto her shoulder and turned her about, pushing her gently toward the cabins where the five actual servents were readying their noble charges for disembarking. "You'd best get back with your own lot, then. We'll need the rails clear for lines."

Chandra shot one last, puzzled glance at the drifting plume of smoke, then walked slowly inside to join the others. She would have preferred to remain at the rail and watch the pilot ship guide them into Ischia's harbor, but now was not the time to toss off the carefully built layers of deception. And anyway, with the dual forts at the harbor mouth sliding by on either side, it was time she worked out her next step.

Quiet kid, thought the mate. *But I reckon that's part of being someone what serves. All six of them were quiet types.* He ran his fingers along a taut lenght of rope and lost the thought in the twists and turns of hemp. *Yep. Five of the quietest landsmen we ever carried. Though it beats the Eighth out of me why two fancy-asses need a half dozen people to take care of them.*

Six

Naked, his hair still damp from the bath, Darvish leaned his forearms on the balcony railing and looked out at the world. The early morning light clearly delineated buildings, gardens, even Yasimina's One abandoned peacocks. *It's like a mountain wine*, he decided, turning his arms so that the beads of moisture glowed, a scattering of tiny crystals. *A libation poured by the Nine onto their mother below.* He couldn't remember the last time he'd seen the sun before noon.

He only saw it today because Lady Harithah had remembered her husband would be arriving this morning and had canceled their assignation. Unwilling to settle for second best, he'd been in his own bed reasonably early and practically sober.

Waking with a clear head. . . . Darvish stretched and smiled. *What an interesting concept. Maybe someday I'll try it again.* Then he remembered that not only Lady Harithah's lord would be arriving today but also the first third of his bride's dowry.

His bride. The word was a bad taste in his mouth and a little of the light went out of the world. *Consider myself betrothed. Thank you very much, O Most Exalted Father.* Maybe he should tell her about the challenge he'd made to the whores of the city, male and female, last year in the middle of the market square. *And if that doesn't disrupt Father's plans,* Darvish smiled sardonically, *I'll tell her how I almost won.*

"Highness?"

He turned slowly. "Fadi."

"Highness, the healer says that she is busy this morning." The young dresser, keeping his gaze carefully level with the prince's knees, held out a squat clay pot securely stoppered with a round of cork. "She said . . ." He took a

deep breath and felt his ears begin to burn. He just couldn't
use the words the healer had used in front of his prince.
Why did she keep doing this to him?

"She said as long as I was up I could spread that stuff
myself?"

"Yes, Highness. Mostly." His prince sounded amused
and for Fadi that was almost worse than anger. Except that
Prince Darvish never got angry. He was difficult at times,
but Fadi knew that was the wine, not his prince. *His* prince
was the best master in the palace and all the things his
friends had said would happen to him when he came to
serve, hadn't. He was a little disappointed about some of
that actually. His ears burned hotter as he felt sure the
thought lay naked on his face for his prince to read.

If it did, Darvish chose to ignore it. "Thank you, Fadi."

As the pot changed hands, their fingers touched and the
young dresser sighed. Managing to stifle a sigh of his own,
Darvish's smile softened as he watched the boy hurry away.
I was never *that young.*

Fadi's adoration depressed him at times. What remained
to adore once the attraction of the flesh had been denied?
And he'd made it very clear that Fadi was too young for
that. Both to Fadi and to others. His smile iced as he remembered the expression on the Lord Rahman's face as that
noble had been informed what would happen to his genitals
if he ever spoke again of laying a hand on the prince's young
dresser.

"And speaking of laying on hands . . ." Darvish worked
the cork from the pot and sniffed at the pale green salve. It
had a clean, fresh scent that cleared his head of the overpowering odor of jasmine rising up from the garden below.
". . . I suppose I'd best get this over with."

At the balcony door, the lord chancellor's man met him
with a silver tray and a carafe of wine. "Highness." He
bowed, his voice straddling the thin line between service
and subservience. "Your wine."

Darvish watched a ruby drop trail a thin line of color
down the chilled metal. It just didn't go with the morning.
"No, I don't think so."

"But, Highness, you always have wine in the morning."

"Don't ever presume . . ." He clasped both hands tighter
about the pot of salve in case one should play traitor and

reach out, out of habit. ". . . that you know what I will always do."

"Highness." The dresser bowed again, the marks of his last beating still visible above the neckline of his vest. He expected another, the knowledge in his voice.

This, Darvish thought with a sudden rush of sympathy, *is the one man in Ischia whose place I would not exchange for mine.* "Don't you have something to do?"

"Yes, Highness."

Darvish watched the dresser scurry thankfully away. Perhaps the lord chancellor would have the man beaten later when he made his report—a pity, still, he wasn't going to drink unwanted wine to prevent it.

The old lord would, of course, see plots and machinations in the decision, but that was hardly surprising as he saw plots and machinations in anything. In everything.

Aaron, sitting cross-legged on his pallet, set aside his empty breakfast bowl and reached for the large goblet of water that Kadira had insisted he drink with every meal. Black silk trousers set off the pallor of his skin and threw the circular pattern of scars into sharp relief. He looked up as Darvish came in, saw the prince had still not dressed, and quickly looked away. It did little good. Over the days of his healing he had seen the prince too many times for looking away to erase the sight from his memory. He felt the blood rise to his face and a pounding start between his ears. *Men were not meant to gaze upon one another,* the priests of his childhood had told him. *That is the beginning of the path to the fire.* He shifted just enough to pull at the scars, welcoming the pain as a distraction.

In the old days, he would have had anger to shield him but he had put that aside with his old life. He had nothing now unless this prince chose to give him death.

Darvish knew his nudity bothered Aaron so he went unclothed as often as he realistically could. Any reaction was better than none at all and that was the *only* reaction he'd seen evidence of. He watched the blush rise and fade, then he set his teeth and approached with the salve.

If he had known when he carried the thief from the Chamber of the Fourth that he carried a stone who, once the initial and still unexplained despair had faded, would sit staring at him from behind walls thicker than those that ringed the palace, he would have left him with the twins.

No, not that perhaps, but the last thing Darvish needed was a man who acknowledged him even less than his father did. His excesses meant nothing to Aaron; at least his father felt disgust.

He meant nothing to Aaron.

I saved your life, he wanted to shout. *Don't I get anything in return?* Apparently not.

Aaron made him uncomfortable in a number of ways. Darvish had thought himself an expert at merely existing from day to day, but the outlander made him appear a rank amateur. And Aaron did it without the wine.

One word and the thief would be there to bother him no more. Darvish knew he could never speak that word. If only to prove his father wrong.

"His life is yours. When you tire of him, he dies."

"The healer's busy." Darvish squatted by the pallet and dipped two fingers into the pot.

Aaron braced himself for the prince's touch. The salve smoothed over the jagged edges between the new skin and the old, but the easing was almost lost in the feel of the strong brown fingers that stroked it on. It seemed as though his heart began to beat to their rhythm. From under lowered lids he snatched a glimpse of the prince's face and the concern there surprised him—as much as it would have surprised the prince had he been able to see it.

The surprise drove a crack into the stone surrounding him and a question wailed free.

"What do you want from me, Darvish?"

Startled blue eyes met equally startled gray eyes for an instant, the question hanging in the air between them. Then the gray eyes cooled back to ice and only the blue acknowledged the question had been asked.

"What do I want from you?" Darvish repeated softly. He had seen, in that instant, a loneliness that matched his own, recognized it from a hundred thousand reflections in a hundred thousand mirrors. It stopped the glib answer and it stopped the leer.

What do you want from me?

Like ripples in a quiet pool, other questions spread out from the first.

Why did you save my life?

Why do you care?

Something. . . .

Darvish remembered the look on Aaron's face the first night on the balcony, the pain that had nothing to do with the injuries that had brought him down. Maybe because his head was clear, without the usual insulation of wine, Darvish suddenly remembered his thoughts from that moment. *This is someone who knows. He'd understand how I feel.*

He looked at Aaron's face now and realized what he wanted.

What do you want from me?

I want you to be my friend.

But he wasn't going to say it. Even though he'd bought and paid for that friendship with Aaron's life. He couldn't take that risk. He asked for the one thing he knew he'd get.

"Nothing." Darvish shoved the cork back into the flared neck of the pot, his voice a soft contrast to the almost violent action. "I want nothing from you."

Aaron nodded, his fingers so tightly interlaced that the knuckles stood out bone white. "I can give you that," he whispered, relieved. One corner of his mouth twisted up and without really meaning to, he smiled. The wrong answer would have shattered him into little pieces. He could feel how close he'd come, but he was still whole.

Darvish stared at Aaron's face. *He's smiling?* Slowly, his own mouth began to curve and, shared, the moment stretched.

"Highness?"

Oham's quiet voice drew Darvish around and Aaron's face became expressionless once again, but a link, tenuous and unacknowledged, remained.

"Highness, His Most Imperial Majesty commands your presence in the small audience chamber. Immediately. He requires also that you bring the thief."

"When you tire of him, he dies."

It wouldn't be the first time His Most Imperial Majesty had changed the rules.

"Well now, Aaron," Darvish said with the false sincerity usually saved for social occasions and members of the court high in the king's favor. He tossed back his hair and stood, crossing the room and lifting the carafe with both hands. Hands that trembled, just a little. "It seems we had our talk just in time." The wine ran in crimson lines down from the corners of his mouth and over his chest. Breathing heavily, he tossed the now empty container onto the bed and grinned, his eyes too bright. "I guess I'd better get dressed."

You gave me his life, Father. At Darvish's sides, his hands curled into fists. *I'll fight you if you try to take him from me.*

Tension filled the small audience chamber, tension so palpable that Aaron almost raised a hand to brush it from his face. Like sheets of lightning before a summer storm, it radiated out from the four who waited for them and lifted the fine hair on the back of his neck.

As they crossed the room, the only noise the light slap of their sandals against the tile, Aaron took stock of the doors, the windows, the guards, the habits of years reasserting themselves. It would be a difficult but not impossible job and probably worth it for the heavy gold lamp brackets alone. Lastly, he noted the people.

The throne in the small audience chamber was rosewood, intricately carved and highly polished. The king, however, was still obsidian and between the gray of hair and beard his expression was black. To his right, the crown prince also showed anger, but it was equally mixed with speculation as he watched them approach. The shaven-headed priest was simply terrified and the lord chancellor—Aaron recognized the fat man immediately, Darvish's drunken ravings were quite accurate—had set his face in no readable expression at all.

From his position a pace behind the prince, Aaron watched Darvish drop gracefully to one knee and mirrored the motion a heartbeat later. His half-healed chest allowed him little grace and his thighs trembled as he rose, but he set his jaw and pretended he hadn't spent the last three ninedays flat on his back. As he lifted his head, a glare from the lord chancellor drew his gaze.

A man's ears don't stop hearing just because he no longer wishes to live, and while Aaron healed he'd listened. He'd listened to the words and to what was behind them. He knew who paid the third dresser.

You're a fool, he thought at the broad sweep of Darvish's back, while returning the lord chancellor's glare with a cold stare of his own, *if you think this man is not dangerous just because he is fat and old.* But then, he already knew Darvish was a fool.

From the expression on the lord chancellor's face, Aaron suspected that the obeisance made to the king by a thief was supposed to differ from that made by a prince. Tough.

"You requested my presence, Most Exalted?"

Darvish had thrown back two additional goblets of wine on the way through the palace and Aaron marveled at how little the amount of alcohol he'd consumed had affected him. His voice sounded clear and his hands hung steady by his sides. Nor did he appear affected by the tensions in the room. The muscles of his back were knotted, Aaron could see that clearly through the thin white silk of his shirt, but he'd brought that tension in with him.

The silence the followed Darvish's ritual words stretched and lengthened and the air became heavier still. It seemed that the colored tiles in the mosaic behind the throne grew both muted and more distinct. Aaron's eyes narrowed. He'd assumed, like Darvish, this meeting had been commanded to tell the prince his thief must die, but now he wasn't so sure. He ignored the faint taste of relief. He wanted to die. He waited to die.

And then the king spoke, thunder to herald the storm. "The Stone has been taken."

"Nine Above . . ." Darvish breathed and Aaron silently echoed it. The Stone held the volcano. Without it, Ischia would die. "Who?"

Slowly, all eyes turned to Aaron.

"It wasn't me," Aaron said dryly, wondering how they expected him to have stolen anything when he could barely walk. "I was with him." He jerked a thumb at the prince and felt strangely pleased when, after an astounded moment, Darvish grinned and stepped back so that they stood side by side.

"That does not necessarily excuse you," the lord chancellor snapped.

"Are you accusing my Most Royal brother of taking The Stone?" Shahin's question was silk, but it was the silk of the garrote. Over the last few weeks, the heir had been discovering more and more how much he disliked his father's omnipresent councillor. That the man was devoted to the throne, he did not doubt, but some of the ways that devotion had been expressed he did not care for at all. In the opinion of the crown prince, the lord chancellor needed to be reminded of his place.

The lord chancellor recognized the tone and hurriedly bowed. "Oh, no, not at all, my prince. But he does share quarters with a known thief. . . ."

"And we all know that if said thief had stirred at any time during the night you'd have known of it a heartbeat later. So let's stop this foolishness," the word was directed equally at the lord chancellor, Darvish, and Aaron, "and get to the point." The hooded eyes pinned Aaron to the spot. He felt not unlike a rabbit must, caught in the gaze of a great hawk. "You could not have taken The Stone, but you will know who did. Tell us."

Aaron considered the other thieves of Ischia. He owed them nothing, after all.

"If The Stone is missing, what holds the Lady?" Darvish asked suddenly, a hint of fear appearing in his voice.

The priest spoke for the first time, her voice a clear, light soprano growing shrill with the strain of remaining calm. "Not even a living volcano constantly erupts. The wizards of both the temple and the palace focus power to block the smoke and smell, hiding the theft from the people. They stand ready should the worst occur."

Darvish nodded. "So the wizards know," he murmured, relieved. "Who else?"

"Only we six and a senior priest at the temple." Her fingers worked against the red and yellow tassels that hung from her belt of office, but her face remained impassive. "If the people find out . . ."

"If the people find out," Darvish repeated, "then the panic will destroy Ischia before the volcano has a chance."

"I'm glad to see the wine has not completely rotted your brain, little brother."

Under the sarcasm, Aaron was sure he heard approval in Shahin's voice, but before he had a chance to ponder it the king spoke again.

"Who has The Stone, thief?"

Aaron had weighed all the thieves of the city and found them wanting. "The thief came from outside Ischia."

The king's teeth flashed in the gray of his beard. Not for an instant did Aaron believe the expression was a smile. "You are very sure."

"I am." *He uses his power like a sword, much as my father used his like a club.* With the thought came memories—a huge red-bearded man, a dark-haired girl crouched at his feet, her blue eyes wide with terror—and with the memories came a storm of emotion—guilt, anger, terror, pain—too thick to breath through. *NO!* He slammed both memory and emotion back down behind the walls where they belonged. *I am through with all that!* He added denial to the walls until nothing remained but the void.

"Aaron?"

The void and Darvish. But Darvish he could deal with. He should never have left the prince's rooms. He should have stayed there, waiting to die.

Aaron avoided the prince's gaze—concern could break the walls again—and spoke directly to the king. "I could not have done it and I was the best."

"The best?"

The lord chancellor's words were a verbal sneer of disbelief.

Aaron merely replied, "Yes." They could believe him or not, he didn't care.

Plump hands spread and the lord chancellor smiled. "And just look where you are."

"That is hardly his fault," Darvish snarled.

"And this is hardly to the point," the priest broke in. "Squabbling like children will not help us to recover The Stone." She suddenly recalled whom she chastised and flushed. "Begging your pardon, Most Exalted."

Aaron barely heard the argument. Hardly his fault? "What do you mean, that was hardly my fault?" He'd failed. Who else could bear the blame?

Keeping a wary eye on his father, Darvish turned and glanced down at the younger man. "Didn't I tell you? Bugger the Nine," he ignored the gasp from the priest, "I thought I had. Your grappling iron had been deliberately flawed. It couldn't have happened by accident and it couldn't have borne your weight."

Deliberately flawed. *Deliberately* flawed. Cold fury rushed in to fill the void—fill it and overflow it. Aaron didn't see Darvish step back. He didn't see king, prince, priest, and lord chancellor watching him, faces wearing nearly identical apprehension. He saw a fat face, smoke-stick bobbing on one full and greasy lip.

When he spoke his voice came out like shards of ice.

"There's only one place in Ischia The Stone can be."

* * *

Not even the strong breeze off the harbor could sweep away the mixed smells of rot and dirt and too many people in too little space. Darvish fought against the urge to breathe through the fabric of his sleeve, as many young nobles did when one thing or another brought them down to this part of town. He scowled at a whining beggar, stepped over a pile of garbage—the bloated flies nearly covering it were so well fed they ignored him—and wondered if the volcano might not be preferable.

Behind him, he could hear the three guards muttering obscenities, they liked this place even less than he did. He, at least, knew they were here for a reason. They thought only that their prince had sold something he shouldn't have, the the prince's pet thief knew where it was, and they were the muscle in case he had trouble getting it back. Not exactly a shining purpose to ease a walk through the worst slum in Ischia.

"Will three be enough?" Darvish had asked.

"Do you ever travel with more than three?"

"No."

"Then more will cause suspicion. Questions will be asked and the more questions the greater the chance the people will find out and panic." The priest shook her head, dark stubble a shadow against her scalp. *"Above all else, the people must not find out that The Stone is missing."*

"How fortunate for us all, Darvish, that your reputation allows you access to such people without raising the type of comments that would lead to questions. You'll have your sword," Shahin added. *"Perhaps you'll have a chance to prove you can use it as well as a bottle."*

Aaron's eyes were too cold to be human. "Herrak has no guards about him—he would have to share his treasures, then. He has the best wards his money can buy. But I have been through Herrak's wards before, they know me. And Herrak thinks I'm dead."

His most exalted father wouldn't have been depending on him, Darvish knew, if he had any other choice. But he didn't, for the priest was right. Above all else, the people must not know. It was Shahin Darvish didn't understand; his words had been almost more a challenge than a dismissal.

Aaron stopped in front of a townhouse that looked as though it were about to collapse under its own weight. Each of the three stories was sinking at different angles and the stone, which might have been white once, now barely held its shape in infinite shades of gray. Only one piece of the obsidian inlay that had long ago made this building the showpiece of the neighborhood remained, tucked up under the perch of a crumbling gargoyle.

The recessed door opened directly onto the filthy street. In its shelter, Aaron spoke practically his first words since leaving the palace; ''They stay out here.''

As one, the three guards turned to the prince.

''You might as well,'' Darvish agreed. ''If he wanted to kill me, he could have done it easier last night.'' One of the guards turned a snigger into a sneeze. Darvish ignored him. He knew what they thought. ''You're not needed inside and I'd prefer not to exit into any surprises.''

Body blocking the exact motions, Aaron worked his fingers against the latch, twisting them with an agility that suggested the manacle scars had not destroyed his skills. The door opened just enough to allow him to slip inside. Darvish, larger and heavier, squeezed through behind with more difficulty. The guards philosophically settled down to wait. This wasn't the first time His Royal Highness had gone into a strange house leaving them to secure the door.

''Course, they're usually not quite so . . .'' The first guard let the comment trail off, moving his foot away from a small unidentifiable mound of gray.

''Yeah? Well, you weren't along when his nibs tucked inta Black Sal's.'' The second smiled with satisfaction as she added, ''They tossed him out just before dawn. We hadta carry him home. Yep, he's bin in places worser than this and come out again. Got the Nine's own luck up his ass does our royal master.'' She hacked and spit, scoring a direct hit on a roach.

The third guard only watched the now closed door and hoped that her prince wouldn't need her.

''Stand still.'' Aaron's voice cut the small anteroom into smaller pieces still. ''Don't touch anything.''

''When will Herrak know we're here?''

''We crossed the first ward at the mouth of the alley. He's known for some time.''

''Oh.'' The outside door slid silently shut and Darvish discovered that the termite ridden boards facing the street were only a thin veneer over solid oak planks. ''Aaron, you can't open this door from the inside." Nor, given the lack of maneuvering room, did he think he could break it down. The trapped air was hot and heavy and Darvish had the sudden uncomfortable thought that they stood in an inescapable oven.

"I can open the outside door." Aaron lifted his hand to knock on the inner door of the anteroom. "but we're going in." As his knuckles brushed the polished wood, the heavy door swung silently open.

"Unlocked?" Darvish asked, loosening his sword in its sheath.

"Shouldn't be," Aaron grunted.

"Right." Perhaps Herrak had already run with The Stone. Perhaps they were walking into a trap. Darvish pulled the scimitar free.

Moving cautiously, they entered a corridor barely wider than the prince's shoulders. The towering walls were composed of Herrak's treasures stacked haphazardly to the ceiling. The hanging lamps, guttering as they used the last of their oil, were almost worse than no light at all. Shadows leapt and lunged and a myriad of dark nooks and crannies drew the eye. An oppressive smell of mold and decay contributed to the claustrophobic feeling and dust motes danced in a glittering fog that thickened every time they moved.

Aaron stopped suddenly, his head up, his expression demonic in the half light. "This is wrong."

Breathing shallowly through his teeth, Darvish dropped into a fighting stance. *And how can you tell what's right in a place like this?* Above his head a lamp sizzled and sighed into darkness. "What's wrong?" he asked, ears straining for a sound, any sound, they weren't making themselves.

"The lamps. He has a servant to tend them."

"Do you think he's left with The Stone?"

The thief barked with derisive laughter. "What? And leave all this?" As suddenly as he'd stopped, he sprinted forward.

Darvish scrambled to catch up.

The narrow corridors didn't change although the building materials did from time to time. Here, almost ten feet packed with bales of clothing. There, furniture jammed tight between floor and ceiling. At the top of a flight of stairs, a statue of a sad-faced man that could only have come from the Nobles' Garden. No rooms, no halls, only the never-

ending maze of Herrak's possessions. The lamps continued
to die.

How much farther? Darvish wondered. He couldn't ask
aloud, he didn't have the breath to spare. Keeping up with
the thin figure of the thief took almost all he had. Worse
news—over the sound of his labored breathing he could hear
an inhuman wail, rising and failing, permeating the maze
like smoke. *I may have to fight that.* For now, he fought the
tremors that shook his body and threatened to shake his
blade like a leaf in a storm. He needed a drink to steady his
arm.

Then the walls began to change. Bookcases now, jammed
with racks of scrolls and heavy leather-bound tomes. Then
the walls stopped. The wailing grew louder.

Weapon ready, Darvish traced the sound to its source.

Tucked up against the base of a heavily laden desk was a
small man, dressed all in dark gray, staring wide eyed at
the stubs of his hands. His sleeves had fallen back and the
jagged ends of his forearm bones jutted charred from flesh
that eased from black to red, angry red lines disappearing
under the fabric of his shirt. Blood dribbled from holes
chewed out of his lips and his chest heaved with the breath
necessary to keep up the constant keening wail.

He shouldn't be conscious. Darvish closed his throat
against the urge to vomit and took a shaky step forward. As
he drew closer, unable to look away, a little more of the
blackened flesh dissolved. There was no smell of burning
or rot, just, very faintly, the bitter scent of the volcano.
When he was close enough, he lifted the man's chin with
the flat of his sword—the eyes were completely and totally
insane.

It took two blows to get the head right off. Panting
slightly, Darvish wiped his sword on the body. *At least the
wailing's stopped.*

But the room was not quite silent and dreading what he'd
see, he turned to face the source of the moaning. Over by
one of the bookcase walls, Aaron stood staring at an im-
mensely fat man, his face expressionless and cold. The fat
man moaned, the sound rolling around the great echo chamber of his belly before being released to thrum against the
heavy quiet. His hands cupped the air in front of the circle
of his face, red to the wrist, the tip of each finger crowned
in black.

"Apparently," Aaron said without turning as Darvish came to stand by his side, "there is a price for touching The Stone."

"Where is it?" Darvish slapped Herrak's hands down with the flat of his blade. He wanted *out* of this place. "Where is The Stone?"

Herrak's eyes showed yellowish white all around and his hands rose back up as though pulled by an invisible puppeteer.

"Answer, you fat fool!" Darvish slapped the hands down again and this time the edge of his sword drew across Herrak's palm. The red flesh parted, but no blood welled up to fill the wound. "Tell me, where is The Stone?"

"Gone," Herrak moaned from behind his rotting fingers.

"Gone where?"

He had to repeat the question a second and a third time before Herrak responded, moaning, "The mirror took it."

"What mirror?" Darvish rubbed his face. It was very hot in Herrak's hidey-hole and the blood of the thief, soaked onto the layers of carpeting, added its signature to the dust and mold and dead air.

Aaron pointed, his long finger appearing whiter than ever.

Almost hidden by Herrak's bulk, was a three-foot oval that Darvish had taken to be a slab of framed obsidian. A closer look and he saw it was a black mirror, its surface absolutely nonreflecting.

One more step and the edge of his sword was at Herrak's throat. Close enough to smell terror, sharp and strong, he breathed the question into the fat man's face. "Where. Is. The. Stone?"

"The wizard has it."

"Wizard?" *Bugger the Nine! We've lost it!* A slight movement of the sword brought another spate of information. Darvish couldn't understand why. Given what Herrak faced alive, death had to be welcome.

"The mirror came to me from the streets. . . ."

"Who brought it?" Aaron snapped.

Herrak's eyes searched the past for a name. "Yaz," he said at last. "Yaz brought it."

"Where did she get it?"

"I don't know. It didn't seem important. I wanted it, you could see eternity in it."

Together, Aaron and Darvish looked again at the mirror. They could see exactly nothing.

"Spelled," Aaron grunted. Darvish nodded.

"You could. You could." Herrak protested. "I saw it. I saw eternity. Then he came."

"Who came?"

"The wizard."

"He came here?"

"No. To the mirror." A spasm of pain twisted Herrak's face and his fingers twitched and danced and grew a little blacker. When it passed, he needed no prodding to continue. "He said he would trade me a thousand precious things for The Stone of Ischia. A thousand for one." For a second he peered out from between rolls of fat, eyes hard, and Darvish caught a glimpse of the power that had made Herrak king of his own small part of the city. He realized that the man barely held on to a tiny fraction of his mind and would shortly be as insane as the dead thief. Suddenly Herrak twisted and fell to his knees, his whole body quivering from the impact. "He sent the thief through the mirror last night," he gasped. "I had The Stone just before dawn. Had to kill Jehara."

"His servant," Aaron supplied.

"She said we killed Ischia." The grimace almost became a smile. "A thousand precious things for one. I passed it through the mirror. I held it." His fingers were black to the second joint. "The thief had already begun to scream." The last word rose in volume until it was almost a scream itself.

The Stone, the heart of Ischia, was gone.

"The wizard," Darvish grabbed Herrak's shoulder and shook him viciously, "where is he?"

"In the mirror!"

Darvish's grip sank deep into the dimpled flesh.

"Where is the other side of the mirror?"

"I don't know!" Herrak wailed. One of the nails on his left hand curled off and drifted silently to the carpets.

Darvish let the fat man go. Ischia was doomed. He lifted his sword.

"No."

The very calm and control of Aaron's voice, so much in contrast to his own raging thoughts and Herrak's tortured whimpering, stopped the scimitar's downward swing.

"The thief is from Ytaili." He held out a small amber

teardrop, the thong threaded through it sticky with blood. "This type, this color is found only in Ytaili, near Tivolic, the capital city. The royal family favors it."

"How do you know," Darvish snorted, not willing to accept a new hope quite so quickly.

"I stole one once."

Ytaili. Six days at sea with good winds. A day to find The Stone. Six days back. A nineday and a half. Surely the wizards can hold the volcano for that long. Perhaps Ischia can live. The relief that came with that conclusion left Darvish feeling physically weak. Then he remembered. *Ytaili. Where Yasimina's brother was king.* He stood for a moment, scimitar point resting against the carpets and watched three nails fall from Herraks' hands. The whimpering had become a constant background noise.

They had the answer, and yet, there was something more. He looked past Herrak to the mirror. Many wizards preferred to scry in mirrors, it wasn't a skill tied to any of the disciplines, but he had never heard of a wizard who could move things through a mirror. *A wizard who can move a solid object through a solid object. . . .* A sudden fear stroked cold fingers down the prince's spine and he allowed himself to be distracted by the fat man rather than search out its source.

We have all we'll get from him, Darvish thought, shifting to a two-handed grip and lifting his sword again.

"No." For the second time, Aaron's cold voice stopped the beheading swing before it had begun. "What has he done to deserve mercy?"

What indeed? Herrak had been responsible for the theft of The Stone. And the loss of The Stone would destroy the Ischia Darvish knew. The nobles could get clear, they had the means and estates elsewhere to retreat to. But Darvish's people, the whores, the wine merchants—he shot a quick glance at Aaron—the thieves would die, if not in the panic, then boiled alive by the rivers of molten rock that would soon follow. And Herrak would have killed them.

Darvish sheathed his sword.

Herrak had done nothing to deserve mercy.

His face blank, Aaron turned silently to lead the way back out through the maze.

They had barely started between the first of the bookcases when Darvish realized that Herrak was trapped. He was far,

far too fat to make it through the narrow aisles of his own house. His treasure boxed him into that one small room and probably had for years.

"He has poison in that room," Aaron said quietly as though he'd been following the line of Darvish's thoughts. "A quick death if he has the courage to take it." His voice was bitter and the line of his back so straight and hard that Darvish felt it would ring like steel if he tapped it.

They were halfway down the first set of stairs when the screaming began.

Seven

Shifting her burden on her hip, Chandra tried to look properly subservient. It wasn't easy. Her head hurt. Fanfares had been blowing at intervals since they left the docks, the bells that dangled from the ornate palanquins set up a constant brassy jangle, the crowds cheered and yelled, and, once they realized that this was the dowry procession, shouted a number of crude comments about her future unintended that set her ears burning. Things they would certainly not have shouted had Chandra been officially present. She hoped. There were a number of things about Prince Darvish that Aba hadn't mentioned.

Remaining with the servants until they were actually in the palace had seemed like a good idea back on the ship, but now she wasn't so sure.

Still, it's not everyone that gets to carry her own dowry. And, she added philosophically, *it could be worse.* The four muscular bearers carrying Lord Assahsem had her complete sympathy as they struggled up the steep streets under the weight of the corpulent ambassador. *"Hang on,"* she thought at their glistening backs as his lordship gave a little bounce and four sets of knees almost buckled, *"we're nearly there."*

The litters themselves she found fascinating. Back home, people who didn't wish to walk, rode or rented a shau, a two wheeled carriage pulled by the man or woman who owned it. After climbing her third, or maybe fourth, set of stairs, she realized that wheels would be completely impractical in a city built on so many levels. Her calves began to ache.

As the small procession—half a company of guard, litters for the two nobles welcoming the dowry as well as the two delivering, the six servants carrying the dowry, the other half a company of guard—crossed the last terrace before the palace gate, Chandra reached out and lightly brushed the wards surrounding the palace with power. If they were too specific. . . .

Might as well use pots and pans and a piece of string, she snorted silently. The wards were predominantly of the Fourth and served only to tell if the wall had been breached. *I could have spelled a notice-me-not against this in my first year of training. Someone in this city must be growing rich selling charms to thieves.*

The gate was not warded at all and in the wake of Lord Assahsem's grateful bearers, Chandra passed unnoted into the palace. She placed her small chest with the rest of the dowry, bowed beside the other servants, stepped back, and then completely surpassed them at fading quietly into the background. Not one of them remembered they had once been six.

A short time later, having gently persuaded a senior servant to tell her where Prince Darvish's rooms were and having discovered that he was not at present in the palace, Chandra headed for the nobles' viewing platforms to get a look at The Stone. Although she could feel great currents of power moving about the volcano, she couldn't feel The Stone and she began to grow uneasy. She was a Wizard of the Nine. Why wasn't it calling to her?

The guard at the entryway surprised her even as she passed him easily. She hoped there wasn't a ceremony of some kind going on. She wanted a chance to really study the artifact without the bother of keeping her presence masked. Moving cautiously, she peered out onto the platform.

Four wizards—one of the Second, one of the Fourth, two of the Eighth—stood at the railing, focus directed down into the crater. Chandra frowned; wizards seldom cooperated across disciplines. Curiosity warred with common sense and curiosity won.

Dropping her minor disguise spells lest her power signature give her away, she slid along the back wall of the platform, the tile mosaic warm against her shoulder blades, heading for a position where she might safely get a glimpse of The Stone. Given time and materials, she could build a notice-me-not so strong not even another wizard could spot her, but as she had neither, she'd trust to luck.

As she moved past the barrier of silk clad backs she could

see, across the crater, a small cluster of wizards on the temple platform as well, their multihued robes billowing in the hot updrafts from the molten rock below. Her frown grew more pronounced. Obviously, she'd stumbled onto some sort of ceremony; one she'd never heard of. She'd studied everything written on The Stone of Ischia and recognized none of what was going on. Something had to be very wrong.

She leaned forward slightly and, yes, there were wizards on what had to be the private royal platform. A quick glance up to the open areas of the rim showed the public platforms were empty.

She could feel the power gathered, waiting to be focused, and she could feel the power spread like a net over the crater's mouth.

Stranger and stranger.

Inch by inch she moved toward the railing.

Then the Wizard of the Second turned and looked directly at her, so close that she could see her reflection in the drops of sweat that beaded his high forehead. His fleshy lips parted and he snarled, "Have you been sent to bring us refreshment? This is hot work."

He thinks I'm a servant! Quickly, gracelessly, she bowed. "Yes, Most Wise." *If wizards are called something different here than they are at home. . . .* "Do you and your Most Wise brethren desire wine or ices or chilled fruit juices?" *Thank the One for this tunic!* She managed to move a hand's span closer to the rail.

"Wine, *and* ices, *and* chilled fruit juices," the Wizard of the Second informed her. "And be quick about it!"

"Yes, Most Wise." A step. A bow. Another inch and she'd be able to see into the seething cauldron of the volcano. Her left foot lifted to step again.

"What is going on here?"

The grip on the back of her tunic almost jerked her off her feet and Chandra found herself dangling from the fist of the Wizard of the Fourth.

"It's a servant, Amarjite," sneered the Wizard of the Second. "Release her so she can get my ices."

Chandra did her best to look obsequious, but her heart beat so loudly she was certain it could be heard over the rumble of the shifting lava. *If they find out who I am, I'll be sent home in disgrace. I'll have failed, just like Father.*

Then she looked up into the completely expressionless face of the Wizard of the Fourth and her throat closed around a fear greater than failure. Wizards of the Fourth learned any number of techniques that Chandra had never been trained to protect herself against; techniques that would shatter crystal as easily as clay.

"A servant," said Amarjite, coldly, "has no business being out on the platforms. Use your head, Simmel, instead of your stomach." He shook her like a mongoose would shake a snake. "What are you doing here, girl?"

He wasn't going to believe her, no matter what she said. She could see that in his eyes. But there must be something she could do. She was a Wizard of the Nine! Failure became unimportant next to what awaited her and she began opening herself to power.

The great metal door leading off the platform of executions slammed back, the crash of iron against rock causing even Amarjite to jerk and turn. Out onto the platform, like two slender black shadows, came the twins. Behind them, a burly guard dragged a bleeding body.

"Nine and One, what now?" Amarjite snarled.

Would this be a chance? Chandra wondered, trembling, and for the moment held the power back.

"They're going to want to drop the body into the Lady," Simmel observed.

"I know that, idiot."

The Wizard of the Second smiled unpleasantly at his colleague. "Then you'd better stop them, hadn't you? Before they destroy the net."

"*I* had better stop them?"

"Well, I can't." Simmel spread pudgy hands and his expression changed to smug triumph. "I'm too fat to walk the path. Besides, you're a Fourth, they *may* listen to you."

With an oath, Amarjite threw his captive down. "Watch her," he commanded, and strode off the platform.

Chandra stayed where she had fallen, peering up at Simmel through a loosened shock of hair. She didn't have to fake the terror.

"Oh, get up and stop looking at me like that," he whined. "I want my ices." Opposition by Amarjite had been enough to convince him, for pure obstinacy's sake, that this child was no more than she appeared. The final command cinched the issue. Wizards of the Fourth had no business giving commands to Wizards of the Second.

Using the carved stone of the platform for support, Chandra scrambled to her feet, her relief so great it made her dizzy. From where she stood, she could see her ex-captor hurrying down a narrow path cut into the side of the volcano, his russet robes billowing out behind him. Turning her head only a little, she could see into the crater.

"My ices," prodded Simmel.

Her face carefully expressionless, she bowed and all but ran back into the palace. She'd seen a golden spire rising out of the molten rock, but its crown was empty.

Where was The Stone of Ischia?

Just inside the door, she forced herself to stop. There was one more thing she had to do before she was safe. With fingers that refused to quit shaking she unraveled a thread from the bottom edge of her tunic, tied a loose knot in it, and waited, peering back through the crack at the platform.

She could feel the Wizard of the Fourth's anger while he was still climbing the path. The instant he backed Simmel into her line of sight, before he had a chance to voice that anger, she shook out the knot.

"Forget."

And then she realized she'd made a major mistake. *Forget* was a spell of the Fourth, one of the few she knew. Amarjite turned his head and looked directly at her.

She focused more power.

"Forget!"

Simmel's face went blank.

The Wizard of the Fourth fought back, his hands clawing at the air.

"FORGET!"

Between one heartbeat and the next, Amarjite's face smoothed and he began grumbling about the twins.

Temples throbbing, Chandra reached out and gently brushed the spell across the two Wizards of the Eighth who had been silently focusing power into the crater the entire time. While she doubted they'd been aware of anything but their own actions, she was too shaken to leave loose ends behind her.

She should leave now, before someone else spotted her. She should slip unseen through the palace and confront Prince Darvish. She should. . . .

Very, very carefully, she slid a finger of power onto the focus of the Wizards of the Eighth, riding it down and through the net. Hiding her power signature within the borrowed focus, she touched the place where The Stone of Ischia should be. And frowned.

Laid over the residual power imprint of The Stone was the taint of another power; like a thin film of grease or a layer of smoke. Too ephemeral for a wizard less powerful to even notice, it told Chandra exactly nothing about who had left it. It came out of no type of power she recognized.

Where was The Stone of Ischia?

And with who?

"Ytaili." King Jaffar rubbed the bit of amber between his fingers. "Are you sure?"

"No, Most Exalted. Not entirely."

"No?" The lord chancellor leaned slightly forward, his expression just hinting at triumph. "Then you have brought us exactly nothing. The Stone, and Ischia, are still lost."

Aaron felt Darvish stiffen beside him and heard what the words and their tone said to the king. *"Darvish has failed again."* He met the lord chancellor's eyes for a heartbeat and then deliberately turned his head away, dismissing him. He spoke directly to the king. "This color is found in small quantities in only one place, just outside Tivolic, the capital. The Royal Family of Ytaili favors it."

"We have only your word for that, *thief*." The fury that throbbed in the veins at the lord chancellor's temples found its way into the last word.

Again Aaron met the lord chancellor's eyes. One shoulder lifted and dropped in the minimal shrug his scars had forced on him. The action said louder than words, *"I don't care what you think. You have no power over me."*

"Ytaili," the king repeated, softly.

With a visible effort, the lord chancellor forced his voice back to calm reason. "A pity His Highness killed the one man who could have told us something."

There it was again, *"Darvish has failed."* From the corner of his eye, Aaron looked up at the prince. *He uses you to consolidate his power with the king, a convenient scapegoat, and you gave him that power over you with your so obvious need to be noticed by your father.* He had walked that path himself. *Don't give him what he wants now.*

But Darvish merely tossed his hair back off his face and said, with an eloquent wave of one hand; "The thief was dying, Most Exalted. To carry a screaming man whose arms had rotted away through the streets—even," he inclined his head slightly, "if *I* were carrying him—would surely cause the questions we're trying to avoid."

The king stared at his third son for a long moment, his expression unreadable. When he finally spoke, sarcasm gave the words a cutting edge. "Then as we have lost one thief, it is fortunate we retain another." He turned his gaze on Aaron. "Give me, thief, the benefit of your experience."

Aaron let the silence stretch, his eyes locked on the king's. He had stopped responding to any power but his own five long years ago when he left his father's keep.

"The old pain rules you still, my lad."

He allowed the faint creak of leather as Darvish shifted beside him to drown out the memory of Faharra's voice. She was—had been—a crazy old woman. When he judged his point had been made, when an outburst from the lord chancellor seemed imminent, he told what he knew.

"The thief who took The Stone had the help of a wizard. That wizard now has The Stone. The thief has been recently in Ytaili, most probably Tivolic. The thief was hired by someone who paid, or was going to pay, him a great deal. . . ."

"How do you reason that?" Shahin stepped forward, away from his place by the rosewood throne and spoke for the first time since Aaron and Darvish had returned to report The Stone truly lost.

"He stole nothing for himself. Therefore, he was paid. The risks were great; he was paid well. He wore a piece of amber that could have only come from a member of the Royal Family of Ytaili. . . ."

"My wife," said Shahin, his voice dangerously quiet, "is a princess of Ytaili."

Aaron had known that, the wedding festivities had involved the entire city, the people rejoicing that the ancient antagonism between the two counties had ended at last. He bowed his head slightly, eyes carefully lowered to hide the thought they held. Powerful help from inside the palace would remove the remainder of the obstacles between a thief and The Stone.

"How dare you," the lord chancellor spat the words at

Aaron, "accuse the Most Blessed Yasimina of involvement in this, this traitorous act."

"He accused no one," Shahin turned his quiet, dangerous voice on the lord chancellor.

Still scowling at the thief, the lord chancellor exclaimed, "I saw his face, my prince." Then his tone and his expression softened. "No one who knows your wife could believe such a thing." He bent slightly and spoke his next words to the king. "She writes to her brother, King Harith, Most Exalted, but surely that does not make her a traitor."

The king looked up at his eldest son, brows drawn down, "She writes to Harith?"

"She's homesick, Father." Shahin turned an expression of loathing on the lord chancellor. "I see the letters, there's no harm in them."

"Just as I said," the lord chancellor pointed out gently.

"Hypocrite!" Shahin used the word like a cudgel. "You insinuate even if you don't dare accuse."

"Would you listen if I did?"

"You've never liked her. You argued against this treaty and our marriage from the first."

"The kings of Ytaili have long desired this land." The old lord addressed the king directly. "I merely suggested it might not be wise to allow them so close, that perhaps the prince should marry within Cisali as you did, Most Exalted." He turned back to the heir. "My prince, the Most Blessed Yasimina's brother *is* an enemy of your Most Exalted father and . . ."

"Was an enemy of my Most Exalted father. My marriage ended that. And even if he landed an army on our shore, that would not make my wife an enemy as well."

"No, my prince, but . . ."

"Enough."

The command dropped Shahin's fists to his sides. He bowed to his father and moved back to stand at his right hand, having almost breached the barrier of the throne.

He loves her, Aaron realized. *He loves his treaty bride and he's afraid the lord chancellor might have been right all along. The prejudices against outlanders he's been raised with, strengthen that fear.* That the people of Ytaili came from the same stock, with the same coloring, language, and beliefs, would help only a very little.

"This amber would be as effective and less incriminating

an identification than a royal seal.'' Darvish offered thoughtfully into the silence.

''So you accuse my wife as well. You're saying she recognized the amber and allowed the thief into the palace?'' Shahin's face held the look of a man who wrestled with inner demons.

''No.'' Darvish took a deep breath. He felt sorry for his brother but sorrier for the fate of Ischia without The Stone. ''I'm saying it's possible that *someone* recognized the amber and allowed the thief into the palace.''

Someone.

Yasimina.

''There is always the possibility,'' the lord chancellor pointed out, ''that the thief had stolen the amber long before and wore it as a momento of his crime. That he has not been near Ytaili or Tivolic in many years.''

King Jaffar's finger tightened on the amber as though he would force it to speak. ''Is this possible?'' he demanded of Aaron.

''Yes.'' It was possible and Aaron would have left it at that—he cared nothing for the city nor the people in it and had, in fact, been deriving some pleasure in imagining Faharra's granddaughter waddling desperately, futilely away from a river of molten rock—except he caught the faintest shadow of triumph crossing the lord chancellor's face. *What do you have to be triumphant about, old man?* Curious, he continued; ''But it isn't likely. The amber could be recognized as stolen and this man was too good to take that kind of chance. He had to have been given it.''

''And this brings suspicion back to my wife?'' Shahin asked the question calmly enough, but his face betrayed his anger and fear.

''No one brings suspicion on your wife, Shahin, but you will speak with her and discover what she knows.''

Although a different response could be seen in the set of his shoulders, Shahin said only, ''Yes, Father.''

''I have thought on this matter,'' the ritual words carried the clash of steel, ''and I will send a force to Ytaili to recover The Stone.''

The lord chancellor leaned forward, plump hand extended almost to the black silk of the king's sleeve. ''Most Exalted, if I may make a suggestion, sending an army to Ytaili would cause the questions we cannot have asked and would no doubt start the war with Ytaili we are anxious to avoid. It would not get back The Stone.''

"Those are criticisms, Lord Chancellor, I have yet to hear a suggestion.''

"Send a small force, Most Exalted. One man perhaps. Or two.''

On the other side of the throne, Shahin gripped the king's shoulder. "Send Darvish.''

Darvish closed his eyes. Aaron could feel him waiting for the laughter that would surely follow.

No one laughed.

"He could travel,'' Shahin went on, still speaking directly to the king, "not as a prince but as a swordsman looking for hire. He could pass with ease. His habits are certainly not those of a prince and even the arms master admits he is uncommonly skilled.''

"Yes,'' agreed the lord chancellor, his eyes alight with sudden enthusiasm, "and send the thief as well in case The Stone must be stolen back. They can be soul-linked so he cannot run.''

Soul-linked, Aaron snorted silently. What a waste of wizardry. Why didn't they just ask? It wasn't as if he had anything better to do. His life before the palace was ash. His life within the palace was only marking time.

Obsidian eyes weighed Darvish silently. "*This* is the only chance for Ischia?''

Darvish winced, a motion too small for any but Aaron to see.

"It is the best chance, Father.''

"And if the people ask where he is?''

"We tell them, Most Exalted, he is in seclusion, preparing for his wedding.''

"And they'll believe that?''

"Again, his reputation works for us, Most Exalted.'' Seclusion in this case would be taken to mean recovering from a lover's complaint he could not bring to a gently bred bride.''

King Jaffar nodded, once. He wasn't convinced but with both his heir and his lord chancellor agreeing for the first time in weeks, he would accept their judgment. "You and your thief,'' he told his third son coldly, "will go to Ytaili and bring back The Stone.''

Darvish bowed. "I am honored to serve, Most Exalted.''

Aaron wondered if any heard, buried deep beneath Darvish's self-mockery, the ring of truth. He suspected Shahin did. The crown prince had just handed his brother a chance to save himself as well as Ishcia.

Soul-linked. Darvish probed at the new and uncomfortable feelings the wizard had left. Every thought seemed to carry with it a faint echo and he felt a sudden desire to scratch he suspected wasn't his. *Soul-linked.* If Aaron moved more than ten of his own body lengths away, he would fall screaming and the pain would continue until the distance was closed.

Darvish had caught Aaron's eye during the short ritual, offering sympathy, camaraderie, he wasn't sure what. To his surprise, Aaron had not rejected him out of hand and his wry acknowledgment of what was being done to them both made the whole thing easier to bear.

Soul-linked. He snorted as he pushed open the outer door of his apartments. *And all I wanted was a friend.*

It had been an afternoon of surprises and the wine he'd drunk on the way back through the halls had not managed to dim the pounding of his heart. His most exalted father had trusted the saving of Ischia to him. To him.

To him. Nine Above!

His laugh sounded forced. "Losing The Stone must have really rattled him."

"Who?"

"My Most Exalted father, of course." The laugh no longer sounded like a laugh at all.

"Why?" Aaron asked, following the prince across the sitting room. "Because he's sending you after The Stone?" The transition from goat to champion couldn't be an easy one. He hoped Darvish could make it. Not that he cared.

"Because he's sending us after The Stone," Darvish corrected. "A thief and a drunk. Nine Above, he must be out of his mind."

"A thief to catch a thief. And perhaps it's time to prove you're more than a drunk."

Darvish stopped and looked back over his shoulder at the younger man. "Am I?" he asked, then sighed and turned away. "I need a drink."

Shahin thinks you are. So does the lord chancellor . . . or he wouldn't have tried so hard to make you into one.

Aaron scowled at Darvish's back and thought suddenly of the brooch he'd been taking to Faharra that last night. *"More good jewels are ruined by their settings. . . ."* For a crazy old lady, she'd been pretty smart.

"I said," Darvish raised his voice above the distant cries of the peacocks, "that I need a drink." He frowned. No dresser appeared from the bedroom, filled goblet on tray, apologizing for making him wait. All was silent and still.

For a panicked instant he feared his father had taken them away, a punishment of some sort he wasn't meant to understand. Then he called himself several kinds of fool and silently pulled his sword. His most exalted father barely acknowledged *him,* his servants were less than nothing.

If they were able, they would have answered his call. Something prevented them.

He motioned for Aaron to continue moving about and, tufted brows high, the thief obeyed. Using Aaron's noise as a cover, he slid along the wall and peered through the arch into his bedroom.

A young woman sat cross-legged on the near corner of the bed, calmly braiding a luxuriant fall of chestnut hair.

The point of his weapon hit the rug with a muffled thud. "Who the One are you?" he demanded. She looked vaguely familiar, sort of pretty in a thin, serious way. Had he asked her to meet him here and then forgotten? It wouldn't be the first time although he generally preferred his women older. He took a step into the bedroom. Behind her, stretched out side by side on his bed, were all three dressers.

The scimitar moved back up into a fighting position. "What have you done to them?"

"To who?" She finished the braid and flipped it back over her shoulder. "Oh. To them. Relax." Unfolding her legs she stood and stretched. The top of her head came no higher than the center of Darvish's chest. "I've put them to sleep. When I'm gone, they won't even remember it happening." Brown eyes flecked with gold rested for an instant on Darvish's face. "Your portrait was accurate enough, I suppose. They left out the baggy bits, but your eyes *are* very blue, aren't they? Now, what have you done with The Stone?"

* * *

". . . and so when I found no one else knew it was missing, I came back here to wait." Chandra spread both hands in a gesture that clearly said her story was finished, and waited for a response. She hadn't mentioned her capture by the Wizard of the Fourth. That she, a Wizard of the Nine, should have been frightened so by a wizard of lesser ability was, was. . . . Well, it wasn't any of their business anyway.

Darvish took a deep breath, opened his mouth to speak, and had a swallow of wine instead. It had been a peculiar sort of a day, to say the least. "Look," he said, pacing the width of the room, "I don't want to marry you either, but at the risk of hurting your feelings, there's more important things going on right now."

"Why should that hurt my feelings?" Surely he didn't think that she'd consider a treaty marriage neither party wanted more important than The Stone of Ischia? "What *happened* to The Stone?"

"It was stolen. Just before dawn." Darvish saw no point in hiding it from her. He could see her storming into the throne room and demanding the information from his most exalted father. If the situation hadn't been so One abandoned serious he'd be tempted to let her do just that. "The thief is dead. We think The Stone is with the wizard who arranged the theft in Ytaili. . . ."

"Of course it's with the wizard, where else would it be? Ytaili's a big place." She raised both brows sarcastically. "I hope you have better directions than that."

Darvish sighed wearily. "All evidence points to Tivolic and someone in the royal family being involved. Aaron and I will start there."

"You and Aaron?" She looked from the tall prince, admittedly muscular but showing definite signs of dissipation, to the slight thief, who for all his breadth of shoulder stood barely taller than she did and who moved as if even breathing hurt. "Why?"

"Because we're the ones who tracked it to Ytaili. Because we've got the best chance to succeed. Because the fewer people who know the less chance of panic. Because. . . ." He searched for another reason. "Because we can slip away without being missed." Say something often enough, forcefully enough, and you could almost convince yourself, Darvish discovered. Almost. *Because they know it can't be done and they're setting me up to fail.*

"Oh." Chandra considered the options. It made sense. Of a sort. She turned to Aaron. "You're soul-linked to him. Why?"

"I'm a thief." He turned his head to face her but let the rest of his body remain still on the pallet. The day had left him weak as a baby. He ached, his head pounded, and they still had to catch the evening tide out of Ischia. "They think I'll run."

"Will you?"

"I doubt it."

"I've never met a thief before."

"I'm not surprised."

"I'd like to talk to you about it later."

"Later," he agreed shortly. She reminded him of Faharra, of how the gem cutter must have been when she was young. He didn't want to like her. He had nowhere to run. Even if Herrak's interference meant he, Aaron, hadn't failed Faharra it didn't, it couldn't, cancel how he'd failed Ruth. Lightly, very lightly, he touched the soul-link. It had been a confusing day.

"Well," said Chandra, in the tone that said this settled things to her satisfaction, "I'm going with you."

"Not if all the Nine showed up and demanded it." Darvish refilled his goblet and took a hasty swallow. "You're going home. Trust me, no one's thinking much about marriage plans right now and your people are going to be worried about you."

"My *people,*" she mimicked with an edge to her voice, "don't even know I'm gone and won't miss me when they find out."

Darvish considered arguing the point, but Chandra's expression told him she wouldn't listen. He decided not to bother. He was hardly the person to be counseling someone about their home life.

"And what are you and Aaron going to do when you find this unknown and, I might add just in case you haven't caught on yet, *very powerful* wizard with The Stone?"

"What do you mean?"

"I mean what are you going to do? Whack him with your sword while Aaron picks his pocket?"

"Something like that." Darvish had another drink. This kid had a vicious tongue.

"It would make sense to take a wizard along."

"We don't have a wizard."

"You have me."

"And *you* can't come."

"Why not?"

"Uh. . . ." Darvish had wanted to take a wizard along, but they were all needed in case the volcano erupted before The Stone was retrieved. The lord chancellor had been most apologetic. "You're too young."

Chandra smiled. What a jerk. "I'm old enough to get married," she pointed out.

"Look, Chandra," Darvish tried being reasonable, "*why* is it so important for you to come?"

Her nostrils flared in an unconscious imitation of Rajeet's expression. "I *told* you. The Wizards of the Nine created The Stone. I'm a Wizard of the Nine and, unless you know another one I don't, the *only* Wizard of the Nine around. That makes me *historically* responsible for The Stone." She tossed her braid back over her shoulder. "And besides, if I help you recover The Stone, I'll be in a better bargaining position to refuse this marriage."

"The marriage won't . . ."

"And if you don't take me with you, I'll tell the whole city The Stone is missing."

"You wouldn't!"

"Try me."

She didn't look like she was bluffing.

Darvish finished his wine and glared at her over the rim of the goblet. She met his eyes, smiling smugly. "Bugger the Nine," he sighed at last. "You win. You can come. Not," he added a little sulkily, "that I could stop you anyway."

"I was wondering when you'd figure that out."

"Figure what . . ."

"That you couldn't stop me."

"Then why. . . ?"

Chandra spread slender hands. "Because I'd prefer we have this conversation now rather than on the deck of a ship or at the palace in Tivolic where you'd give the whole mission away."

Darvish had never liked being patronized and he liked it even less when it was done by a girl half his size and seven years his junior. "They never told me you were a wizard," he growled.

Chandra shrugged. "They never told me you were a drunk. I'd say we're even."

"Yeah? Well, you're . . ." A strange, strangled noise cut him off.

Aaron, his arms wrapped tightly about his body in a futile attempt to keep his chest from moving, rocked in the grip of helpless laughter. It sounded slightly rusty, as though it had been a long time since it had been used. And it sounded just a little desperate.

Darvish and Chandra turned identical faces of aristocratic disdain on the writhing thief.

Aaron didn't know why he laughed, unless it was at the thought of the three of them—a drunken prince, a runaway child-wizard, and a failed thief—taking Ytaili by storm and returning in triumph with The Stone of Ischia. *Soul-linked. I can't get away. I'm going to have to go through with this.*

Perhaps he laughed because he'd forgotten how to cry.

Eight

"I'll meet you at the docks" had been such an easy thing to say back in the quiet of the palace. Chandra shifted her weight and wove the notice-me-not tighter around her. Her un-betrothed and his thief were leaving from the temple, from the prince's "seclusion," so she couldn't leave with them and besides, hadn't she traveled to Ischia on her own?

"I'm a wizard, remember," she'd snapped at Darvish's warnings. *"Remaining unseen is one of the most basic of disciplines."*

When the prince had looked to Aaron for support, the outlander had studied her for a long moment and said, *"There's a row of seven warehouses just in front of the docks, meet us at the western end."*

Darvish had protested and Aaron had replied, *"She's a wizard."* His tone had added, *let her prove it.*

She'd bridled at the prince's grin and stomped from the room. Then she'd had to return to lift the sleep off the dressers. She couldn't remember the last time she'd been so embarrassed.

"I'll get his stone back for him," she muttered, her voice lost under the screams of a thousand seagulls, "and then he'll be sorry he laughed. He'll see. *I* am a Wizard of the Nine."

The rough, undressed stone of the westernmost warehouse dug into her back and the docks of Ischia spread out before her.

Sailors swaggered everywhere, rolling their weight from one hip to another as though they still walked decks, gold gleaming in ears and noses and teeth, every second word a curse. Merchants, either comfortably fat or cadaverously thin, spoke with pursers and captains arranging cargoes and payments and bribes. Whores kept heavily kohled eyes open for opportunity and as Chandra watched, a skinny girl, younger than herself, followed a laughing sailor down between two large piles of rope. Common men and women of Ischia searched the docks for bargains—a bit of silk barely salt stained, a fish not quite freshly dead. Nobles, perfumed sleeves lifted to mask the constantly changing smells of the area and the ever present reek of the less fortunate, searched for thrills, with their guards present in case those thrills got the upper hand. Just at the edge of her hearing, a beggar whined for alms but received, from the shrieks of pain that followed, a less gentle reward.

For over five years Chandra had lived on a quiet country estate with her teacher, her servant, and her old nurse. Once a month her father traveled to her. Once or twice a year she traveled to her father's court.

The docks of Ischia swarmed—there could be no other word for it—with people. Too many people.

In the midst of the procession she had been part of a larger whole. Here, she sat alone. Not that she was frightened. She was a wizard. And a Wizard of the Nine, besides. There was a certain, raw power in it all. There were just so many people. . . .

When the prince and the thief finally arrived, she almost didn't recognize them. The movement of the crowd around them drew her attention, but it took a moment of puzzled staring before she realized who the lithe outlander and his huge hireling were.

Darvish, his hair cropped swordsman short and whiskers a dark shadow along his jaw, looked much less pretty than he had in his long hair and exaggerated court fashions and *much* larger. The heavy cotton and plain sweat-stained leathers showed well-defined muscles, and the grubby white sunrobe he wore could've been poled to make a tent. He still looked like he drank too much, but he didn't look as weak as he had surrounded by silks and softness. He looked nothing like a prince.

Aaron did. Not a single movement was wasted. He looked neither to the left nor the right, his expression hidden within the shadows cast by the stiffened edges of his sunrobe hood. Chandra knew much of his bearing came from his recent injuries—movements were restricted in many ways by burns not quite healed—but he still looked as if he owned the city. Like he stood alone at the top of a mountain and nothing could topple him from the peak. Chandra was impressed in spite of herself; her father had once been a man that strong.

"There's the warehouse." Darvish waved a hand in its direction, studded wrist guards flashing for a moment in the wide sleeves of the sunrobe. He knew he shouldn't be enjoying himself, that his city and its people were in great danger, but he couldn't help it. For at least a nineday, maybe longer, he was free. Free of the palace, free of the plots, free to prove himself to his father. "Where's that girl?"

"Here."

Darvish couldn't stop the jump back, so he added a glare and dropped his hand to his sword hilt. He was not going to look ridiculous in front of this girl he was not going to marry.

Chandra allowed herself a smug smile. She wasn't fooled. And up close, he still smelled of wine. "Your eyes are brown," she said peering up at his face. "A good idea although I could have cast a stronger spell. I doubt this will hold much past morning."

"It doesn't have to last beyond the docks," Darvish snarled, shifting the weight of his shield on his back. It caught on the small pack he wore and, brows down, he yanked it free. "And there won't be much left of a good idea if you tell the whole city."

"My words were pitched to carry only to you."

"Next time, O Awesome Wizard, spare me as well."

"Next time . . ." Chandra looked beyond his bulk, saw Aaron regally indifferent, blushed and fell silent.

"I'm going to find us a ship," Aaron said, his voice as expressionless as his face. "Stay here." He slipped easily into the movement of the crowds although the press of people set his teeth on edge. If they wanted to go on bickering, they could do it without him for a time. Even as a small part of him envied their ability to say what they thought, he despised the waste. Their constant sniping served no purpose, it only wasted time, wasted words.

"One Below, boy, you count out your words like a miser."

Aaron had looked down at the old gem cutter from his perch on her window ledge. "Didn't one of your own poets say that empty words show an empty mind and silence speaks most eloquently of all?"

Faharra had snorted and waved one clawlike finger at the thief. "It wasn't meant to be an excuse for never holding up your end of a conversation."

The pain of Faharra's death had burned down to a gentle ache during his anger at Herrak. His failure to gain the emerald for her tomb, although it still tormented him, no longer weighted every breath. Without it, the walls had weakened and it was getting harder to maintain the void.

"I don't want to know their thoughts," Aaron muttered, deftly sidestepping two whores and a bleeding beggar. He could see danger in that, for what if the thoughts they started speaking began to concern him. If the thoughts Darvish began speaking. . . . *I must be out of my mind; I should've told them to find their own Stone, stayed at the palace and been quietly tortured to death. Before Faharra died, I had my life under control. This is all your doing, old lady.*

From out of memory, he heard her laugh and he allowed himself a small smile in answer.

Darvish watched Aaron cut his way through the crowds like a sword through silk. He moved with an intensity that easily marked his progress in spite of his lack of height. *I could do that,* Darvish realized suddenly. *Just walk the docks like a normal man.* No one expecting a performance from the prince. No one reporting that performance back to the lord chancellor. There were no guards at his back, no spies in the shadows, just him and Aaron and . . .

Chandra. He looked down at the girl who stood arms crossed and foot jigging against the smooth stone of the paving blocks. Maybe a wizard *would* be a help. The poor kid had her own problems and Darvish had never been good at holding a grudge.

"That's the ship you came in on, over there," he told her, waving a hand at a sleek vessel moored toward the eastern end of the harbor. From her masts, she flew the royal colors.

Chandra glanced briefly at the ship and said, "I know."

So it's to be that way, is it. He grinned and added, "I'm sleeping with the captain's wife."

This time Chandra glanced briefly up at Darvish, her eyes hooded with boredom. "I know," she said again. To her surprise, after an astonished second, Darvish threw back his head and roared with laughter and just for an instant he looked like a very nice man indeed. Chandra found herself smiling in response.

At the sound of the laughter, one or two people turned but when they saw a brown-eyed swordsman, not their blue-eyed prince, they went back to their own concerns.

"Your pardon." Even behind the illusion Darvish's eyes twinkled. "That was a boorish thing to say, wasn't it?"

He was inviting her to share the joke, Chandra realized, a joke at his own expense, and the apology had actually sounded sincere. Her smile broadened, she couldn't help it, but by the Nine he confused her.

Then suddenly, the laughter vanished, and the prince's expression turned inward.

"What . . ."

He chopped off Chandra's question with the edge of his hand. Something tugged. . . . He almost had it. Something just this side of pain. Eyes narrowed against the red-gold light of the setting sun, he scanned the crowd for Aaron. There . . . then he jerked, and swore, and raced toward the slight figure who had taken one step too many and crumpled to the ground.

Darvish could feel only the echo of Aaron's agony, not the pain itself, but he knew what Aaron felt and although it eased as he drew closer, the soul-link still screamed though his head like the wrath of all Nine Above.

Scrambling to keep up, Chandra found it difficult to believe that a man of Darvish's size and habits could move so quickly. The crowd scattered, shrieking.

"I didn't touch him, I swear it on the One Below. I never laid a finger on him!" The sailor backed away, hands raised protectively.

Darvish ignored him.

Aaron knelt, forehead resting against the paving stones, body shuddering with each shallow breath. Teeth clenched, he raised his head, then carefully sat back on his heels. A circle of curious faces swam around him and he heard Darvish say, as though from a great distance, "He's not used to the heat." It was a voice only a complete idiot would argue with and no one in the crowd seemed willing.

He tried to rise and the motion sent aftershocks of pain slamming through his body. Strong hands caught him, and held him. Where they gripped, it hurt a little less and then it hurt a lot less and unbidden came the strange thought that, here, he was safe. His vision cleared. He realized he was resting in the circle of Darvish's arms. He pulled away.

"I can stand," he said, and he did.

After a moment, the world steadied. "Perhaps," he said, pulling the hood of the sunrobe back over his face, "we'd better stay together."

Darvish drew in a deep breath and slowly, very slowly, let it out. "Perhaps," he agreed.

"That's it?" Chandra asked, brows up and hands on hips.

"No, not quite." Darvish wiped damp palms on his trousers. "I need a drink."

Chandra rolled her eyes. "Of course you do," she sneered.

"And your business in Tivolic?" the purser asked, counting out the small pile of silver and copper coins into three stacks, one for each passage. When the young man made no answer, he looked up, his lips parted to repeat the question. The words stuck behind his teeth. The outlander's eyes were very pale, almost silver-gray, and nothing, absolutely nothing, of the man showed within them. He felt completely overwhelmed and it didn't make much difference that, even sitting, the purser was almost as tall.

Aaron held the purser's gaze for a moment longer and then, because the question was one he had every right to ask, he answered it. "We're looking for someone."

It was not an answer calculated to make the purser feel more secure and the outlander's clipped accent made it sound more dangerous still. But they had a cabin empty and the captain liked the *Gryphon* to travel full. . . .

His gaze flicked back to where the young outlander's companions stood by the door. "A swordsman, you say?"

"Yes."

"And a girl?"

"Yes."

"The swordsman's?"

"Her own."

More emotion in those last two words than all the others that went before it. *Which,* the purser wondered, *did this outlander lay claim to, the swordsman or the girl? Given the strange prejudice of outlanders, probably the girl.* "She's a wizard?"

"As I said."

"What discipline?"

Aaron could almost feel Chandra's eyes boring circles into his back as he answered. "She hasn't decided yet."

"You bring no trouble on board."

Aaron nodded once.

"And if we're attacked, your swordsman and possibly the wizard will fight."

"Attacked?"

"Pirates," the purser said shortly.

Aaron nodded again and this time the purser echoed it, scooping the coins off the table and into his belt pouch. "Ship's the *Green Gryphon*. We sail with the tide. If you're not on board, you get left behind. No refunds."

Aaron nodded again, flipped the hood up on his sunrobe, and silently the three left the warehouse.

The purser watched them go, whistling tunelessly through his teeth. Outlanders, who could fathom them. This one looked honed to a razor sharpness and ready to cut at the wrong word.

"Use my own name?" Darvish muttered as they headed across the docks to the *Gryphon*. "Are you crazy?"

"I know of four other Darvishes," Aaron told him, "a tavern keeper, a tailor, a gardener, and a blind beggar. They're all about your age. When a prince is named, the common folk are encouraged to use the name as well."

"Why?" Darvish asked. He'd never heard of this.

"To confuse curses. Have Chandra strengthen the illusion that keeps your eyes brown." He almost smiled. "The best lie holds a part of the truth. You'll be just one more Darvish named for the prince."

"What about me?" Chandra pulled on Aaron's sleeve.

"People usually steer clear of wizards. They'll ignore you until they want something."

"Do I use my own name?"

"Is anyone looking for you?"

Chandra thought of the golem waiting patiently for her to return. Of her father who hadn't even realized she was gone. "No."

"Then use the name you'll answer to. It's safest."

Thieves, Chandra realized, narrowly avoiding a pile of fish guts, *have a lot of specialized information.* "Why a merchant ship?" she asked a few minutes later as they neared the *Gryphon*. "Aren't we supposed to be in a hurry?"

"It's leaving tonight," Darvish snapped. He'd been thinking about the blind beggar with his name, trying to compare their lives. "What did you want me to do, commandeer a warship? We're trying not to attract attention."

"Well, maybe," Chandra sniffed, put out by his tone, "you're trying too hard."

Are we? Aaron wondered. Why hadn't they been given, not a warship, but a courier? The crew need only be told they were on a mission for the king, the small, sleek ship could get them to Tivolic in half the time of a merchanter, and it would be there, waiting for them when they needed to escape with The Stone. With a princess of Ytaili in Ischia, royal couriers would frequently go between the two countries. No questions would be asked if one went out tonight.

He supposed someone had their reasons. He would have given a great deal to know who that someone was and what the reasons were.

The salt sea air, the smell of tar and sun-warmed wood giving up its heat into the night—Chandra drew in a deep breath and let it sigh back out in pure contentment. Below her feet she could feel the gentle slap, slap of waves against the hull. Above her head, rope and canvas creaked and billowed as the great square sail trapped a bit more wind. As far from any of the ship's lights as she could get and remain on board, Chandra leaned back and watched the Nine dance across the sky. She would have preferred a faster ship, a ship that could dance across the water, but this would most certainly do.

She would return The Stone to Ischia. A Wizard of the Nine was greater than any single discipline even if she couldn't figure out what exact discipline they faced. Even if—she pushed aside a moment of doubt—the wizard who stole The Stone could do things with mirrors she'd never heard of. *That* would put an end to any stupid marriage plans and give her time to deal with the problem of her cousin and the inheritance.

For the present, she would learn what she could of her companions, their strengths and weaknesses, so she could put them to the best use when the time arrived.

Darvish leaned against the stern and looked back at the lights of Ischia, breathing in the last scents of his city as the offshore breeze pushed the *Gryphon* out to sea.

I'll make you proud of me, Father. The thought had more the tenor of a threat than a promise.

He lifted his wineskin in salute, then half drained it to drown the fear that even returning The Stone and saving the capital would not be enough.

Up in the bow, Aaron stared into darkness, remembering the way the pain had eased in the circle of Darvish's arms.

It was the soul-link, he told himself. *The soul-link made it safe. Nothing more.*

Out of the darkness came voices from his childhood, stern priests who invoked an unforgiving god. *Man and man is a sin and a blasphemy. That way lies the fire.*

What kind of god makes love a sin? Faharra had asked. *Too little of it in the world as it is.*

It was the soul-link, Aaron told them both. *The soul-link made it safe. Nothing more.*

"Not another bloody letter."

The page shrugged and handed the small leather pouch embossed with the royal seals of both Ytaili and Cisali to the courier's captain. "I don't know what it is, ma'am. I was told to emphasize," he stumbled a little on the unfamiliar word, "that it had to be in Tivolic as soon as possible. That you're supposed to catch the evening tide."

"I can see the urgent cord, boy." She tapped one callused finger on the red silk string sealed around the pouch. "And don't tell me how to sail. I've been doing it for longer than you've been alive."

"Yes ma'am. I mean, no ma'am." He skipped back as the captain barked an order, the ropes were tossed clear, and the courier slipped the dock. Shoving his hands deep in his trouser pockets, he lingered for as long as he dared. That was the life; racing across the ocean, daring wind and wave, getting the message through whatever the cost. He sighed and headed back up the innumerable terraces to the palace. Maybe he should apply to the navy. Nothing ever happened in Ischia.

Safely clear of the harbor, the captain turned the package

over and frowned at the royal seals. ''Well, all I can say is, if it's from Her Most Blessedness, and if she wants more bloody peacocks, she can find another ship to carry them.''

''Tired of beating on the crew?''

Darvish threw himself down by Aaron in the shade and grinned at Chandra. ''Nine, no,'' he answered, ''I got tired of them beating on me.'' The last two mornings, Darvish had picked out the largest men in the crew and challenged them to spar. He said he did it to stay in training, but his companions suspected he did it for fun, the no-holds-barred, gouging, biting type of fighting the sailors did couldn't be called training by any stretch of the imagination. The last two nights, he'd gotten drunk with them, having passed rapidly from landsman to compatriot.

''I know he's supposed to be pretending to be a swordsman,'' Chandra had sniffed at Aaron, ''but does he have to do it so well? He's still a prince and he should act more like one.''

The demon wings had risen. ''Why?'' Aaron had asked. ''You don't.''

''I am a Wizard of the Nine,'' she'd replied haughtily.

Aaron had gestured at the prince, surrounded by sailors, teaching them a soldier's song with impossibly lewd lyrics. ''This is what he is.''

Aaron and Chandra, the crew ignored. They returned the lack of interest.

Mopping his face with a double handful of his sunrobe, Darvish shot a questioning glance at the small silver bowl tucked into the curve of Chandra's crossed legs. ''Have you found The Stone yet?''

''Not exactly,'' Chandra frowned. ''I can tell it still exists and that we're heading toward it, but any details it burns out.'' When she'd last tried, just before sunrise, the power surge almost destroyed her scrying bowl. But she wasn't going to tell Darvish *that*. Nor was she going to mention the touch that had stroked lightly across her focus and diverted it. This was between her and that other wizard.

''At least we know we're going in the right direction and that it hasn't been destroyed.''

''I keep telling you, no wizard in his right mind would destroy The Stone of Ischia.''

''What if this wizard isn't in his right mind?''

Chandra snorted. "You're just saying that to be annoying!"

"Probably," he admitted, unrepentant. He prodded Aaron gently with a bare foot. "You put that salve on yet?"

"Hmm?" Deep in the protection of his sunrobe hood, Aaron's eyes were closed. The motion of the ship and the heat of the sun had filled the void and it just wasn't worth the effort to empty it out again. He was warm, he was comfortable, nothing even hurt very much.

"The salve?" Darvish repeated.

He'd brought the small pot up on deck, but, no, he hadn't applied it. He managed a single shake of his head.

"Do you want me to do it?"

A lazy flick of a pale finger seemed to indicate that Darvish should go ahead.

Shaking his own head, Darvish knelt and pried the cork from the pot. "There isn't much left," he warned, flicking Aaron's sunrobe open. The yellow silk trousers—"If I have to look less like a prince, you have to look less like a thief."—were low on Aaron's hips and he hadn't bothered putting his shirt on at all. *And a good thing, too,* Darvish thought with a wry smile. *I don't think I'm up to undressing him. And stopping.* He watched the brown of his fingers against the white of Aaron's chest and tried not to think of anything in particular.

The salve was cool against the scars and the gentle circular motion was the final thing Aaron needed to relax him completely. He felt like he didn't have any bones.

"You know what you need, Dar?" he murmured. "You need a war."

It took Darvish a moment to get past the diminutive. No one had called him Dar since his grandmother had died. He ran a line of salve carefully down the join of new skin and old, taking enough time for the lump in his throat to dissolve. "I thought it was war, amongst other things, we were trying to prevent," he said at last.

"No, no, you *personally* need a war." Darvish got the impression Aaron was speaking almost to himself. "I had a cousin like you once, a great fighter; soldiers, common people would follow him anywhere. Father said Joshua was the best *kar kleysh* he'd ever had."

"*Kar kleysh?*"

Eyes still closed, Aaron frowned. "You'd call it a war

chief, uh, a commander.'' One corner of his mouth twitched upward. "Of course, the tricky part was commanding Joshua. You're like him, Dar. You need a war to be appreciated.''

"Maybe I should start one when we get to Ytaili?''

The same corner twitched upward again. "Maybe.''

"*Kar kleysh*,'' Chandra repeated thoughtfully. "I've never heard that language before. Where exactly are you from?''

Aaron sighed deeply. "A very, very long way from here.''

"But where exactly? And why did you leave? And why become a thief, for the Nine's sake? You're an intelligent man, wellborn, I can't imagine anything so drastic that it would force you to make that kind of choice.''

Between one heartbeat and the next, stone walls slammed back into place, muscles tensed, and Aaron returned to the real world. *No,* he thought, *I don't imagine you can. Ruth was three years younger than you when she died.* In one fluid motion he gained his feet and without speaking turned and walked to the bow where he could be alone with the memory of the screaming.

Darvish savagely shoved the cork back in the pot and thought about how much he'd like to wring Chandra's neck. "That was just brilliant,'' he snarled.

"What?'' Chandra protested. "I just asked him some questions.''

"Well maybe next time, O Awesome Wizard,'' Darvish stood and glared down at her, "you'll think about the answers you might get and then you'll think again about asking. And now, just so you have ample time to disapprove, I'm going to get drunk.''

Alone, Chandra chewed her lip and picked at the tarred end of a piece of rope. The rules governing people made the most difficult wizardry with its chants and measurements and potential for disaster look both easy and safe. At least the rules of wizardry never changed. "It wasn't my fault,'' she told her shadow. Her shadow didn't look convinced.

"Courage, little sister.'' In the red-gold light of The Stone, the man's expression appeared deceptively kind. "Win through, prove yourself worthy, and you need never be alone again.''

* * *

"I feel sorry for her," Darvish said, as the two men leaned on the rail and watched the sun extinguish itself beneath the horizon. "She's so busy saying, *If you don't need me, then I don't need you* to her father that she's never acknowledged how much he hurt her."

Aaron grunted and Darvish continued. "She's hiding that hurt behind anger." He grinned. "And occasionally an obnoxious personality." The light of the sun gave his skin a ruddy cast and turned the brown illusion over his blue eyes almost purple. "I wish there was something we could do to help her."

Aaron turned, looked steadily at Darvish for a moment, then shook his head in disbelief. "The blind leading the blind," he snorted and walked away, still shaking his head.

The gentle roll of the ship sent the huge figure crashing into a wall, where it rested for a moment before going on. It squinted against the night and the fine misting of rain, spotted its destination, and lurched determinedly forward. Two tries opened the door and, ducking under the low lintel, Darvish fell into the tiny cabin.

"Get off me, you ox! You're all wet!"

Slowly and carefully, Darvish stood and then reached out and considerately stopped the wild rocking of Chandra's hammock. "Though you'd be a . . . sleep."

"I was until you landed on me!"

Darvish thought about that for a moment. "Oh," he said. "You asleep . . . Aaron?" He peered into the dark shelf of the cabin's narrow bunk.

The thief's pale eyes glimmered eerily. "I was."

"Oh."

As Darvish continued to loom over him, Aaron stirred uneasily. "You stink," he said. "Go to bed."

The prince sighed and straightened. "Go to bed," he repeated morosely, somehow managing to find his hammock and get into it. "Go to bed alone. I'm in the . . . middle of th' ocean. Risking my . . . life . . . an' I'm witha virgin ana stone. Aaron doesn't like boys," he added after a second, "an' I respeck that."

You're not a boy, Aaron thought.

And the priests said, "Man loving man is foul in the sight of the Lord."

"An' Chandra's justa child. A baby. Only sixteen. S'okay to be a . . . virgin when you're still a baby. I unnerstand. Really."

"Look," Chandra said suddenly, "it's nothing personal." Maybe if she explained, he'd drop it. This might not be the best time nor place, but the darkness made it easy so she continued. "It's because I'm a Wizard of the Nine."

"Wizards," said Darvish, from the shadowed depths of his hammock, "don't have ta be . . . virgins. I know tha fer a fact. Four facts, in fact. Five if you figger . . . one of 'em was twice."

"But not all wizards are the same." It had become very important that they understand. "Wizards make themselves a focus for external power, channeling it into the forms they choose. Most wizards can focus only a small amount of the power available and the forms they can channel to are limited by the discipline that makes them Wizards of the First or the Second or the Ninth. Wizards of the *Nine* are capable of focusing *all* available power and the forms are limited only by their level of training."

"But virgins . . ."

"I'm coming to that. To focus that kind of power, the wizard must be strong. Sex weakens you. Marriage weakens you. Love weakens you most of all. I won't lose my strength, myself, in another person. I won't do it. I won't."

"Then don't." Aaron's voice was steel and stone and ice.

"We'll get The Stone," Darvish said around a yawn, "and that'll show them all." He yawned again and almost instantly after his breathing slowed.

Chandra took a deep breath of her own and shakily released it. As much as his habits disgusted her, she found herself liking Darvish much more than she'd have ever liked the pretty princeling she'd expected. We'll get The Stone, he'd said. We. Her and Darvish and Aaron. If Aaron wanted to be part of a we. . . .

Then, over the prince's gentle snores she heard him say, "Good night, Wizard."

She smiled. *We'll get the stone.*

"Good night, Thief."

". . . but Gracious Majesty, if you want it done away from the harbor—we search for a single ship and the ocean is large."

King Harith stabbed a beefy finger down on the map, a square cut ruby flashing deep red in the lamplight. "How hard can it be?" he demanded. "The *Gryphon* sails from here," the finger moved, "to here. You tell a ship to wait here, and when *Gryphon* sails by it's ours. Simple."

"Most ships, Gracious Majesty," the Lord of the Navy tried again, "cut over to the north current somewhere along here. . . ."

"Good." The king nodded his heavy head. "The perfect place for an ambush."

"But, Gracious Majesty, we have no way of knowing where they will cross to the current."

"Of course we do," the king snorted. "Take a Wizard of the Seventh along, find out where the winds blow tonight. You can have a couple of ships in the area by tomorrow morning?"

The lord nodded. It hadn't really been a question.

"Good, anyway, have the wizard find out where the winds would put the ship onto the current and be there. Seventh is a god of storms, after all, he should be able to figure out a few One abandoned winds. I want that ship and everyone on it destroyed completely. Take a Wizard of the Fourth along as well, they're good at that sort of thing."

The Lord of the Navy took a deep breath and said in the most innocuous voice he could manage. "Could that not be interpreted as an act of war, Gracious Majesty?" Not only could Ytaili not afford a war at this time, but to break a treaty just less than a year old would panic other treaty partners and start something they couldn't hope to control.

"Of course it could be interpreted as an act of war, you One abandoned idiot," King Harith growled. "And that's why," his eyes glittered in the lamplight and he smiled, "you're leaving no witnesses." One way or another, treaty or no treaty, he would get Cisali, if not by the war his people refused to fund, then by less overt means. To that end, he had helped the wizard Palaton steal The Stone and now, he would prevent Ischia's heroes from stealing it back.

Nine

Head pounding, guts heaving, miles away from a cure, Darvish staggered to the rail to throw up.

"Now a sailor'd time it t'the swell, so it don't splash back on the ship."

"The Nine can time it," Darvish muttered, and spat. He straightened up and glared at the mate, who grinned genially back at him. "What the One were we drinking last night and may She have mercy on me for doing it?"

"Rice wine."

"What wine?"

"Rice wine." The mate's grin broadened and the early morning sunlight gleamed on a pair of gold teeth. "You bought a keg out of cargo."

"Good for me." He clenched his teeth on another spasm, and managed, barely, to keep control. "Charged me double, did you?" he asked hoarsely when he could speak again.

"You didn't *have* quite double. We cut you a deal."

"Thank you." A callused hand clapped him jovially on the shoulder and the shock of the blow echoed through his head. Only his death grip on the rail kept him standing. The mate, while not quite the prince's height, had shoulders and arms so heavily muscled that he appeared in constant danger of tipping over. Darvish had sparred with him twice and he hoped never to meet the man in a serious fight. "If you're looking for some exercise, I don't think I'm up to it."

"Nay, I wondered if you wanted somethin' to eat. We've a fine mess of roe fried up with big chunks of onion."

Darvish growled out most of a curse before he had to heave his guts over the rail again. "You have a sick sense of humor," he snarled when he could.

"You're not the first to say it," the other man admitted,

laughing. He leaned his massive forearms on the rail and squinted into the distance. "Now then. What's that there?"

Suspecting that he'd already found The Stone, that someone had slipped it into his skull during the night, Darvish peered in the direction the mate seemed to be looking. "It's land," he said at last.

"Aye. It's the Ytaili coast. There's a strong current north the captain likes to ride close in. But look there," he pointed, "by that great white lump, what do you see?"

The dark bank of land merged into the sea at one edge and rose up to disappear into a gray veil of morning mist at the other. Darvish, attempting to ignore the additional pounding that focusing caused, finally found "the great white lump." It was probably a cliff, and an immense one to be visible even as a blotch of color from this far out. He could just barely see a tiny black speck, no, two specks bobbing up and down on the waves before it, silhouetted against the white at the top of each crest.

"Ships?" he guessed.

"Can't think of what else it could be. Can you? But the question is," he continued without waiting for an answer, "what're they doing just sitting out there?"

"Fishing?" Darvish asked and winced as that brief enthusiasm sent a spike through his head.

"Could be. 'Cept there ain't nothin' to catch in there; too close to the current." He scowled and pushed back off the trail. "Captain'd best be told." Another scowl into the distance and he was gone.

"What are you looking at?" Chandra had done a finding for one of the sailors who'd lost a new awl and had been paid with a bright red silk shirt. She didn't usually care much about clothes but she'd never had to wear the same plain brown tunic for almost a nineday before. Her new wide sleeves billowed in the wind as she leaned over the rail beside Darvish.

"Ships," Darvish told her shortly, his attention more on keeping his stomach quiet.

She narrowed her eyes and leaned forward to the edge of safety. "Where?"

"That way." Aaron had come up on her other side and now he pointed. "By the white cliffs."

"How can you tell it's a cliff?" Darvish wanted to know, curious if Aaron could actually see clearly that far.

"What else could it be?"

Darvish shrugged and immediately regretted it.

"That doesn't look like much fun," Chandra observed when he'd finished and was wiping his mouth.

Darvish glared at her over the back of his hand. "And you only studied for five years to figure that out?"

An errant breeze crossed the distance between them and Chandra vigorously fanned the air in front of her nose. "Why do you do it if this sort of thing happens afterward?"

"Why do I do it? You mean why drink?"

"Yes. Why?"

He smiled viciously. "Because I do it so well." Then with a mocking bow he turned and walked away.

Chandra sighed and bit her lip. "I did it again, didn't I?"

"You ask too many questions," Aaron said quietly, his eyes still apparently locked on the ships in the distance.

As the sun rose and the mists burned off the land, the *Gryphon* drew closer to the white cliffs. The strange ships, slightly larger but still not large enough to be identified, remained where they were, riding the swell and waiting.

"Can they see us?" Darvish asked, back at the rail, a ship's biscuit in one hand and a wineskin dangling from the other. At that moment he was as close to contentment as he'd been in years. The court had receded into the past and he could do nothing about The Stone until they reached Tivolic.

"Aye, they can see us but no better than we can see them." The mate refused the offered wineskin.

"Could it be pirates, waiting to draw us into a trap?"

"Aye, could be. Could be ships in trouble. Be better to stay out here and avoid them entirely, but the captain don't want to miss the current. It's a bitch of a row without if the wind drops." He hacked and spit over the side. "Can't tell from here. We have to go in."

"But if it's pirates and you go in. . . ."

"We'll be in a wind abandoned heap of shit for sure. And if it ain't pirates, if they're in trouble and we don't go in that's the same kind of help we'll get when we need it."

"So it might be ships in trouble or it might be pirates pretending to be in trouble to lure you closer?"

"Aye." His massive hands twisted around the rail and the wood creaked alarmingly. "Sailed with a captain once who had a brass tube with circles of glass set in it. Forget what she called it, but when you held it to your eye you could see for miles. Wish we had one now.''

Darvish chewed thoughtfully on the biscuit. "Was it magic?"

"Nay, just something she'd picked up in the east."

"I wonder if there's something magic can do. . . ."

"Aye, mumble a deal of nonsense and charge more'n you've got for it." The mate pursed his lips and rubbed at the sweat on his chest. After a moment he sighed. "Go ahead. Ask her. Even if she doesn't do any good, I don't imagine a slip of a thing like her could do much harm."

As Darvish headed back to the stern and their cabin, he noticed that the crew worked with one eye on the job at hand and the other on the ships in the distance. No one sang, growled orders were reinforced with muttered threats, and the loudest noises came from the *Gryphon* herself; the wind straining against her sail, the sea slapping against her hull. Darvish glanced up onto the sterncastle and saw the captain standing by the great sweep oar, one hand resting lightly on its secured end. Although a braided gray beard covered most of the captain's face, what little remained visible did not look pleased.

Better you than me, Darvish thought as he ducked and went into the cabin.

The hammocks were slung against the wall and Chandra lay on the bunk, hands behind her head, getting lost in the grain of the wood above her.

"Chandra, we need you to scry those ships."

She blinked and slowly came back to herself. "What?"

Darvish hooked the cabin's one small stool out of the corner it had been shoved into, pulled it over to the bunk, and sat down. "We need you to scry those ships," he repeated earnestly.

Chandra swung her legs out and sat up carefully, the bunk left her a little headroom but not enough for enthusiasm. "The ships by the coast?" she asked.

"Yes. We need to know if they're pirates soon enough for the captain to change course if he has to. And I might add, he doesn't want to."

"Well, I'd like to help. . . ." Darvish opened his mouth. Chandra stopped him with an upraised hand. "But I can't. I'd need a piece of the ships to scry them."

"Bugger the Nine!" Darvish stood, and kicked the stool aside. "We have to know what's going on." He slammed a fist into the cabin wall. "Where's Aaron? Pirates are just thieves in a boat, maybe he'll know how to identify them."

"I don't know."

"How can you *not* know? This isn't that big a ship."

Chandra looked up from buckling her sandals and frowned. "He wanted to be alone. I'm sure *you* could find him if you looked, *you're* the one with the soul-link, but Darvish," she stood and tossed her braid behind her shoulder, "there might be something else I can do."

He paused, bent over to clear the low lintel, and half turned. "What?"

"There's a spell, a distance seeing spell." Her chin came up. "I don't see so well in the distance, so I use it a lot. I could cast it and take a look at those ships."

"And how could you tell if they were pirates?" he asked, not unkindly.

"Well, there must be some way of telling."

"There is; they swarm screaming over the side, swords drawn and start hacking the crew to bloody bits." He grinned, shrugged, and came back into the cabin. "Could you cast it on someone else?"

She never had, but . . . "Yes, of course I could."

"Could you . . ." Darvish took a long pull on the wine-skin while he tried to slap an idea into shape. "Could you cast it on *something* else?"

"What?"

Quickly, Darvish explained the brass tube the mate had mentioned. "So if you could make something like that, a distance tube that anyone could look through. . . ."

"It isn't a hard spell," Chandra said thoughtfully. She'd used it often enough that she could probably cast it in her sleep. A spell she knew less thoroughly she wouldn't dare to modify. Rajeet, her teacher, had warned her time after time to follow the parameters of a spell exactly, but new spells had to come from somewhere. And Wizards of the Nine were not meant to be tied as other wizards were. She took a deep breath. "Get me a small piece of coal and a little bit of dry sand."

"Sand? Chandra, we're at sea!"

"Ask the cook," came Aaron's quiet voice from the door. "He banks his coals with sand."

"Aaron, that's brilliant!" Darvish turned the full force of his smile on the younger man, then pushed past him and ran for the bow.

"It is very clever," Chandra agreed.

"I notice details," Aaron muttered, trying to get his traitorous heart to start beating again after being caught in the vise of Darvish's smile. When he felt the heat had faded from his face, he pushed back his sunhood and came into the cabin. "*Can* you make a distance viewer?"

"Of course I can, I'm . . ." She stopped and wilted a little under Aaron's gaze. He didn't accuse, he didn't even look like he didn't believe her; he just looked. "I think I can," she amended with a sigh. "It should work."

"Is it dangerous?"

She opened her mouth to say no, then closed it again. Magic worked through well defined rules to focus power into something entirely new which—and realistically she had to admit there was a slight chance things could go wrong— might not hold it. "There's a possibility of danger. . . ."

"Then why do it?"

This time there was only one answer. She could say "to help the ship" or "because Darvish asked me to," but she didn't think Aaron would believe either. "To prove that I can."

Aaron grinned. Chandra returned it. Just for a moment they understood each other perfectly.

"All right, I got the coal and I got the sand and the cook thinks I'm out of my mind," Darvish rushed back into the cabin and his excitement made the tiny room seem smaller still. "Anything else?"

Chandra took the dish of sand and the pieces of coal and placed them carefully in the center of the stool. "I need a tube; it has to be fairly stiff, but it can't be metal. . . ."

"Why not? The mate talked about a brass tube."

"If I mark on a brass tube with charcoal, the symbols will rub right off and as soon as they're gone, so's the spell. I need something hollow that charcoal will stick to that's about this long." She held her hands about six inches apart.

"I had thought of the perfect item," Darvish waggled his eyebrows rakishly, "but it turned out to be too big."

"And she'd have to remove it," Aaron put in dryly from the bunk, where he'd tucked himself to get out of the way. "You wouldn't like that much."

"What. . . ?" Chandra looked from one to the other. "Oh." She scowled up at the prince, who winked. "Is that all you ever think abou . . . no, it isn't! Give me that!" She pulled the wineskin down off his shoulder and shook it.

"Hey!"

"Never mind!" She shoved it back into his hands. "Finish it!"

A little bemused but willing to oblige, Darvish did as he was told.

"Now cut the neck off, here," she drew a line on the leather just below the thickened spout with her thumbnail, "and here." A second line was drawn just above the bell.

A few moments later Chandra peered through the narrow end of the flared tube and said, "Now get out."

"Get out?"

She put her hand in the small of Darvish's back and pushed, waving Aaron up from the bunk and out the door in the same motion. "I need to be alone to work. You're too much of a distraction."

Darvish beamed back over his shoulder at her. "That's the nicest thing you've ever said to me." Then he followed Aaron out onto the deck. As she pulled the door closed, she heard him say, "My sword, your brains, and her talent . . . that wizard with The Stone doesn't stand a chance."

It could have been the wine talking, it *probably* was the wine talking, but it was nice to hear anyway.

"It's a what?" The mate looked suspiciously at the piece of wineskin dwarfed by Darvish's hand.

"A distance viewer." Darvish held it out to him again, his thumb and forefinger carefully in the places that Chandra had indicated.

"It's a chunk of One abandoned wineskin with black marks on it."

"Yes it is," Darvish agreed. "But it's also a distance viewer.

The mate snorted and spat, his opinion obviously clear.

"I thought you wanted a closer look at those ships?"

"Aye."

"This will give it to you. You saw me look through it, it won't hurt you."

"Ain't afraid of it."

"Then take it. I've seen the ships, but I don't know what

I'm seeing." At his most charming, Darvish could persuade a frog to sing. "Just try it. What have you got to lose? Hold it here and look through the narrow end."

The mate grunted and, obviously humoring the other man, placed his fingers by Darvish's and lifted the cylindrical bit of leather, still smelling strongly of fermented grape, to his eye.

"Nine Above and One Below," he breathed. Through the flaring end of the wineskin he could see the ships they'd watched through most of the morning only now, instead of a vague silhouette impossible to identify, he saw two masts, the sails down but not secured, a hull narrower and higher than the merchant ship, an anchor rope running taut down into the sea. The second ship could have been cast from an identical mold. "Nine Above, they're navy!"

He spun away from the rail and bounded for the stern-castle, waving the distance viewer over his head like a very small and grubby flag. "Captain! Captain!"

"What's that all about?" Chandra wondered, jolted out of her fit of the sulks by the mate's strange behavior. Darvish had insisted *he* present the viewer to the mate;

"Please, let me. You're a wizard, you have other skills."

"You think if I gave it to him he wouldn't take it."

Darvish looked down at the mutilated wineskin. "Well, yes."

He hadn't exactly said she was tactless, but he'd implied it. It hadn't helped her mood to realize he was probably right.

Darvish raised a questioning brow at Aaron, but the thief only shrugged. "I have no idea," the prince admitted. "But before we go and find out, let me see your hand."

"My hand?"

"Your palm, let me see it." He smiled down at her. "Aaron isn't the only one who notices things, you know. You've been holding your left hand like it hurts you since you came out of the cabin."

"It's nothing."

"Let me see."

The tone said, *let me help,* and it was the kind of voice her father had used when she was young and had hurt herself, a voice he'd used before her mother had died and he'd. . . . But Darvish was weak, nothing like the strong man her father had been then, much more like the man he'd become.

"Hand wounds are the most difficult to tend yourself," Darvish said reasonably. "You're going to need both hands if we're to get The Stone."

He had a point. Chandra turned her palm up and held it out.

An angry red circle, both like and unlike a burn, cut across the mound of her thumb and curved around the base of her fingers.

"Aaron? Do we have any salve left?"

Aaron, who'd stood quietly in the background through the testing of the distance viewer, nodded and said, "A little." He slipped off to get it.

"What happened?" Darvish asked, gently flexing the fingers. The bones of Chandra's hands were so tiny and delicate they reminded him of bird bones and her wrist slid with room to spare through a circle of his fingers.

Chandra shrugged. "I had to block the open end to set the spell. I guess," she added ruefully, "I shouldn't have used my hand."

"I guess not," Darvish agreed solemnly, unsure of her reaction if he laughed.

They stood awkwardly for a moment almost but not quite holding hands.

His hands are warm. And rough, not like a courtier's hands at all. And they were so large, Chandra realized, that he could probably completely enclose her fist in his. *Why doesn't he say something?*

Darvish couldn't think of anything to say. All the glib and clever phrases he used at court didn't apply to someone who'd become a friend; although it was a strange and tentative sort of friendship, really more like comrades-in-arms. He'd never had one of those before either, well, not before Aaron and he wasn't likely to end up holding Aaron's hand. Not if Aaron had anything to say about it.

"Dar." They both jumped and shot Aaron looks so identically relieved that he had to hide a grin. He held out the squat clay pot. "There's a little left in the bottom."

"Right." Darvish shoved Chandra's hand in Aaron's direction. "You do it, I'm going to see what the captain has decided. We seem to have changed course." He smiled strangely down at the wizard, spun on his bare heel and almost trotted off.

"What was that all about?" Chandra wondered, the lines smoothing out of her forehead as the salve soothed the pain out of her hand.

"I think he likes you," Aaron told her, his voice expressionless, his heart strangely heavy.

Chandra remembered a number of the things the crowd had shouted as the dowry procession had made its way to the palace. "I can't see why," she sniffed.

A moment later they followed Darvish to the sterncastle where a great sweep oar had been untied and the two steersmen had turned the *Gryphon* to the very edge of the wind. The captain still peered through the distance viewer, his legs braced against the roll of the deck and his gaze locked on the navy ships. When he lowered his arm, he stood quiet for a moment longer, then nodded once at Chandra and said, "My compliments, Most Wise." It was the first time anyone on board had used the honorific. "You have saved us from a great disaster."

Behind him, sunlight gleamed on gold teeth. The mate beamed as though it were all his idea.

"You have my thanks, Most Wise," he continued. "For the losses you have saved us, your passage price will be refunded. Now, about this viewer. . . ." His eyes glittered. "Will it work for anyone?"

"Yes, of course," she answered, tossing her head. "The spell is in the tube, but it will only last as long as the symbols on the outside do, so be careful. Why?"

"If you had a brass tube and proper etching tools?"

Chandra shrugged, she was getting a little tired of explaining. "Then it would last a lot longer. Not forever, but longer. Now," she crossed her arms and frowned, daring him to cut her off again, "why are you running away from navy ships?"

The captain's expression froze and the glitter grew harder. Behind him, gold teeth disappeared. The mate flexed his massive arms and waited for orders.

Aaron and Darvish stepped up to stand beside her and Darvish, who had been trying to think of a tactful way to ask the same question, muttered, "You do like to live dangerously, don't you?"

The silence grew.

The two steersmen, the captain, and the mate. Not completely impossible odds if it comes to it, Darvish thought.

There was an almost imperceptible change in the captain's expression and Aaron knew the balance had tipped. As he didn't know which way, he kicked out the fulcrum. "They're smugglers," he said. "There's four bags of ground kerric nut in with the spices."

"But kerric nut kills!" Chandra exclaimed.

"In large enough doses," Aaron agreed.

"Well, I'm glad we've got that settled." Darvish spread empty hands and grinned his patently irresistible grin. "We'd prefer to stay clear of the Ytaili navy ourselves."

The captain glared at Aaron. Aaron stared steadily back. Although it was difficult to tell for certain, down in the depths of the captain's beard, one corner of his mouth may have twitched in a rueful acknowledgment. "I bet you would," was all he said.

"Captain, Sir!"

"What is it, Ensign?"

The ensign leaned as far over the edge of the fighting top as she dared. "They've changed course, Sir."

The captain of the *Sea Hawk* turned and, shading his eyes, peered in the direction of their quarry. The ship, facing them dead on all morning, now angled about forty-five degrees to port, paralleling the coast rather than heading straight for it.

"Sink the Nine," he swore. "Most Wise!"

Both wizards looked up at the bellow.

"Is that soul-link still on board?"

The Wizard of the Fourth closed her eyes for a moment in concentration. "It is," she sighed. She had come only because the king had ordered it. Ships made her sick.

"Then the waiting is over." The captain rubbed his hands in anticipation. *Pretend you're in trouble, let them get in close, then take them.* He hated that sort of order. The *Sea Hawk* was meant to swoop down into battle, not sit like the cheese in a trap.

"So there's honor amongst thieves after all," Chandra observed, picking at a sliver of wood.

"Not at all," came the answer from the shadowed depths of Aaron's sunhood.

''Then why . . .''

''Are we alive?'' Aaron finished. ''The captain figures he can use us.'' It had been a calculated risk mentioning the smuggling. ''He could have easily decided if we weren't for him we were against him,'' he explained. ''Now he knows whose side we're on.''

''They're raising their sails,'' Darvish called out, running up fully armed. ''They're coming after us.''

''We need a wind,'' the mate added, right behind him. ''The captain wants to see you, Most Wise.''

The captain wanted a wind. ''One in my sails, one that they'll have to tack across to reach us. Can you give me such a wind?''

Chandra pulled at the end of her braid and thought about it. Gentle breezes to cool a garden or a sleeping room, she'd called many times. A wind was a difference in intensity not form, easier in that than the distance viewer. She tossed her braid behind her shoulder. ''Of course I can.''

''What do you need?''

''Another piece of coal, a dagger,'' she held her hands apart, ''with a blade about this long, a ribbon,'' the distance between her hands lengthened, ''about this long and,'' she looked down at her feet, ''a circle of the deck off limits to everyone but me.''

''They have a wizard.'' The Wizard of the Seventh held his face into the freshening wind and sniffed. ''This wind is power called.''

''Well, turn it,'' commanded the *Sea Hawk*'s captain.

''They have a wizard,'' Chandra gasped. ''They're trying to turn the wind.''

''Can they do it?'' Darvish asked, taking a long pull on the wineskin that dangled from his sword hand.

''I don't know.'' Her brow furrowed and the ribbon, beginning to tangle, flew straight and true once more.

The *Gryphon* surged forward; the sail belled taut.

''I thought I ordered you to turn that wind.''

''It isn't as easy as all that,'' the wizard panted. ''Their wizard is *very* powerful and responds to everything I do by pulling in yet more power.''

''I don't care what you have to do,'' the captain roared.

He had never failed in a commission for his king and he had no intention of starting now. "Stop that ship!"

The wind rose and above the *Gryphon* the sky grew black.

"It's too much," the captain screamed over the protests of his ship. "The mast is about to come down. Stop it!"

"I can't!" Chandra's hair, free of the braid, whipped around her. "There's too much power!"

"Why are you stopping?" The captain glared down at the Wizard of the Seventh. "I thought your god controlled the winds."

"Storms," corrected the exhausted wizard from the deck. He raised a shaky arm and pointed over the captain's shoulder. "And it's in His hands now."

Chandra's ribbon tied itself in a knot.

The storm broke.

The *Gryphon* bucked and wallowed as frantic figures crawled over her, lowering her sail, securing lines and hatches.

"Get below!" The mate dragged Chandra to her feet and thrust her at Darvish. "The last thing we need now is landers on deck!"

"I can walk!" Chandra protested with what little energy she had remaining.

Darvish ignored her and lurched toward their cabin. He grabbed at a line as the ship rolled and a wave sucked at his feet, then dove through the door that Aaron had wrestled open. Shoving Chandra onto the bunk, he lunged back at the door and, adding his strength to Aaron's, dragged it closed.

Inside the tiny room, it was like being in a drum as the wind and waves beat at the ship, trying to drive her down. Strained timbers shrieked and moaned. They couldn't talk. They could barely think.

Darvish emptied the wineskin he carried. Then he sat, wedged in a corner, and worked the leather in his hands. Pulled it. Twisted it. Waiting. He hated waiting. He didn't do it well.

Aaron, his feet braced against the bunk, his back against the wall, sat wrapped in the void and waited to die. He was good at it. He'd been doing it for the last five years.

"If you truly want your cousin's death, you're not going about it the right way."

"Any death will do now, Faharra."

He shoved the small voice that dared suggest he couldn't die while Darvish needed him, back behind the walls and drowned it out with Ruth's screams.

Chandra turned her back on the two men and chewed her lip, blinking rapidly to clear the heat building behind her eyes. She'd failed. She'd never failed before. *She* was a Wizard of the Nine.

The ship dropped out from under them. Even Aaron cried out as it slammed back up to meet them as they fell.

"That is it!" Darvish pulled himself to his feet and settled his sword on his hips.

"What are you doing?" Chandra yelled. She could hardly hear herself over the howl of the storm.

The prince unhooked his shield, slipped his arm through the strapping, crashed into the wall, and said in a sudden lull, "I'm going out for a drink."

"You're what?" Chandra couldn't believe her ears, then the storm struck again and nearly threw her from the bunk.

Aaron dove for Darvish's legs, but the deck heaved and he grabbed at air.

The wind whipped the heavy wooden door out of Darvish's hands and slammed it up against the outside wall. A smaller man would have been pulled from his feet, but Darvish only laughed and staggered into the storm.

Aaron scrambled upright and, clinging to the wall, somehow made his way outside. The world had become a seething mass of gray, clouds and wind and rain and sea, impossible to tell where one ended and the other began. He squinted and could just make out a darker mass by the rail and beyond that a line of black. Darvish? And land? With arms made strong from a thousand midnight climbs, he inched his way forward, hand over hand, scarred chest muscles protesting as more than once they held his entire weight, feet having been swept or blown out from under him.

The ship rolled and he watched the rail and the prince-shaped shadow beside it, slowly, majestically, go under. Then the *Gryphon*, like a great dog, shook herself upright again. By some fluke of the storm, he could see that section of the rail clearly. It was empty.

Aaron let go of his hold and took one step, two; by three

he was running. Then the storm picked him up and dashed him against the rail. He sucked in salt water, coughed, and pulled himself to his feet.

Someone grabbed at his arm.

"Are you crazy?" he screamed at Chandra.

"Are you?" she shrieked back.

Then the ocean reached up and took them both.

Barricaded into her bunk, the Wizard of the Fourth wanted to die and it didn't help that the Wizard of the Seventh kept declaring in a smug voice that no one ever died of seasickness. She could care less that the soul-link had left the *Gryphon* and not if the king himself commanded it would she leave what she *knew* was her deathbed to give the information to the captain.

Ten

The sunrobe tangled around Aaron's legs, wrapped about him like a shroud, and he struggled desperately to be free of it. The world had no up nor down, only surging gray waters that threw him end over end, a giant's plaything with no will or direction of his own. His lungs screaming for air, he fought free of the clinging fabric and, able to use his legs at last, kicked frantically for the surface. Just as he thought he must breathe or die, that even water would be better than the burning pressure behind his ribs, his head broke through into air.

Rain and spray drove into his face, alternating sweet water and salt. He gasped and coughed but managed to ride to the crest of the next two waves. To his right he thought he saw a dark circle of water; Chandra's head perhaps or even Dar's, he had no way of knowing how close or far the prince might be, only that he was not yet ten body lengths away. Then a seething white wall crashed down upon him and again he fought the ocean for his life.

"Well, if you really want to die, young Aaron my lad, why don't you just stop fighting?" The Faharra of memory spread scrawny hands. *"No, wait, pardon me, that would be giving up and One forbid you should give up."*

Another gasp for air. Another wave hurling him deep and around and over. He could no longer tell if the constant roar came from the storm or from inside his head. The pouch at his waist—their remaining money and his tools—grew heavier and heavier, dragging him down. He clawed at the water, broke free again, and slammed into a spinning body with enough force to throw stars against the water and knock him limp.

For an instant they were tangled, arms and legs moving together in a violent dance, then the storm caught them up and swirled them apart.

"Dar. . . ." Aaron realized it almost too late, and just managed to hook a finger under a bit of leather harness. The larger man was limp, the weight of his sword pulling against the body's natural tendency to float, only the strength of the waves keeping him from sinking to the bottom. Aaron couldn't tell if the prince moved on his own or if his limbs thrashed about at the mercy of the storm. He could only hold on and struggle to keep them both on top of the waves that lifted them and threw them toward the shore. And he could only hope that the ocean hadn't already won, hope that he didn't drag a corpse by his side.

I don't care for him, he told the god of his father. *I don't care. There's no reason for him to die.*

Almost contemptuously, the ocean spit Chandra up on shore. She cried out as a rock gouged into her knee, grateful to have the air to cry out with. The waves still sucked and pulled at her legs and she knew she had to move, that the ocean could take her back as easily as it had let her go, but she didn't have the strength. Water ran from her nose as she coughed and choked. Her arms and legs felt as though the bones had dissolved and washed away.

A wave surged beneath her, lifted her and she clutched desperately at the rocky shore, not caring that sharp edges and broken shells cut into her fingers. Panic pushed her forward, scrambling on her hands and knees, head bent under the weight of sodden hair, eyes half closed against the sheets of rain that continued to lash her face.

When at last she thought she should be safe, when only the spray could reach her, she collapsed, cheek pressed into the rock.

That was when the terror struck, when she realized she could have died. Not all her wizardry could have saved her and even the bright and shining father of her childhood would have been helpless before the fury of the storm. She started to shake and couldn't stop, her teeth clattering in her head like loose pebbles in a bag. She couldn't catch her breath, her heart raced, and without her willing it her knees curled up to her chest.

One Below, I could have died. . . .

The warm lines of tears brought her back. She was a Wizard of the Nine, and wizards don't cry. She'd vowed that at ten and she clung to it now. Breathing deeply through her nose, she forced her body to calmness, clenched her jaw to still her traitorous teeth, straightened her legs, and sat up.

The world was gray from her feet to the horizon; rocks and water and rain and sky. She couldn't see the ship. She couldn't see much beyond the great gouts of spray that veiled the shore. She'd never felt so alone.

And then something heaved itself up out of the water.

The scream broke through before Chandra realized it was Aaron. He stood, stumbled, and fell back to his knees. One arm stretched out behind him, he crawled for land.

Afterward, Chandra couldn't remember how she'd gotten to Aaron's side, how she'd dared go back into the waves she'd so narrowly escaped. She could only remember grabbing Darvish's other arm and the two of them pulling his dead weight up onto a gravel beach. Together, they heaved him over on his stomach and Aaron began to push the water from his lungs, his lips moving in what Chandra assumed was a prayer.

An eternity later, Darvish gasped, gagged, and vomited bile.

They waited out the rest of the storm under the dubious shelter of a rock overhang. Darvish staggered to it mostly under his own power and then lapsed into semiconsciousness, moaning softly from time to time. They found out why when Chandra lifted the prince's head into her lap—he'd begun to thrash and she didn't want him spilling what little brains he might have left out on the rock—and her palms came away red with blood.

The cut wasn't large, but it crowned a nasty bit of swelling that covered almost the entire back of Darvish's head.

The storm ended about midafternoon, almost as suddenly as it had started. One moment they were pinned in their shelter by sheets of rain and driving wind, the next a broad beam of sunlight bathed the shore in golden warmth and behind the scattering clouds the sky was brightly blue.

Aaron pulled himself to his feet and staggered out onto the rapidly drying stones. His wet clothes clung to him and he shivered. "We can't stay here," he said wearily.

Chandra crawled out from under the overhang and sat back on her heels. The sky still glowered an ugly purplish gray to the north and neither the *Gryphon* nor the two ships chasing her were in sight. "Are we stranded?" she asked, her voice sounding thin and tired.

"They won't be back for us."

"Aaron, what should we do?"

She sounded young and scared. Aaron shuddered. Ruth had sounded much the same.

"Aaron, what should we do?"

That had started it all. He heard her scream. He heard the whip come down.

"Aaron?" Chandra touched him lightly on the arm and he jerked away and almost fell, his expression equally twisted with guilt and pain. She didn't understand. He was the strong one. "Are you all right?"

He managed a breath and slammed the wall back into place, ignoring the cracks and weakened areas because he had to. Later, he could strengthen them. Later. Now, Dar and Chandra needed him and that need was weakening the walls and how had it happened? He hadn't let anyone need him for so long. . . .

"Aaron?"

"We can't stay here," he said again, what remained of the walls firmly in place.

Somehow, working together, they moved Darvish back away from the sea into a small sheltered hollow crowned on two sides with spindly wind-warped trees. His head had stopped bleeding, but he was never more than half conscious and when they got him lying down again, he lost his hold on that.

"We'll need water," Aaron panted, blinking sweat from his eyes. He skinned off his wet shirt and spread it in the sun to dry. "And a fire, and food." After a moment's hesitation, he unbuckled the pouch and laid it by the shirt.

Chandra waved a hand back past the trees. "I can make a fire once the wood dries and call water, too." She sighed, and added, "If there's any so close to the sea to call." Even out of sight, the crash of the surf was a steady background noise. "I don't know what to do about food." Her eyes dropped to Darvish. "Or him."

"I'll take care of the food," Aaron said shortly. "The gods will have to take care of him." Then he climbed out of the hollow and back toward the shore, the scars on his chest standing out in angry red circles.

It hurts him to care, Chandra realized, stripping off her

own wet clothes and spreading them out to dry. *I don't know why, but it hurts him to care.*

She looked down at Darvish and saw he was shivering. Squatting by his side, she began working at the straps and buckles of his harness, slipping the sword belt out from under him and laying the whole thing to one side. It surprised her a little how heavy it was; had the sea been any less violent she had no doubt it would have taken him straight to the bottom. His harness clear, she pulled off his sodden half boots and worked him carefully out of his shirt. Without even thinking of what she was doing she picked the knots out of his trouser laces, hooked her fingers in the waistband, and tugged the wet cotton down over his hips.

Oh, she thought a moment later. *So that's what it looks like. How . . . bizarre.*

When Aaron returned, he carried a dozen or so oysters and a handful of oval rocks from the beach wrapped up in the wet bundle of his sunrobe. He'd found the robe floating just off shore like a great undulating mat of cream colored seaweed and waded out to retrieve it. It was just at the edge of the soul-link. As he'd bent forward to scoop it up, the pressure had begun to build behind his eyes and he'd hurriedly retreated, dragging the robe through the water until he reached safety.

He stood at the edge of the hollow and looked down. Tented in the silken strands of her drying hair, the ends just brushing the ground all around her, Chandra sat cross-legged, staring into a hollow she'd scooped in the stony soil. Aaron could see the tension in her hands, tendons ridged and spread fingers straining, and could just barely hear— no, feel—a low murmur of sound repeated over and over. Wizardry. He shot a glance at the sky, but it remained clear. Then he realized that her hair was all she wore and he jerked his gaze away.

To Darvish. Who wore less, his hair having been cropped short back at the palace.

Aaron's knees trembled and he sat, quickly, before he fell. He'd seen the prince a hundred times since the night he'd failed to get the emerald, but that didn't seem to matter now. He couldn't go down there. His mouth grew dry and sweat prickled up and down his sides. He could feel the heat of the sun on his shoulders like warm hands and could see it touching all down the length of Darvish's body. He swallowed hard and closed his eyes.

A pair of men, bound to the same stake, writhed in the rising fire. Both had been warriors, one had a wife and six children, but they'd been caught together by the priests and condemned to the pyre. Aaron's father had made him watch until the blackened ruins had resembled nothing human. He'd been seven.

He opened his eyes again.

Suddenly, Chandra sagged forward. The bottom of the bowl-shaped depression before her darkened as water welled up from its center. The water level rose, lapped at the symbols scratched around the edge, and stopped. She smiled down on it proudly, despite the pounding behind her eyes that threatened to bounce them from her head. The water had been deep and she'd had to focus a painful amount of power to bring it up.

When she'd caught her breath, she leaned forward and scooped up a handful. It was so cold it made her teeth ache. This was what her father wanted to take from her; he wanted to force her into a marriage that would weaken her until she no longer had the strength necessary to tap the kind of power magic of this complexity needed. Perhaps—the thought pushed her heart up into her throat—perhaps with no strength of his own, he resented hers. No. She shook the water off her hand and wished she could as easily shake off the thought. Lower lip between her teeth, she caught up her nearly dry hair and began to braid it.

A twist of her head to catch a loose strand and she spotted Aaron up on the ridge. He was staring down at Darvish, hunger and horror chasing each other across his face. Chandra frowned and her fingers stopped moving as she tried to understand. As though he'd become aware of her gaze, Aaron turned, emotions shoved hastily away, and looked right at her.

The color came up on his pale skin like a sunrise, red and hot.

It took Chandra a moment to realize why he blushed.

"Oh," she said and hoped her darker skin hid the answering flush as she reached for her dry clothes. Aba's warnings about "nasty boys" sounded in her ears and she hushed it sternly. She knew she was in no danger from

Aaron. And Darvish, well, she'd be in no danger from Darvish either even if he were conscious. It was just that with Aaron looking at her in such a way, she wasn't . . . comfortable. And she'd always been comfortable in her skin before.

She tied her trousers, tucked the shirt in, and checked on Aaron. He didn't look ready to move. Picking up Darvish's clothes, she took a step toward the prince.

This is stupid, she decided suddenly. "Hey!" she called. "I'm going to need help getting him dressed, he's too heavy to wrestle with alone."

Aaron swallowed. *This is stupid,* he decided. *This is weak.* His head came up and his jaw set. *Nothing controls me like this, nothing.*

"The old pain still rules your life."

"SHUT UP, Faharra!"

He scooped up the sunrobe and, every muscle in his body tight, walked down into the hollow.

"Darvish? Can you drink this?"

Darvish peered suspiciously into Chandra's scrying bowl. It had been tucked into the deep pocket of the wizard's trousers and was now the only container they had. "What is it?" he croaked.

"Just water."

"I need wine."

"You need water." She balanced his head against her chest and put the bowl to his lips. "Drink."

"I need wine."

"Well, it's the middle of the night and we're in the middle of nowhere, thanks to you, so where am I supposed to get wine?"

"I don't know." His head pounded so he couldn't think. "You're a wizard. Make some."

"It doesn't work that way." She let his head fall back on the folded sunrobe, not really caring if it was thick enough to cushion the wound. This was all his fault and the first thing he did was whimper about wine. Some prince.

"Aaron?" Darvish tried to look into the flickering light by the fire, but the small movement became a violent jerk, his head whipping about out of control. "Aaron?" Aaron would understand.

"I'm here."

"Aaron, I need a drink." *That's not my voice,* Darvish protested silently. *I don't sound like that.* But those were his words, so it had to be his voice.

"Drink water." Worry sharpened his tone more than he'd intended. Aaron had hoped the prince would sleep through until morning even though he knew the craving would be stronger then. A full night's sleep would have given Darvish additional energy to fight it with. He supposed he should be grateful that Darvish had woken up at all, given the crack he'd taken on the back of the head.

"It isn't fair," Darvish moaned into the sunrobe. He hurt all over and he needed a drink. A drink would make him feel better. "It isn't fair," he moaned again.

Chandra made a disgusted noise and joined Aaron by the fire. "It isn't the bump that's making him like this, is it?"

"No." Aaron threw another branch onto the fire. They didn't need it for warmth, the night was sultry, almost as warm as it would have been in Ischia over the heart of the volcano. The fire was a comfort, and a dubious one at that.

"It's the wine, isn't it?"

"Yes."

"When we get going in the morning . . ."

"Going?"

"To rescue The Stone."

"Oh, right." Aaron hadn't thought of The Stone in some time. He listened. Darvish's breathing had lengthened into sleep again. "We won't be going anywhere in the morning."

"Because of the bump on his head?"

"No. Because of the wine."

"Here, Wizard? This is where they went over?"

The Wizard of the Fourth peered at the map. It all looked like lines on parchment to her, but the king had listened intently to the Wizard of the Seventh's explanation of the storm, had questioned the captain of the *Sea Hawk* at length and seemed to know what he was talking about. "Yes, Gracious Majesty," she agreed, "that is where I felt the soul-link leave the boat."

"Ship," snarled the *Sea Hawk*'s captain in the background.

She ignored him.

"Then why, by the Nine and One, didn't you tell the captain at the time?" King Harith slammed his fist down on the map, rocking the table and making the candle flames dance.

"The captain was endeavoring to save his boat and his crew, Gracious Majesty." She drew herself up to her not considerable height. "I did not think it opportune at the time."

"I don't pay you to think! I pay you for results!"

"I am a Wizard of the Fourth," she reminded him. "I belong in His chamber, Gracious Majesty, not bobbing about the ocean in a boat."

"Then go back to your bloody chamber!"

With a slightly less than gracious bow, she swept by him and out of the room.

"Wizards," he muttered to himself. "Use them when you have to and ignore them the rest of the time. Now then," a blunt finger tapped the parchment, "if they went over here," he frowned intently, "and if they survived, they'll make for the south trade road and they'll have to go through this area," he laid his hand down flat, "here."

"No. I don't want it." Darvish tried to push the bowl away, but his hand shook so badly he couldn't even make contact.

"Drink it anyway," Aaron told him. They'd been getting as much water into him as they could; he didn't know if it was helping.

Darvish drank; he didn't have the strength to avoid it, but a good portion dribbled out the sides of his mouth. His stomach clenched around it and he hoped he wasn't going to be sick again, it hurt too much. He felt terrible. He couldn't stop shaking. He was so cold.

They used his shirt for a pillow so the sunrobe could be spread out over him. Even the slight weight of the thin cotton seemed to mute the shaking. Aaron stayed in the shade as much as he could.

Aaron threw himself over the thrashing prince, but his weight was too little to do much good and Darvish's flailing arms and legs were printing new bruises up and down the length of his body. They had no way to restrain him and he had to be restrained before he broke something.

Suddenly, Chandra dropped to her knees beside them, narrowly avoided a random blow, and tossed the contents of her scrying bowl in Darvish's contorted face. When it seemed to have no effect, she slapped him as hard as she could, and screamed, "Sleep!"

Darvish bucked one final time, his back arched painfully high, then slowly he relaxed.

"It won't last long," she explained to Aaron as they caught their breath. "Four hours at most. He's not enough in his right mind for it to hold."

Aaron carefully straightened Darvish's right arm. "Then hopefully four hours will be long enough."

"I'm not eating that. It's a rat."

Aaron didn't look up from messily disemboweling the small animal with Darvish's sword. "It's a ground squirrel."

"It looks like a rat," Chandra insisted.

Aaron shrugged. "There's always more raw oysters and steamed seaweed."

"Rat. Hummph. You're lucky you're sleeping through this," she muttered in Darvish's direction.

"You can't keep me prisoner here! I want to get up!"

"So get up." Aaron moved back and watched as Darvish actually made it to his feet, where he stood and swayed like a tree in a gale.

"You see!" he panted. "There's nothing wrong with me!"

His eyes were red, even through the strengthened illusion. Huge circles beneath them were darkly purple.

"You're hiding it, aren't you?" He took two swift steps to Aaron and hauled the smaller man up by his shirt front. Aaron breathed shallowly through his mouth. Darvish had been sweating heavily and he stank. "Where is it? Where are you hiding the wine?"

"There isn't any wine."

"There's always wine!"

"Not this time," Aaron said coldly. He felt Darvish's arm tremble and he kept his balance easily as the prince thrust him away.

Darvish squeezed his eyes shut tight and wrapped his arms around his gut as sudden cramps twisted his insides into knots. When they were over, he felt Aaron's gaze and opened his eyes.

"I'm sorry," he panted. "Did I hurt you?"

"No."

"You shouldn't be out of bed. Healer'll skin me if those blisters break."

Another spasm hit and he whimpered with the pain.

"Lie back down, Dar."

Yes, that was what he needed. He needed to lie down. Lying down made it a little better. He fell to his knees and crawled back into the depression his body had made in the ground, scrabbling the sunrobe around his shoulders.

Hot tears rolled down his cheeks. "I am sorry," he said again.

Aaron nodded, once. "I know."

"Was he drunk all the time?" Chandra asked, poking the fire and watching the sparks rise into the night.

"No. Once or twice a week. I heard it used to be worse."

"Before you came?"

Aaron lifted a shoulder and dropped it again. "Maybe. He drank all the time though. From the moment he woke until he went to sleep. He drank in the bath. He drank on the way to the training yards. He drank on the way back."

"And it made you angry." In all the days since she'd met him, Aaron had never made a speech that long.

Angry. Aaron hadn't been angry, not really angry, in five years. Anger. It certainly filled the void. "Not then," he said quietly, looking across the fire to where Darvish slept fitfully, "but now."

Chandra sighed and tossed her braid back behind her shoulder. "Don't you just feel like going off and finding The Stone yourself? Just leaving him?"

"No. Not this time."

"Three times pays for all."

"You never said that, Faharra."

The memory snorted. *"I'm saying it now."*

"But, Father . . ."

"No, Shahin. I have said my final word on this. You may leave with your wife if you choose to do so. I am remaining in Ischia."

Only by a great effort of will did Shahin manage to hold

his tongue and when they had bowed from the king's chamber he turned on the lord chancellor.

"You were no help at all," he growled.

The lord chancellor looked confused. "My prince?"

"No one will think you a coward if you leave the city, Most Exalted." He mimicked the older man's voice. "Of course no one will think him a coward, no one knows anything about what's going on. But you *must* have known the effect that would have on him."

"I'm—I'm sorry, my prince." The lord chancellor rubbed at his temples and took a deep breath. "I wasn't thinking. I'd just come from the viewing platforms. . . ."

"And. . . ."

"The level has risen another body length."

"Can the wizards hold it?"

"For now, my prince, but. . . ." He spread plump hands wide.

"But we haven't much time."

The lord chancellor bowed his head in agreement.

"Make them shut up!" Darvish flung himself forward, his eyes wide and panicked. "Make those One abandoned peacocks shut up!"

"I will." Aaron laid his hand on Darvish's shoulder. The skin felt like it was on fire. "Lie down."

"You make them shut up!"

"I will. Lie down."

Chewing his lip, Darvish slumped back and raised his hands up before his face. "They're rotting away," he howled. "I touched The Stone and they're rotting away! I didn't mean it, Father! Make it stop!"

"Chandra, sleep him again."

The young wizard pulled at the end of her braid. "Again? It's dangerous."

Aaron watched a pulse pound in Darvish's temple, the blood banging up into it with frightening force. "So is this," he said. "Sleep him."

Frowning, Chandra pushed the prince back into oblivion, watching the tension leave Aaron's shoulders as it left Darvish's, hearing both hearts slow to a less punishing beat.

"He's draining your strength through the soul-link to help survive this, you know."

"I know."

"I think I could block him. . . ." She let the offer trail into silence, reading her answer in the silver-stone of Aaron's eyes. *Fine,* she thought. *But if you both die and leave me here alone, I'll never forgive either of you.*

"What is it? I don't want it!"

"It's an egg. Eat it."

"I don't want it. The sun's too hot."

"Eat it anyway."

"It's raw!" Darvish protested. "How can you force me to eat a raw egg!"

"So drink it." Aaron tipped the bowl between Darvish's lips.

Darvish choked, swallowed, and seconds later brought it back up again.

For the first time in four days, Chandra felt some sympathy for him. She'd have done much the same thing. Raw gull eggs were beyond what anyone should be expected to stomach.

He drank as much water as they could get to him and just before sunset, he managed to keep an egg down. A little while later he managed another.

"Darvish?" Chandra raised her head and peered sleepily out through the veil of her hair. Darvish, hollow cheeked and gray, squatted by the ruins of last night's fire, tearing at the charred remains of a gull. "Darvish?" She pushed her hair back and sat up. "Are you all right?"

He smiled sheepishly, swallowed, and said, "Yes, I think so." He waved the piece of meat still in his hand. "Uh, this is really good."

"Thanks, Aaron brought down two with his sling. We stuffed the body cavity with wild plums. Are you sure you're all right?"

Darvish flushed and lowered his eyes. "Yeah. I'm sure."

"Does Aaron know."

"No, he was gone when I woke up."

"He won't be far."

"No." Darvish touched the edge of the soul-link. "I guess not." He wanted to apologize, or explain, or say thank you, or something. All the things he'd done before—the drinking, the whoring—seemed to culminate in what had happened here and all the shame he'd ever felt—all the shame he'd ever denied while searching for a life that his father would notice—made its presence felt. This morning, with only vague memories of the last few days, he felt more ashamed then he would have believed was possible. It tied his tongue in knots.

Chandra watched him, her head to one side, with a speculative, almost neutral, expression. This man's weakness had been responsible for her near drowning and had kept him flat on his back and raving for three days. Because of him, she'd been battered, cast adrift, and forced to fend for herself. She'd been furious with him, disgusted that he could do such a thing to himself and, worse still, involve her, had once or twice felt sorry for him. Now she didn't have the words to describe how she felt; although hungry and tired of the whole mess formed the basis.

Darvish wondered why Chandra remained silent. He writhed internally at what he imagined must be her thoughts. *If only she'd scream at me, it wouldn't be so bad.* The silence grew and he struggled to carry it. Finally, because he could think of nothing else to do, he devoured the gull meat he still held. Although his stomach gave out mixed signals, he was ravenously hungry.

After he finished and drank three handfuls of water from the spring, he stood and stretched. He felt as weak as a kitten, a strong breeze could toss him on his butt, and his head throbbed a quiet background to every movement. A quick touch discovered the bump and healing gash and for a moment he allowed himself to believe that the wound and not the wine had been responsible for the humiliating bits and pieces he could remember. He didn't allow the delusion to last long; for all his other faults Darvish seldom bothered to lie to himself about himself. He was an irresponsible drunken buffoon. He'd heard his father and his father's lord chancellor say it often enough.

"So."

Aaron's voice added a new edge to the shame and drove it into Darvish's heart. *I was the prince, the rescuer, the provider; if only in my mind not in his. What am I now?* Would the nothingness Aaron had shown in the palace be back? The "I care too little for you to even feel disgust." Or would the disgust be there at last, wiping out even the prickly relationship that had begun to grow? Not knowing was the worst. Darvish turned around.

In his bright yellow trousers, cream shirt, and copper hair, Aaron was a blaze of light on the hillside. Darvish squinted and remembered the stories his old nurse had told him of the Fire Lords who came to burn up bad little boys. They were easy to believe in just now.

Aaron's expression was unreadable but it wasn't nothingness at least. "Are you all right?" he asked.

Darvish thought of several clever comments. "Yes," he said quietly.

As Aaron came closer, Darvish saw that the younger man's eyes were circled with purple shadow and that the flesh he had gained during his long convalescence had been pared back to bone. His face and hands were red with sunburn. Darvish flushed and looked down at the sunrobe that would have at least prevented the latter.

"Would it help if I said I was sorry?"

Aaron's brows rose and he looked openly skeptical. "Would you mean it?"

"Yes."

"Then it would help if you proved it." Aaron pushed past him, scooped up the soiled sunrobe, shook it out and put it on. It had a ragged edge along the hem where Aaron had torn off fabric to make his sling. He nodded at Chandra, who tied off her braid and picked up her scrying bowl, tucking the small silver vessel back deep in her trouser pocket.

They've come to an understanding, Darvish realized. Their silent companionship shut him out and that hurt, but he knew it was his own fault. The knife twisted.

"Well?" Aaron looked pointedly at Darvish's shirt and sword belt.

Darvish scrambled to dress, ignoring as best he could both the weakness and the pain in his head, suddenly reminded of why they'd left Cisali and how much time had passed. As he fought with water stiffened leather, he had a vision of Ischia drowning in molten rock while he lay delirious and sick by his own hand. He could feel their eyes on him and he waited for the accusations that had to come.

"Take a good long drink before we go," Aaron instructed, fitting action to the words. "We may not have water again until we stop and Chandra can call another spring." He stood and wiped his mouth.

Chandra knelt and drank, willing to follow Aaron's lead, just as anxious to get this over with.

Darvish dropped clumsily down, sucked up as much water as he could hold, and rose awkwardly again. *Would you please scream at me,* he wanted to plead. Righteous anger would help to lance the shame.

"If you can't keep up, say so." Aaron stood and looked at the prince for a moment, throwing all his strength into the walls that kept him from alternately shrieking and sobbing in both anger and relief. Then he turned and started up the slope, needing to get away from this place that would always be haunted with images of Darvish twisting in pain.

Chandra followed him, wondering if Aaron knew why he was running away or what he was running away from. *More of those questions I'm not supposed to ask.*

And Darvish followed her.

Would it help if I said I was sorry?

It would help if you proved it.

It looked like that was all the relief, the release, he was going to get, and for the first time in his adult life it became important to prove himself to someone besides his father.

He had to rest often and although he was desperately thirsty most of the time, he never once mentioned that he needed a drink.

Eleven

"I don't think those navy ships were after the *Gryphon*. I think they were after us."

"Us?" Carefully pushing her hair away from her face with the back of her hand, keeping greasy fingers well out of it, Chandra looked up from her haunch of ground squirrel.

"Not you," Aaron corrected. "Dar and I. The man who stole The Stone couldn't have gotten through the palace carrying the equipment he'd need in the crater without inside help. And he certainly couldn't get back out carrying The Stone. That help sent a message to Tivolic, told them what ship we'd be on." He tossed Darvish a baked root that Chandra swore was nonpoisonous.

"How?" Darvish asked, juggling the root. "We didn't know what ship we'd be on."

"Easy enough to have us followed."

"No." He shook his head. "Then they'd have known about Chandra."

"So? To a palace spy, what's unusual about Prince Darvish joining an attractive young lady? Nothing. They wouldn't recognize her as your betrothed. I saw her miniature and *I* wouldn't know her from that. Even now."

"He made me look simpering," Chandra broke in, seething. "I hated that picture. Stupid artist."

"They won't know she's a wizard, either," Darvish said thoughtfully. "And if they ever caught up with the *Gryphon* and found we went overboard they'll think we're dead. That puts us two up."

"But they'll know you're traveling with a wizard now, the sailors on the *Gryphon* will tell them."

"I doubt it. The *Gryphon* will tell that lot exactly as much as they have to, no more, and even if they do mention you, with the storm you called up they'll think you're a Wizard of the Seventh.''

"But the distance viewer isn't a Seventh, it's more First or Ninth.''

"They won't mention the distance viewer to the navy,'' Aaron said with his twisted grin.

"Did you know they were smugglers when you bought us passage?'' Chandra asked him, suddenly suspicious.

Aaron shrugged. "I suspected. Smugglers don't ask questions. We didn't need questions.''

Chandra took a bite of squirrel and looked almost cheerful. She'd been useful lately in a way she'd never been before. She liked it. A lot. "Look at the bright side. We're alive and we've got resources they don't suspect. Even if there is a traitor back in Ischia, we're doing all right.''

"We're also half starved, barely equipped, and walking to the capital,'' Aaron reminded her.

And that's all my fault, Darvish added silently, gouging at the ground with a stick. He had to add it. The others wouldn't. He'd tried to apologize for that specifically, for being so stupid as to walk out on deck during the storm; Aaron had said nothing, Chandra had rolled her eyes and said, "Don't do it again, okay?'' One Below, he was going to do his best, but he still wished they'd scream at him.

"Could be worse.'' Chandra threw the bone into the fire.

"If you say it could be raining, I'm going to throttle you with your own hair,'' Aaron said mildly. It was safer to talk than to think. His thoughts kept chipping holes in the wall.

Darvish couldn't join in the banter. He felt like he had to prove he belonged again. So he turned the subject back to Ischia. "Who do you think the traitor is?'' Aaron's demon wings took off and Darvish nodded. "Yasimina,'' he said with a heavy sigh.

"Most likely,'' Aaron agreed, although he'd respected what he'd seen of Shahin enough to hope he was wrong.

"Who's Yasimina?'' Chandra asked, wishing for the first time she'd paid more attention to talk of King Jaffar's court.

"My eldest brother's wife,'' Darvish told her. "It was a treaty marriage a little over a year ago. She's the second youngest sister of the King of Ytaili.'' He paused and smiled a bit sadly. "Shahin loves her. She likes peacocks.''

* * *

The soft shush, shush, of leaves stroked together by the afternoon breeze surrounded them. Up ahead, a dead branch tapped and creaked, hanging at a crazy angle from the tree. Boots and sandals crunched through last year's growth making the three of them sound like an army on the march. Even Aaron was unable to move with his customary quiet.

The dry, dusty smell of dead leaves that rose up with each step and then lodged in the back of the nose became mixed with the more potent scent of cedars off to the right. Insects danced in each slanting greenish-gold ray of sunlight, humming their own accompaniment.

Sweat dribbled down Darvish's back and he loosened his sword in its sheath. Something was wrong. Something was missing. He lengthened his stride, moving quickly past the other two and waving Chandra's question quiet. To his surprise, she cut it off. He'd expected an argument, having abdicated any right to command when he fell from the *Gryphon.*

Chandra was a little surprised herself, her mouth having obeyed before her mind had a chance to ask why.

Darvish could smell something now, something that didn't belong. Char. Men. And animals. Very close. The trees stopped suddenly, a cluster of fresh cut stumps marking the edge of the clearing. Darvish dropped behind cover and peered out.

Directly in front of him, he could see where the wood had been dragged into the camp, could see that the grass had been cropped short, could see—and smell—the pungent signature of draft animals, could see that the camp was deserted. Carefully, his hand by his sword, he moved out into the open.

The clearing was larger than he'd initially thought, but the camp seemed to have filled all available space. Evidence remained of at least five wagons, each with an indeterminate number of people. A huge fire pit had been dug in roughly the center of the clearing and Darvish made his way across the trampled ground toward it.

"Whoever they were," he called as Aaron and Chandra came out of the trees, "they were here until at least this morning. They drowned their fire, but there's a coal still hot."

"Shoi," Aaron said, pushing the hood of his sunrobe back. His face was peeling, the proud hook of his nose especially badly. "Wanderers."

"I've never heard of them." Chandra bent and picked up a scrap of bright green cloth ground into the bottom of a wheel rut.

"Neither have I." Darvish began to move toward the far side of the clearing where he could see a well defined track heading off to the northeast.

Aaron snorted. "You live on islands. Wagons make lousy boats."

"They *live* in wagons?"Chandra asked.

"Yes."

"Does Shoi mean anything?" She threw the bit of cloth back on the ground.

"It means People. Others, non-Shoi, call them Wanderers."

"What do they do?"

Aaron turned to look at her and both tufted ginger brows rose. "They wander. Wha. . . ?"

A brilliant blue bird swooped across the clearing screaming insults.

"No birds. . . ." No birds. No birdsong. For the last little while, things had been entirely too quiet. Darvish drew his sword clear seconds before the first man charged into the clearing, blade whistling down in what he obviously hoped would be the killing stroke.

Silently, teeth clenched, Darvish attacked. There were two, three, no, five of them and only one of him. For any chance at all, he had to keep them off balance.

Steel sang against steel and as the swords hissed apart, Darvish kicked the man in the knee as hard as he could. Inhaling, he ducked a wild swing. Exhaling, he cut through to guts with a backhanded slash. This was his one chance to redeem himself; he put everything he had into the fight. A left-handed swordsman had the advantage and he stretched it to the limit and beyond.

A point dragged down the length of his right arm, deep enough to hurt but no deeper.

One Below, I want my shield! He dropped, rolled, and from the ground, using both hands, cut a man off at the knees. Bouncing up inside another's guard, he slammed his weighted pommel into a temple and shoved the body away. When he turned, the man first into the clearing waited, favoring one leg. A parry, a dodge, Darvish forced him around to his bad side, swung and hacked through neck, collar-bone, and into ribs.

He yanked his blade free, spun about, and there was no one left to fight.

Three men were dead, two were down and dying. As Darvish watched, Aaron gave the grace blow to one, using the man's own dagger, and moved toward the other. Two of the three dead, Darvish had killed, the third had been flung onto his back, his face a bloody ruin. A stone from Aaron's sling, Darvish guessed.

He ripped free the torn shirtsleeve and used it to wipe most of the gore from his sword before sliding the smeared blade back into the scabbard.

Then he started to shake. His legs threatened to buckle and he sucked in great lungfuls of air.

I need a drink. Oh, One Below and Nine Above, I need a drink.

At nineteen, he'd killed three men in battle while in nominal command of a squad sent to clean out a pirates' nest on Cisali's south shore. In not much more than a dozen heartbeats, he'd just doubled that.

Chandra kept her mouth covered with both hands and tried very hard not to be sick. There was so much blood, black where it had soaked into the ground and red, bright red, dark red, every kind of red, where it clung to the bodies. And those men were so very dead. Not quietly dead, like her mother, welcoming the release from pain, but brutally dead and hating every second of it.

She didn't realize the first whimper had escaped until she heard it. She couldn't stop the second nor the third. She wanted to wail or cry or keen or something.

Then warm arms enfolded her and a large hand stroked her back.

"Look away," Darvish murmured softly into her hair. "Look away, gain some distance. The less immediate it is, the less horrible it is. I know."

"So much blood," Chandra said dully, neither fighting against his arms nor relaxing into them. They were a comfort that she couldn't quite seem to find how to accept.

Slowly, Darvish turned her, pulling her gaze away from the bodies. When she faced him rather than the battlefield, she gave a strange little sigh and collapsed against his chest, dry eyed and shuddering.

''I never saw anyone die like that before,'' she said.

Neither have I. Darvish felt the memory of each blow in his hands, the meaty resistance of flesh, each jar as steel hit bone.

Aaron moved carefully among the bodies, fighting against the memories that threatened to overwhelm him; memories of a life he'd left behind, released as he'd released the stone from the sling. He'd killed his first man at eleven in a raid on a neighboring keep. One of the defenders had stumbled and fallen and Aaron had slammed a hand ax into his throat. After the battle, his father had lifted the head on a spear point and proudly proclaimed the Clan Heir a man. There had been a lot of blood on his father's hands, and a good bit on him as well.

He'd killed this morning for the first time since he'd left his father's keep. He'd killed without thinking, protecting Darvish's back.

''A fine shot, my son!''

''I am not your son any longer.''

''I couldn't have done it better myself.''

''Shut up, Father!''

But denial wouldn't take back the stone nor the sudden falling into violence that was his father's way. He had allowed himself to relax and his past had tried to reclaim him. He would have to be stronger until the past could be destroyed.

For now, however, denial was all he had.

''They're dressed like outlaws,'' He flopped one over on its back with a well placed foot. ''Ragged, dirty. Too well fed, though.'' He squatted and rubbed the base of a sword blade clean, frowned, reached for another, and drummed his fingers against the steel. ''They all carry swords and daggers marked with the insignia of the King's Guard.''

''What?'' Darvish's head snapped up.

''They were sent by the King of Ytaili.''

''Now that puts a different shine on things,'' exclaimed a voice from the clearing's edge. ''Any enemy of imperial guards is a friend of ours.''

The speaker was a short, heavyset man, dressed all in greens and browns. Beside him stood a young woman, a little taller, dressed much the same. They both carried long knives and the man held a thick staff bound at both ends with brass. Their skin was darker than Aaron's but lighter than both Darvish's and Chandra's.

Aaron stood slowly, hands out from his sides. "They have an archer in the trees," he said over his shoulder. "The Shoi never travel in less than threes."

Chandra pulled out of Darvish's arms. She was a Wizard of the Nine and wasn't going to have these Shoi think she needed comforting. Darvish, like Aaron, stood with his hands out from his sides. An indifferent archer at best, even *he* could hit them shooting from cover and at that range.

While the woman scowled, her visible companion leaned forward on his staff and studied Aaron. "You're a long way from your rocks and winds and cold, Kebric," he said at last.

"I am," Aaron admitted.

"Now I've never been that far north myself," his accent lengthened the words, emphasizing their musical lilt, in direct contrast to Aaron's which clipped them off, "but I have heard that a clansman who leaves his keep, let alone one who leaves his bleak and inhospitable land is a rare bird indeed."

"I left." Aaron's hands spread wider and his tone left no room for further discussion.

"So you did," agreed the older Shoi. "So you did." He nodded genially at Darvish. "Fine sword work, young man. Can't remember when I've seen better."

Darvish flushed. His sword masters had always said he was good. He'd never quite known whether he should believe them, but this man had no reason to lie.

"The proof is in the pudding as they say," he continued. "Here you stand, barely scratched—although you should have that arm seen to. I wouldn't trust any kind of imperial lackey to keep his sword clean."

The shallow cut down the length of Darvish's right arm, now brought suddenly to mind, began to throb and burn. He'd forgotten it was there.

"And there they lie, dead." He spit in the general direction of the bodies, his head darting forward then back, the movement precise, the rest of him remaining completely still.

They hadn't moved since they'd entered the clearing, Darvish realized, not even making gestures when speaking.

Even Aaron moved more, but where Aaron looked controlled, the Shoi merely looked . . . still.

"And Most Wise." A gracious nod at Chandra. "What is a gently-bred lady wizard doing out in the woods with these ruffians?"

Chandra's brows drew down. "Don't patronize me," she snapped.

Both Shoi smiled broadly and the young woman spoke for the first time. "My uncle begs your pardon," she said, her accent, although similar, much less florid.

Not quite mollified, Chandra nodded a prickly acceptance.

"You must be very powerful," she continued, her tone not quite neutral, not quite friendly. "Your power shines like a beacon."

"I *am* very powerful." Still frowning, she asked, suspiciously, "What do you mean shines like a beacon?"

"The Shoi," Aaron explained without taking his eyes off the two at the tree line, "are power sensitive. Some say they're a race of wizards."

The older man sighed. "And some say the Kebric are a brutally violent, not overly intelligent, race of inbred maniacs. But you don't hear us spreading *that* around."

Although Aaron's lips thinned to a white-edged line, he kept silent. His father would have roared in anger and charged to the attack at the insult, at the string of insults. Aaron was not his father. He had remade himself in his own image. He held tight to that image now.

"Uncle. . . ."

"Yes, you're completely right, Fiona, that was completely, well—almost completely uncalled for. Now, if you would be so good as to retrieve Grandmother's knitting."

She nodded and moved quickly across the clearing. At the far side, by one of the wagon marks, she swung herself up into a tree and dropped back down seconds later with a handful of green wool.

"One of the children hid it," Fiona's uncle explained as she returned and handed it back to him. "Grandmother'll be glad to get it back." He smiled genially and slid the wool into his belt pouch. "And now, chance met by the trail, you may call me Edan. And this, my sister's daughter, you may call Fiona." He made no mention of the third Shoi, the archer Aaron had said remained in the trees. "You three will, of course, accompany us to our new camp. We're always eager to entertain the enemies of our enemies.''

Not even Chandra needed Aaron to tell her this was not an invitation they could refuse.

The walk to the Shoi's new camp took two days, although the Shoi could have done it in one. Any energy Darvish had managed to regain had been used in the fight and to his intense embarrassment he had to rest often or fall over.

The first time this happened, Fiona had squatted beside him, pushed up his chin with one strong finger, sniffed, and said, *"Topasent."* Then she frowned and looked up at her uncle.

Edan pursed his lips and thought a moment. "Wine-chains," he translated at last. "About as close as it comes."

She nodded and, releasing Darvish's chin, asked, "How long have you been free?"

Free? What was she . . . then suddenly Darvish understood. How long since his last drink. How long since the wine-chains had come undone. He had no idea. He remembered emptying the wineskin while the storm raged and tried to breach their tiny cabin, but he didn't know how long ago it had been. Nine Above, it seemed like an eternity.

"Six days," said Aaron softly behind him.

Fiona pulled a drinking skin off her shoulder and tossed it in Darvish's lap. He jerked back and his breath caught in his throat. "Relax, it's water. Drink as much as you can and piss away the poisons." She stood and shook her head. "Six days . . . and you fought five men and won. You must have the strength of an ox. Just fighting free of *topasent* has killed others." She drew in breath as though to continue, then shook her head, turned on her heel and strode off into the trees beside the trail. They almost seemed to open and close around her so silently did she move.

"It killed her father," Edan told them, his cheek resting against the smooth wood of his staff. "He got free twice, but the third time stopped his heart."

Chandra moved to stand by Aaron so that the two of them were a shield against Darvish's back. "Well, it isn't going to kill Dar," she declared.

Darvish, lifting the waterskin to his mouth in trembling hands, wasn't so sure.

That afternoon they reached a road of sorts that followed

the banks of a good sized stream. That night they camped by its side and the third Shoi came out of the trees. Once he'd set his short curved bow carefully down and had tossed two rabbits to Edan, it was next to impossible to tell him apart from Fiona in the uncertain light of the fire.

"Twins," their uncle said proudly, "very lucky. Fion and Fiona, a blessing to the family."

The younger man laughed, his teeth gleaming white in the shadow of his face. "That's not what you said when we were children, Uncle." He threw himself down on the grass with the grace of a giant cat. "He said we were demon spawn and kept threatening to abandon us by the side of the road."

Edan grinned as he gutted the rabbits. "Yes, but your poor misguided mother would never let me."

He reminds me a bit of Darvish, Chandra realized as she watched Fion help his sister string the rabbits over the fire. Although he shared the economy of movement that seemed a Shoi trait, he somehow made it seem flamboyant. *Darvish at his best, as he should have been without the wine.* She shook her head. Twins as a blessing? The Shoi were strange indeed; everyone knew twins shared only one soul between them and so had to be carefully watched.

While the rabbits roasted and sparks and fireflies danced short-lived duets, the three Shoi heard the story of the shipwreck and what happened after. It was almost impossible not to respond to a direct question from one of them. Chandra scanned for power but found nothing. Whether it was because there was nothing there or because she had no idea of what to look for, she didn't know.

"So the two of you and a sick man survived with nothing, no supplies, not even a waterskin for six days." Edan chewed thoughtfully on a piece of meat. "Difficult to believe."

"We had a sling and a wizard," Aaron said dryly. "What more did we need?"

Fion laughed, Fiona smiled, and Edan threw up his hands in defeat.

The next morning, Fiona picked up the bow and slipped away into the trees.

As they walked, Darvish leaned closer to Aaron and said quietly, "Did you notice, they never once asked us why we were heading for Tivolic in the first place."

Aaron nodded. "That usually means they already know."

They reached the camp just before sunset and the twilight followed them in, giving everything a softer and faintly unreal appearance. The circle of wagons seemed larger than it could possibly be and more children than those wagons could hold swarmed about their legs, shouting questions in the language of the Shoi and the common language of the area. The food smells from the communal fire reminded them of how long it had been since they'd eaten a real meal and Aaron and Chandra both had to swallow sudden mouthfuls of saliva. Darvish caught the scent of something else and clenched his fists.

"About time you got here!" An elderly woman, not quite fat, stomped down out of one of the wagons and waved a dimpled hand imperiously at Edan. "Come on, then. Grandmother wants to see you." She paused then added. "*And* them."

Fion slipped away, to Edan's muttered "Coward," and the four of them walked across to the central area. Except for the children, no one paid them much attention.

Darvish had to both duck and turn sideways to make it through the wagon door, but once inside there was a lot more room than he'd expected. It was stuffy though, and the air smelled stale as if it had been in the wagon for a very long time. A combination of the lamp's position and the lines of the wagon drew the eye instantly to an incredibly old woman wrapped in a pile of shawls and blankets. The remains of her hair were pulled back into a tight steel-gray knot emphasizing the skull-like delineation of her face. Her eyes, sunk deep into the bone on either side of a pinched nose, were barely open. Her skin, dry and crossed and recrossed with a multitude of fine lines, reminded Darvish of a lizard's. He'd never seen anyone that old before. Out of the corner of an eye, he checked Chandra and Aaron for their reactions.

Chandra merely looked intrigued. Aaron had gone completely blank.

The old woman's voice, in direct contrast to her frail appearance, was surprisingly strong. "Have you got my knitting, then?'

Edan laid the bundle of green wool on her lap. "Yes, Grandmother. Here it is."

She sighed and it sounded like more air than that wasted

body could possibly hold. "I can see where it is, Edan, you *kokta*. Get out."

"Very well, Grandmother." He didn't exactly scurry for the door, but it was close.

"Now then." She pointed a twisted finger at Aaron and paused for a moment for her breath to whistle in and out. "You. Relax. I'm not going to die on you."

Aaron started but showed no visible signs of relaxing. The Shoi—not this family but their northern cousins—had traveled every year to the great fair that marked a moon's truce between the warring clans. He *knew* that many of their seemingly magical pronouncements were based on no more than observation and a deep understanding of human nature. It didn't help.

She stared from one to the other, her gaze still sharp enough to cut despite her age, then clicked her tongue. "So," she said, after rocking a moment in thought. "The Stone of Ischia has been stolen and you three have been sent to get it back. Don't you think an army would be more practical, Your Royal Highness?"

"A race of wizards" Darvish said softly. He couldn't decide if meeting the Shoi was the best or worst thing that could have happened.

Aaron's eyes narrowed. "Common sense," he corrected harshly. "They felt power move from Ischia to Tivolic. The only relic with that kind of power in Ischia is The Stone. They heard no rumor of war and then a warrior, a thief, and a wizard show up on their way to Tivolic from Ischia. They know the King of Ischia has a blue-eyed son. Here we have a blue-eyed warrior."

"But my illusion," Chandra interrupted. "His eyes look brown."

"Illusions seldom work on the Shoi."

The smug expression on the old woman's face had turned to one of deep annoyance. She spat a question at Aaron in a language that seemed mostly made of consonants.

"No," he answered.

She scowled, openly disbelieving.

"There was a wizard involved," Chandra attempted to change the subject. Making the matriarch angry didn't strike her as a particularly good idea, not when they needed so many things.

"Of course there was." Gnarled fingers picked peevishly at the knitting still on her lap. "There always is."

"And whoever took The Stone seems to know we're coming."

"Whoever indeed." A cackle of ancient laughter threatened to turn to coughing, but with a visible effort the old woman regained control of her body. "With imperial guards rotting out there you needn't blather about whoevers. If His Most Gracious Majesty doesn't have The Stone now, he most certainly knows who does." She turned to Darvish. "Didn't one of your brothers just marry a princess of Ytaili?"

"Yes."

"Well, there you have it."

Darvish shook his head. He hadn't wanted to believe it was Yasimina. Would have rather it was anyone else.

"You don't know that," Aaron said suddenly, his voice stone.

"So you defend the little princess, do you, Kebric?" Lips pulled back off nearly perfect teeth, intensifying the skull-like resemblance. "It won't do either of you any good. The only way to defeat a traitor is to keep him or her in the dark. You will therefore be traveling with the family to Tivolic."

Darvish pushed the thought of Shahin aside or a time. "What?" he asked, a little lost.

"Are you deaf, boy? I said you're traveling with the family to Tivolic."

"Oh." It would take a braver man than he to argue with that pronouncement. "Why are you helping us?" he asked.

"Because we want to." Her tone stated there need be no better reason than that."

"Then we thank you." Ignoring the pounding behind his temples, he bowed his most gracious bow and pressed the back of her hand to his lips. It felt a bit like kissing a lizard, dry and leathery.

"Flatterer." She looked pleased. "Now get out. I'm tired."

As they reached the door, she called out, "Prince!"

Darvish turned.

"You touch one drop of wine in my camp and I'll have your fingers broken."

"What a lovely old lady," he muttered to Aaron outside.

The demon wings flew, a silent comment weighted in sarcasm.

''What did she ask you?'' Chandra wanted to know.

''She asked if any of my ancestors were Shoi.''

''You made her angry.''

Aaron shrugged. The old woman's first words had cut too close. He'd slashed at her pride. They were even.

That night when the fire blazed high, Chandra stood in the shadow of a wagon and watched as Darvish divided his attentions between Fion and a girl with close cropped curls who laughed low in her throat. She'd seen him overcome his need and recognized the strength it had taken to drink water instead of wine and she couldn't argue with his right to take other pleasures when they were offered, but. . . .

But what? She didn't know exactly, so she stood and watched and chewed on the end of her braid. And wondered.

''He's such a *haus*.'' Fiona's low voice barely carried over the sound of a Shoi and the fire.

Chandra spit out the wet end of her braid. ''A *haus*?''

''A slut.''

Darvish slipped a hand behind the girl and lifted his mouth to Fion.

''Yes. He is.''

''I meant my brother.'' Chandra could hear the smile in the other woman's voice. ''If you care about him, you could be there. They would both give way.''

''No.'' Chandra sighed. ''I don't care about him like that.''

''Oh.''

''I don't care about anyone like that. I'm a Wizard of the Nine.''

Fiona shook her head. ''Power is a cold companion in the night,'' she said and left as silently as she had arrived.

''Well, maybe it is,'' Chandra muttered, shoving her hand deep into the pocket of her trousers to wrap around the comforting shape of the scrying bowl. ''But it's a lot more interesting in the daytime.''

From the other side of the fire pit, where the flames danced strange shadows in the darkness, came the eerie wail of a reed pipe. Chandra recognized the instrument but not the tune. The shepherds who surrounded her father's country estate had never played anything so wild. A drum joined in and then another deeper pitched and then something she didn't know at all that surged through the rest, caught them up and carried them crazily along.

The music sizzled along her skin and Chandra had the ridiculous thought she must move or burn. Others had the same idea and in the light of the fire she saw the young men and women of the Shoi answer the wild call. One, two, then a surging mass of bodies circled the flames. They stamped and spun, holding her motionless watching. The music grew more frenzied and so did the dance. She knew what the call was now and with gritted teeth refused it.

I am a wizard of the Nine, she told it. *This want is not mine!*

And then a slim white shape leapt and whirled before the fire.

''Aaron?'' She took a step forward, squinting.

His hair blazed red and gold like a cap of flame as he whirled and leapt impossibly high. The fire danced in reflection on skin wet with sweat. Even the scars on his chest seemed some bizarre barbaric decoration. His eyes were closed, or almost closed, and he gave himself over totally to the music. Bare feet slammed down into the dirt, the walls tumbled, and all the passion behind the walls blazed out.

The beat came faster, harder, and he followed it.

Chandra searched for Darvish and spotted him at last moving with the two Shoi into the greater privacy behind the wagons.

Turn around, she pleaded silently. *Look to the fire!* If Darvish looked, she knew he'd understand who Aaron danced for.

But he didn't turn and he didn't look.

When the music ended, chest heaving, hands fisted at his sides, Aaron disappeared into the darkness alone.

Twelve

"Have you heard, Aisha? Have you heard?"

The sandal maker continued to placidly stitch, not even glancing up as old Cemal tottered in through the open front of her shop. Two or three times a nineday he picked up a hot rumor from his cronies and gleefully spread it about the marketplace. Aisha had long ago ceased to get excited. "Have I heard what?" she asked, eyeing her work critically.

"Well. . . ." Cemal carefully lowered his brittle bones to the rug, then took another moment to rearrange his robe over his skinny legs. These trousers that the younger people were wearing; he just couldn't see the point. "Well, Barika—you know her, the sausage maker's youngest daughter—has a friend, Habibah, who has a little brother who is a page to His Excellency the Lord Chancellor at the palace."

He paused and Aisha grunted, measuring out a length of leather strapping.

"Well, Habibah's little brother, the page at the palace, told Habibah, who told Barika, who told her father, who told me."

"Told you what, Cemal?" Aisha asked, because she knew it was expected of her, not because she wanted to know. It was possible she had enough of the tooled leather left for one more pair.

"Told me that The Stone is missing."

Her reaction was all that Cemal could have wished. She actually stopped working and looked at him, her eyes wide and her mouth open.

"Missing," he reiterated with a cackle of humorless laughter. "We're all going to die."

Aisha closed her mouth. The Stone missing? "Nonsense," she snapped.

"Not nonsense." Cemal shook his head, his few remain-

ing strands of hair flapping emphatically. "And they sent
Prince Darvish out to get it back."

"Darvish?" The sandal maker smiled. "That proves it's
nonsense, old man. No one in their right mind would send
Prince Darvish to the well for water."

"He hasn't been seen in the usual places for over a nineday," Cemal muttered peevishly.

"No mystery there, he's in seclusion in the temple.
Something about his upcoming marriage and a case of
crotch."

"But Habibah's brother. . . ."

"Is a kid. Besides," she reached over and patted his knee,
"the King, and the Heir, and even His Excellency the Lord
Chancellor are still at the palace. You think they'd still be
there if there was any danger of the Lady blowing?"

Cemal sighed. "You're right," he admitted, heaving
himself to his feet. "The Stone missing and Prince Darvish
gone after it. I must be getting old to believe that." And
shaking his head, he tottered out of the shop, an occasional
muttered, "Old," drifting back over the noise of the market.

Aisha finished attaching a buckle with tiny meticulous
stitches, then set the strap down beside the almost com-
pleted sandal. Drumming her fingers against her thighs for
a moment, she frowned. From where she sat, she couldn't
see beyond the stonework edging the building across the
way and it had suddenly become important to see farther.
Still frowning, she rose and stepped out into the street, waving an absent greeting to the basket maker in the shop next
to hers.

She couldn't see the palace, the street angled too steeply
for that, but she could see the spreading edge of smoke that
had been hanging over the city for days. It was a very little
smoke, but, born and raised in Ischia, the sandal maker
could not remember smoke like it before. There could be
no truth in old Cemal's words, but she felt a strange sense
of disquiet touch her nevertheless. She had seen an execution at the volcano, seen what the molten rock would do to
flesh if it ever broke the bonds that held it captive in the
crater.

Her brother, long moved to a village on the south shore,
had always said she would be welcome. Perhaps now would
be a good time to visit.

* * *

"My prince."

"Lord Chancellor."

"The lava has risen another body length. The wizards say it will soon be up over the cup and when that happens," the lord chancellor spread plump hands, "they may not be able to hold it further."

Shahin scowled. He knew the wizards had been using the golden cup The Stone had rested in as a focus point for their power. He hadn't realized they were so dependent on it. The cup was a good distance away from the rim of the crater and if they could hold the molten rock only that far, it drastically cut the time they had remaining. And when the captive volcano finally broke free, the wizards would be the first to die. "Will they stay? If any one of them breaks and weakens the block. . . ."

"The wizards will live or die as one, my prince." The lord chancellor's bearing was smug. "Their powers are now woven too tightly together for any single strand to break free. They may give in to terror as they wish, but they cannot withdraw their power."

"You knew that would happen?"

He bowed his head, the expression on his round face unreadable. "I have always excelled at planning ahead, my prince."

So the wizards were trapped. Shahin tapped his thumb against his lip and came to a decision. "We must begin evacuating the city. Immediately."

"My prince! And cause the very panic we have been trying to prevent?"

"Better a panic now than a thousand deaths later," Shahin snapped, rising and striding to the windows.

"You would sacrifice your people now for a later that may never come?" the lord chancellor asked quietly.

The prince turned and, just barely visible beneath his beard, a muscle jumped in his jaw. His voice had the brittle edge of a man holding onto calm by strength of will alone. "You seem to have great faith in my brother considering you have never had much use for him before."

"Your royal brother, my prince, is not meant for court life. He is not now at court."

It sounded reasonable, it was the truth after all so it should, but. . . .

"We begin evacuation. Now. The guards will do what can be done to prevent panic."

"I am sorry, my prince," and he both looked and sounded sorry, "but that is your most exalted father's command to give. Not yours."

Shahin drew in a deep breath and let it out slowly. It would do him no good, it would do Ischia no good, if he antagonized this man who held the king's trust. It was a lesson Darvish had never learned. "Then I will go to my father."

"I am sorry, my prince," the lord chancellor said again. "But he will not see you."

Out in the gardens, the peacocks screamed.

"He will not see me?" Shahin repeated.

The lord chancellor stepped back, away from the expression on the heir's face, suddenly reminded of how much like the king this eldest son was. "He feels, my prince, that until the crisis is over, given the suspicions against your lady wife. . . ."

Shahin's eyes narrowed and one fist came up. With an effort so great it left him trembling, he managed to hold his reaction to that. "You will never speak to me of my wife again." His voice cut off each word and threw it at the lord chancellor. "Now, you and I together will go and see my most exalted father."

The small room in the king's apartments did not contain a throne, but it held a high-backed chair that served. The king sat, fingers steepled, his brows drawn down so that his eyes were hidden deep within their shadows.

His own eyes blazing, Shahin touched his knee to the carpet, then hurriedly stood. "Most Exalted," he began but the king raised an imperious hand and cut him off.

"Do you realize how close to treason you come?" he asked.

Shahin jerked back, blinking as though he'd been hit. His chest felt as though a block of marble had been dropped on it from a great height. He fought against the weight for the breath to speak but only managed a single word. "Treason?"

"Or were you not told that I would not see you?"

"Yes sir, by the lord chancellor, but. . . ."

The lord chancellor came forward, knelt, then rose and moved to stand behind King Jaffar's chair.

"He speaks with my voice in this."

"But why, Father?" Shahin spread his hands, anger overcoming shock. "We must work together if Cisali is to survive."

"Do not tell me what we must do!" The king rose a little out of his chair, then settled again, his face the expressionless mask he ruled behind. "I can no longer trust you. Your wife. . . ."

"I sent Yasimina to the country a nineday ago and even were she here, I do not make her privy to state secrets."

"Did you not allow her to write to her brother, King Harith, before she left?"

Shahin felt a coldness growing in his gut. Until this moment, he had heard that tone only when the king spoke with Darvish. It was all king and no father and in all ways denied any blood tie. "She wrote only to tell him she was going to the country. I read the letter, Most Exalted, there was nothing treasonous in it! He is her brother. She was homesick."

"To write to such a man at such a time is treason; the contents of the letter do not matter. To allow her to write the letter is treason. To come here to me when I have ordered that you will not is treason. Thrice you stand accused."

When Shahin had given in to his pleading bride, he had known trouble would come of it. But this, this he had not, could not have, foreseen.

Behind the throne, the lord chancellor bowed his head, his expression unreadable.

"I will be merciful. This time. You will remain in the palace and you will continue to perform those duties that do not include the throne. You will not speak with me nor in any way contact me until this crisis is over and the traitor has been found."

Shahin dropped again to his knee, but his chin came up as though he answered a challenge. "Am I suspected of being the traitor, Most Exalted?"

The two men locked eyes and after a long moment, King Jaffar looked away. "No," he said. "But you have been tainted by your outland bride. I can no longer trust you."

"Ytaili is hardly outland, Most Exalted!" Shahin protested, even though he knew it would have been wiser to keep silent.

"Ytaili tries to destroy us!" the king roared, rising to his feet. "What I do, I do for the good of the realm!"

Knowing he must choose his next words with care, lest his father reject them out of hand, Shahin laid his forehead on his upturned knee, the position of the penitent. "Then for the good of the realm I ask a boon before I am denied your presence."

Still breathing heavily, the king lowered himself back into the chair. "Ask."

"For the good of the realm, Most Exalted, order the evacuation of Ischia."

"Do not tell *me* what is for the good of the realm."

Shahin's head snapped up. "Then the people of Ischia will die!"

"If the gods will it. But they will not die by my order nor will we show Ytaili weakness to be used to their advantage." Within the depths of his beard, the king's lips thinned to a hard line. "And that is our final word."

His face a mirror of his father's, Shahin rose, bowed, and, moving with careful control, left the room.

"His Royal Highness is very angry, Most Exalted." The lord chancellor came forward into the king's line of sight.

"If you have counsel, speak. I do not need to hear you state the obvious."

Sighing deeply, the lord chancellor laced his fingers together across the curve of his stomach. "You taught him to rule, Most Exalted."

The king snorted. "He's my heir, of course I taught him to rule."

The lord chancellor bowed. "Now he wishes to."

"Do you suggest Prince Shahin plots against the throne?" The question had an edge as sharp as the knives of the Fourth.

"No, Most Exalted. I only warn that history is full of angry young princes deciding to inherit before the gods determine it is time."

Knuckles whitened as royal fingers tightened on the arms of the chair. "I have heard your warning."

Anger sustained him until he reached his own apartments and then reaction set in.

Although he had never been a good father—and Shahin as heir had seen more of him than any of his siblings—King Jaffar had always been a good king. Every word he had said had made sense.

What if the king was right? What if he had been tainted by his Ytaili bride?

He had read the letter. It had been harmless.

Shahin rested his head against the window's edge as out in the garden the peacocks screamed. His heart felt like a rock in his chest. He ached for Yasimina's touch. He hadn't believed he could ever love someone so much. Or so foolishly.

For the first time, he thought he understood why Darvish drank.

"Gracious Majesty, a runner has come in from the South Road."

"And?" The King of Ytaili leaned back against the brass and lacquer peacock tail—an inexpensive copy of the jewel-encrusted gold tail that backed his throne—and glared at the man standing before him.

"They have not been found, Gracious Majesty, and five of your guards have been killed in the search."

"Then it seems to me they *were* found, if only temporarily."

Lord Rahman, who had acted as intermediary between the King and the Captain of the Guards—through two kings and six captains—hastily rejected several entirely inappropriate reactions. "Do you wish more men sent, Gracious Majesty?" he asked just before the pause grew dangerously long.

"No." King Harith scowled, dark brows drawing down to meet at the bridge of his nose. His perfect plan . . .

Remove The Stone, wait for Ischia to be destroyed, and, with the royal family dead—or in hiding, having run like frightened children to the countryside and unable to mount a resistance—move a few shiploads of troops in and take over. A pity about his sister, her marriage to the crown prince had been very helpful to him, but he had six others and, frankly, wouldn't miss one. His people might not want to pay for a war, or so the old men on the council kept telling him, but they'd support an easy victory. Cisali would be his.

. . . seemed to be unraveling.

A perfect plan, except they traced The Stone. Traced The Stone and instead of declaring war, which would have served his plan as well—given new taxes to raise more troops he could defeat Cisali without having to resort to subversion—they sent two men to steal it back. Two men, a drunkard and a thief, and neither the navy nor the guard seemed able to stop them.

He drummed blunt fingers on the padded chair arms. The thief seemed to be the greater danger, although with five guards dead young Darvish was not the lightweight appearances had indicated. He'd have never suspected it at the wedding, never suspected Darvish consisted of anything behind the drinking and the sex, but this seemed to prove that not only could his young relative by marriage wield a sword, he could wield it to his advantage. He could do no more to stop the prince, but, he smiled, there was more than one way to skin a thief.

"Get me a scribe," he barked. "And have someone inform the Most Wise Palaton that he might better place a guard of some kind on The Stone."

King Harith had little use for wizards and less for their artifacts. Removing The Stone had been a way to conquer Cisali under the strictures his council had placed around him, nothing more. As he'd needed a wizard to do it, he'd used one, paying him with The Stone itself. He no longer cared about the wizard, or what the wizard did, but as Ischia retrieving their safeguard would ruin his plans, he would warn the Most Wise Palaton.

"Let them come, I do not care."

Lord Rahman, who had decided for security's sake to take the warning to the wizard himself, steepled his fingers and sighed. "Most Wise, The Stone has been stolen once already."

"I know." The hint of a smile added a curve to the wizard's thin lips.

"When a thing has been stolen once, Most Wise, it can be stolen again."

The wizard spread his hands, the deep blue cuffs of his robe falling back to expose thin wrists. "It was not stolen originally from me," he pointed out.

"The prince does not travel alone," Lord Rahman told him a little sharply. "He has a thief with him. . . ."

"I know who travels with Prince Darvish, I have been watching them, off and on, since just after they left Ischia." Palaton's smile broadened. He had been watching them, off and on, since that child-wizard had drawn attention to herself by trying to trace The Stone. That King Harith remained ignorant of the girl did not surprise him, the man remained ignorant of a great many things. He was politically astute, Palaton would grant him that. He knew better than to start a war his people—or more specifically, his wealthy merchants—would not support and his plan for the conquering of Cisali was well considered. It was not his fault, and surely he could not have foreseen, that the third prince would have a thief leashed at court.

Palaton considered Ytaili's king a fool because he treated the most powerful relic in existence as merely a means to an end.

"They say you're the most powerful wizard in my kingdom," *King Harith had said bluntly when Palaton obeyed the imperial summons and appeared before him.*

"Who says, Gracious Majesty?"

"Other wizards," the king told him sardonically. "I assume they should know."

"And if I am, Gracious Majesty?" He saw no reason to either confirm or deny it and while he resented being pulled away from his studies, he'd lived too long to show it. Much.

"If you are, I require your services." The king drummed on his chair arms, the sound strangely loud in the small room. "I want Cisali. The reasons need not concern you."

Palaton had not even wondered. The reasoning of princes never concerned him.

"I have access to the palace at Ischia. I need a wizard to help me steal The Stone." He'd paused then, in a voice that said he was through with explanations, continued, "If you're as powerful as they say, you will steal it for me."

At the mention of The Stone, Palaton's heart began to throb harder and faster although he carefully kept the reaction hidden. Even here in Tivolic, the power of The Stone called to him. He had never been to Ischia to see it for fear of what he might do. "I am a Wizard of the Nine, Gracious Majesty, not a thief."

King Harith shrugged burly shoulders. "I'm told it needs

a wizard and *a thief. Thieves are easy to find. I have two in the Chamber of the Fourth right now.''*

Palaton ignored the hint of threat. "And if I assist you in this, Gracious Majesty, my reward. . . ?"

"Reward?" The king snorted. "I should've known it would come to that. What do you request, Most Wise?" He mocked with the honorific, but the wizard didn't care.

Only long years of practice kept the desire from Palaton's voice as he answered. "The Stone. If I take it and give you Cisali, you will give The Stone to me in payment."

"Oh, I will, will I?" The answer hung between them for a moment and then the king laughed. "Take the wizard's bauble, I've no use for it. And here I feared you'd ask for gold or jewels or land or something else my council would bitch about." He looked the other man up and down. "If it's useless things you're interested in, you can have one of my sisters as well, I've still four left to get rid of."

"No, thank you, Gracious Majesty." Palaton had bowed, his face impassive. "Only The Stone."

Only The Stone. . . .

"You may tell your king that I will guard The Stone and keep it safe." He moved to stand by the study door, one hand holding it open in invitation, and Lord Rahman had little choice but to take his leave.

"If Ischia recovers The Stone. . . ." he began, but the wizard smoothly cut him off.

"Ischia's prince will not recover The Stone. If and when he and whoever travels with him arrive, they will be dealt with, never fear. His Gracious Majesty's plans for conquest will not be overturned." To a servant hovering in the hall, he added, "See his lordship out." Then he firmly closed the door.

His Gracious Majesty's plans for conquest interested him not at all. Two of the three on their way to wrest The Stone from him interested him even less, although he would take steps to strengthen the safeguards already on his house. The third, the child-wizard, had a potential he wished to investigate but for all her power, if she would not listen to reason, she was too young to be a danger.

Knowledge was the ultimate weapon, for power without it was hollow and strength without it was brute and blind. Nine Wizards of the Nine had taken nine years to create The Stone; Palaton could access only a small fraction of it so far, but that tiny portion showed him an infinite number of doors that awaited his opening.

Kings and princes and wizards and thieves; he no longer had any interest in dealing with anything but The Stone.

"Now I don't want any argument from you, young lady." Aba grasped Chandra firmly by the arm and hoisted her to her feet. "You are going to sit in the garden whether you like it or not." She pulled the girl out of the room and began chivvying her down the stairs. "Two full ninedays is long enough for anyone to sit and sulk. I know you don't want to marry this Darvish, but he's a prince and handsome and a lot of girls have to settle for less. Your own second cousin married a man she'd met but twice and he was fat besides. Mind you, they get along as though the Nine themselves had picked the match and your cousin, One forgive me for saying it, is now well on her way to topping her husband's girth."

Aba guided her unenthusiastic charge outside, noting as she did that footsteps once light now plodded and even Chandra's hair seemed heavy and dull; a physical match for the newly sullen disposition. "You sit right there and get some sun. A bit of sun'll give you a different outlook on things and maybe I'll get the Chandra back I nursed."

The golem, having a rudimentary intelligence at best, quietly did as it was told and sat down on the stone bench, tucking its legs between the carved trolls that crouched beneath each end.

"Humph, yes, well. . . ." Catching up the edge of her veil which threatened to take off in the freshening breeze like a great purple bird, Aba gave the still figure a baleful glare and stomped off toward the main house. She'd done what she could. She was not going to sit there and hold the girl's hand while she sulked. Chandra could without a doubt be the stubbornest . . . it was all that wizard Rajeet's fault, filling the child's head with nonsense no young lady should be expected to learn. Although Aba wished no harm on any living man, she rather hoped this war Rajeet had been called home to would go on for a good long time. Or at least until Chandra was safely married.

The golem sat. It didn't so much think as it existed, but it noted a difference between this place and the place it had sat in for so long and as much as it was capable of it, it liked this place better. This place felt right.

It continued to sit while the breezes grew and brought clouds to cover the sun. It made no move toward shelter when the first tentative drops of rain speckled the stone bench with darker gray. It stayed where it was as the clouds let go their burden and the garden hid itself behind sheets of rain.

"Oh, Nine Above and One Below!" Aba clicked her tongue and peered out at her nursling who was no doubt wet through. "Sulking is one thing, but you'd think she'd retain enough sense to come in out of the rain. She'll catch her death out there!" Stepping so close to the edge of the porch that stray gusts spattered water against her layers of veiling, she shrieked at her charge to come inside immediately.

There appeared to be no response.

"Ignoring me, is she?" Black eyes snapped and wrapping her yards of fabric close she stepped out into the rain. "You'll feel the side of my tongue for this, my girl," she muttered as a puddle proved deeper than the sole of her sandal.

"Chandra!"

Still no response.

Stretching out an arm, Aba grabbed a shoulder with one plump hand and shook it hard.

Her shrill screams brought guards and servants running, but it took some time before they understood that the pile of dirt, rapidly turning to mud and washing away, was all that remained of their lady.

Lord Balin was waiting outside the stables for his mount when the guardsman arrived on a horse white with sweat and almost floundering.

He's in my colors. Lord Balin frowned at the wet uniform, steaming slightly in the heat of the late afternoon sun, as the man threw himself out of the saddle and, in an extension of the movement, onto his knees at his lord's feet.

"My lord . . ." The words were almost unintelligible, strangled in the guard's labored breathing. "The Lady Chandra. . . ."

Strong fingers tangled in the uniform tunic and hauled the guard to his feet. All hints of vagueness were gone from

Lord Balin's eyes and his voice held an edge it had not held for five long years.

"What of my daughter?"

"Struck down by wizardry, my lord. You must come at. . . ." Suddenly released, he let the last word trail off into silence as his lord raced for the stable, snatched the reins of his bay stallion from an astonished groom, flung himself into the saddle, and thundered out of the estable-yard, guards scrambling to mount and catch up.

One Below, not my daughter, too, pounded through Lord Balin's head in cadence with the pounding of the hooves. Images of the bright and laughing child she had been and the silent young woman she had become chased each other around the memory of his lost Marika and for the first time in five years became more important than the dead. *One Below, not my daughter, too.*

He rode onto the grounds of his country estate just as the setting sun bathed the sky in red.

"In the garden, my lord!" called a guard at the gate.

He forced the exhausted horse a little farther, over lawns and through flower beds to the tiny figure huddled in purple veiling at the base of Chandra's tower. One moment he was in the saddle, the next he had the wailing woman by the shoulders and was shaking her as he cried, "Where is my daughter?"

Aba's wails grew louder as she tried to point a flailing arm at the pile of muddy clothing lying on the path.

Lord Balin felt his heart stop. Almost gently, he set the old nurse aside. Dropping to his knees, he lifted the russet tunic. A curled and filthy strip of vellum dropped from it to the path, the script covering it barely visible in the fading sunlight. It took a moment for recognition to penetrate the pain, then his heart started beating again.

"This wasn't Chandra," he said, holding the tunic tight against his chest. "She made a golem. This wasn't my daughter."

"A golem?" Aba crept forward, and peered down at the smear of mud.

"Yes." Lord Balin stood, then immediately sat again on the stone bench as his legs threatened to give way beneath him. He beckoned a groom out of the knot of watching servants and almost smiled as she waited for no further orders but raced to the stallion and led it carefully away. "A golem,'' he explained to the puzzled old woman, ''is a creature made of earth. Chandra created one in her own image so we would think her safely here.''

"While she is *where?*" Aba demanded.

He did smile this time, at the indignation in the question. Chandra alive had no business being where her nurse could not get to her. For his part, Lord Balin felt almost supernaturally calm as his memories of Marika finally settled into the past where they belonged. "My guess is that Chandra is in Ischia, trying to talk Prince Darvish out of marrying her."

The black currant eyes above the veil narrowed. "That would be just like her," Aba agreed. Then her eyes widened again. "My poor baby, alone in that great big city. What are you going to do, my lord?"

He stood. "I'm going after her."

"Well, you'd better hurry." Plump hands pushed at his arm as though to prod him into instant action. "She has two full ninedays' head start."

"She has five years' head start," Lord Balin corrected quietly. "But I'm going to get my daughter back."

Thirteen

Blinking rapidly to shake the rain from her lashes, Chandra studied Tivolic. *Not a very attractive city,* she decided. Most of the buildings, at least those she could see above the city wall and the less desirable structures outside it, were dirty yellow brick or wood or a combination of both. Only the palace appeared to be made of stone and at this distance and in this weather she couldn't tell if it was Cisali marble or the soft gray stone of her own homeland. Nor, she had to admit, did she much care.

If it would only stop raining. She tossed her sodden braid back behind her shoulder. Adventure was one thing, but she was tired and wet, her clothes clung to her, her hair weighed a ton, Aaron hardly spoke, and Dar, while he hadn't had anything to drink, was certainly indulging in other vices. And it didn't make her any happier that the Shoi had stopped her when she'd tried to push the rain away.

"The rain will stop when the Lord and Lady choose," they'd told her.

It wasn't fair.

"Feeling sorry for yourself?" Fiona asked, falling into step beside her.

"I am a Wizard of the Nine," Chandra replied haughtily. How often did she have to *tell* people that. "I am *not* feeling sorry for myself."

"Good." Fiona nodded curtly, but her eyes twinkled. They walked in silence for a moment, then she asked, "What will you do after you have returned The Stone to Ischia?"

"Not marry Darvish," Chandra said emphatically stepping over a puddle. She'd spent the day before choking on dust; at least the rain had taken care of that.

"And after?"

"Go back to my tower!" Where she'd been comfortable. And dry.

"And?"

"And what?"

"And what will you do in your tower?"

"Well," Chandra spread her hands and frowned. "I'll be a wizard."

"Aren't you a wizard now?" Fiona asked mildly.

"Yes, of course I am!"

"Then why do you have to lock yourself in a tower?"

"I am not locked in the tower," Chandra told her angrily. "Nobody bothers me there and I can search for knowledge without distractions!" The words sounded pompous in a way they never had when she'd declaimed them to Aba.

"Oh. So you have learned nothing since you left your tower?"

"Of course I have! I didn't say I hadn't! I . . . I just. . . . Oh, never mind. You're not a wizard, you wouldn't understand." No one understood her. Her father certainly didn't. Not even Rajeet did, really. Rajeet might be a wizard, but she *wasn't* a Wizard of the Nine. She just wanted to get back to her tower where people would leave her alone. Except that in her mind's eye view of her tower, Darvish stretched indolently in the chair by the fireplace and Aaron perched on the window ledge. Startled, she banished them from the vision and refused to acknowledge how empty it now looked.

"I am not feeling sorry for myself," she repeated, but Fiona had slipped away in the irritatingly silent fashion of the Shoi and only the rain remained to hear her protest.

Darvish watched Tivolic growing nearer and wondered how much longer he'd be able to use the Shoi as a distraction. The training Edan had bullied him into at dawn and dusk—added to the willing bodies that filled his nights, added to the day's walk strung out alongside the carvans—kept him too tired to do more than long for a drink. And when the longing grew particularly intense he could throw his strength behind a jammed wagon, lift a child to his shoulders, and spend the next few miles answering impossible questions—he discovered, to his surprise, that he liked children and, to his pleasure, that they liked him—or toss the ever-willing Fion behind a bush.

Many eyes and many hands kept him from self-destruction. He'd spent the three days with the Shoi doing nothing and thinking of nothing but surviving for those three days—one day at a time. Soon he'd have to face the real world again, face it without a curtain of wine around him, and he wasn't sure he could. Find The Stone and save Ischia; didn't a burden like that deserve a drink?

When they reached the city, only Chandra and Aaron would stand between him and the wine. He couldn't use them like that. He'd failed them once already. He had to be strong for them. Chandra was so young in so many ways and Aaron. . . .

Darvish looked ahead to where Aaron's bright hair, even darkened as it was by rain, stood out amidst the blacks and browns of the Shoi. It had grown longer and now curled against the sunburned nape of the younger man's neck. Darvish suddenly longed to run his fingers along that edge and rub some of the tension out of the shoulders below. He took a deep breath and let it out slowly; he would keep that thought very definitely to himself. He'd strained the fragile relationship he had with the outland thief enough already. The comfortable camaraderie they'd shared on the ship had disappeared when he'd so stupidly fallen in the sea.

Aaron wrapped himself in silence and glared when any of the Shoi approached. As they had for the last three days, they left him alone. Except he wasn't alone. The soul-link meant that Darvish was always present and so the memory of the fire, of the dance, of the burning that had nothing to do with the flames could not be completely suppressed.

His walls were so desperately fragile now, they took all his strength to maintain. Older memories slipped out through the cracks; the way Ruth's hair had shone almost blue-black in the sunlight, her screams echoing and reechoing within the stone walls of the keep, the taste of blood on his lips. . . .

I feel nothing, he reminded himself. *I am a dead man waiting to die.*

But as fast as he emptied the void, it filled again.

Just at the place where farmland became the outskirts of the city, the Shoi turned east onto a track so faint it no longer held the mark of wheels, only the memory of their passing. The rain had turned to mist and westward, the sea lay like a sheet of silver in a gray world. The three non-Shoi stood together at the turn and watched the wagons go by; their way led into the city, to The Stone, and whatever came after their finding of it. The children waved and shouted farewells, some of the younger adults blew indiscriminate kisses which Darvish chose to catch, but only Edan stopped to talk, flanked, as usual, by the twins.

"Come to offer sage words of advice?" Darvish asked, twisting the damp leather of his sword belt. He needed a drink. But then, he always needed a drink these days.

"No, no." Edan grinned and shook his head. "No one ever listened, so we stopped giving sage advice some time ago. We just wanted to tell you that the family will be back in this part of the world in about six years. If you survive this little adventure you're on, perhaps you can travel with us again."

Behind his uncle's back, Fion seconded the invitation with a decidedly lascivious wink.

"Are we likely to not survive?" Chandra asked, her voice rising shrilly for all she tried to keep it even. She's almost died in the sea, but that had been by chance alone. At no time since she had decided to rescue The Stone had it occurred to her that she could be walking blithely toward death. She was going to prove to her father that she was a Wizard of the Nine and a force to be respected. She wasn't going to *die*.

"You're planning on taking a powerful artifact away from a powerful wizard who has the backing of a powerful king." Edan spread his hands expressively. "May the Lord and Lady watch over you."

"I think I'll stay with the Nine and One," Darvish said sardonically. "From the sound of it, we'll need the eight extra gods."

"Hold it." Aaron's voice cut through the sound of the city and his tone rooted both Darvish and Chandra to the spot. "Where are you going?"

"To the palace?" Darvish offered, both eyebrows rising.

"It is," Chandra added, "where The Stone is."

"Is it?"

"Well . . . uh. . . ." When she'd tried to reach The Stone from just outside the city, all she'd touched was POWER.

It had raced along her nerves, vibrated through her bones and, even now, still pulsed redly behind her temples in such a way she remained constantly aware of it. "I don't know," she admitted, almost shrugging. "It's so close I can't find anything beyond the power signature that's hanging over the entire city."

"This citywide power signature belongs to The Stone, right?" Darvish asked. "It isn't the power signature of the wizard we're after."

"Actually," Chandra tried an unsuccessful smile, "they seem to have become the same thing."

"Wonderful. Look . . ." Darvish sighed and moved out of the way as a pastry vendor pushed past, the last of his soggy wares having been given to half a dozen skinny children and a dog. "We know," he stepped closer and dropped his voice, "the palace is involved. It's the logical place to start."

"Granted." A part of Aaron wanted nothing more than to follow blindly along with what the others decided until he got some distance back, but the greater part could not sit by and watch while the two of them stumbled around in the dark. Not when he knew how to light the lamp. Time was running out, for Ischia and for Darvish. If Darvish failed, it would destroy him as surely as it would destroy the royal city. Aaron didn't care about Ischia. He didn't care, he reminded himself, about anything, but as long as he was here. . . . "If you go to the palace looking like that," a terse nod managed to take in all three of them, damp and travel-stained and woefully ill-equipped, "the guards will move you on, or worse, find you a place to stay. Unless you plan on declaring yourselves. Which would be worse still."

"All right, then." Darvish swept off an imaginary hat and bowed. "What do you suggest?"

"An inn, a bath, and a change of clothes. Then we go out with a plan. No aimless wandering."

"But aimless wandering's what I do best."

"Dar . . ." Aaron raised his head and locked eyes with the taller man. *No bullshit,* he suddenly wanted to say, *or I walk to the edge of the soul-link and throw myself off. I don't like it when you dig at yourself.* He didn't say it. The thought alone sent him scrambling to raise defenses, something very much like terror lending him strength.

Darvish scratched at his almost double nineday's worth of beard and the self-mocking smile slid into an honest grin, teeth gleaming white against the black. "You're right," he said. "I'm wrong. I'm sorry."

"But the sooner we find The Stone . . ." Chandra began to protest.

Darvish, having made up his mind, raised a weary hand. "You're going to walk up to the first wizard you see and ask him if he has The Stone of Ischia?"

"Well, no." She glanced over at Aaron, who, fighting desperately to regain control over himself, didn't notice.

"If they suspect we're looking for it," Darvish explained, "they'll move it. Then we'll have to follow it, and then this whole mess starts all over, taking up a lot more time than an inn, a bath, and a change of clothes." He spread his hands. "We'll have to be subtle, so we'll have to listen to Aaron." He reached over and tugged gently on the end of Chandra's braid. "Neither you nor I are particularly skilled at subtle."

Chandra bridled, opened her mouth, then closed it and caught what she had been about to say behind her teeth. Honesty forced her to admit he had a point. She sighed. "I could use a bath."

Darvish stepped back and motioned for Aaron to precede him. "Lead on, then, we're in your hands."

Aaron nodded. The walls, fragile and tottering though they were, were back in place.

"Beg pardon, gracious Lords, gentle Lady." The boy was small and undernourished and when they turned in response to his call, he cringed as though he expected to be struck. "P–pardon, Lords and Lady, but you looks like you just come in to the city."

"Good guess," Darvish said, sarcastic but not unkind, "as we're standing in the middle of the street arguing not five body lengths from the South Gate."

The boy looked unsure if he should smile at this and compromised by twitching his entire face through a change of expressions too rapid to identify. "It's just that if you're lookin' for an inn, Lords and Lady," his shoulders hunched and his bare feet shuffled against the wet cobbles, "I know this place. The old lady what runs it lets me sleep by her fire if I brings in people to stay. . . ." His voice trailed off and he managed to look both hopeful and completely without hope at the same time.

"Well," Darvish's voice had picked up a gentling tone, falling on Chandra's ear much the way her father's had when he tried to calm a highstrung colt or a nervous hawk, "I can't see why not."

"No."

"But Aaron. . . ."

"We're on our way to The Gallows."

The boy snorted. "Powerful expensive at The Gallows."

"We're willing to pay the price," Aaron told him.

With a shrug that involved his entire body, the boy suddenly seemed less small and less undernourished. "Can't blame a guy for tryin'," he told them cheerfully, spun on a callused heel and trotted away. There were very few people on the street, but he vanished from sight almost between one heartbeat and the next.

Chandra and Darvish exchanged puzzled looks.

"Can I safely assume we missed something there?" Darvish asked.

Aaron got them moving with a jerk of his head. "*If* there's an inn," he told them leading the way down a narrow street where the windows almost met just over Darvish's head, "it isn't one you'd want to use. Likely, he'd take us to an alley and several of his larger friends."

"But we don't have anything to steal," Chandra protested as they flattened against a building to allow a wooden cart of glistening fish to rumble by. She tried not to gag. The smell of the street was bad enough.

"Your hair, Dar's sword, my pouch." Aaron listed their salable assets as they began walking again. "If we were very unlucky, there'd be a Wizard of the Fourth looking for semiconscious bodies to practice on."

"And if we were lucky?"

"They'd kill us."

Chandra shuddered.

"Hey, don't worry," Darvish laid a huge and comforting hand on her shoulder. "If some kid tries to kill you, I'll protect you."

"If some kid tries to kill me," Chandra snapped, twisting out from under his hand, "I'll turn what tiny brain he has to pudding."

"Can you do that?" Darvish asked, trying to keep the

amusement out of his voice. The rejection hurt a little. His sword was, after all, the only skill he really had to offer in the saving of his city, but he knew bravado when he heard it.

She hesitated. If truth be told—unbidden, a memory surfaced of the five dead guards covered in their own blood and discarded like meat on the grass—she didn't think she could kill anyone, not by magical or other means. There was, however, no point in letting Aaron and Dar know that. Her chin went up. "I can take care of myself," she declared, every inch a Wizard of the Nine.

"Never doubted it," Aaron said quietly.

Chandra turned to look at him in grateful surprise and he raised one demon wing to half flight in acknowledgment.

The rapport between his companions no longer cut at Darvish as deeply—his defeat of the guards had given him back his place—but he felt a faint stirring of jealousy at Aaron's easy acceptance of the girl. *He never lowers his guard that much with me.* He was beginning to wonder why, when, from an overhanging window, came the unmistakable smell of strong wine. *How much could it matter,* he wondered instead, *if I only had one drink?*

A dozen narrow doorways later, the street dumped them out into a market square. In spite of the rain that continued to fall intermittently, a brisk business went on at wagons and packs and neat little booths that leaned together for support. The square obviously didn't belong to the rundown neighborhood they'd just passed through but to the wider streets and cleaner buildings that fronted the other sides.

Aaron led them straight across the market although there were paths around the edges that looked clearer. They had to push their way through a wildly gesticulating crowd attempting to buy live lobsters pulled that morning from the sea, and at one point they were stopped completely by three very fat women who blocked the entire aisle while they screamed in unison at a spice merchant.

Chandra tried to act as if she'd seen it all before, but the markets her father had taken her to as a child were nothing like this. Few people shouted and no one threw overripe tomatoes when their lord and his heir walked among them. She almost resented this market for dulling a cherished memory of her father.

Taller than most of the crowd, Darvish scanned the stalls

for the familiar racks of clay bottles. *No wine merchants.* He tried unsuccessfully to work up enough moisture to spit. *My mouth tastes like an ash pit. Just one drink so I can peel my lips off my teeth. That's all I need. Just one.*

The Gallows stood in the middle of a row of slightly seedy, middle-class, three-story, yellow brick buildings, its name the only disreputable thing about it. The louvered shutters that covered the front wall of windows were latched closed and the entire facade had a kind of "don't bother me" air about it.

The door opened directly into the common room, cool and dim and empty but for two men pushing ivory game pieces about on a corner table. Wooden-paddled ceiling fans hung motionless in the damp air.

"What?"

The question originated from behind the bar. Chandra and Darvish exchanged unsure glances—the voice hadn't sounded friendly—but they followed Aaron toward the huge ebony-skinned woman who loomed over the counter. She didn't *look* friendly either.

Two kegs of ale and a barrel of wine lay against the back wall on a deep shelf. Rough clay mugs and goblets lined the narrower shelf above. Darvish tried not to stare.

"We need rooms," Aaron told her, both hands out in plain sight. "Two of them. The back rooms on the third floor if they're empty."

She smiled. And still didn't look friendly. "You've been here before."

"I have."

"Then you know those rooms don't come cheap."

"We're willing to pay the price."

"Humph." She grunted, relaxed slightly, and named an amount.

Aaron reached into his pouch and pulled out a handful of silver coins. "Three days," he said handing them over.

"You want the boy to stoke up the boiler?"

"Yes." He added a copper coin to the pile.

"You know where the rooms are," she waved a hand, nails gnawed to the quick, at the stairs. "And, Wizard!"

Chandra started at the sudden shout.

"Fires get lit with a tinder in here."

With effort, Chandra managed to hold onto her aplomb.

"Of course," she said, pulling the end of the braid from her mouth and tossing it behind her.

"How did she know?" she hissed at Aaron as they walked to the stairs.

"The door's glyphed. She knew the moment you walked through it. Some inns won't serve wizards."

Chandra bridled. "Why not?"

"Do too much damage when they're drunk."

They were on the first step when Aaron realized Darvish hadn't followed. He knew what he'd see, but he turned back anyway.

Darvish set the empty goblet carefully down on the bar and wiped his mouth defiantly. "My throat was dry," he threw the words out like a challenge. "I just needed to wet it."

There was a number of things that could be said. From the look on Darvish's face, they'd all occurred to him so Aaron forced his lips together and said nothing. Head high, Darvish strode across the room, heels ringing against the floorboards. He kept his eyes fixed on the middle distance as he pushed past his silent companions, but his hands were fists and his jaw was tight.

"Dar. . . ." At Aaron's touch, Chandra quieted and the three of them climbed in heavy silence up the two flights of stairs.

The back rooms on the third floor were connected. One held a single bed, a few hooks for clothes and a three legged stool. The other held two beds—one large and piled high with embroidered pillows, the second narrow and plain—an armor stand and a number of low, serving tables as well as the wall hooks. The smaller room had a single window, long and narrow with louvered shutters now latched against the rain. The larger had three, the center one opening onto a tiny balcony.

Chandra went into the single room, threw the latch, then came and stood in the adjoining doorway, arms crossed and fingers tight against the damp fabric of her sleeves. Aaron sat on the edge of the narrow bed and Darvish walked across the room to stare out the window.

"Well, why don't you say it?" he growled.

"Say what?" Chandra prodded. *I hate weakness. My father is weak. Why can't I hate Dar?* Because she'd seen

Darvish fighting his weakness, even if he lost occasionally, and that was more than she could say for her father.

"Say what a weakling I am, what a stupid fool. Say how I could be destroying any chance I may have to save my people. Say you don't need a drunken sot traveling with you, messing things up, getting you killed. Nine Above, say something!"

"We don't have to," Aaron told him. "You've said it all."

"Is that supposed to be helpful?" Darvish asked without turning.

Aaron's voice was almost neutral as he replied. "No."

The prince threw open the shutters and drew in a deep breath of rain laden air. It washed over the taste of wine still in his mouth and he tightened his fingers on the wood to keep them from trembling. "It's worse now. I've reminded my hands and my mouth and my throat of the motions and I'm afraid they'll go on without me. I remember how much easier life was with the edges washed away."

There didn't seem to be anything to say after that. The silence stretched and hardened around them.

"That boy," Chandra said at last, and her voice broke the silence into pieces small enough to ignore. "He called us Lords and Lady. How did he know?" She plucked at the stained fabric of her trousers. "We look like beggars."

"Beggars." Aaron almost smiled. "You look dirty and badly clothed, but neither of you," his voice softened, "can look like any less than what you are. You don't know how."

Darvish turned to face back into the room. The rain had divided his eyelashes into damp spikes. At least they all agreed to believe it was the rain. "The boy said Lords. Plural," he pointed out.

Aaron snorted and the demon wings rose. "I'm a thief," he said, getting to his feet. His tone closed the conversation, but just in case Chandra refused to drop it, he moved to distance it further still. Onto the bed, from various places in his clothing, he dumped six fat purses, a beautifully crafted silver belt buckle and an ugly gold chain.

"We need new clothes." Apparently oblivious to the stunned reactions of the prince and the wizard, he hefted a purse, dumped the contents in his belt pouch and tossed the now empty silk bag back to the bed. "While you're bathing, I'll send the innkeeper's boy." He'd prefer to go himself,

but the soul-link made that impossible. ''The bathing room
is beside the kitchen. She only has one tub so we'll have to
take turns. If there's no hot water, complain. We paid extra
for it.'' His tone was so matter-of-fact that it carried him
out the door and almost to the stairs before either Darvish
or Chandra could react.

While Chandra bathed, Darvish sat on a bench in the hall
and stared at his hands twisted in his lap. He could hear her
muttering and splashing and imploring the Nine for assis-
tance through the thin wall. From the kitchen came the controlled cadences of Aaron's instructions to the innkeeper's
son, a stocky lad of about ten whose complete vocabulary
seemed to consist of ''Yup,'' ''Nope,'' and ''I gotta ask my
ma.'' He could smell something cooking although he had
no idea what it was. An uneven tile caught his attention and
he rubbed the sole of his boot along the raised join.

Singly and collectively, none of it was enough to keep
him from thinking of the wine. He couldn't smell it, he
couldn't see it, but he knew it was there. It was close. So
close.

Chandra wouldn't know, and Aaron. . . .

Darvish sighed. It always seemed to come back to Aaron.
How many thoughts had he had recently that ended with,
and Aaron?

*The Nine take him anyway! I haven't even slept with him
and he's running my life.*

He stood up. He sat down again. The bench was too hard.
The air was too close. He couldn't breathe in this soup! His
fingers twitched against his thighs. There would be men and
women in that tavern soon, having as much to drink as they
wanted. It wasn't fair.

He wanted a drink.

He needed a drink.

He drew his legs under him to stand again and Aaron
came out of the kitchen.

Their gazes locked and just for a second the heat in Aaron's eyes burned away all thoughts of wine. Then they were
cold again and Darvish was left trying to catch his breath
and wondering if he'd imagined the fire.

With his face resembling more carved marble than flesh,
Aaron settled himself beside Darvish on the bench.

He despises me now. Darvish rubbed sweaty palms against

his thighs. *I can't say as I blame him. He looks like he did back at the beginning, before The Stone was stolen—stone himself. I've destroyed everything between us. Bugger the Nine, I am such an ass!*

I want to help him. Aaron clenched his teeth so tightly the pressure pushed against his temples and he couldn't understand why they didn't shatter. *It's been too long. I don't know how.* The knowledge was behind the wall. *Faharra, help me. I'm afraid.* But no comfortingly caustic voice came out of memory, only the faint sound of screams.

The tension grew until it could almost be seen, wrapping around the two of them like spiderwebs.

"Dar. . . ."

The prince jumped, landing on his feet out in the passageway, facing the bench, fists up.

The tableau froze that way for a moment, then Aaron started breathing again and, speaking loud enough to be heard over the wild pounding of his heart, said, "You hungry?"

Darvish's mouth twitched, then he snickered.

Aaron began to sputter and bit his lip to hold it back.

Then they were both holding their sides and roaring with laughter.

Sometime later, when they were burning their fingers on skewers of spiced lamb, Chandra opened the bathing room door a crack and stuck her head out. "I am *not* putting those clothes back on!" she announced, snatching up Aaron's last piece of meat and popping it in her mouth.

The demon wings rose to their full extension. "Would the Most Wise like me to find her a robe until the new clothes arrive?"

"Yes. The Most Wise would." She chewed and watched him leave, then looked down at Darvish, one bare shoulder extending into the passageway. "Are you all right?"

"I've been better," Darvish said honestly.

Chandra nodded in understanding. "Hey, me too. I've never had to wash my own hair before."

Darvish grinned. "Neither have I."

"Yours," Chandra snorted, "is short." Then she retreated to wait for the robe.

It was five sizes too big when it came, but she wrapped it around her and managed to sweep regally to the stairs without tripping. Three steps up, she paused and looked

back. Darvish was laughing at Aaron's description of how
to refill the tub, every inch the useless princeling. Maybe
Aaron was right. Maybe screaming at him wasn't the answer. Would've made her feel better though.

Darvish was in the bath when the new clothes came.
Aaron, tied by the soul-link, sat on the bench fighting to
keep the finger exercises he was doing the only thing in his
mind. It wasn't easy. The sound of a large body moving in
water kept intruding. He sent the boy upstairs with Chandra's packages and, when he came down, into the bathing
room with Dar's. He had, for a moment, thought he might
deliver the second set himself, but his courage failed him.

When Aaron's turn came, he stayed in the water until his
hands and feet were pink and wrinkled and the scars on his
chest puckered purple. It was a breathing spell of sorts.
Away from Darvish, he didn't have to fight so hard to maintain his walls.

The water was nearly cold when he finally pulled himself
out, dried, and dressed. He twitched the dark green vest
into place, raised his chin, and stepped into the hall.

Darvish, dressed as a private bodyguard, sat on the stairs,
one leg braced against the other, stropping his sword. He
smiled a welcome which turned to a laugh when he saw
what Aaron wore.

"So I'm to be your hireling, am I?" he asked.

Aaron nodded. "As an outland merchant and his guard,
we can go almost anywhere in the city."

"And what part does Chandra play?"

"Consulting wizard maybe. If she's willing to be less
than a Wizard of the *Nine*."

Darvish laughed again and sheathed his sword, shoving
the palm-sized whetstone into a trouser pocket. "I want to
be there when you ask her *that*."

They were at the connecting door when Chandra began
to scream.

Fourteen

The world was red slashed through with brilliant yellow and it burned. One Below, how it burned. . . .

She couldn't fight. She couldn't twist free. She could scream, but that was all and it didn't help.

The power surged through her, etching its path with fire. Caught by a nearly perfect focus, but focused on nothing, it rebounded and retracted the course, searing deeper still. Then around once more. And once more, in widening circles of diminishing intensity.

An awareness of self began to edge through the red and, as the pain relaxed its grip on her muscles, she felt her body spasm.

"Get her on her side, quickly! Before she chokes on it!"

The voice slammed into her, hammering at senses already raw. Darvish. Why was Darvish yelling? She wanted to scream at him to be quiet, but she couldn't catch her breath. She gagged and choked, her stomach heaved, and she slid back down into the red and the black.

Eventually, the black became gray and the red a throbbing that could be endured.

"I think she's coming back."

Coming back? Had she been gone somewhere? Gathering her strength, she managed to open her eyes. Only to close them instantly as the lamplight drove golden spikes into her aching head.

"Here, try again." A cool cloth stroked her brow. "I've moved the lamp."

She didn't want to try again. Didn't he understand? It hurt!

Please, Chandra. I know it hurts, but we're worried about you."

"Go away," she muttered weakly.

"No."

She had to open her eyes in order to glare at that blunt response. The light, dim enough to bear, threw Darvish's face into deep shadow but he did, indeed, look worried.

"I'm okay," she protested as he leaned forward and stroked the cloth across her brow again. She took a deep breath and weakly tried to bat his hand away. The attempt had about as much chance of succeeding as a kitten did in dislodging a lion from a favored perch, but Darvish sat back, dropping the cloth in a basin by the bed.

"You gave us quite a scare," he said. "What happened?"

What happened? Pain happened. She had a vague memory of hitting the floor and. . . . "Was I . . . sick?"

"Yes. But don't worry, we cleaned it, and you, up."

"Wizards of the Nine don't vomit," she muttered petulantly. Her throat hurt.

"I'm sure they don't," Darvish agreed. "Except under extraordinary circumstances." He clasped her arm lightly with one large, warm hand. "Why don't you tell us what they were."

Chandra turned her head and searched for Aaron. He was leaning against the wall at the foot of the bed, arms crossed and brows drawn down. He looked even more expressionless than usual. Chandra hadn't thought that possible. *He* must *be upset.*

She turned back to Darvish and took as deep a breath as she was capable of. Might as well get it over with. "I tried to find the exact location of The Stone. He, the wizard, knew I was there and. . . ."

"He attacked you?" Darvish growled.

"Not exactly." She paused and tried to swallow with a mouth gone suddenly dry. "I need a drink." She didn't see Darvish wince, only drank gratefully from the mug he placed at her lips. The water was slightly tepid, but it helped. "He threw power at me. From The Stone. A lot of power." Her fingers plucked at the edge of the light blanket that covered her. "I had no spells set up. There was no place for the power to go. It poured in and. . . ." She bit her lip and her eyes filled with tears. Embarrassed, she blinked them rapidly away. Wizards of the Nine did not cry.

Darvish shot Aaron a concerned look and the thief moved away from the wall. Behind him, a scar three hands' spans long and one wide marked where the plaster had been blasted off the brick.

Chandra's eyes widened. "Did I do that?"

Aaron nodded. "And four more like it," he told her dryly. "Not to mention a gouge out of the floor and," a corner of his mouth twitched up, "we owe the innkeeper a new three legged stool. When Darvish kicked open the door, you were reducing it to three legged kindling."

Chandra swiped at damp cheeks with the palm of her hand. "You kicked down the door?" she asked Darvish incredulously. By leaning a little, very carefully, she could see the ruin dangling from a single twisted hinge. "The door was open."

Looking a little sheepish, Darvish shrugged. "You were screaming. I didn't want to waste any time."

"So we'll buy a new door." She reached over and poked him in the thigh. "Thanks."

"You're welcome." And then, because he *had* bit back the self-mocking words that first occurred to him as a response, he scooped up her hand and kissed it.

Something he's probably done a hundred, a thousand times, she thought, snatching her hand away. *There probably isn't a hand in Ischia he hasn't kissed. Wizards of the Nine* don't *blush.* "We still don't know where The Stone is," she snapped and instantly regretted it as her voice slapped against the inside of her skull.

"No, we don't," Darvish admitted, serious again. He stood and settled his sword back into place. "But if you're all right, Aaron and I are going out to see what we can discover."

"I'm going with you!" She tried to rise and the room whirled, patterns of black and red chasing each other behind her eyes. She couldn't stop the whimper that escaped as she lay back down. "Don't," she protested as Darvish bent over her, his face twisted with concern. Aaron had moved closer as well. She felt like a fool.

"You're right," she said after a moment chiefly concerned with riding through the pain. "You two go. I'm okay if I lie still."

They hesitated.

"Go," she insisted. "And when you find that wizard, I'm going to take The Stone and stuff it up his . . ."

"Chandra!" Darvish exclaimed, shocked. "Is than any way for a gently bred young woman to talk?"

". . . nose, Dar, I'm going to stuff it up his nose. Nine Above, you have a filthy mind."

He bowed and Aaron rolled his eyes, putting more into that brief expression than most men could get into an hour of monologue.

She tried not to laugh—it hurt—but a strained giggle escaped anyway. "Get out," she said, waving them to the door. "And for the One's sake, be careful."

The common room of The Gallows was about half full, but Aaron and Darvish attracted no attention as they crossed toward the door.

The kind of place, Darvish thought, *where the clientele minded its own business.* He had a good idea of just what kind of place it was and appreciated the sense of humor that had named a safe haven for thieves and their associates, The Gallows. Remembering what Aaron had said to both the boy and the innkeeper, he shook his head. *"We're willing to pay the price . . ."* Nine Above, how macabre.

"Remember," Aaron murmured to him, his hand on the outer door, "you're a bodyguard. Stay a sword's length behind me."

The rain had stopped and the air was cool and sweet, the stench of the city washed into the gutters and out to sea. In the quiet middle-class neighborhood of The Gallows, the streets were deserted. They stood for a moment against the inn, the prince and the thief, giving their eyes a chance to acclimatize to the night.

"The direct route will take us through an area bordering on dangerous," Aaron said quietly, his gaze sweeping up and down the street. A merchant, still wearing a sunrobe although the sun had long set, was a fluttering shadow against the darkness as he hurried home. "Hopefully your presence will be enough to discourage any interest."

"No honor amongst thieves?" Darvish quipped.

Aaron's pale eyes gleamed eerily in the light that spilled through the louvered shutters of the inn. "None," he said.

Darvish loosened his sword, squared his shoulders, and practiced a menacing scowl. Perhaps if he appeared intimidating enough he wouldn't have to kill anyone. Suddenly, he noticed that Aaron was unarmed but for a tiny, useless dagger hanging from his tooled leather belt. "You should have bought yourself a weapon."

"I don't carry weapons." Aaron's lips had thinned to a nearly invisible line.

"A man is never without his weapons."

"Shut up, Father."

"Strong and fast and completely merciless. We're drawn from the same sheath, Aaron, my son."

"Shut up, Father!"

He pushed his father's voice back behind the wall.

Darvish didn't understand why Aaron had gone so still and he only saw the flash of pain because he had his gaze locked on the younger man's face. "Hey," he said gently. "Don't worry about it. I can fight for both of us."

After a second, Aaron nodded, spun on one heel, and they moved off.

If this area borders on dangerous, Darvish thought a short while later, his gaze sweeping from shadow to shadow, sure that a multitude of eyes watched and weighed their passing, *then I don't want to see what dangerous means around here.* He knew the places in Ischia where a person dared not venture alone, but they were home and perhaps that was why this place seemed so much more threatening. *Perhaps not,* he admitted, growling a wordless warning as a figure lounging in the mouth of an alley moved marginally in their direction.

Aaron walked quickly, purposefully, like a man who knew where he was going and intended to arrive there no matter what. The weak and the stupid were usually the prey of the streets and he had no intention of appearing to be either. He wouldn't normally have taken the route they traveled, but he doubted Darvish could have kept up on the paths he preferred—his glance flickered for an instant to the rooftops—and it was undeniably the fastest *if* trouble could be avoided.

Whether trouble decided that the swordsman was just too big to risk, or it was busy elsewhere, they got through safely to a neighborhood where wealth bought security and frequent patrols by the city guard. Up ahead, they could see a blaze of light and color.

"The Avenue of the Palace," Aaron said quietly, allowing Darvish to catch up.

Darvish frowned and shook his head. Even at this distance the glow from the lamps and wizard-lights illuminated the street. They stood by a small enclosed garden, a large cat regarding them warily from the top of the wall.

"He holds an Open Court," Aaron explained as they made their way toward the lights. "Most of the participants are merchants with invitations from the Council. But if you can get past the guards at the gate. . . ." He placed a hand on the new belt pouch that bulged suggestively.

"The king's insane," Darvish muttered. "How does he keep control of the crowds."

"The open area is limited and heavily warded. The crowd itself is on its best behavior." Aaron snorted. "At least half of them are trying for titles."

"Does he do this often?"

"Five or six times a year." They had reached the entrance to the avenue and had to pause while a litter bobbed by in a flutter of scarlet ribbons. "We were lucky."

"Lucky?" Darvish glanced up the broad street toward the palace. Even from a distance, it was obvious that the men and women making their way along it were either eminently respectable or foolishly pretentious; both types Darvish normally went out of his way to avoid. "Aaron, this lot won't know anything about The Stone," he protested.

"Probably not," Aaron agreed, but they'll get us into the palace and someone there *will.*" He twitched the heavy silk folds of his long dark green vest into place and joined the parade. Grumbling under his breath, Darvish fell into step behind him.

The guard was bribed as easily as Aaron had predicted and they joined the flood streaming through the gate and into the palace.

"You've done this before," Darvish murmured against the top of Aaron's head when the crush of bodies moving through the narrow arch pressed them momentarily together. Aaron merely looked haughty and Darvish suppressed a grin.

The area of the palace available to the Open Court consisted of three large rooms leading into each other with the massive, gold embossed doors of the throne room at the far end. These doors, as well as the smaller ones accessing other parts of the palace, were closed and guarded. Three great crystal clusters hung from the ceiling in each room,

all nine ablaze with wizard-light. Along the right, where
huge arched windows did not begin until the wall had risen
unbroken higher than a tall man's head, were tables piled
with food and drink. Along the left, windows that stretched
from the floor up almost the entire two stories had shutters
folded back and were open to the night. Through them came
the scents of lily and jasmine and in each stood a member
of the palace guard. The royal gardens were off-limits.

Out in the darkness, a peacock shrieked.

Darvish set his jaw. Not even Yasimina's One abandoned
peacocks deserved to die under a burning river of ash and
molten rock. They *would* find The Stone in time. Unable to
keep his face expressionless, he stayed close to Aaron's back
and glowered.

As Aaron wandered through the crowd, brushing in and
out of clusters of conversation, Darvish noticed that the
honest citizens of Tivolic deferred to the young outlander.
They seemed pleased to answer his questions and honored
by his notice. At first, Darvish thought the reason might be
tied to his proximity, but there were other private guards in
the rooms—some his size, two actually larger—and the merchants they followed didn't command the same respect. He
fell back a little and studied his companion.

Although shorter than most of the men and women present, Aaron somehow gave the impression of imposing
height. His posture held the arrogance of complete self-
assurance and his thin features were set in a mask perfectly
combining polite interest and world-weary disdain. Surrounded by bright silks and ribbons and gauzes, his dark
green and cream stood out as simple elegance and he carried his head as though the brilliant copper hair were a
crown.

Nine Above and One Below. Darvish caught his breath in
admiration. *My little thief plays a better prince than I ever
could.*

Respectfully acknowledging a cluster of shaven-headed
priests, Aaron strolled into the third of the rooms. During
his last time in Tivolic, he had darkened his hair and skin
and used the Open Court to make a survey of possible prey.
A young woman back in the middle room used it for the
same purpose tonight. They had saluted each other warily
and continued their separate ways; after a certain level of
skill, the profession held no strangers. Tonight he needed

information so he became, for the men and women attending, a part of the experience of the Open Court. It didn't matter that they'd remember him, he wouldn't be working in Tivolic again.

Ignoring the guard, Aaron drifted to a window and looked up at the night sky. He took a deep breath and marked where the black edges of buildings blocked the stars. As he exhaled, he turned and continued his slow circuit, a possible route to the heart of the palace carefully filed away.

He skirted a pair of wizards, bowed to a shriveled old woman, who gazed after him in surprise, and tried to ignore his buzzing nerves. *I didn't used to have nerves.* He could feel Darvish following respectfully behind him. Nerves used to be buried with everything else, behind the wall. He hadn't realized things had gotten so bad. *I used to work alone.*

So far, no one had mentioned The Stone or Ischia although rumors of a war were rife and the merchants were grumbling of revolt should the king increase taxes to pay for it.

"The rooms are well filled tonight, Gracious Majesty."

"The rooms are always well filled for these One abandoned things," King Harith grunted, squinting through the spy hole. "I see Lord Fath is down there."

Lord Rahman bowed, in case the king could see him from the corner of an eye. "As you commanded, Sire."

"Well, he'd better be telling stirring tales of victory and honor, by the Nine, if he wants those land grants." He scowled at the distant figure of the young lord who appeared to be holding half the room enthralled. There was no way of knowing exactly what he was talking about, but it seemed to involve a great deal of arm waving, that the king supposed could represent sword thrusts. Lord Fath had been instructed to work on building popular sentiment for a war. The more volunteers he had from the merchant class, the more sons and daughters willing to put on a uniform for the glory of it, the more the parents would be willing to pay. His council would be ecstatic if he could take Cisali without the need to pay for mercenaries.

Grumbling under his breath, the king scanned the rest of the crowd. He was *not* looking forward to walking the length of the rooms and back. The Open Courts were a success. There'd been much less squawking about taxes since they'd begun, but he hated them with a passion. He never knew what to say.

Fortunately, I'm too good a king to allow my personal preference to outweigh the chance of getting this lot to cheerfully pay for a. . . . "Nine Above!"

"Gracious Majesty?"

"I wasn't calling *you,* Rahman. You always did think highly of yourself." He stepped away from the spy hole. "But as long as you're here, have a look at the young man standing under the wizard-lights."

Lord Rahman peered through the tiny aperture and clicked his tongue. "Very striking, Gracious Majesty," he agreed. "Hair that brilliant a color is rare."

"It's not just the color, Rahman." King Harith waved the elderly lord back to his place. "Look at how he holds himself." The king took his own advice. "Nine Above, but I'd be happy if my son had half that much presence."

"Your eldest son, Gracious Majesty, is but seven years old. And although the outlander does indeed have presence, he looks to me, Sire, as if a sharp blow could shatter him completely."

"Nonsense. He looks strong, in control . . . familiar." The king straightened up and frowned. "An outlander with hair like beaten copper. Why do I feel I should know him?"

Lord Rahman pulled reflectively on the pointed end of his short white beard. "An outlander," he murmured. "Hair like. . . ." He released his beard and bowed. "The thief that travels with Prince Darvish is an outlander with red hair, Gracious Majesty."

"Thief?" The king studied the outlander again. "He does fit the description at that. Nine Above, but the boy has balls, standing there as arrogant as you please. If this is the lad, I don't see Prince Darvish."

"No, Gracious Majesty, nor did I. And he would be very evident if he were here." Lord Rahman had met Cisali's third prince at the treaty wedding the year before. He had not been impressed by the drunken fop.

"Have the guards pick up this bold young thief, Rahman. Carefully though, we don't want to have to chase him through half the merchants in Tivolic. Oh, and Rahman." The old lord stopped, one hand on the door. "Have him brought to me here. I like his looks and I want to speak with him before he's executed."

* * *

Darvish was finding the evening easier than he'd expected. He had, after all, been playing a role at his father's court for years and hovering protectively was certainly less wearing than the contortions he went through in Ischia. Although he desperately desired a drink, he forced himself to approach that desire from the point of view of a private guard. *I am on duty. I cannot drink.* It helped. It made him feel like he had his life under control. *Maybe I should keep the job.* He hooked his thumbs in his sword belt. *I seem to be better at it than the one I was born to.*

He studied his reflection in an ornately framed wall mirror just as Aaron looked up and met his eyes in the glass. Darvish's heart lurched and he took an involuntary step forward.

Aaron felt caught, trapped; he couldn't look away. Nor was he sure he wanted to. Then his jaw dropped and whatever stretched between was shattered by the sudden realization that they were in serious trouble.

He spun on a heel and, with a jerk of his head indicating Darvish should follow, strode quickly for the exit, the length of three rooms away. *It may already be too late. . . .*

"What's his hurry?" asked a young matron, watching the outlander and his guard leave with some interest.

"Probably heading for a dark corner," her husband said suggestively, piling three oysters on a biscuit.

"But he's by himself," she protested.

Her husband, who had been close enough to see what had passed in the mirror, only grinned and reached for a pomegranate.

"Why are we leaving?" Darvish demanded in an undertone as they reached the first room and were slowed by the crowd still arriving. "We haven't learned anything yet."

"The king is about to walk the rooms," Aaron muttered, glaring down an elderly man who looked too curious. "He mustn't see you."

"He won't recognize me, Aaron." Darvish grabbed the smaller man by the shoulder and spun him around, not caring how it looked. They were walking away from their best chance to find The Stone. "Look at me, I still have Chandra's illusion on my eyes and I've grown a beard!"

"Look at yourself," Aaron snarled. "With brown eyes

and a beard you're a slightly larger image of the crown prince. I think he'll notice that!''

Darvish almost threw Aaron to one side, grabbed a silver tray from an astounded servant and held it up to his face. ''Bugger the Nine,'' he said softly. *After all those years of trying to belong, was this all it took; an illusion and a beard?* ''I didn't realize.'' He lowered the tray and shook his head. ''I never looked like any of them before.'' Breathing deeply, he managed a wry smile. ''As usual, my timing is impeccable. Let's get out of here.''

They were at the gate, a single guard between them and freedom, when a shout from the room behind told them that their leaving had not gone unnoticed.

''I don't care what warned them! Go after them!''

The gate guard turned at the shout, saw two men approaching, and lowered his pike to block their way.

Aaron broke into a run, twisted at the last second, and slithered eel-like between the pike and the wall. Darvish didn't bother trying to go around. He grabbed the haft of the weapon, yanked it from the guard's grip, and smacked him hard in the chest with the butt end. The guard slammed up against the wall and slid to the flagstones, gasping for breath.

Suddenly, every hair on Darvish's body rose and his skin crawled.

''The wards!'' Aaron shouted.

Cursing, Darvish dove forward just as the gate wards snapped into effect. He hit the ground, rolled, got to his feet, stumbled, and cursed again. His right foot had gone completely numb. Gritting his teeth, he broke into a staggering run. Fortunately, some feeling remained in his ankle; mostly pain, but that was better than no feeling at all. At least he retained some control.

''I wasn't quite fast enough,'' he grunted as Aaron dragged him off the brightly lit Avenue of the Palace and into the deep shadow of an ornate wall. He pounded his boot, trying to beat sensation back into the flesh it covered, and prayed for feeling to return. The pain spread down from his ankle. ''One Below,' he grunted, biting his lip at this answer to his prayer, ''you deal in mixed blessings at best.''

Aaron frowned as guards spilled out of the palace. Were they going to course blindly through the streets with no idea of the direction their quarry had taken? Then he growled wordlessly as the guards were joined by a robed Wizard of the Fourth. The ward. They could track Darvish by the ward.

Tersely, he explained the situation to the prince.

"So until the ward wears off. . . . It will wear off?" Aaron nodded and Darvish continued, "They know where we are?"

"Yes."

The wizard's hand was up and sweeping the avenue. At most, they had minutes remaining.

Darvish stood and deliberately put pressure on the foot. He couldn't feel the pavement under it. "What do we do?"

"We walk a path they can't follow. Can you climb?"

Darvish set his jaw. "I can do anything I have to."

He wasn't so sure of that two gardens and a rooftop later as he followed Aaron along an uneven ledge half a brick wide. It wasn't so much the width of the ledge, it was the two-story drop should his scraped fingers lose their grip. He reached for a new hold and lifted himself forward in an awkward hop, dragging his numb foot along the wall. Another two hops and he ran out of brick.

"Aaron?"

"Shh!"

The admonishment came from below. Darvish squinted under the curve of his shoulder and saw Aaron standing on a balcony one story down and five feet across open air, gesturing at him to jump. "Forget it," he muttered, searching for an alternative. There didn't appear to be one.

Two gardens, a rooftop, and the One abandoned ledge away, he could hear a woman's voice—the wizard?—yelling, "Go up, I said! Then go around, but don't let them get away!"

"I definitely need a drink." He dangled for a moment on one arm and then with a combination of brute strength and luck, managed to turn so that his back pressed against the wall. *It's not far,* he thought, looking down at Aaron and blinking sweat from his eyes. *I could just fall forward and not miss it.*

Muttering a brief prayer to the Nine and One, he jumped.

He hit the balcony standing, then dropped to his hands and knees, biting back a cry as the warded foot shot daggers of fire all the way up to his hip. Aaron pulled him erect and he leaned on the thief's shoulder for a heartbeat, catching his breath. As the pain faded, he realized he could feel the brick through both soles.

"Good," Aaron whispered when told. "The ward is fading. Stay close." And he sped, a silent shadow, down the length of the balcony.

Stay close. Darvish shuffled after him as quietly as he was able. *And all this time I thought he didn't have a sense of humor.*

One of the louvered doors swung slowly open and he froze.

Rubbing her eyes, a little girl of no more than five wandered out onto the balcony. She saw him and stopped. "I heard noises," she told him sleepily.

"Everything's under control, little Mistress." Darvish forced his voice to remain low and soothing. "Go back to bed."

Her lower lip went out. "Will you tell me what happened in the morning?"

He smiled. "If you go back to bed now."

"Promise?"

He hated to make a promise he couldn't keep. "I promise."

She nodded, satisfied, and padded back inside.

Darvish gently pushed the door shut and hurried to catch up with Aaron, his heart pounding so loudly he was sure it must wake the rest of the household. He leaned forward and placed his mouth close to the other man's ear. "She must have thought I was one of her father's guards."

Aaron, all too aware of warm breath against the side of his head, pulled a little away. "If her father has guards," he said quietly, "I suggest we leave."

Darvish looked at the iron pipe running to the roof. "Up that?"

Aaron nodded.

"Will it hold my weight?"

Teeth glimmered briefly in the darkness as Aaron smiled. "It should."

It did, but only just.

Darvish's foot had regained almost all feeling when Aaron suddenly dropped flat on the narrow top of a crumbling wall. Darvish dropped as well and then inched forward until he could grasp Aaron's ankle. "What's wrong?" he hissed.

They were in a poorer neighborhood now, looking down into a narrow yard that stretched behind a row of tenements.

"They've cut down the tree that used to be here," Aaron said tightly. "We need it to get up there, to that row of balconies."

Darvish tightened his grip on Aaron's ankle until the thief turned to glare at him. He let go and smiled. "I don't think I'm up to scrambling through a tree anyway. Why don't we take our chances on the ground?"

Aaron studied the yard. It was completely enclosed, and the buildings facing it were quiet. It might be safe. He nodded, slid over to hang his full length, and dropped noiselessly to a clear patch of packed dirt.

Breathing a prayer of relief, Darvish followed. He'd had quite enough of the high roads of the city. Straightening, he unstrapped his sword from his back and buckled the belt about his waist where it belonged. The familiar weight reassured him as he crept after Aaron through piles of debris. They'd gone half the length of the yard when he noticed he was walking normally. His foot tingled faintly and then that, too, was gone.

"Aaron," he called softly.

A low growl answered and from out of the darkness stalked the biggest dog he'd ever seen.

"Aaron?" Darvish backed away slowly.

Stiff-legged, the dog followed.

"I see it," Aaron said quietly from behind him. "Keep coming, there's a gate in the far wall."

Darvish risked a glance back over his shoulder. The far wall was a considerable distance away. His hand dropped to his sword hilt. He didn't want to kill the dog and he wouldn't if he could avoid it. They were the intruders, after all. "Aaron, give me your vest." Slowly, very slowly, he reached back. There was a rustle of silk and then the fabric touched his hand. He got a good grip and just as slowly brought his arm forward again.

The dog growled louder and charged.

As the dog's feet left the ground, Darvish flung the full folds of the vest in its face. Even braced, he staggered as the massive front paws hit his chest, scrabbling through the silk. Wrapping the fabric around forelegs and head, he heaved the dog as far as he was able. It wasn't far.

Wondering how one dog could make so much noise, he turned and ran.

Aaron reached the gate and yanked back the latch, diving through into a pungent alleyway. Darvish charged through seconds later and together they pushed the heavy wooden barricade closed and held it as it trembled and shook under the big dog's charges. The gate bowed and jerked about like a live thing, but they finally managed to slam the latch down again.

"Not much point in being quiet," Darvish shouted above the frenzied barking. The neighborhood was coming awake around them. "The ward has worn off."

"Then let's head home," Aaron panted, wiping a smear of dirt off his jaw.

"There they are, by the dog!" The mouth of the alley filled with guards.

As one, they spun and took off in the other direction. Down the alley, across the street, and, out of sight for the moment, down another alley so tiny it barely deserved the name. It ended in a blank wall.

"Bugger the Nine! Trapped!" Darvish spun around and drew his sword. They could only come at him one at a time. There were worse places to make a stand.

"Dar! Through here!"

What he had taken to be shadow was a narrow passage-way between the wall and the building it joined, where the soft bricks had rotted and crumbled away.

"The guards are in heavy leather," Aaron explained as he slid into the darkness. "They can't follow."

"Aaron," Darvish assumed it was exhaustion. Things weren't funny enough to merit the laugh he couldn't contain, "*I* can't follow. Even without heavy leathers."

They could hear the guards on the street, coming closer.

Darvish turned again to face them, then half turned back, his eye caught by a glimmer of light. A door, set flush with the alley wall, almost invisible.

"Aaron, what's through there."

Aaron frowned. "The tavern we passed. But there's people . . ."

Darvish grinned. "Oh, I know there's people." He sheathed his sword and pulled the thief forward. "Now it's your turn to follow me."

The cook almost killed them when they burst into the

kitchen, but Darvish wrapped an arm around her ample
waist, whispered something in her ear, and moments later
they were slipping out into the common room, two handfuls
of ash having dimmed the brilliance of Aaron's hair.

"Can you get your hands on a sword and two sunrobes?
One for each of us?" Darvish murmured scanning the noisy
crowd; laborers for the most part, a few outlanders, and
one or two off duty sword-for-hires, all well primed. From
where they stood, he could see at least three arguments tottering on the brink.

Completely out of his depth, Aaron nodded. "What will
you be doing?" he asked.

Darvish rubbed his hands together and looked positively
gleeful. "Keeping the guard busy," he said. Then he walked
across to the biggest, loudest man in the place, tapped him
on the shoulder, and, when he turned, punched him in the
stomach.

A few moments later he pulled himself out of the melee
and met Aaron by the door. Aaron ducked a flying stool and
handed over the larger of the two sunrobes.

"Put the sword on," Darvish told him, shrugging into
the filthy garment.

"Guard!" bellowed the tavern keeper. "Guard!"

Beginning to understand, Aaron obeyed, covering his own
clothes with the other stained robe.

"Now, then. . . ." Setting his teeth, Darvish picked up
two mugs of wine that had miraculously remained un-
spilled. He looked down at them for a heartbeat, then
squared his shoulders and threw the contents of one in Aaron's face and the other in his own.

"Shall we?" he bellowed, over the sound of a table splin-
tering into kindling.

Aaron nodded. He could hardly believe Darvish had done
what he'd just done. Given the cravings he knew the wine fumes
must be prodding awake, he'd never seen anything braver.

Arm in arm, they staggered into the street.

They were two buildings away, helping each other stum-
ble home, when the guard ran past them without a second
look.

With the door barely closed behind them, the lamp flame
still flickering in the draft, Darvish began stripping off his
clothes. He couldn't endure the wine smell a moment lon-

ger. They'd tossed the sunrobes over a convenient wall on the way back to The Gallows, but his shirt, and even his pants, still reeked and every breath reminded him of how long it had been since he'd had a drink. Naked, he walked to the window and threw the bundle out. They could get him new clothes in the morning; he couldn't stand to have those in the room.

His hands were scraped raw, his right ankle throbbed with every movement, he ached in muscles he didn't know he had, they were no closer to finding The Stone . . . *and all I can think of is how much I want a drink.* He braced his arm against the window frame and let his head fall forward. *One Below, but I am a disgusting excuse for a man.*

He heard the connecting door open and straightened up. The last thing Aaron needed to see was him feeling sorry for himself.

"Well," he said, turning, "you certainly know how to show a fellow a good. . . ." Then he caught sight of the look on Aaron's face. "What is it? Is something wrong with Chandra?"

"No." Aaron's voice was as emotionless as Darvish had ever heard it. "She's sleeping."

"Then what? What's wrong?" He watched as Aaron crossed stiffly to the smaller bed and sat down, then he walked over to stand beside him. "What is it?"

"It's nothing. I'm just tired." Aaron grabbed at the end of his shirt and went to pull it over his head, but the thin silk stuck against his chest.

Darvish squatted to get a better look and sucked his breath in through his teeth. The red-brown patterns he had thought embroidery were actually blood. "You've reopened your scars," he said softly. The fabric had dried into the wounds.

"It's nothing," Aaron repeated, yanked the shirt up over his head, and threw it across the room. A muscle jumped in his jaw, but that was his only reaction as the dried blood tore free and fresh began to run red against the pallor of his chest. The scars were an ugly inflamed purple. The skin had cracked in four places.

"Nine Above, are you out of your mind?" Still crouched at Aaron's feet, Darvish twisted and stretched a long arm back for the pitcher of water. Dragging Aaron's old sunrobe off the end of the bed, he tore off a strip, moistened it, and reached for Aaron's chest.

"No." Aaron struck his hand away.

"Don't be stupid, Aaron, you're covered in blood."

"It doesn't matter."

"It matters to me." Darvish reached out again and when Aaron lifted his hand to push him back, he grabbed it. They grappled for a moment, and then Aaron yanked his wrist free and tried to rise. Darvish pushed him back.

"What's wrong with you?"

Aaron grimaced. "You could have died out there and it would have been my fault!"

Darvish sat back on his heels. "What are you talking about?"

"In the alley. The crack. I should have known you wouldn't fit."

Darvish reached out and shook the younger man gently by one thin shoulder. "Aaron, you are not responsible for my size. Now, please, sit still and let me take care of this." When Aaron made no protest, he began to wipe away the streaks of red. "You don't *have* to live in pain," he murmured lightly, then froze as something warm and wet dripped onto the back of his hand.

Aaron began to tremble as another tear fell. And then another. He couldn't stop them.

"Aaron, what is it?"

Aaron fought for control and lost. "I always fail the ones I. . . ." Desperately, he caught the last word.

"You let the old pain rule your life, Aaron, my lad."

"Faharra?" He could see the old lady as she lay dead on her couch, her eyes staring forever into darkness.

"You let the old pain rule your life."

"No. . . ."

"Aaron, please, tell me what's wrong."

The pain in Darvish's voice drove through the last of the walls and they came crashing down.

"Ruth!" Aaron slid forward onto his knees and cried as he had not been able to cry for five long years.

Tears streaming down his own face, although he had no idea why, Darvish gathered the slim body close and held it safe. Slowly, a word at a time, the story came out.

Aaron had fought all his life to live up to his father, Clan Chief, warrior, a man whose strength of body and will was legend. Then, at thirteen, he fell in love with his cousin, Ruth, and fighting and mayhem didn't seem as important any more. His father, disapproving, promised Ruth to a Clan Chief three times her age who had used up and buried two wives already. She ran to Aaron for comfort. He gave it. His father caught them together.

Damaged goods could not be given to a fellow Clan Chief. As a warning to the other women of the keep, Aaron's father beat her to death in the courtyard. Aaron, on his knees, his uncle's hand in his hair, was forced to watch the entire thing.

"She screamed my name until the screaming stopped. . . ."

Then his father had presented the bloody whip and demanded Aaron kiss it and reswear his allegiance.

"I couldn't. I vomited. He pushed me down in it and called me no son of his. I left the keep that night and have been no son of his ever since."

Darvish tightened his grip and Chandra, who had been standing silently in the connecting doorway, stepped back at the look on his face.

"It wasn't your fault," he whispered, his voice a soft contrast to the expression of murderous rage that twisted his features. "It wasn't your fault."

"I failed her. I failed Faharra. I failed you." *If I am not my father's son, what am I? What is left?*

"What could you have done for her? Died with her? Wouldn't she rather know you lived? And as to Faharra, you were betrayed. You didn't fail her. And believe me, Aaron, you *did not* fail me."

Wrapped in the warm haven of Darvish's arms, he had to believe the last. And if that was true, perhaps the rest of what Darvish said was true as well. Perhaps. He shuddered and sighed.

Darvish felt him relax and, greatly daring, brought one hand up to stroke the copper hair.

Chandra propped the damaged door closed and, wiping her cheeks dry, climbed thoughtfully back into bed. In her opinion, the best thing for both of them now would be to admit how each felt about the other and go on together from there.

They wouldn't.

Men.

She threw herself back on the pillow, heard again the raw pain spilling out in Aaron's voice, and had a quiet cry.

Fifteen

"It's an ugly city up close, too." Chandra leaned against her window frame and frowned out at the morning. She could hear the rumble of wooden wheels against cobblestones and the musical call of the water seller as he made his rounds through the streets below. Breezes were heavy with the scent of fresh baked bread and her stomach grumbled in response. The sky was a brilliant azure blue and the light had the kind of clarity that comes only early in the day.

But the buildings were still a muddy yellow brick and besides, she wanted to be home. She missed her tower. She missed her studies. She missed her garden. She even missed Aba and being taken care of so thoroughly that she never had to consider the day to day business of living.

And she missed her father. She had realized it lying sleeplessly in the dark, wanting him to come and make everything all right.

Except he couldn't. She realized that in the cold light of day. He was only her father, and a man, and nothing he could do would make the situation they were in any better.

But, oh, it hurt to let go of the idea that he could.

She combed through her hair with her fingers and brought it forward to braid. *He was only her father, and a man.*

"Good, you're up." Darvish stood in the doorway to his and Aaron's chamber, one hand preventing the abused door from crashing back against the wall, the other clutching the folds of Aaron's old sunrobe where it was wrapped around his waist. "I wonder if you could do me a favor?"

Chandra, her hands still busy with the pattern of her braid, lifted her eyebrows in silent inquiry.

"The new clothes. . . ." Darvish felt his face flush under her regard. He hadn't thought himself still capable of blushing. "I, uh, threw them out the window last night and I, uh, was wondering if you'd go talk to the tavern boy about getting more.''

"You threw them out the window?" Obviously interesting things had been going on before Aaron's wailing cry to his cousin had awakened her.

"It's a long story."

Chandra smiled pleasantly and crossed the room to perch cross-legged on the end of her bed. "I think I deserve to hear it," she pointed out. "Unless it's," she paused significantly, "personal."

Darvish finally managed to force the door upright on its own. "It's not personal," he sighed, getting a better grip on the sunrobe. "It's just long."

Chandra waited patiently, looking as expectant as she knew how.

"Oh, all right." He crossed to the window and squinted out. Chandra obviously planned on staying right where she was until he told all. "King Harith was holding an Open Court. . . ."

The catalog of the previous night's disasters didn't go as badly as Darvish had expected. To his surprise, he found Chandra an attentive and intelligent listener, perhaps the best he'd ever had. She interrupted seldom with questions and when she did they were always to clarify a point he'd missed or skimmed over.

". . . and after I threw them out the window, Aaron. . . ." He paused and took a deep breath. "Aaron," he tried again, but anger rose up and choked off the words.

"It's all right." She reached out and grabbed his elbow, stopping his staccato pacing. "I heard that part." She shrugged, apologetically; Wizards of the Nine did not eavesdrop. "He called out rather loudly."

Darvish met her eyes, nodded once—an unconscious echo of Aaron's minimalist body language—and threw himself beside her on the bed, somehow managing to maintain sunrobe and dignity. "It's a real pity," he ground the words out as if he was grinding an edge onto his blade, "that I'll never have the chance to meet Aaron's father so I can kill the One abandoned son-of-a-bitch."

"I'd thought that myself," Chandra told him, blinking rapidly to clear the tears from her eyes.

"Hey." Darvish reached up a large finger and traced the

moist path down her cheek. "I thought Wizards of the Nine didn't cry?"

Chandra jerked her head away and scowled. For the second time in maybe eight years, for the second time that morning, Darvish felt his face flush. "I'm sorry," he said. "Sometimes I'm a facetious jerk."

"Sometimes," Chandra agreed, throwing her braid behind her shoulder. When she thought she could speak without a betraying quaver in her voice, she asked, "Is Aaron okay?"

"He's still asleep. I thought he should sleep as long as he could."

There were dark shadows under Darvish's eyes, but Chandra didn't mention them. She remembered what she'd last seen as she'd slipped back into the darkness of her own room; Aaron cradled in the protective circle of Darvish's arms and Darvish's mouth pressed against the copper hair. She felt her cheeks growing hot and she stirred uncomfortably.

"No," Darvish told her softly. He had a pretty good idea of what she was thinking.

"Actually," she said, realizing it as she spoke, "I didn't think you would. You wouldn't take advantage of his vulnerability like that. He needed a friend, not a lover."

Darvish stared at the girl in silence for a moment and wondered if she knew the compliment she had just paid him. No one at court, from his most exalted father to the most supercilious noble would have doubted for a moment that he'd taken Aaron to his bed. Tears burned behind his lids and he tossed his head to clear them away. "Thank you," he said at last.

She sensed what it meant to him, smiled self-consciously, and lightly touched his hand. "I'll go see about getting you some clothes." Unfolding her legs, she slipped off the bed and sped out of the room.

A few moments later, she was back.

Darvish, still seated where'd she'd left him, looked up in surprise. "That was fast."

She bit her lip and looked sheepish. "We, uh, we forgot about money."

Darvish looked momentarily blank. "Money?"

One Below, we're going to save Ischia and we don't know how to buy breakfast? "Wizards of the Nine," Chandra managed, before she collapsed against the door, helpless with giggles, ''don't . . . worry . . . about money.'' It wasn't *that* funny, but she couldn't seem to stop laughing.

Darvish grinned and shook his head. ''Neither do princes, obviously.'' He stood, made a last minute save of the sun-robe, and headed for the other room. ''Good thing we're traveling with a thief.''

''Good thing,'' Chandra agreed, wiping her eyes and managing to achieve a shaky control.

Wizards of the Nine don't laugh at themselves either, Darvish thought with satisfaction, and he paused on the threshold. ''Chandra, why don't you want your cousin to inherit? Is he an evil man?''

''No.'' Although she had no idea where it came from—she hadn't thought of her cousin in a nineday or more—she tried to answer the question. ''He's just a, well, a man.'' She frowned. Admitting that, the next step was easier. ''It's not that he'd do a bad job, exactly, it's just that . . . that. . . .'' She clutched at air, searching for the words.

''That he wouldn't do as good a job as you would?''

''Well. . . .'' Her chin rose defiantly. ''Yes.''

Darvish smiled and, leaving the confused wizard to puzzle over their last exchange, went into the other room to look for Aaron's belt pouch.

''A thousand pardons, Gracious Lord.''

Lord Balin waved his guards back and studied the pudgy merchant who, racing along the docks, had almost slammed into him. ''It's of little importance,'' he assured the man. ''No harm was done.''

The merchant stopped bobbing obeisances. ''Thank you, Gracious Lord.'' He wiped a sweating forehead with a handkerchief so heavily scented with lime that even from a distance it overcame the fish and salt and tar smell of Ischia harbor, then shuffled impatiently, waiting for the foreign lord to move on.

The foreign lord stayed right where he was. ''Where were you heading in such a hurry?''

''A ship, my lord. I have passage on a ship.''

Lord Balin frowned. There were a great many ships in the harbor that seemed to be loading the citizens of Ischia as cargo. ''You're leaving the city, then?''

''Only for a time, Gracious Lord.'' He glanced up at the

taller man, saw interest, and almost visibly swelled. "There
is a rumor, Gracious Lord," he confided, "that The Stone
is missing and Prince Darvish has been sent after it."

"Surely you are too astute a man to listen to rumor,"
Lord Balin said evenly, neither voice nor face giving any
indication of the sudden fear clamped around his heart.
*Chandra. If The Stone is missing and Darvish gone after it,
where is my daughter?*

"Ah, my lord, but there are facts as well." He began
counting them off on heavily ringed fingers. "All platforms
to the Lady—the volcano, Gracious Lord, we call her the
Lady—are closed, not only the public ones, but I have a
nephew, a priest, who tells me that temple platforms are
closed as well—and there are wizards on all of them. A
great cloud of smoke—you can't see it from here, Gracious
Lord—hangs over the palace and the temple and begins to
move down over the nobles' townhouses. My nephew is
certain that the temple suite Lord Darvish is said to be in
is empty. And most telling of all, Gracious Lord, the earth
has moved. Not once, but twice."

"Is there panic?"

"Not yet, Gracious Lord, for His Most Exalted Majesty
and His Royal Highness Prince Shahin, the Heir, are still
in the palace and the people feel if they remain. . . ." He
waved his hands, unable to articulate exactly what the people felt. "But if the earth moves again, Gracious Lord. . . .
You have not picked a good time to visit Ischia." He flushed
as he realized his last words might have been thought to be
a criticism. "Begging your pardon, Gracious Lord."

Lord Balin waved a silent dismissal and watched the
pudgy man scurry thankfully away. Then he turned and
looked thoughtfully up the steep slope of the city to where
the white marble of the palace gleamed in the sunlight. He
had sent no word that he was coming, not did he now wear
any visible insignia showing his name or rank. He wanted
to storm into the throne room and demand his daughter
but. . . .

"We walk," he said to the four guards he'd brought from
the ship.

Silently, they moved into formation around him.

By the time Lord Balin reached the last set of terraces
leading to the palace, he could see the smoke. Half expecting thick black clouds, he was relieved to see it was no more

than a thin haze. And he was dismayed to see it at all. The city, if not panicked, certainly seethed on the edge and it would take very little to turn the questions and confusion into riot. Business seemed to go on as usual, despite rumors, but the mood felt brittle and likely to shatter at any moment.

He personally didn't care if the entire country sank into the sea, as long as he found his daughter first.

A small crowd stood in clumps scattered about the square before the palace. Fruit and candy vendors wandered among them, and a juggler, perched on the steps of the central fountain, threw four daggers and a pomegranate in a glittering cascade.

As Lord Balin entered the square, the conversations closest to him stopped and the silence spread out behind him like a banner. His dress, his bearing, his guards, proclaimed him noble; it didn't matter that he wasn't of Cisali. Even the juggler caught his knives and stood quietly watching.

"Gracious Lord!" A woman's voice stopped him at the palace gate. "Is it true? Has The Stone been taken? Are we all going to die?"

Her questions hung in the hot air like the haze of smoke and Lord Balin thought for an instant that the smell of sulfur had grown stronger. These were not his people, but they were people and they deserved an answer. If he could not give them the truth, neither would he add to the tensions.

"Your king," he said, half turning to face the square, "remains. And *I* have just arrived."

"But, Gracious Lord, they say. . . ."

"*They* say a great many foolish things." He forced a smile. "I try not to believe what *they* say."

As he passed through the gate, he heard the babble of conversation rise again and he wondered how much longer such wordplay would suffice.

An official of the court stood by the gate guard, an ingratiating smile plastered across her broad face. "Gracious Lord," she intoned bowing slightly, "that was very well done. You are. . . ?"

"Lord Atam Balin." He stretched out his left hand with the heavy gold signet. "I wish to see your king."

The bow was repeated, much deeper. "Gracious Lord, if we had but known. Your messenger. . . ."

"I sent no messenger. I am not here for ceremony. I wish to see your king." His tone added, *Don't make me repeat this a third time.*

"Lord Balin."

The official started at the voice and dropped to one knee.

"My most exalted father is unavailable at the moment," Shahin continued, stepping forward. "Perhaps I would do instead?"

Sometime later, behind the closed doors of the crown prince's suite, Shahin shook his head and said quietly, "I don't know where she is, but as far as I know she never made it to the palace. I'm sorry."

Lord Balin felt the blood drain away from his face and the world went dark. *She never made it to the palace. . . .* Strong hands on his shoulders guided him into a chair. *She never made it to the palace. . . .* Unresponsive fingers were wrapped about a metal goblet. *She never made it to the palace. . . .*

"Drink," a voice commanded.

He drank and, slowly, the world came back. With a steady hand, although the knuckles were white, he set the goblet carefully on the small table beside his chair and stood. "You have been most helpful, Your Royal Highness, but as I must now search elsewhere for my daughter, I must leave and begin."

"Wait." Shahin studied the older man for a moment and came to a suddenly decision. "You say your daughter is a wizard. Could she have come and gone again unseen?"

He offered hope and Lord Balin grabbed for it. "She could have. She's very powerful."

"The day your daughter would have arrived to speak with my brother, he left to search for The Stone of Ischia."

Lord Balin sat down again. "Then the rumors are true."

Shahin nodded. "They are."

"Where. . . ?"

"To Tivolic, the Ytaili capital."

"Then I must go after. . . ." His voice trailed off.

Shahin remained silent while Lord Balin thought, watching the man's expression as he turned possibilities over in his mind.

"No one must know," he said at last. "If the people of the city discover it, the panic will destroy Ischia as surely as the volcano. The Prince Darvish goes to Ytaili to recover

The Stone in secret to prevent war between the two countries, which would again destroy Ischia as surely as the volcano. If I sail in to Tivolic, demanding my daughter, I could, myself, be responsible for destroying Ischia.'' He passed a shaking hand over his face and looked up at Shahin pleadingly. ''Can I at least be sure that she was with him?''

''I remember the day well, Your Royal Highness,'' Oham's voice was impassive.

''Before your prince went into the temple, did a young woman visit him in his rooms?''

''No, Your Royal Highness.''

''The young woman is a wizard,'' Lord Balin broke in. ''She would have been disguised in some way.''

''I do not remember any visitors that afternoon, Gracious Lord.''

''Your Royal Highness?''

Shahin looked down at the young dresser kneeling trembling by Oham's side. ''What is it?''

''I don't remember that afternoon at all.''

Oham stiffened. ''Please excuse him, Your Royal Highness.''

''You don't understand, Your Royal Highness. I remember that morning. And that evening.'' Fadi's voice cracked under the stress. He blushed and went on. ''But I have no memory of the afternoon at all.''

Shahin turned to Lord Balin. ''Could Chandra do this?''

''Yes.'' The word was almost lost in the great sigh of relief.

''Thank you both. You may go.''

Oham rose fluidly off his knees at the crown prince's dismissal and began backing from the room, but Fadi stayed a moment longer.

''Gracious Lord?''

Lord Balin looked down into the boy's dark eyes and surprisingly found comfort in his expression. ''Yes?''

''You needn't worry about your daughter, Gracious Lord. If she's with Prince Darvish, he'll keep her safe. He's . . . I mean. . . .'' Suddenly overcome by confusion, Fadi stammered into silence.

Lord Balin lightly touched his hair. ''Thank you,'' he said softly.

As close to scarlet as a young man of his complexion could get, Fadi backed quickly from the room.

"You are, of course, welcome to stay," Shahin told him, "until they return. Of course, if they don't return," he spread his hands helplessly, "you're welcome to die with the rest of us. Your own people, might prefer that you live."

"I don't know your brother, Prince Shahin, but I'll take that boy's opinion over some I've heard. It takes a special kind of man to inspire love like that. And you, Prince Shahin, don't know my daughter." Lord Balin's head went up proudly. "She's a Wizard of the Nine and I choose to believe that between the two of them, you'll get your Stone back. I *will* be here when she returns."

Shahin smiled. It had been so long since he'd done it, it felt strange on his face. "There's more to the story."

Lord Balin nodded. "There always is. You can tell me while we wait for your most exalted father to see me."

"Prince Shahin takes much upon himself."

"I am glad he told me, Most Exalted. His story keeps me from blundering in and destroying your carefully laid plans."

King Jaffar's eyes narrowed, but he couldn't deny the truth of what Lord Balin said. "A hue and cry raised for your missing daughter would certainly attract unwanted attention," he admitted.

"As I understand what is happening, I am willing to wait here, quietly."

"Surely, Gracious Lord," the lord chancellor stepped forward, his brow creased, "you will return home. Your people will need you. You can await your daughter there without the danger of dying with Ischia."

Lord Balin studied the lord chancellor for a long moment. "I know what my daughter is capable of, Lord Chancellor, and I do not think she and your Prince Darvish will fail. Your counsel leads me to believe you fear otherwise. I wonder, given those fears, why *you* stay?"

"I remain by the side of my king." The lord chancellor bowed deeply toward the throne.

"Would it not make more sense for you to escort your king to safety, from which he may continue to rule in health no matter what happens here?"

"My king chooses to remain with his people."

"Enough." King Jaffar leaned forward and both men returned their attention to him. "You are no subject of mine, Lord Balin, and I will not command you as though you were. If you wish to await your daughter's return here in Ischia, my palace is at your disposal. You will, of course, remain silent about The Stone."

"I will, of course, Most Exalted." Lord Balin watched the lord chancellor, hands tucked within the sleeves of his robe, move back to stand behind the rosewood throne. "And I hope my continued presence will help to reassure the people of Ischia that all is well."

King Jaffar almost smiled. "That had occurred to me." Then his face grew hard again. "Prince Shahin is not presently in grace with the throne. It would be best if you spend little time with him."

Lord Balin inclined his head. "I hear your words, Most Exalted."

"Well?" Prince Shahin asked, offering the older man a drink. He'd made it very clear that he expected his servants to be busy elsewhere while he and Lord Balin talked.

Nodding his thanks, Lord Balin accepted the goblet. "If the lord chancellor was a little fatter," he sighed wearily, "you could drop him into the volcano and solve most of your problems with a single stroke."

"You have sent a message to the wizard?"

"Yes, Gracious Majesty. The Most Wise Palaton has been informed that Prince Darvish and the thief are in the city."

"I want those two found, Lord Rahman."

The elderly lord spread his hands. "The patrols continue to search, Gracious Majesty, but Tivolic is a large city and if the young thief has friends amongst his kind. . . ."

King Harith drummed his fingers on the arm of his throne. "His kind," he snorted. "Offer a purse of gold and a full pardon to anyone who gives information leading to their capture and that should take care of *his kind*."

"I'm sorry. I can't. It hurts."

Darvish reached out and shook Chandra's shoulder gently. "Hey, it's all right. With the beard gone I don't look like Shahin anymore and with the illusion on my eyes I don't look like me. I'll be fine."

Chandra lifted her face up out of her hands and glared at him. "You'll be fine? What if I can never focus power again?"

"Don't worry," Darvish said reassuringly. "We'll come up with another way to get The Stone."

"I'm not talking about The Stone, you overmuscled moron! I'm talking about me!" Her voice cracked on the last word and she buried her face again. *I'm not going to cry. I'm not!* She hadn't cried when trying to change Darvish's appearance had sent her writhing to the floor in pain and she wasn't going to cry now.

"You just need time to heal," Aaron said calmly. "Consider the violence of the attack you survived. Is it any wonder you still have a few open wounds?"

"It'll get better?" Chandra was heartily embarrassed to hear the quaver in her voice.

"If you stop picking the scab off it."

"That's disgusting, Aaron." His right shoulder lifted slightly and fell in a minimal shrug and she managed a weak smile. This brown-haired, brown-skinned, brown-clothed little man with Aaron's voice and Aaron's manner would take some getting used to. Walnut stain; she studied him critically. Aaron managed without power. And Dar . . . well, Dar managed, too, more or less. So she couldn't focus power for the moment. Her legs and her brain still worked fine. She pulled a long breath in and out through her nose and got briskly to her feet. "Well," she said. "Let's go."

On the stairs, when she'd bounded down out of earshot, Darvish murmured, "You made her feel a lot better. I didn't know you knew so much about wizards and power."

"I don't."

"You don't? You lied?"

"I made her feel a lot better, remember?"

Darvish couldn't think of anything to say to that, so they descended the remainder of the stairs in silence.

"Well?" Aaron asked as they caught up to Chandra on the street. "Where to?" Darvish had said he had a plan and Aaron was glad of it. He wasn't up to planning; he felt as if his life had been suspended somehow, cut loose and floating. He felt very exposed. To his relief, Darvish and Chandra had treated him no differently when he'd finally staggered out of bed, heavy-eyed and tired after a dream-filled and restless night. He couldn't have borne it if they'd offered sympathy or comfort. He didn't need either. He needed them unchanged and he needed time to convince himself that he didn't have to carry the guilt for Ruth's death any longer. It wasn't going to be easy to let that go.

"We're going down toward the harbor," Darvish explained, squinting into the setting sun and flipping up the hood of his sunrobe. "I'm looking for a wineshop."

"Why?" Chandra asked, peering out from under the stiffened brim of her own hood.

For a moment, Darvish heard not, "Why?" but, "Going to drink yourself into a stupor?" which is what the question would have meant in Ischia. Then he realized, if Chandra asked, she wanted to know. If she meant something else, she wouldn't bother with sarcasm.

"I'm going to find myself." He smiled the old self-mocking grin that had put any number of hearts at court in a flutter. Chandra's didn't appear to be fluttering.

"I beg your pardon?"

"Not me, exactly. But someone like me. A younger son with too much time on his hands and nothing to do, no place to belong. But wanting to belong so badly he's willing to play the part they set out for him of drunkard and fool."

Her face softened with sympathy. "Now that you know that," she said, reaching out and briefly squeezing his hand, "you can stop."

The grin grew a little sad but no less self-mocking. "Chandra, I *always* knew it."

They didn't travel all the way to the harbor but to the street just back of the docks and warehouses where the sailors and dock workers went to spend their pay. A thousand exotic things were for sale there, from silks to spices to an hour's pleasure, and buyers and sellers haggled cheerfully at the top of their lungs. Aaron could understand why Darvish went to the Ischia equivalent rather than stay at court. At least here if he were a drunkard and a fool it was because he *was* a drunkard and a fool and not because the people expected him to act as one.

"Any particular wineshop?" Chandra wanted to know, her head swiveling from side to side as she tried to see everything at once.

Darvish shrugged. "It doesn't matter. He'll be in one of them."

"Will he be able to help?" Aaron asked as they plunged into the crowds.

"He may not know where The Stone is, but I guarantee he'll know something that will lead us to it. Gossip and speculation are a favored pastime at court and no one thinks to watch their tongue around his type."

Aaron nodded thoughtfully. He'd seen that himself during the short time he'd been with Darvish in the palace. He opened his mouth to ask another question, then snapped it shut as he closed his hand about a small wrist whose fingers were attempting to dip into his belt pouch. The failed pickpocket, a skinny, sexless child of no more than seven was pale with terror under the dirt but knew better than to attract attention by fighting to get free.

"I didn't mean nothin'," it squeaked.

Aaron stared at the small thief for a number of heartbeats, then said, "You should have waited until the crowd ran interference for you." With his free hand he reached into the pouch and flipped a Ytaili silver wheel into the air. The coin flashed once in the sunlight, then a grubby hand shot out and it disappeared. Aaron released the wrist he still held and the child scrambled away.

"No honor amongst thieves?" Darvish asked.

"None," Aaron snorted and his expression added, *Don't bother me about it.*

"*You're too good a thief, Aaron, my lad.*"

"*Not now, Faharra. Please.*"

"There!" Darvish stopped suddenly, a hand on each of his companions' shoulders. "He's just turned onto the street, short man, slender, in bright green and gold."

"I see him," Chandra said.

Aaron nodded.

Although the sun had not yet set, the young man was weaving as he made his way down the street. He tossed long dark curls back off his face, smiled charmingly, and greeted everyone as if they were friends of his heart he had been too long parted from.

Which, Darvish mused, *was entirely possible.*

They watched as he made his way into one of the less reputable looking wineshops, passing by the tiny patio and its kicked in the corner piles of debris for the dark and secret interior. His pair of guards, not bothering to hide either their boredom or their disapproval, followed.

"He's just a kid," Chandra murmured. "I wonder who he is?"

"We should know," Darvish agreed. "Wait here." It only took him a moment to find out; the whores were well acquainted with the young man. "He's the king's nephew. Too close to the throne to be allowed his own life. Too far to have any sort of official duties."

"And by encouraging this," Chandra's wave took in the whores, the wineshop, "it keeps him unable to build a power base."

Both men turned to look at her in some surprise.

"I *am* my father's heir," she pointed out sharply.

As they moved toward the wineshop, Darvish felt his shoulders begin to tense. They reached the edge of the patio, and the smell of the place hit him, not just the wine but the sweat and the smoke and the close dark comfort of it.

"I can't go in there." The muscles of his shoulders and back were tied in painful knots. His teeth were clenched so tightly his ears ached.

Aaron slipped an arm under Darvish's elbow and got him moving again. To hesitate, to appear weak in this neighborhood invited trouble. He steered the unresponsive prince between two buildings and into a quiet alley, then he let go and stepped back.

Darvish managed a shaky grin and jerked his hands up through his hair. "Sorry." He gulped in great lungfuls of the fetid air, which at least didn't smell like his past. "I—I thought I could do it. I thought it wouldn't bother me. I was wrong."

"We need you, Dar. You can get him talking. We can't."

"He's our only lead to The Stone, Dar," Chandra added.

"You think I don't know that!" He turned suddenly and drove his fist forward, hard enough to split a knuckle and mark the yellow brick with red. When he pulled his arm back for a second blow, Aaron slipped between him and the wall. Gray eyes met brown and held them. Slowly, Darvish's hand unclenched.

"I think I know a way," Chandra said softly. "Use the soul-link."

Grateful for the chance to break an eye contact that had acquired a life of its own, Darvish pivoted back to face her. "What are you talking about?" he snapped. "You can't use a soul-link for anything. It's a leash, nothing more."

"Oh, no." Chandra disagreed, "that's what it's used for, that's not what it is." A sudden noise out on the street, caused her to move forward and lower her voice. "Don't you remember when they first put it in? You were having weird thoughts and feelings that you knew weren't yours?"

"They stopped," Aaron pointed out. His face had fallen into the completely expressionless mask he wore when he was most disturbed. That the soul-link was a physical tie to Darvish he could handle, barely. That it might be an emotional joining as well. . . .

"No, they didn't stop. You just stopped noticing them. Dar, you can draw on Aaron's strength to get through this. You did it before, when you were fighting the wine."

"I drew on Aaron's strength?"

"Yes."

Darvish remembered how Aaron had looked the morning he'd finally come back to himself. *So I was responsible for that as well. One Below, but I have a lot to answer for.*

"You can do it again."

"No."

"Why not? Aaron doesn't mind."

The barb in her voice pulled Darvish up out of the melancholy he had fallen into. He took a step toward the wizard and hissed through his teeth, "Are you crazy? You *heard* what he went through last night."

"Dar. . . ." The last thing Aaron wanted was for Darvish to have access to what he thought, what he felt. At the same time, he had never wanted anything so badly in all his life. "I've strength enough for *this.*" He twisted his lips up into the closest he could come to a smile as Darvish faced him again. "I'm good at self-denial."

"So you're to carry my weight again tonight?" Darvish's words were bitter. He hadn't thought he could despise himself more than he had that morning by the sea. He could. He did.

"So he's willing to help a friend." Chandra met both the gray eyes and the brown with a steady stare of her own. "We don't have time to dance around your ego, Dar." She put her hands on her hips and glared. "Say thank you and let's get going on this."

After a moment, Darvish stopped gaping at her. "Thank you," he said, a little stunned.

"Yeah," Aaron replied, in much the same tone. "No problem."

They glanced at each other, saw identical poleaxed expressions and began to laugh.

Chandra rolled her eyes. Men.

Merchants, sailors, and whores moved sullenly out of the way as the patrol of city guard moved the length of the street.

As far as the patrol leader was concerned, she and her men were wasting their time. This neighborhood held a thousand hidey-holes and few friends of authority, and an evening spent searching vermin infested wineshops would leave them with nothing more than queasy stomachs and flea bites on their ankles. They sure as the Nine wouldn't find any sign of the two men twisting the king's tail.

But, she hitched up her sword belt, *orders are orders*. "Stay together, and keep your eyes open. If anyone wants to claim the reward, bring them to me." Choosing a wineshop at random, she waved the patrol toward the door. She'd lead them into battle but she'd be damned if she'd lead them into that.

"May we buy you a drink, my lord?"

The young lord looked up and smiled broadly. He had a charming pair of dimples and thick eyelashes that swept coquettishly against the curve of his cheek. "You certainly may," he told them, inspecting each with obvious approval. "One big drink, or three little ones?"

"Your preference," Darvish said cheerfully, sitting down and matching the smile. Behind it, he held tight to his end of the soul-link.

"Three big ones, then." He tossed blue-black curls back off his face. "Why waste time?"

It wasn't difficult to turn the talk to Cisali, to Ischia, to The Stone.

"I don't know nuthin' 'bout no Stone." He leaned forward and a delicately embroidered sleeve dragged through a blood-red puddle of wine. "Bud I betcha I know who would. Uncle Gracious Majesty King gets lots of letters from Ischia." Poking his finger into the puddle, he quickly sketched a likeness of the king on the splintered wood of the table, then sat staring down at it proudly. "It's good, isn't it?"

"Yes," Darvish told him gently, "it's good." And it was, even considering the media and the shakiness of the artist. He'd captured exactly the king Darvish remembered from Shahin's wedding and captured exactly the look Darvish himself remembered receiving. "Has King Harith been sent any letters lately?"

"Course he has. Lots."

"In the last nineday?"

"Lots. At least one."

"I bet you don't know where he keeps them."

He poured another nearly full goblet of wine down his throat. "Bet I do," he coughed out at last. "Keeps them locked in his gracious private ocif . . . office. Saw them when he was yelling at me yesterday." His brow furrowed. "Maybe today. Uncle Gracious Majesty King yells a lot," he confided sadly.

"I'm sure he does."

"Are you goin'? I thought you could stay and we could, I mean, all of us could, we could. . . ."

"We have something we have to do."

The young lord sighed. "Everyone has something they have to do."

Darvish reached out and tenderly brushed the black curls back. "I know," he said.

He managed to follow Aaron and Chandra outside and got clear of the inn before he had to stop and hug himself hard, waiting for the trembling to run its course. The solid feel of Aaron in his mind helped. The warm, physical touch of his and Chandra's presence helped more.

"Dar." Aaron's voice was soft but insistent. "We have to move on. There's a patrol searching the street."

Darvish nodded. He couldn't trust his voice. With Aaron holding one arm and Chandra the other, he somehow got his legs to move and, one step at a time, they headed back to The Gallows.

"We have to get the letters," he said when he could. "If they were written in the last nineday, they're not likely to be from Yasimina asking for another set of One abandoned peacocks. Ischia will never be safe if we don't find the traitor. Aaron, can you break into the palace? Into the king's private office?"

Aaron smiled strangely at a memory he didn't voice. All he said was, "Yes."

"Milord?"

He looked up from the picture he was drawing in the spilled wine and smiled charmingly. "Yes?"

"We're looking for two men. . . ."

"Two?" He sighed. "I'd settle for one. Or a woman. Or a large dog. Small horse." He giggled. "Most Gracious Uncle hates it when I say that. Thinks I'm a pervert." Suddenly, he reached out and anxiously clutched at the patrol leader's arm. "I'm not, you know. 's just a joke."

The patrol leader pulled sticky fingers off her wrist brace. "I'm sure, milord."

"Should we take him with us?" one of the guards asked her as she turned away in disgust.

She snorted. "He wouldn't thank us. Let's go, people. There's nothing here."

The young man watched them leave, then raised his hand for another drink. On the table, the sketch he'd done of Darvish dried and disappeared.

Sixteen

"It won't work." Aaron's voice was flat. "You're just too big."

Chandra looked up from the pieces of apple peel she'd been trying to lay out in a single strand. The imported fruit had cost almost as much as the rest of the meal. "You'll have to let me remove the soul-link," she said, not for the first time. "You haven't got a choice."

"And what if it knocks you out?" Darvish snapped, pushing away his low table and slopping coffee out onto the polished wood. "How is Aaron supposed to get over the wall if you can't punch a hole through the wards?"

"Aaron won't be going over the wall if I don't get rid of the soul-link," Chandra pointed out. They'd argued in circles all through the meal and she was tired of it; she preferred having her brain power-burned than having the argument continue. "I can live with a little pain. We *don't* have a choice."

"No." Darvish shot to his feet and stamped over to the window. "It's too dangerous for you. I won't allow it."

"You won't . . ." Chandra began, teeth showing, but Aaron shook his head gently and she bit the rest of the comment off.

"Dar." Aaron moved silently up to stand behind him. Darvish continued to stare out at the lights of Ytaili. "If we have to enter another tavern, I'll—we'll—be there for you. You won't have to face it alone."

"Is that what you think I'm really worried about?" Darvish laughed bitterly and turned. "Well, you're right. As usual. This must be getting awfully tiresome for you; always being right where I'm concerned." He reached out and grabbed Aaron's chin. "Afraid you're going to be my new crutch? That I'll suck you dry just to get through all those bits of life I'm too much of a coward to face on my own?"

Aaron remained perfectly still in Darvish's grip, fighting and winning against the urge to twist free. "You can lean on me without the soul-link," he said softly.

"Lean on you?" Again the bitter laugh. "I don't know if you've noticed this or not, but lately you've been a little unstable yourself."

"I've noticed." There were no walls left to hide behind. "You lean on me. I'll lean on you."

And why can't I think of a single witty thing to say to that? Darvish wondered, searching Aaron's face for hidden meanings or sarcasm he knew he wouldn't find.

"Well?" Chandra asked at last, strongly suspecting that if she didn't do something about it, they'd stand and stare at each other all night.

So slowly that it was almost a caress, Darvish released Aaron's chin. "Do it," he said.

"We've got another problem." Chandra peered over at the wall of the palace, barely visible even though her eyes had grown used to the night, and twirled the wet end of her braid between two fingers. "I'm going to have to go in with Aaron."

Darvish muttered something unintelligible—and, Chandra suspected, uncomplimentary—under his voice. Aaron quite clearly said, "No."

Chandra ground her teeth and squirmed around behind the low parapet until she could see the two men lying beside her on the roof. "I can't open the wards from here," she explained, snapping each word out. They had a lot of nerve refusing before hearing her reasons. "I'd need to use too much power. A lot of good it would do, Aaron sneaking over the wall, if I'm going to be lying here screaming."

"Oh, I don't know," Darvish mused. "It might be a good distraction. I'm kidding," he added hastily, his teeth flashing white in the shadow of his face and one arm raised to fend off Chandra's fist. "Can't you make him a charm to get him through?"

"I suppose I could fake it if I could touch the wards." She shrugged, wasn't certain they saw it in the darkness, and said, "Same result as removing them though."

Darvish slammed his fist lightly against the brick. "Bugger the Nine."

"But I *can* get us both through. With my eyes closed and

one hand tied behind my back. It's a different kind of spell, takes almost no power, and the Nine," she waved a hand at the stars in case they were unsure which nine she referred to, "will be in a perfect position in a very few moments."

"You can do it without hurting yourself?"

"Yes."

"That's what you said about removing the soul-link."

"I never did," Chandra told him indignantly. "I said I could stand the pain. And," she pointed out, "I did stand it."

"I know you did, Chandra." Darvish spoke soothingly. He in no way wanted to negate what the young wizard had already gone through, but he needed to make sure she understood that accompanying a thief over the palace wall was not the same thing as sitting safely in their room at The Gallows. "But you screamed."

"Only once."

"Once would alert the guard."

"I *told* you, this is a different kind of magic."

"What will you do inside?" Aaron asked suddenly, leaning across Darvish so that he didn't have to raise his voice.

Chandra rolled her eyes. "I'm a Wizard of the Nine, not a thief. I'll sit quietly at the base of the wall weaving a notice-me-not until you come back."

"You'll destroy yourself," Aaron said bluntly. "You don't know how long I'll take."

"So I'll sit in a shadow!"

"Shh!" Darvish cautioned.

Chandra pointedly ignored him, but lowered her voice again. "You'll have to come back to me. You'll need me to get out."

"How well and how fast can you climb?" Darvish surrendered. It was time to start making the best of a bad situation. He certainly didn't want Aaron to take Chandra over that wall, but even less did he want the traitor in Ischia to go free and that's what would happen if they couldn't steal those letters.

She studied the wall, this time actually seeing the physical structure and not the intertwined lines of power rising from it. It was a little over twice her height and the stones looked smooth and set flush. "Up that?" "Not very," she admitted grudgingly.

"Dar, could you throw her to the top?"

"We have to go through the wards together," Chandra interjected before Darvish could speak. "Holding hands at the very least."

Darvish sighed and shook his head. "Aaron can climb to my shoulders and take your hand. From there he can get himself through the ward at the same time as I toss you up and when this is all over we can make a living as street acrobats. Come on," he rolled to his feet and, crouching low, started for the stairs, "let's get this over with before my brain convinces me how One abandoned the whole idea is."

"You may have to distract a guard," Aaron pointed out, scuttling along beside him.

"I'll sleep with the One abandoned guard," Darvish grunted. "if that's what it takes to get on with this." For the first time in over a nineday he didn't feel embarrassed at needing a drink. Any sane man would need a drink under these circumstances. *Ischia may be dying under a river of molten rock and I'm throwing a mouthy wizard into the palace of Ytaili. Nine Above and One Below, why me?*

He touched the emptiness where the soul-link had been and a muscle jumped in his jaw. *In a few days,* Chandra had told them, *you'll forget you ever had it.* Glancing over at Aaron moving down the stairs beside him, he doubted that. He doubted that very much.

"Are you all right?"

Chandra wiped at the blood dribbling from her lip and managed a weak nod. Then her legs gave out. She slid down the wall to land knees at her chin and back braced against the cool stone; crumpled but basically upright.

Aaron squatted in front of her, the center tufts of his brows pulled down so tightly they touched. "You said it wouldn't hurt," he accused.

She smiled wanly. "I lied."

He didn't bother asking her why; the answer seemed self-evident. They'd still be on the roof arguing if she'd admitted how much opening the wards would take out of her.

Senses straining for any indication that they'd been heard, Aaron glanced around the small courtyard; it hadn't changed since the last time he'd visited. The statue of an ancient king rose up dark and foreboding in the center of the tiny square and at his feet curved a single stone bench flanked by squat pots of ivy. There were obvious signs the courtyard had been larger once, but internal pressure from the palace had forced expansion almost to the wall. The old king fought a losing battle for space with buildings and bureaucracy.

The pale glow of a lamp shone through one of the upper windows, but the night absorbed its light long before it hit the ground. At the base of the wall, the shadows were impenetrable.

"Wait here," Aaron told her, his lips against her ear. She smelled vaguely like apricots and as a silky strand of thick brown hair brushed against his nose, he forgot for a moment what else he was going to say and asked instead, "Are you going to be all right?"

Chandra rubbed at her temples and wished that Aaron would stop breathing quite so loudly. "I'll be fine," she whispered irritably. "All I have to do is sit here and. . . ,"

Aaron's finger stopped the final word.

Chandra stiffened, then froze as the slap of sandals against paving stones and a brusque, 'You there! What are you doing here?" sounded clearly from the street side of the wall.

"I'm waiting for you," Darvish's voice had gone low and throaty, holding both an invitation and a promise.

"You're what?" The guard now sounded more surprised than threatening.

"I've been trying to meet you for some time. I bribed one of the other guards to find out what section of wall you'd be walking."

"You what?"

As much as it hurt her head, Chandra had to smile at the new tone in the guard's voice. She wondered what Darvish was doing in order to inspire such ragged breathing.

"Why don't I walk along with you and we'll talk."

"My wife. . . ."

"Doesn't have to know."

The double footsteps faded along the wall and the murmured words were lost to distance.

Aaron's face was unreadable in the darkness. Chandra wished she could call enough power to see if he needed reassurance, but she suspected that for the moment even so small an amount would knock her writhing to the ground. His voice gave nothing away.

"Stay here," he said, and vanished.

She knew he didn't actually vanish—not even she could

sustain the focus necessary for that and *she* was a Wizard of the Nine—but one moment he was beside her and the next he was gone. For a heartbeat, an Aaron-shaped shadow became visible against one of the buildings, and then she was alone.

At first, she concentrated on regaining her strength, on soothing the raw channels that felt as though she'd taken ragged-edged nails and clawed at the abraded surface. She watched the dance of the Nine, all but the Sixth visible over the edge of the palace, and used their cool light as a balm.

Then she counted the dark on dark windows that faced the tiny courtyard, beginning with the one still glowing faintly with light.

Then she fidgeted.

She realized suddenly she had no idea how long Aaron should take and thus no idea of how long she should wait before finding Darvish and mounting a rescue. He'd been gone a very long time, but surely she'd hear if a thief were captured within the palace. Maybe not. Aaron had said this courtyard was far away from anything important; which was why he used it. Perhaps he heroically resisted betraying their mission in a Chamber of the Fourth even now.

Carefully, she stood, sliding her back up the wall, remaining in heavy shadow. She took a deep breath.

You're being ridiculous. Look at the Nine. He hasn't been gone that long.

A horse passed by out on the street and she found herself thinking of Ischia, where, because of the terraces almost no one kept horses and litters were the preferred transportation of the wealthy. Which made her think of home and how ridiculous a litter would look at home where almost everyone rode. Which made her think of her cousin inheriting. Which made her angry. She was the heir, not him. He'd never even made an effort to learn about the common people he might one day be ruling.

And how much have you learned about the common people in the last five years, asked a little voice.

Her shin banged into the edge of the bench and she looked up in astonishment at the worn features of the stone king. She hadn't realized she'd moved away from the wall. Eyes darting from side to side, she checked the surrounding buildings. All the windows were dark and shuttered against the night, including the one that had been open and lit a short while before.

Almost trembling with relief, she turned, intending to retreat back to the wall where Aaron expected to find her.

"Ahh!" The man-shaped shadow leapt back with a great fluttering of robes and a lot of white showing around his eyes.

Chandra mirrored his motion almost exactly. The bench caught her behind the knees and she sat down, hard, the jolt stabbing pain up behind the bridge of her nose.

The shadow gathered itself together and stepped aggressively forward. "What are you doing here?" it demanded, the effect a little lessened by a sudden octave change on the last word.

A wizard, Chandra realized. The outline of the robes was unmistakable. He didn't sound dangerous, but he was certainly capable of calling the guard. What was she supposed to answer? *What would Aaron say. Aaron wouldn't get himself into this kind of a situation. All right.* She took a deep breath, *What would Darvish say?*

"I'm, uh, waiting for a man." Darvish would have gotten the delivery smoother, *had* gotten the delivery smoother, but then Darvish practiced.

The young wizard came close enough to acquire a face and his scowl slipped into embarrassment. "Oh. I'm sorry, milady, it's just that I've never seen anyone else in this courtyard."

"That's why we chose it," Chandra told him. It certainly sounded like a logical reason.

"Oh," he said again.

Chandra was fascinated to learn that a blush could be heard.

"I'll just be going then, milady."

"No, wait." This was her chance to learn about the wizard who had The Stone. Even this . . . this young man, should have noticed the power signature hanging over the city. "He's late and I'm a little afraid of the dark." She patted the bench beside her, beginning to enjoy herself. "Please, would you stay?"

He hesitated a moment, feet shuffling against the flagstones, then he sat. He was pleasant looking enough, although he should have shaved and given the mustache another try in a few years.

"Oh, you're a wizard!" she exclaimed as though she'd just noticed. It sounded ridiculously false to her ear, but she had to say something to keep him from asking who she waited for.

He visibly preened. "I," he said, "am a Wizard of the Fifth."

She stretched her mouth into a smile and wondered if batting her eyes would be taking things just a bit too far. "I feel much safer now."

He returned the smile and ducked his head away, suddenly shy, realizing that "milady" was no older than he was.

"You must do lots of important work."

The self-important tone strengthened. "His Most Gracious Majesty depends on me."

Chandra recoiled a little, trying to make her expression fearful. She had no way of telling if the young man had augmented his night sight. It was an easy spell, but he was only a Wizard of the Fifth, after all. "You aren't that new, really powerful wizard the court is buzzing about?"

"No, no," he hastened to reassure her. "That is, I'm . . . I'm powerful, but I'm not new. I came into my powers years ago."

"Oh." Most wizards came into their power at puberty and although Chandra herself as a Wizard of the Nine had been an early developer, she doubted this wizard had had his power for "years."

He took her silence for continued trepidation. "Don't worry about old Palaton," he scoffed. "He almost never comes into the city."

Chandra hoped she looked sufficiently awed. "You know him?"

The young man, himself considerably in awe of a wizard whose power signature had suddenly flared and now hung over the city like a storm cloud, never stopped to consider how a person without talent would find Palaton any more than a peculiar old man. "Of course, I know him. *I* am a Wizard of the Fifth."

"Oh. Yes, of course." *Pompous little twit.* She looked down at her fingers laced on her lap and wondered how to end the conversation. *His name is Palaton and he lives outside the city. We should be able to find him with that.*

"Um, look, if your, uh, man isn't coming, perhaps I. . . ."

"No. I don't think so." She shook her head, thinking furiously. "Sometimes it just takes him longer to get away. And he has to be so careful in case Her Gracious Ma . . . oh." She covered her mouth with both hands and turned away in what she hoped was believable confusion.

His mouth worked wetly, but no sound emerged.

"Uh," he managed at last, and stood. "I'd, uh, better be going then."

"He would so hate to be seen," Chandra agreed.

Seconds later, she was alone in the tiny courtyard once more.

"The king's mistress?" asked a quiet voice behind her."

Heart in her throat, she whirled around. The statue of the ancient king stared down at her, one hand raised as though in benediction. Then a shadow separated itself from a fold in the stone robe and dropped to the bench beside her.

"One Below." It was most definitely a prayer. She tried to remember how to breathe again. "Aaron, if you ever. . . ."

Teeth flashed in the walnut stain. "Sorry."

"No, you aren't," Chandra muttered but relented when he really did look upset. "Did you get it?"

He touched his breast and she heard the faint rustle of parchment.

"Good, let's get out of here." She stood, took two steps forward and stopped. "Aaron, how are we going to get over the wall without Darvish?"

Without Darvish. Aaron touched the empty place where Darvish had been. Except that Darvish had been in more than that one place for some time now. He shied away from the thought, the voices of childhood priests suddenly grown loud in memory.

"If I boost you to the top, can you hold the wards open long enough for me to get through?"

Hold the wards open; not just slip through, but hold them open. Her head began to throb and her nails bit into her palms in memory of the pain. From what she could see of Aaron's expression he realized what he asked her and she trusted him enough to know that meant there was no other way. Hold the wards open. "Be quick," she said, just barely managing to keep the quaver from her voice.

He moved as quickly as he could, but that was almost not quick enough. The fire began to burn and sear again and she couldn't prevent a whimper from escaping. She felt a scream building and knew that in another heartbeat it would be too strong to hold back.

Then she was falling.

Then she was caught in strong arms that held her close and whispered with Darvish's voice, "Hush, little one, you're safe."

It didn't seem worth it to argue with the form of address.

The crowd outside the palace gates surged back and forth like an angry sea. Its numbers had been growing since early evening as the frightened men and women of Ischia gathered to demand answers. The smoke rising from a hundred torches mixed with the smoke from the volcano, thickening it, darkening it, adding to the rumors and the fear. A constant ebb and flow of sound rose with the smoke and beat against the palace walls.

"Show us The Stone!"

"The Stone!"

"The Stone!"

The cry came from a thousand throats, in a thousand voices. It would grow angrier as the night progressed and if there were no answer—and there would not be—it would feed on itself, turning to panic and riot.

The lord chancellor stood in the gatehouse, gazing out over the square, able to see and remain unseen. He had dismissed the guards who normally stood watch in the small airless room, needing to be alone with his thoughts. Plump hands tucked in the loose green sleeves of his robe, he frowned at those thoughts and hoped he hadn't made a crucial mistake.

"My Lord Chancellor."

He turned slowly and bowed, graceful despite his bulk and his age. "My prince. And my Lord Balin." He smiled apologetically. "I am sorry, my lord, that His Most Exalted Majesty has no time to spend with you. He has," fingers waved toward the window slits, "other things on his mind just now."

"I am aware of those other things," Lord Balin said shortly.

"Yes. Of course." The lord chancellor studied the foreign lord. "His Royal Highness told you. I remember now. So awkward to explain the absence of your future son-in-law otherwise."

"Since you bring it up," Lord Balin's lips curved in a smile that more closely resembled a scimitar's edge than a gesture of friendliness, "I was wondering why you suggested Prince Darvish for a mission of such importance, one on which the entire fate of Ischia depends, when he has a reputation as a drunkard and a fool."

"And yet, with that reputation you betrothed your only daughter to him," the lord chancellor pointed out mildly.

Lord Balin flushed, but his voice remained steady as he replied, "I did not know His Highness's reputation at the time. You did, my Lord Chancellor."

"Ah, but a reputation may not be all there is to a man. Is that not right, my prince?" Shahin's eyes narrowed as the lord chancellor continued placidly, "Did you not place young Fadi, the beloved son of one of your own people in your brother's service, sure that there he would remain unmolested? In spite of your brother's reputation?"

"I did," Shahin growled. "But then I never believed him abusive, only weak, and of late I've been able to see the man Darvish might have been if not for your attempts to destroy him. Or do you deny you guided him toward what he became?"

"Deny it?" For the first time the lord chancellor's voice held passion. "No, my prince, I will not deny it. Do you think *I* could not see the type of man your brother might have been? At fifteen he was well on his way to it when I began to, as you say, destroy him. He was large and strong, almost beautiful yet still masculine. He had the potential to be the best swordsman this part of the world had ever seen and, in spite of my *destruction,* still almost managed it. He was intelligent, kind, gentle by choice, and strong when he had to be. And," the lord chancellor was almost shouting at the astonished crown prince, "he had something your most exalted father does not and had it stronger, my prince, than you. He had the common touch. Even as he has become, even as they have seen him, the people love him still."

Shahin retreated a step before the older man's vehemence.

"Most dangerous of all, he is a third son! You, who stand to inherit a kingdom, have no idea what that means, my prince. He has nothing. Nothing.'' His voice dropped and the two men listening openmouthed had to strain to hear the next words. "The rest of your siblings had found diversions, but Darvish had potential—was potential, my prince. Had he become the man he should have been, he could have taken it all. Had he tired of his nothing, and what man would not, the people of Cisali would have given him the throne.''

"But Darvish would not. . . .''

"Perhaps he wouldn't have. But a powerful man with no power is dangerous.'' The lord chancellor sighed and for a moment looked old and tired. "My duty is to your most exalted father, to the throne, and I have done my duty. The people may still love him, but they will not follow him. Your inheritance, my prince, is safe. And now,'' he drew himself up, becoming once again the self-assured states-man, "I must carry out his Most Exalted Majesty's com-mands concerning this.'' Once again, fingers waved toward the window slits.

On cue, came the sound of rocks striking the outside wall of the gatehouse.

"What has my most exalted father commanded?'' Shahin asked, stepping back out of the chancellor's path.

"The guards are to be doubled before the barricades on the public platforms.''

Shahin frowned. "But that will only further convince the people that The Stone is missing.''

"Do you question His Most Exalted Majesty's com-mands?'' the lord chancellor asked mildly, pausing in the doorway. "If I may remind you, my prince, you have al-ready been pardoned for treason. I would not suggest you try your father again.'' Then he was gone.

Shahin sagged against the wall and rubbed his temples. The diatribe on Darvish he had not anticipated.

Lord Balin shook his head. "The lord chancellor seems to have an answer for everything and everything he says makes logical sense.''

"It always has,'' Shahin said bitterly, turning to peer out at the angry mob. "I never questioned him myself until he began attacking Yasimina. And now, for perfectly logical and completely unfounded reasons he is almost the only one with access to the king.''

"As you say,'' Lord Balin mused, "for perfectly logical

reasons. And yet, he never did answer why he sent Prince Darvish to retrieve The Stone. . . ."

"You can put me down now," Chandra muttered. "I'm fine."

"I'll put you down on your bed," Darvish told her, starting up the second flight of stairs, "and not before."

Chandra sighed, but as she'd already discovered squirming had absolutely no effect on Darvish's grip she let her head fall back against his shoulder. The play of muscles under her cheek intrigued her. Although she'd been conscious for only the last little bit of the trip, he'd apparently carried her all the way from the palace and still seemed to show no signs of flagging. After a half dozen steps she said, "You're very strong."

He smiled. "Thank you. You're very brave."

Chandra accepted that as her due.

"And very stupid."

"What?" she yelled, twisting up to face him and immediately wishing she hadn't. When the red cleared from her vision she saw he was frowning down at her.

"You could have killed yourself."

"I found out where The Stone is," she protested.

"Dumb luck. You lied about what opening the wards would do to you." He shifted her weight a little. "Okay, that was brave. But if you'd died, or screamed, you'd have trapped Aaron behind warded walls and left him to the mercies of the Fourth. Not considering *that* was stupid. And how do you think we'd have felt if you died?"

"I found out where The Stone is," she repeated sulkily. The big ox was right, but everything had worked out fine so what was he complaining about. "Aaron wasn't trapped and I didn't die."

"Thank the Nine and One for that." It wasn't the first time Darvish had thanked the gods that night. He'd thanked them pretty much continuously from the moment Chandra's limp body had slid off the wall and into his arms. He'd thanked them for Chandra's sake. For Aaron's. For his own. He turned sideways, carried her through the door Aaron held open, and laid her gently on her bed. Then he pushed her back into a horizontal position as she tried to sit up. "Lie down," he commanded squeezing her shoulder gently, "and rest."

As lying down was infinitely preferable to sitting up, Chandra stayed put.

Darvish watched her for a moment and, when he was satisfied she wasn't going to move, held out his hand to Aaron.

The packet of parchment was thick and Darvish spread it out on the end of Chandra's bed in some puzzlement. Government documents made up most of it. "Aaron, why didn't you just bring the letters from Ischia?"

Aaron's brows raised. "They aren't exactly stamped with the royal seal," he pointed out. "I brought everything in the desk."

Darvish shook his head, eyes sweeping over the page in his hand; a list of merchants likely to protest a further tax. "Sorry. I forgot you weren't in a position to read through this garbage."

"Dar." The prince glanced up and Aaron spread his arms. "I can't read."

Chandra tried to look as though she'd known it all along, while Darvish slowly turned a deep red.

Aaron only smiled. "It's not that common a skill. You're a prince, Dar. You've had a better education than most."

"But you can read your own language," Darvish sputtered. "I mean, from the north. . . ."

"It's a priest's skill where I come from." He reached down and pushed a new parchment into Darvish's hand. "And not all of them learn it. *Are* the traitor's letters in there?"

"Uh. . . ." Hurriedly, Darvish shuffled through the pile. His face grew grim as he pulled a letter free. "Yes," he said through clenched teeth, "one of them at least."

"Do you recognize the writing?" Chandra asked. She'd raised herself up on her elbows to see better, to the Nine with the pain in her head. "It's a good thing you wouldn't use a scribe for this kind of thing."

An accurate, although not complimentary, description of Aaron filled the page in a flowing, cursive script. Darvish jammed a hand back through his hair in frustration. "It looks familiar," he admitted, "but I just don't know. I just don't know! Bugger the Nine!" With a sudden vicious movement, he crumpled the parchment and flung it across the room. "Let's thank the One you took that chance," he snapped at Chandra, rising and striding for the door. "It looks like you got the only information we can use. Get some sleep, we go after this Palaton at dawn.''

Chandra decided not to protest that they didn't know exactly where Palaton was. From the expression on Darvish's face that wouldn't be the case for long. She lay back against the pillows and concentrated on rehealing her tattered power channels.

Aaron retrieved the letter, smoothed it, slipped it into the front of his shirt, and, picking up the lamp, silently followed Darvish from the room.

He caught up to him at the foot of the stairs. Darvish had taken two steps toward the bar and the wine barrels and stared across the remaining distance, naked longing twisting his face.

''I need a drink,'' he said softly as Aaron came up beside him.

Aaron thought of a hundred, a thousand things to say. He touched Darvish lightly on the back of one bare wrist and settled for, ''I know.''

Just for a moment, Darvish had the strangest feeling that the soul-link was back. That Aaron's strength was there for him if he needed it.

The lava was a hand's span below the golden cup. The wizards were failing. It would all be over soon.

''I have your word you will rescue me?''

Palaton had smiled. ''You present me with The Stone and I will rescue you in such a way that you will be a hero to the people.'' He'd looked thoughtful. ''Provided any survive.''

''A hero?''

''That will make your task of rebuilding, and ruling under His Gracious Majesty much easier, won't it?'' Long, thin fingers had laced together. ''I'll make it look like the last thing the wizards manage to do is fling you to safety.''

''Will you have power to do that?''

''With The Stone I will have power to do anything.''

''Then you will have The Stone.''

Palaton had bowed, a slight graceful movement. ''And you will have Cisali. Although you will have it without Ischia.''

It would all be over soon. And then, it would begin.

Seventeen

"We go through his front gate? That's it?"

"That's it," Darvish agreed, watching the few remaining stars disappear in the spreading gray of dawn. "And we keep going until we get The Stone."

"Not much of a plan." Aaron closed his pouch and then settled the belt around his waist. Although he'd been up for much of the night, he'd found no information at all on the Most Wise Palaton's house or grounds or habits. Sources that made it a point to know who held every item of worth in the city, and how easy those items of worth were to obtain, knew nothing and expressed a distinct lack of interest in knowing more. Nor did they question their lack of interest which to Aaron best indicated the Most Wise Palaton's abilities. "You know, we'll probably die."

"I know Ischia will *definitely* die unless I, we, bring back The Stone." The last star went out and he turned from the window. "I haven't been much of a prince up until now, but if I have to balance my life against Ischia. . . ." He let his voice trail off, took a deep breath, and started again. "I can't ask either of you to come with me. This isn't your fight."

"The One it isn't!" Chandra snapped. "Nine Wizards of the Nine created The Stone to keep Ischia safe and now some other wizard has run off with it. As a Wizard of the Nine I should think that involves me." Her tone dared either of them to suggest it didn't.

"You could die," Darvish reiterated, bluntly.

"I could've died any number of times since I started on this, this . . ." She frowned and searched for the right words. Adventure, sounded as if she weren't taking it seriously enough and only bards could use quest with a straight face. ". . . rescue mission. If I die attempting to retrieve The Stone, at least my death will have meaning." Drawing herself up, she tossed her braid back over her shoulder. "I'll die like a Wizard of the Nine."

At any other time Darvish would have smiled, or laughed outright at such a bombastic pronouncement, but he knew she meant it so he only inclined his head and said, "Thank you." The prince was glad of the wizard. He stood less than no chance without her along. The man, as much as he wished her to be safely out of it, was glad of her company.

He turned to Aaron. Pale gray eyes regarded him steadily, and Aaron's expression seemed to indicate that the option of not going didn't apply to him. Between one heartbeat and the next Darvish realized it didn't. And why.

Nine Above, he . . . I mean, I . . . We. . . .

"Why not wait until night?" His eyes now hooded and his expression carefully blank, Aaron bent to buckle on a sandal.

"It wouldn't make any difference," Chandra broke in. Any more long, soulful, *silent* looks between those two and she was going to bash their heads together. "Palaton has The Stone. I've felt its power and I know what *I* could do with it." Cautiously, she tested her focus; it was tender but no longer painful although the power of The Stone was a continuous background thrum. "Night, day; it won't matter to him."

"Then we don't wait." Darvish strapped on the small guardsman's buckler. "We go, now."

Aaron nodded. "Then if everyone knows we're coming, this is how I suggest we get through the gate. . . .

Back in the center of the city, the bell in the temple tower rang twice and it was officially dawn. At each of Tivolic's five gates, guards gave the go-ahead to brawny young men who put their backs to the windlasses that would open the city for another day.

The senior guard at the North Gate yawned, scratched at the placed where his leather jerkin bit into his armpit and wondered why they bothered. What with the houses of the rich stretching along the river and the houses of the not-so-rich stretching along the road, not to mention the new temple that had just gone up, there were almost as many buildings outside the city as in it. He squinted east where streaks of pink and gray were giving way to blue and the great golden ball of the sun seemed to be sitting in the middle of

the Duce Florintyn's olive groves. Then he squinted up the
long empty length of the North Road and sighed. Give him
the East Gate any day. At least the steady stream of market
traffic kept a man awake.

Yawning, he wandered back in under the wall and propped
his shoulders against the cool stone. The first of what would
soon become a steady stream of men and women headed
out to a day of service amid the estates of the wealthy. A
heartbeat later he jerked erect and tried to yank the night's
creases out of his tunic.

"M–most Wise." Frantically, he motioned his partner
over. Two years seniority or not, he wasn't going to face a
Wizard of the Fourth on his own. It was the same wizard
who had stood at the gate the day before, he noted. Not that
that helped.

She stared at them both with barely concealed disdain,
not so much angry at them as at the circumstances that ordered her out to this gate at dawn for a second day when
she'd have much rather still been in bed. The circumstances,
however, were not available to be angry at and the guards
were.

"If there's anything we can do, Most Wise."

"Stay out of my way. Both of you." She twitched her
red-brown robes closer around her legs and sneered at three
young women as they passed, their chattering silenced by
her gaze. "You will continue to watch for the outlander and
his companion."

It wasn't exactly a question, but the senior guard figured
it would be safer to answer it than ignore it. "Yes, Most
Wise. A small man with red hair and pale skin and a large
man, dark but with blue eyes."

"I know what they look like, idiot!" she snarled. "Now
take up posts and watch. And don't interfere with the servants." Her voice became a dangerous purr that put both
men more in alliance with her. This anger was not only
directed away from them but toward something they could
understand. "One forbid that the merchant-princes should
have to wait to have their asses wiped."

The servants hurried by in ones and twos, young and old,
men and women, and the Wizard of the Fourth scowled at
them all indiscriminately.

*"The description is useless. Even an outlander and a
drunk will have brains enough to disguise themselves when*

they know they are discovered.'' The two other wizards with her in the small office nodded in agreement.

"You will watch for the soul-link," Lord Rahman had replied mildly. *"We know the soul-link is still in effect. You said so yourself; that you sensed it while trailing the ward."*

"They could have had it removed since," she snapped.

"You three have assured me that you are the only Wizards of the Fourth in the city at present and as you all are in the service of His Most Gracious Majesty I assume you would inform me if you had been approached by enemies of the throne."

During the answering pause, she glanced sideways at her companions. Neither of them looked guilty. Nor, however, did they look about to speak.

"There was a wizard on the Gryphon,*"* she said pointedly.

Lord Rahman tapped the parchment on the table before him. *"A Wizard of the Seventh creates storms,"* he said, *"not a wizard of the Fourth. If the wizard from the* Gryphon *survived the sea and if she still travels with the two we search for, she will not be able to remove the soul-link."*

"Palaton could remove it." She put all the loathing felt for someone new and powerful into the name. That he had not become involved in the power struggles around the palace somehow made it worse.

"Palaton, as you well know, is a Wizard of the Nine and is not relevant to this discussion." The genial sarcasm left his voice and it grew cold. *"I have had enough argument, Most Wise. If you wish to leave His Gracious Majesty's service, tell me now. If not, you will keep watch at the gates to ensure that the king's enemies do not leave the city should they evade the patrols now searching for them."*

"There are three of us and five gates." Her voice was equally cold. Wizards of the Fourth feared no man but neither did she wish to find a new patron.

"You will watch at River, North, and Dawn Gates."

"Day and night?"

"No." Lord Rahman smiled tightly. He hated dealing with wizards. *"At night you may rest. The gates are locked then, after all."*

That had been two nights ago and this was her second morning staring into the stupid common faces scurrying out to their stupid common jobs. Carefully, she rehearsed the words of the binding spell and tied and untied knots in the bit of string that went with it.

"Let them come through this gate," she prayed to her stern god, "and they'll pay for every bit of discomfort I've had to endure."

"This is stupid!"

"Milady, please."

"I will not be quiet. This is stupid! Stupid! Stupid! Stupid!"

The Wizard of the Fourth watched curiously as a young woman of obvious middle-class merchant lineage approached the gate. Beside her scurried a small, harried man in a clerk's robe that almost exactly matched in color the nondescript brown of his hair. Following the required two paces behind was a private guard, listening to the conversation of his betters with every sign of enjoyment. The wizard frowned. A small man and a large one. She reached out with power. No soul-link.

"If Father wants his business blessed, why can't he go to the temple we always go to?"

"The oracle, milady . . ." The small man kept his voice low and soothing. It seemed to have no effect. As they came closer, the wizard saw he had cut himself shaving and a tiny piece of cloth still adhered to his narrow jaw. The shape of his face declared he had outland blood, but in a city that depended heavily on trade, so did a large part of the population.

"Of course, the oracle." Her voice dripped with loudly expressed scorn. "A priest tells Father that all signs point to the new temple and *I* have to get up at the crack of dawn and walk forever out into the country! *I* think it's just to get Father's money out there to pay for having built it!"

The wizard tended to agree with the sentiment. In her experience, money commanded most of the oracles read by priests. The large man, as though aware of her interest, caught her eye and winked. *Well, he certainly has nothing to hide.* The guilty—guilty of anything—did not make themselves known to Wizards of the Fourth. She scanned his tight leathers appreciatively. *And he certainly isn't hiding much either.* His eyes, she noted—large eyes, long-lashed—were brown. A soft inviting brown.

"Milady, please, lower your voice."

"Why?"

"People are sleeping."

"So?"

The wizard's frown deepened. There was something about the girl she didn't like. . . . Not entirely certain why, she reached out again with power.

And slid right into the power signature that had been hovering over the city and on the edge of every wizard's consciousness for a double nineday. Palaton! How dare he interfere with her work! She would have words to say with Lord Rahman about this.

Furious and fuming, she glared at the backs of the girl and her companions as they walked up the North Road toward the gleaming bulk of the new temple. One last, "This is stupid!" drifted back. Come to think of it, it was pretty obvious what she didn't like about the girl.

"I wish you joy of her," she muttered at the two men and began devising suitably scathing epithets about the *Most Wise* Palaton to deliver to Lord Rahman.

"You were right, Aaron."

"Of course, he was right." Chandra tried to convince her heart it could now start beating more slowly and fought the urge to turn and see if the Wizard of the Fourth still watched them. She had no real understanding of what she had done to the wizard's probe; somehow she had slid it through her own channels and into The Stone and done it without the wizard noticing. As it would only demand explanations she couldn't give, she decided not to tell Aaron and Darvish. "My father says that if you're going to hire an expert," she gave her brightly colored cotton sash a tug just to have something to do with her hands, "the least you can do is take his advice. No one would have believed we were servants and even if they did, you'd look ridiculous trying to sneak out with a sword."

"We're through the gate," Darvish told her acerbically, wiping damp palms against his thighs. "You can stop babbling now."

"Babbling? Huh! I was great." She glared up at him. "All you had to do was look big and mean."

"We were lucky," Aaron told them shortly. He realized that their stretched nerves found release in the bickering, but he couldn't listen to it any longer. He'd give his right arm for something, anything, resembling a plan.

They walked in silence for a time, then Chandra spit out the end of her braid and said, "I wonder why he hasn't tried to stop us."

Aaron shrugged. "We haven't been a threat."

"Or he doesn't think we're a threat at all." Chandra frowned. She hated not being taken seriously.

"A point in our favor," Darvish mused, loosening his sword in its sheath as they arrived at their destination. "He's overconfident."

"Or he's right." Aaron squinted up at the property's double gates, the delicate filigree bathed in the pale gold light of the rising sun. It didn't look like a gate designed to keep people out.

The gate was unlocked, not surprising as the thin decorative metal wouldn't have held against a determined assault. To their surprise, it was also unwarded.

As far as Aaron could see, the garden appeared empty. The frenzied barking of a dog sounded down the road and from beyond the wizard's house came the constant mutter of the river. Metallic wind chimes danced in morning breezes and rang an almost tuneful cacophony. Tall lilies rustled along the path. Nothing looked threatening. Nothing sounded threatening. Yet the knowledge of threat hung so precisely over Palaton's estate that Aaron felt he could draw a line across the gateway to define it. He *hated* working without a plan.

"Shouldn't we go over the wall?" Chandra whispered.

Aaron shrugged. "If he knows we're coming, why make it more difficult for ourselves?"

Chandra shuddered as she passed between the carved pillars of pale stone that bracketed the gateway. The signature of The Stone was now so overpowering she could see it, pulsing red-gold, if she closed her eyes. Almost, she could see it with them open. And she wanted it. The desire was so sudden and so strong that for a heartbeat it was all there was in the world.

It took nine Wizards of the Nine nine years to create the artifact. *And, oh, what I could do with it.*

"Chandra? Are you all right?"

Darvish's soft question brought her back to the garden and she turned her head just enough to see his worried frown. Unsure of her voice, she managed a vaguely reassuring smile. She didn't want him getting the wrong idea.

*Of course, I'm all right. Why wouldn't I be? I'm not the one
with the problems.*

The wide drive curved slightly northward from the gate
to the door, the crushed limestone already reflecting back
the early morning light. As Darvish unbuckled his sword
belt, he squinted, marking the distance they'd have to travel.
No obstacles. *Not likely.* He took a deep breath and tightened his right hand around the warm leather of the scabbard.

The drive was untrapped. Aaron realized that wasn't
unusual, not even the most paranoid of homeowners wanted
to risk sending legitimate visitors into a spiked pit, but it
made him nervous. He longed for the night and shadows to
wrap him about in obscurity. This reminded him too much
of his father's attacks on neighboring keeps which usually
began with smashing down any barricades and moved on to
mass slaughter by both sides. What was a thief doing here,
in the light of day?

"You're too good a thief, Aaron, my lad."

"Good enough for this, Faharra? He flexed damp fingers.
I doubt it."

Chandra fought the urge to say, "It's too quiet." or something else equally inane and reached into her pocket for the
handful of rice she'd gotten from the kitchen of The Gallows. Rice was not the usual medium for the spell, but it
was the only thing resembling a grain or a seed available.
Murmuring under her breath, she began to pour it from one
hand to the other.

They'd rounded the curve of the drive when the six fight-
ers stepped out of nothing.

Darvish drew his sword and tossed the scabbard and belt
to one side.

"Now then, lad, let's have none of that." A grizzled vet-
eran stepped out of the line of guards and beamed genially,
her expression of goodwill lessened somewhat by the angle
of her nose and a scar that puckered one cheek. "There's
six of us and only three of you. One of you," she amended
after a swift examination of Aaron and Chandra. "We'd
rather not have to kill you, so why not just throw down your
sword?"

"We'd rather not have to kill you either," Darvish told
her with his most charming smile. He wondered how much
longer Chandra needed for her spell and how long he'd last

if she wasn't ready soon. He really *didn't* want to kill anyone but suspected the guards would not be fighting under that handicap. "So why don't you just let us by and we'll forget we ever met."

She shook her head. "Sorry, lad."

As they charged, Chandra threw the rice.

Four guards fell.

"Two to one," Darvish said softly as, moving too quickly to stop, the older woman and a very young man closed with him.

He caught the first strike on his blade, the second on his buckler. His first and second blows were blocked as well. After a moment, the young man stumbled, a long line of red running diagonally across his thigh. He swore and swung around to protect his injured leg.

"Sleep," Chandra told him, and threw the last of the rice in his face.

Like his fellows, he was asleep before he hit the ground.

Teeth clenched against his weight, Chandra pulled him clear.

Aaron watched as a vicious backhanded swipe sliced into the rim of Darvish's buckler. He should help. The curved swords were useless to him, but there were daggers in plenty on the guards. His father preferred the hand ax but had trained him with daggers as well.

"You've the best eye and steadiest hand in the keep, Aaron, my son. I'm proud of you."

"I don't want you to be proud of me, Father."

Daggers belonged to the past.

Darvish, used to exploiting the advantage of being a left-handed swordsman, found everything he threw blocked with a grim intensity and a joyless smile. The woman was good. She was very good.

He grunted in pain and looked down with some surprise as her sword slashed through his leathers and slid along his ribs.

She was better than he was.

He fell with the blow and came up under her guard.

Almost.

The last four inches of his edge took her cleanly across the throat, drawing another joyless smile below the first.

Her eyes had just enough time to register disbelief before she died.

"Darvish! You're hurt!"

"I know." He drew in a long shuddering breath and gingerly touched his side. There was less blood than he expected, but it hurt like all Nine Above. "I don't suppose you can heal it?"

Chandra blushed. "No, I. . . ."

"Never mind." He tried a grin that didn't quite work. "You took out five of them. You've paid your way."

Aaron moved silently to Darvish's side. The wound was long but shallow and angled in such a way that it didn't cut off the use of his arm. He'd seen worse, but not on Darvish and he found that made all the difference. "Take off your sash," he commanded Chandra over his shoulder.

She frowned but obeyed. Aaron was a thief, not a fighter, but she still thought he should have done something to help. After all, he'd helped the *last* time.

Shaking out the long piece of fabric, Aaron wound it quickly around Darvish's ribs, up over his shoulder, and secured the fringed end. "Better?" he asked, forcing his hands not to tremble at the pain he knew he'd caused.

Darvish carefully raised his right arm to block an imaginary opponent. "Not really," he winced, sucking air through his teeth.

Aaron's lips thinned, but he tried to match Darvish's matter-of-fact tone. "At least you won't bleed to death." He slid out of the clerk's robe. "Shall we get on with this?"

Wiping his sword with the offered robe, his movements exaggeratedly precise, Darvish nodded. "Let's."

Chandra decided to allow them the look they then exchanged. They'd kept it short and she figured they both needed it.

The door to the house was locked but whether in response to the fight or because of the hour they had no way of knowing. Aaron loved the complicated mechanical locks of the rich. They gave access to a thief the way a lowly bolt or bar did not. He slipped a long flexible tool from his pouch and bent to work.

In six heartbeats, maybe seven, the door swung open.

The interior was dim and cool, light passing through the thick stone latticework that made up the front wall and lying in broken patterns on the tile floor.

* * *

Palaton smiled into the mirror that showed, not his reflection, but the three at his door. "I will call the girl to me," he told his companion, running his hands gently around the gilded edges of the mirror's frame. "And then you will put the other two away where they can be forgotten."

"Where to now?" Darvish whispered.

Touching the red-gold pulse that had wrapped around her like a cloak as she passed through the door, Chandra let her need for The Stone answer. "Up," she sighed. "We have to go up."

"All right." He made his way to the nearest set of folding doors. "Then we look for stairs."

The very proper servant about to open the doors from the other side was as astonished as Darvish, but the prince recovered faster. Throwing his sword to his right hand, he lunged forward, yanked the man against his uninjured side, and clapped a massive palm over a mouth just about to open in a terrified yell.

"Now what do we do with him?" he asked, breathing a little heavily as the motion jerked his wound around.

"Slit his throat."

"Shut up, Father."

Chandra stepped forward, feeling as though she moved through a dream, and touched the man just between his rolling eyes. "Sleep," she told him, and wasn't surprised when he slumped against Darvish's hold, although without a grain or seed to help focus and form the power the spell shouldn't have worked. "The Stone," she said by way of explanation, and, stepping over limp legs, followed the call deeper into the house.

"You'd think a wizard would protect his people against things like this," Darvish muttered as he let the sleeping servant slide the rest of the way down his body and onto the floor.

Chandra paused and looked back at him. "Why? Wizards aren't in the habit of breaking into each other's houses. Do you arm your servants against attacks by other princes?"

Darvish looked a little concerned at the defensive tone in her voice and Aaron's brows were high as he moved to Darvish's side, asking, "Should I scout ahead?"

"No, we stay together. We've enough potential for disaster without dividing it by three."

Aaron nodded, that made sense to him, but Chandra only shrugged, turned, and once again began following the call of The Stone. Exchanging worried looks, the two men followed.

Drawn by the inner call of The Stone, Chandra walked the length of the new room and went through the double latticed doors at its far end, heading deeper into the house. Eyes straight ahead, completely unaware of her surroundings, she crossed another room and came face-to-face with a large mirror in a gilded frame. There had been mirrors in both of the previous rooms she realized suddenly; they were important although she couldn't remember how or why.

The mirror hung in a wide corridor that ran the width of the house. It took her a moment to realize that her expected reflection was not present, just a broad expanse of silvered glass with a red-gold fire burning in the heart of it. She moved closer. The fire grew.

"Chandra, be careful!" Darvish didn't like the way Chandra stared at her reflection nor did he much like the way she advanced on it. His own reflection stared back at him, brows drawn down in worry.

"I know what I'm doing," Chandra said without turning. The red-gold fire had become a jewel that spun just beyond her reach. She moved closer and laid one hand against the cool glass. "I'm a Wizard of the Nine." If she just reached a little, she knew she could get it.

"Chandra!"

As fast as the two men moved, the mirror moved faster. By the time they reached it, only a red-gold glow remained and that too faded, leaving them staring at their aghast reflections.

Darvish raised his sword to strike at the glass, but Aaron grabbed his arm and dragged it down. "Dar, no! If she's in the mirror and you smash it, you may kill her. If she's gone through it, you may trap her where she is." He held his grip until the trembling left Dar's muscles and they began to relax, then he released the sword arm and stepped back.

Breathing heavily, nostrils flaring, Darvish jerked away from the glass that seemed to mock him by being nothing more than it appeared. "She isn't dead." He wouldn't allow her to be dead. "We find Palaton. And if she's been hurt, we make him pay." *But she isn't dead.* He started down the corridor, coldly furious at Palaton, at himself. "I should've warned her. He brought The Stone to Ytaili with a mirror. I knew he used them. I should've warned her.''

Aaron fell into step behind him. ''I should have warned her, too.'' And with the words, the walls had slammed up again, fully formed, trapping emotion behind them. They'd been a part of him for so long and he'd been without them for such a short time that he couldn't knock them down. Nor did he try. After all, he'd failed Chandra. ''As much my fault as yours.''

''No. The responsibility was mine.'' Too wrapped up in his own anger and guilt he didn't hear the echo of the void in Aaron's voice. His greatest fear was that Palaton had taken Chandra hostage and would offer to trade her life for The Stone. *She knew that she could die but, Nine Above, don't make it my choice.*

Their sandals whispered quietly against the tiles as they hurried along the corridor, deeper into the house. At a cross corridor, they paused, listened, but heard nothing more than their own labored breathing and the soft chink of metal against stone as Darvish rested his sword point against the floor.

''That way,'' he said, and pointed. ''Keep moving away from the door. We'll have to pass another mirror. Don't look in it.''

But they both glanced quickly as they sped past. First Darvish, then Aaron. Hoping they'd see Chandra staring out at them. Terrified they'd see Chandra staring out at them.

They saw their own reflection scurrying single file down the hall of a wizard's house, nothing more.

When Aaron's image stepped beyond the mirror's range, its surface grew brightly silver and a single ripple ran top to bottom down the glowing length. The man-shaped creature that stepped through into the corridor should have been too large to fit between the borders of the gilded frame. The floor should have trembled under its weight. Aaron should have felt its fetid breath on the back of his neck.

It fit easily through the borders of the frame.

It made no more noise than the fall of dust in an empty room.

It had no breath to give it away.

Aaron felt the hair on the back of his neck rise and he half turned. His mind had no time to understand what he saw before blackness claimed him.

Darvish heard the sound of heels thudding against wood. He whirled about in time to see Aaron's feet disappearing into the mirror.

"NO!"

Diving forward, sprawling his full height along the floor, he grabbed out desperately as the ripple shimmered up through the glass, bottom to top, and screamed as a quarter inch of his index finger was sliced cleanly off. Blood sprayed against the mirror as he snatched his hand back and bundled the fringed end of Chandra's sash around it. Then he sat for a moment on the floor and tried to calm his ragged breathing. Panic would help neither his companion nor himself.

He'd screamed more from Aaron's loss than the loss of his fingertip, the latter having happened too quickly and too cleanly to do more than send a jolt up his arm. The pain radiating out from it now, sending every muscle from wrist to shoulder into weak spasms, more than made up for that, but it remained nothing beside Aaron's loss and the feeling that an essential part of him had been ripped away.

Gingerly, he unwrapped the end of the sash. From what he could see through fresh blood welling up, the mirror had cut through flesh and nail and bone, crushing nothing, merely evening the index finger with the two flanking it. *Thank the One, it's not my sword hand.* Bracing his sword against the wall, he awkwardly cut free a piece of cloth. More awkwardly still, he got it around his finger and tied it with a bit of fringe, using his teeth to pull the knot tight and put pressure on the wound. The rough bandage was already soaked through, but it was the best he could do and he wouldn't waste more time on it. Palaton's servants must have heard the scream and above all else he had to avoid getting into a fight he couldn't win.

Finding Palaton is still the best idea, he thought, standing and wiping sweat from his forehead with the back of his sword hand. *Find the stairs, I find Palaton.* He started on in the direction he'd been going, deeper into the house.

The corridor ended in a brilliantly executed mosaic and another cross corridor, both of which showed the silver shiver of a mirror centered in their end walls.

Bugger the Nine! He flattened against the tiles. *Perhaps if I keep my reflection out of the glass. . . .*

Hearing voices to his right, he sidled cautiously toward a pair of latticed doors, folded open. The sunlight spilling

through them bathed a heavy wooden door set in the op-
posite wall with bright gold. Riding the light came the sharp
scent of fresh cut oranges and a quiet conversation.

". . . . less tense if you're going to serve in a wizard's
kitchen, boy." The voice was a woman's, the tone dry and
almost disapproving.

"But I tell you, I *did* hear someone scream." The last
word cracked and jumped an octave.

"And I tell you, unless they're screaming about the food,
ignore them. Get me a larger bowl."

Silently, Darvish moved out into the sunlight. Surely there
would be stairs by the kitchens to take food up to the wizard. He could see ovens and the end of a large table, but
the cook and her helper were out of sight and as long as he
couldn't see them. . . . He studied the latch of the wooden
door and paused. The hinges were metal. Could he risk the
noise of the door opening giving him away? Could he risk
not opening the door when the stairs he sought might be
behind it?

And then the decision became moot as he stepped away
from the wall and his reflection touched the closer of the
two mirrors.

It shivered.

In one fluid movement, he crossed the hall and flung the
door open with his mutilated hand.

The stairs behind it stretched down.

For less than a heartbeat, dust motes danced as the brilliant sunlight spilled into the darkness below. Then the door
was closed again with Darvish behind it, forehead resting
against the heavy wood, straining with all he had left to
hear the wizard's guardian approach.

He heard nothing except his blood pounding a distraction
in his ears and began to think that he had moved in time.
Then the feel of the of the corridor changed. The fine hair
on the back of Darvish's neck rose. Something was out
there. Something. . . .

Muscles tensed, he prepared to throw himself forward the
instant the door began to move. If the One was with him,
he could slam the heavy wood against his opponent and gain
a slight advantage.

And then the feeling went away.

But it didn't go far.

"What are you doing in here?" The cook's voice rose to

such a volume that it defeated walls, corridor, and door, and Darvish heard her as though she stood beside him. "Go back to your master! Go on! Get!"

Her voice grew louder as she pursued the creature out of the kitchen. "Oh, no, right off of this level! You go back into your nasty mirror before I take a broom to you."

There was a long pause while the heaviness lifted out of the air.

"That's better." Although he heard no sound, Darvish imagined her dusting off her hands. "Wizard promised me no magic in my kitchen and I'll hold him to that promise, by the One. There's nothing to be afraid of, boy." Her voice trailed off into reassurances.

Slowly, very slowly, Darvish pushed the door open and squinted into the sunlight. The corridor was empty. No creature of magic stood waiting for him. Weak with reaction, he leaned against the cool wall of the stairwell and breathed a heavy sigh of relief.

Up from the depths came the unmistakable smell of wine.

He swallowed and found himself descending.

So there's wine. That doesn't mean Aaron is not there as well. A wine cellar is a perfectly logical place to hide captives.

Another step, and then another, and then two more. His head remained in sunlight, his feet in shadow. Three more steps and he waited while his eyes grew accustomed to the dark. Enough light followed him down the stairs that he was able to make out a small table holding a squat pitcher and a mug. Against the far wall he could just barely differentiate the rounded shadows of barrels in the darkness.

The last step and the cool stone of the cellar floor pressed up against his sandals. The air didn't so much smell of wine, as it was wine, and Darvish drew in great lungfuls of it. The pain of his wounds receded before a need so strong that his sword lay on the table and the pitcher was in his hand before he was aware of moving.

One drink, to give me strength. I've lost a lot of blood. Nine Above, surely I deserve that much. Perhaps the wine would fill the aching emptiness where Aaron had been.

Working by touch, ignoring the torment that rode up his arm when he knocked his fingers against the wood, he shoved the thumb of his wounded hand through the ring on the cover of the first barrel and yanked it up. The smell of the wine grew thicker, wrapping like a heavy blanket around Darvish's head. He plunged the pitcher into the darkness and brought it up dripping.

To prove he still had control, he carried it untasted back to the table and filled the mug. Then he sat on the bottom step and raised the mug to his lips.

Just one. To give me strength.

Eighteen

Aaron regained consciousness slowly, aware first of the cool tiles below and the brightly colored mosaic on the ceiling above. Cautiously, he laid his palms flat against the floor and pushed himself up into a sitting position. The room swam in and out of focus. After a moment it settled, and he took a look at where he was.

The room was small and square. Heavy wooden doors were centered in two of the walls and a third wall was made up of the stone patterning that fronted the house. He had no idea what the room was normally used for as the only thing in it besides himself was a tall metal urn filled with long stalks of dried grasses.

He stood, waited again while the room shifted focus, then checked both doors. Bolted. His pouch of tools still hung around his waist, but it would do him no good.

He peered through the opening in the stonework, scanning the garden. The stone was more than a foot thick and he could no more hope to go through it than he could go through the solid stone of the walls. Returning to the center of the room, he sat. He was trapped. There was no way out.

Behind the walls in his mind he could feel grief and guilt and terror battling to get free. Outside the walls, he felt nothing, not even a physical reaction to whatever had rendered him unconscious before bringing him here. He vaguely remembered a huge misshapen man, decided it must have been magical and, with no reason to care, left it at that.

So I've failed one last time and finally get to die. He didn't know how he knew but he was sure, with a terrible certainty, that no one would come to release him, that slowly, hunger and thirst would bring the end he'd waited for for so long.

"The Clan Heir never surrenders, remember that, boy."
"Shut up, Father."

"If you want your cousin's death, Aaron, my lad, you're going at it the wrong way."

"Shut up, Faharra."

He pushed the voices of the past back behind the wall but one rose up loud and strong to take their place.

NO!

It was Darvish's voice, but Aaron couldn't remember ever hearing the prince cry out the word with such desperation, such pain, such incredible loss. It echoed through his head and the walls trembled.

"Leave me alone," Aaron whispered, his hands curling into fists on his lap. "I failed you, too."

NO!

"I left you alone. I was taken when you needed me. Ruth, Faharra, Chandra, you. I fail everyone. Let me die."

NO!

He threw back his head, the white column of his throat exposed and vulnerable, and wailed, "I have nothing to live for!"

NO!

"You don't understand!" he screamed at the voice, leaping to his feet. "It doesn't matter, I can't get out!"

Aaron stood panting in the silence, listening to his breath, listening to his heart pounding in his chest, and staring at the huge metal urn. The doors were solid wood and bolted, but the brackets holding the bolt were secured only in the wood, not bolted in turn themselves or it would show on his side of the door. There was a way out.

His father's way.

Moving with exaggerated care, much the way Chandra had moved when she was following the call of The Stone, Aaron walked across to the urn and tipped out the grasses. It was large and heavy, but he'd always been stronger than he appeared and he lifted it with little trouble. Slowly, he approached one of the doors.

His father's way. The way of mindless violence, of brute force. The way he'd turned from so many years before when Ruth screamed his name.

And now I prove myself my father's son.

The urn slipped from lax fingers and rang against the floor.

I can't.

NO!

"SHUT UP, DAR!"

But Darvish didn't shut up and the voice kept denying, over and over again, its incredible loss.

Aaron remembered arms that had held him when he cried and he picked up the urn by its fluted neck and slammed the solid metal base into the door.

The reverberation of the blow almost flung it from his hands, but he hung on and struck again.

And again.

And again.

He didn't know when he fell into the rhythm he'd last heard being beaten into a young girl's back by a length of leather. He didn't know when the tears started pouring down his cheeks. He didn't know when he began screaming Ruth's name. He didn't know when the blood from the scars on his chest soaked through his thin shirt.

He only knew the door, and that Darvish was on the other side of it, and that he'd do anything he had to to ease the pain in that cry.

When the wood finally surrendered and splintered and released the bracket; when the bolt clattered to the floor and the door flew open; when silence fell again. . . .

Aaron looked down the empty corridor. Arms trembling, he set the battered urn gently on the floor. He felt strangely calm, and empty. For the first time in five years, Ruth had stopped screaming his name. He didn't think he'd ever hear her again. Or his father. Or Faharra.

"I'm my father's son," he said softly. But then, he always had been. He drew a deep shuddering breath and went to find Darvish and Chandra and The Stone and a reason for living.

Darvish licked his lips and stared down into the mug. He had been sitting like that, not drinking, for longer than he cared to think. The wine fumes teased him, wove seductive spells around him and yet somehow, every time he brought the mug to his mouth, he lowered it, contents untasted.

"I deserve this drink," he said to the darkness. "I've fought for it, bled for it, risked my ass for it."

Around him, the wine agreed but then, that was the beauty of wine. It always agreed.

He shifted his mutilated hand in his lap and sucked air

through his teeth at the pain. "This," he lifted the cup, "was the one thing that was mine."

Again, the wine agreed.

"I wanted a friend, Aaron." It didn't really matter that Aaron couldn't hear the answer. He'd probably forgotten the question. "Just a friend. That was all." His voice grew rough. "I thought you'd understand and you did and now they've taken that from me, too." The wine would ease the loss, mask the ache, bring forgetfulness. "Nine Above!" The curse bounced off the back wall and echoed through the cellar. "What kind of prince has to rescue a thief from the Chamber of the Fourth to find a friend?"

This kind of prince, said the wine.

"It wasn't my fault! They never gave me anything to do. Nothing meaningful. Nor would they let me live a life of my own. Do you know," he asked the mug he clutched so tightly, "what that does to a man?" His laugh held the old self-mockery and he lifted the battered mug in a gay salute. "Yes, I suppose you do."

By accident, he tilted the liquid at exactly the right angle and could, in spite of the dim light, see himself reflected in its smooth surface.

"They never gave me anything to do," he repeated softly. His hand trembled. The reflection wavered and dissolved. Although he tried frantically, he couldn't find himself again and this frightened him.

As he continued to stare into the wine, the fear changed, his lips twisted into a snarl, and an unexpected anger rose to take its place. The anger lifted him to his feet, throwing the mug as hard as he was able against the far wall.

"Except this once! They shit on me for eight years and then they expect me to do the impossible." The rage burned through him and out. "I never wanted to be a hero! I only wanted to belong!" He snatched his sword up from the table. "So I'm going to save Chandra and Aaron." A vicious backhand swing sent the pitcher slamming into the stone, spraying wine. "And I'm going to get The Stone." He brought his blade down on the table like an ax and wood chips flew. "And my most exalted father can take the One Abandoned chunk of rock and choke on it!"

Still burning, he spun on the ball of one foot and bounded up the stairs.

The cook looked up in some surprise when the tall warrior strode into the kitchen, but she carefully and immediately schooled her features, ignoring for the moment, young Ahmid, who had dropped her second best mixing bowl and was now opening and closing his mouth like a landed fish. "How may I help you, milord?"

"The stairs, going up—where are they?"

It was not her business to protect the wizard from swordsmen. Her duty was to prepare and serve the food. Besides, he had a weapon drawn and looked likely to use it. "The stairs are at the other end of this hall, milord."

Darvish nodded his thanks and left. As he broke into a trot, he heard the cook snap, "What are you staring at, standing there in a pile of broken crockery? Clean it up."

The stairs were where the cook had said, rising, shadowed and cool, into the upper story of the house. Turning slightly to one side and shifting his grip on the sword, Darvish began to climb. The anger had faded a little although its heat still kept his thinking clear. He felt remarkably calm. This would finish things, one way or another.

". . . functioning as a power storage, it also focuses the power it stores and this enables it to draw in more power as it needs it."

Chandra nodded thoughtfully. "That would make sense if it was created to hold the volcano of Ischia in check permanently.

"Ah, but because of The Stone's ability to focus, once a Wizard of the Nine is in tune with it there is no longer any need for elaborate preparations." Palaton's dark eyes almost glowed with his enthusiasm. "Any spell, of any magnitude, can be instantly performed."

"Without pain?" Chandra asked, frowning up at the older wizard.

"The only pain occurs while tuning yourself to The Stone." He sat down in the wood and leather armchair facing The Stone and rubbed his temples with long fingers. "You actually came through that better than I did. It is possible your power potential is higher. We will have to test it, of course."

"Of course," Chandra agreed absently, peering into the red-gold heart of The Stone. It rested in a cup atop a delicate spire of gold much as it had in Ischia except that this spire rose up from a golden base, not a cauldron of molten rock. *What an opportunity. To work with The Stone, to dis-cover its secrets, what it is capable of. To discover the knowledge of the ancient wizards and to be able to use it again.*

"Chandra!"

She started and whirled. It took her a moment to pierce the red-gold veil and find a memory to match the large, sword-wielding figure by the door, then it took her another moment to reconcile the changes. The memory had never looked so grim, nor had such lines drawn deep by the corners of his mouth. "Dar? You look terrible. Are you all right?"

"Are you?" His heart had given a sudden leap at the sight of her, then had settled back into the angry pounding that had driven him from the wine cellar. She appeared to be physically unharmed but. . . . He moved farther into the room, noting and discarding the huge open windows, the profusion of plants, and the few pieces of heavy old furniture scattered about. The only items of importance were Chandra, The Stone, and the man who had to be Palaton.

Chandra rolled her eyes at Darvish's scowl. "Of course I'm all right."

He frowned; she was obviously enchanted. Hopefully, dealing with Palaton would deal with that as well. "Move away from The Stone," he commanded quietly.

"Dar!" She shifted to better shield The Stone with her body and began to weave a gentling spell just in case. She didn't think he'd attack her, but he had such a grim expression on his face she couldn't be sure. "It isn't like you think. We've been wrong all along."

"And the attack at the inn never happened?"

"It wasn't an attack. I misunderstood. He had to be sure that I was a Wizard of the Nine, so he offered me the power of The Stone."

"And nearly killed you."

Darvish stepped sideways and Chandra moved as well. "He didn't mean to," she told him. "Palaton isn't a bad person, he's a Wizard of the Nine. He's like me."

"He's like you?"

She didn't understand his tone but hoped the question indicated he was willing to be reasonable. "Yes."

"Really." The word dropped into the room like a thrown dagger. Darvish, while continuing to keep part of his attention on the man seated behind the glow of The Stone, locked his eyes on Chandra's. "Then ask the Most Wise what he's done with Aaron."

"Aaron?"

"You do *remember* Aaron?"

"Don't be stupid, Dar," she snapped. "Of course, I remember Aaron. He's fine. He's somewhere safe until Palaton can deal with him."

"Deal with him?" The sword point came up.

"Oh, for the One's sake, not like that!" It was her turn to glare. "I think Palaton's been pretty understanding about the whole thing considering we broke into his house."

Aaron was safe. The iron band around Darvish's chest loosened a little and his voice was less like a weapon as he asked, "Can the Most Wise Palaton not speak for himself?"

"He can." Palaton came to stand by Chandra, resting one thin hand lightly on her shoulder. He towered over the younger wizard but then, he towered over most people and noted with interest that this prince of Ischia could look him right in the eye. "We have work to do, Chandra," he reminded her impatiently.

"Palaton." Chandra twisted to smile up at him as she said his name and Darvish felt his stomach knot. It wasn't the smile of adoration he'd feared but an even more dangerous smile between equals. "This is the Prince Darvish I told you about."

Palaton inclined his head a barely perceptible amount.

Ignoring the introduction, Darvish dove forward and slammed his sword so hard into an unseen barrier that his entire arm went numb and he barely managed to keep his feet.

"DARVISH!" Chandra's eyes blazed. "You haven't been listening to a word I've said! Palaton is not an enemy! He's a Wizard of the Nine. Like me!"

"Then what's he doing with The Stone of Ischia?" Darvish snarled, backing a little away and searching for the parameters of the barrier.

"He's studying it. Look," she continued in a more reasonable tone of voice, "this," a sweep of her hand indicated The Stone, "is an artifact of the Wizards of the Nine. It holds an incredible potential for knowledge."

"So he's studied it. He's also stolen it and now I've come to take it back."

Chandra sighed. "Dar, you don't understand. He hasn't finished. And *I* haven't even started."

"And Ischia will die for your longing for knowledge?"

"Well, no, but. . . ."

His brows drew down. He was no longer entirely certain that Chandra was under an enchantment. "Then you will give me The Stone," he growled. "Now."

"No, we. . . ."

"Then Ischia will die."

"But. . . ."

"Unless you two Wizards of the Nine," the title was as bitterly sarcastic as he could make it, "know another way to stop the volcano."

"No, not yet, but that's my whole point. Working with The Stone, we might find a way."

"And the people of Ischia will pay for that knowledge with their lives."

"No."

"Yes, Chandra! They die! All of them!"

"But. . . ." Confused, she looked up at Palaton. This wasn't the way it was supposed to be. This wasn't the way he had explained things would happen when he'd thrilled her with the reasons he'd taken The Stone and now offered her a place at his side.

"There will always be more people, Chandra," Palaton said quietly. "But there is only one Stone. If you turn your back on a chance to study it, to study your heritage, it will not come again. You are a wizard of the Nine, are you not?"

Her chin came up. "Yes, I am," she declared emphatically. But she wouldn't meet Darvish's eyes. Everything was so much clearer before he showed up.

"Will you turn your back on knowledge? Will you turn your back on what you are?" Palaton demanded.

"Will you turn your back on the people of Ischia?" Darvish asked grimly. "Because if you would, then I'm very glad tradition will make your cousin your father's heir."

"What?" That got her attention as nothing else he had said had, and she whirled to face him, hands clenched into fists. *How dare he judge her.*

"You're trading the certain death of hundreds of people

. . . of *my* people, for the chance to play with a new toy. Oh, a very powerful toy,'' he conceded with a sneer, ''but that's all it is to both of you. A toy.''

''It isn't like that, Dar,'' she pleaded with him to understand. The constant pulse, pulse, pulse of The Stone made it difficult, almost impossible to think of anything else.

''Hundreds, thousands of men, women, and children will die. Your fault, Chandra. And you don't care.''

Dying? Hundreds, thousands dying? Had she forgotten that? ''I *do* care.''

''Ha!'' She flinched back as though he'd physically struck out at her. His voice remained a low merciless growl as he continued. ''If *this* is a Wizard of the Nine, if *this* is what your father saw you growing into, I'm not surprised he chose to live in the past.''

''Don't!''

Darvish ignored her pained wail although it added another wound to the ones he carried already for his people's sake. ''Is *this* what you are, Chandra?'' He pointed with the sword point at Palaton. ''A Wizard of the Nine? A murdering, friendless . . .''

''Enough. You are wasting our valuable time.'' Palaton raised a hand, The Stone grew brighter for a heartbeat, and. . . .

''No!'' Tears rolled down Chandra's cheeks, but she caught the power Palaton threw and twisted it aside.

A square section of the parquet floor to Darvish's right flared and the next instant became charcoal and ash. Darvish remained where he was but shifted his weight onto the balls of his feet, his blade pressing against the barrier surrounding both wizards. When it went down, Palaton was his.

''Dar's right.'' Chandra straightened her shoulders and faced the other wizard squarely. ''You made me forget the people.''

''I did not make you forget anything.'' Palaton sounded vaguely amused. ''I reminded you of what you are: a Wizard of the Nine.''

She sniffed, looking both absurdly young and strangely dignified. ''But that's not *all* I am. If it's all you are, then I'm sorry for you. We're taking The Stone back to Ischia.''

''No.'' He shook his head. ''You are not.''

Again, The Stone grew brighter.

Chandra paled and swayed, then visibly pulled herself together. Her brow furrowed in concentration.

The Stone grew brighter still.

Eyes wide with surprise, Palaton jerked as though stung. "Amazing," he murmured. "The amount of power you can conduct is truly amazing." The furrows in his brow grew deeper. "You may be the stronger, but I think you will find that the knowledge you threw over for *people* is not to be so casually despised."

Sweat glistened on Chandra's skin, rivulets gathering along her collarbone to run down between her breasts.

The barrier disappeared.

The moment Darvish felt his sword tip press on nothing, he threw his weight behind it for the killing blow.

Massive, misshapen hands clamped his arms to his sides, gripping so tightly he cried out. His sword clattered to the floor as his fingers spasmed in pain. Caught fast, Darvish could only watch as the two wizards fought their silent battle and The Stone blazed. He threw back his head and howled in frustration.

The sound echoed through the room. Lost in it was the noise of a slight body sliding over a broad window sill.

Standing silently in the dappled shadow of a broad leafed plant, Aaron knew Palaton would soon deal with him as well. He was too good a thief not to recognize a man with all the angles covered. If it wasn't another monstrosity, like the one that held Darvish, he had no doubt it would be something equally effective. Where, then, to throw his strength? At the creature holding Darvish? At the wizard himself?

He squinted at The Stone.

One chance.

Removing his belt pouch, he stepped out into the room and with all his remaining strength threw it—not at the creature, not at the wizard, not at The Stone—at the thin golden spire below The Stone. The spire snapped off at its base. Impossibly slowly, The Stone began to fall.

"No," Palaton gasped and spun out of the power lock with Chandra.

Chandra gulped air, raised a trembling hand, and destroyed the creature holding Darvish.

Darvish dove forward, caught up the broken spire, slammed the jagged end up and into Palaton's heart.

As the Wizard fell, he stretched out desperate hands for The Stone and together they crashed to the ground. When Chandra reached him, he wasn't quite dead. He gazed at the red-gold glow between his fingers, wearing an expression close to contentment and said quite clearly, "Almost worth dying to touch it at last." His voice grew wistful. "It was what I always wanted to do."

Exhaling very, very slowly, he died.

Darvish got carefully to his feet. Aaron walked slowly forward to stand by his side. The three of them stood looking down at Palaton and The Stone which had grown, perhaps, a little less bright.

The silence that fell seemed to isolate them in that room, push them outside of time. The light appeared sharper, the air cleaner. Like being caught in crystal, Darvish thought. He touched Aaron lightly on the shoulder and said, "Are you all right?"

The crystal shattered. The world returned.

Aaron nodded. Now was not the time to tell just how all right he was—despite the open wound his chest had again become. They'd have time for that later when there'd be a number of other things to be told as well. He noted the new bandage and the darker stains on the old one. "You?"

"Yeah." Slowly he lowered himself to the floor beside Chandra.

Her eyes bright, Chandra lifted her head. "I'm sorry," she whispered. "It was just that he . . . he. . . ." Her lower lip began to tremble and tears ran silently down her cheeks. At first, she resisted the pressure of Darvish's arms; then, with a strangled cry, she threw herself against his chest and sobbed.

"He was the first person to understand what it meant to be a Wizard of the Nine," Darvish finished gently, holding her close. "It's okay. Most people would do worse than you did for understanding."

"What's worse than betraying your friends?" she asked, her voice tight.

Darvish pushed her chin up until she had to meet his eyes. "Not stopping when you realize that's what you're doing."

Chandra looked from Darvish to Aaron and managed a watery smile in return.

The new silence had all the world in it and although there

were a thousand more things to say, the silence seemed to say them all.

Aaron squatted by the body and took a closer look at The Stone. "How do we get it back to Ischia?" he asked, lacing his fingers together to prevent them from reaching out and touching it. While he could sympathize with Palaton's desire, he vividly remembered the thief in Herrak's chamber with his hands rotting away and he had no intention of becoming the newest resurrection of that thief.

"And is there an Ischia to get it back to?" Darvish bent carefully and retrieved his sword.

"I can find out."

"What?"

"Palaton. . . ." Taking a deep breath and rubbing her nose against her sleeve, she began again. How could a man she'd known for such a little time have made so much of an impression? "Palaton told me The Stone can be used for scrying. Distance doesn't seem to matter." She knelt across the body from Aaron. Palaton's eyes were open, staring at The Stone. Lower lip between her teeth and a tear trembling on a lower lash, she brushed them closed. "I can find out about Ischia."

"Nine and One, yes!" Darvish got stiffly to his feet and moved to stand at Aaron's back. "Hurry, Chandra. Please."

The Stone grew brighter.

The guards fell back before the howling rush of people without a blow being exchanged. The few that attempted to hold their posts were overwhelmed by numbers and pushed aside, the rest threw down their weapons and joined the citizens of Ischia in tearing down the barricades.

"The Stone! The Stone! THE STONE!" The cry rang hoarsely from a thousand throats as the public platforms were gained at last. The rush forward sent three in the front rank over the edge and their screams still sounded when shouts of "The Stone!" stopped and a wail rose from those near enough to see.

The molten rock seethed and boiled not a finger's span below the golden cup, a cup empty of The Stone of Ischia.

Almost as though the unwilling sacrifices had strengthened it, the volcano surged against the weakening bonds that held it. The wizards began to sway. On the royal platform, the heir spoke impassionedly with a slightly older

*man who shook his head in emphatic refusal and attempted
to pull Prince Shahin back into the palace.*

A great cloud of smoke boiled up. The crater twisted.

*One corner of the public platforms crumbled and a dozen
more people fell screaming to their deaths, the rest scrambling frantically backward in hysterical panic.*

*On the royal platform Shahin crumpled to his knees and
the face of the man with him became clearly visible for the
first time.*

"Papa, no!"

The Stone blazed.

Coughing and choking in air suddenly heavy with smoke
and sulfur, Darvish rubbed the back of his injured hand
across his eyes, attempting to clear away the afterimages of
red-gold fire.

"Darvish?"

He blinked furiously and his brother's face swam into
focus. "Shahin?" He stared incredulously around. The
three of them, plus the body of Palaton still clutching The
Stone, were on the Royal Platform although a heartbeat before they had been in Ytaili. "Nine and One," he breathed.

"And then some," Aaron agreed, slowly straightening.
He reached down a hand to help Chandra up. "Are you all
right?"

"I think so." She shook her head, trying to clear it. While
whatever she'd done hadn't exactly hurt, her entire body
resonated to the pulsing of The Stone and the enormous
amount of power she'd focused had left both radiant trails
and an annoying throbbing between her ears. "I think
I'm. . . ."

"The wizards," came the wail from the public platforms.
"The wizards are falling!"

Barely visible through the smoke, the gaunt and exhausted men and women who had held the volcano at bay
for two ninedays, collapsed one by one. The last to fall, for
an instant holding the power net alone, buckled slowly to
the frighteningly clear sound of her spine shattering.

Chandra whirled to face the volcano, arms wide, fingers
spread. Caught in mid swell, the molten rock lapped against
the lip of the golden cup, then sullenly receded. Hot winds

lifted the smoke up and away and no more rose to take its place.

"Aaron, look at The Stone. She's not drawing on its power!"

Aaron's gaze flicked from Chandra to The Stone to Chandra again. "She's holding the Lady of Ischia on her power alone," he said.

"Chandra, what are you doing?" Darvish could see lines of strain on her face already. "Use The Stone!"

"I can't," she grunted, forcing the words out through clenched teeth. "Too close. It was . . . made for this. If I used it now, it would pull me in. I'd get lost . . . in it. You have to put it back." The corners of her mouth trembled as she tried to smile. "Hurry?"

"Darvish!" Shahin grabbed his brother by the arm. "Where did you come from. What's going on?"

Darvish shook himself free. "We're saving your ass," he snapped. This was not the time for long explanations. They still had to figure out *how* to return The Stone to its place. "Any ideas, Aaron?"

"Just one," Aaron told him and he pointed to the Platform of Execution and the cage. He watched Darvish measure the angle of the support beam and the amount of available chain and knew that he understood, both the plan and the part each of them would have to play.

"Should work. How do we carry The Stone?"

Aaron prodded Palaton's rigid corpse with his foot. The journey from Tivolic, however it had been accomplished, seemed to have fused the body into one solid, inflexible piece. "Palaton can carry it. We've no time to be more creative."

"Granted," Darvish admitted grimly. He swung his sword up over his head and chopped down with all his strength. And then again.

Lips tight with revulsion, Aaron quickly scooped up Palaton's severed hands and with them The Stone. The wrists remained stiff and the fingers curved. If he held them carefully together, they should suffice.

The path between the royal platform and the cage more resembled a decorative ledge than something meant to be traveled. It curved, narrow and treacherous, along the inside of the crater with no room for mistakes—on one side sheer rock, on the other, the Lady waited. Aaron and Dar-

vish ran it at full speed, ignoring the danger, ignoring
Shahin and Lord Balin, ignoring the shouts from the crowd
as they recognized their missing prince. *What good saving
Ischia,* they both thought and each knew the other thought
it, too, *if Chandra falls?*

At the platform, Aaron set Palaton's hands down and
joined Darvish in wrestling the heavy cage out of its rests.
With no one to work the winch, they balanced it on the very
edge of the stone itself. It took them a frenzied moment to
work the bolts free and then another to drag the front half
away from the back.

"You okay?" Darvish asked as Aaron climbed inside.

Aaron nodded. "Let's do it." He wanted to sound unaf-
fected for Darvish's sake, but he couldn't seem to get his
teeth unclenched.

Darvish heaved the front of the cage shut and secured the
bolts. He didn't look at Aaron while he did it. He couldn't
have done it and look at Aaron; not for Chandra, not for
Ischia. Palaton's flesh felt heavy and cold and Darvish's skin
crawled as he carried the hands and their pulsing burden
over to the caged thief.

With his own hands crammed through the bars to just past
the wrists, Aaron had almost no maneuverability. His fingers were as white as Palaton's as he gripped the grisly
calipers.

"Can you hold them?" Darvish asked.

"Just do it," Aaron snarled. He couldn't hear the scrape
of steel on stone over the frenzied pounding of blood in his
ears. Then, thankfully, all he had room to think of was
keeping hold of The Stone as the cage swung out over the
pit. For one heart stopping second, the cage, Aaron, The
Stone, fell free. A jerk and a grinding of chain later, all
three hung an equal distance between the wall of the crater
and the golden cup.

Darvish played out the chain until the top of the cage was
level with the platform and Aaron's pale face was out of
sight, then he raced for the support beam. The thief would
have danced along it. The prince scuttled on hands and
knees. At the end, he lay on his belly, locked his legs around
the ironbound wood, and reached for the chain. The links
were warm and slightly gritty under his hands. The muscles
in his arms and back straining, he began to swing the cage,
slowly at first, then in ever lengthening arcs.

Pressed as tightly as possible against the heated metal, Aaron narrowed his world to the flash of gold below him at the apex of his swing. His feet and lower legs were burned from the radiant heat of the volcano and he could feel blisters rising where his bare skin touched the metal cage. None of that mattered. On his second pass over the cup he began to count. On his third, he dropped The Stone.

The only sound as it fell was the grinding shriek of the abused chain as every man and woman watching held their breath. It tumbled, growing brighter as it drew closer to the molten rock, then suddenly flared, a miniature red-gold sun. When the afterimages died and thousands of pairs of watering eyes strained toward the golden cup, The Stone of Ischia was back where it belonged—the captured fire captive once again.

After a moment of complete and absolute silence, the crowd went wild; screaming, shouting, weeping for joy. The crater echoed with the sound.

"The Stone! The Stone! THE STONE!"

Nineteen

On the royal platform, Chandra lowered her arms.

"Chandra?" Lord Balin, oblivious to everything except his daughter, touched her lightly on the shoulder.

She half turned and began to speak, then her eyes rolled up and she pitched forward into her father's arms.

She saw his terror when she opened her eyes, felt his love, his pride, his fear; knew it was all for her. For a heartbeat, she felt a sense of power as strong as the power of The Stone. With a word or a motion she could ruin this man who so desperately held her. A heartbeat later, she reached up a trembling hand and tentatively touched his cheek.

"Papa?" she asked.

They cried together for a time.

Moving with frantic haste, Darvish dragged the cage up onto the platform. His blood slicked fingers fought desperately with the bolt while Aaron watched, head lolling slightly to one side. Teeth clenched with the effort, he forced the front and back of the cage apart and pulled the younger man free.

Aaron swayed but managed to stay on his feet.

"How badly are you hurt?" Darvish demanded, wanting to touch him, afraid to touch him.

"I don't know." He was, in fact, strangely disinterested in the whole thing and what pain there was seemed to come from far away. "But I don't think I want to do that again."

"You won't ever have to," Darvish promised softly, brushing a flake of ash from one high cheekbone. They stood staring at each other until the sound of the crowds chanting Darvish's name reminded them where they were.

"Sounds like you're a hero," Aaron told him, one corner of his mouth twitching up into a smile.

Darvish snorted and jerked his head toward the royal platform where a portly figure in deep green had just appeared.
"It won't last. Can you walk back up there? The path isn't
wide enough for me to carry you."

"Sure." He'd walked narrower ledges, hadn't he? And
nothing hurt too much. Of course, he couldn't really feel
his legs and that might prove a bit of a problem, but he'd
get by. He waved a hand at the blood that dripped sporadi-
cally from the sodden bandage around Darvish's finger.
"Can *you?*"

"As long as I don't walk on my hands." Gently he steered
Aaron toward the path. "You first." He could catch him even
if he couldn't carry him. "What did you do with. . . ?"

"I dropped them. Why? Did you want me to keep
them?"

Darvish winced. "Aaron. . . ."

Shahin met them at the edge of the royal platform. "You
should have waited," he chided, helping Aaron through the
narrow gap in the railing and holding out a hand to his
brother. "I sent guards to open the doors."

"Doors," Darvish repeated. He twisted and looked back
at the Platform of Execution.

As they watched, the huge ironbound doors slammed
open, the crash of the metal striking the rock audible even
above the noise of the crowd. Trumpeters dressed in royal
livery emerged, blowing a fanfare as they came.

Darvish cocked an eyebrow at his brother, who shrugged.
"I sent a pair of guards," Shahin told him. "This isn't *my*
idea."

Then a figure in robes of brilliant white appeared, daz-
zling in the sunlight. A huge ruby set amid the gleaming
gold of the crown blazed on his brow, almost outshining
The Stone itself. He raised his arms and the crowd fell silent.

"The Stone has been returned!" King Jaffar's voice filled
the crater, echoing faintly between the palace and the temple. "Ischia has been saved!" With a flourish that seemed
to encompass both the people and The Stone and still direct
the attention to himself, he lowered his arms.

Shahin shook his head. "It looks like he was about to
face the crowd when you three appeared and he decided to
wait. He's just managed to tie the throne to the recovery
of The Stone." The heir's voice held a trace of admiration

as he added, "Everything he does, he does for the good of the realm."

The chanting began again but this time, they chanted the king's name.

Darvish sighed and, although he knew His Most Exalted Majesty wouldn't be able to hear, said quietly, "Hello, Father."

Shahin heard and lightly touched his brother's shoulder. Finding he had nothing to say, for there was nothing he could say, he shook off the mood and peered into Darvish's face. "Your eyes are still brown."

"Chandra," Darvish said shortly, turning away from the crater. "Is she all right?"

Lord Balin looked up—his daughter's head resting on his chest, her body curled within the circle of his arms—and nodded. His eyes were bright and his cheeks were damp. "She says she just needs to rest."

"Don't listen to her," Darvish cautioned. "She needs a healer."

Lord Balin smiled at the protective tones in the young prince's voice. "Thank you, Your Highness. Your brother assures me that healers are on the way." He pressed his lips against Chandra's hair.

The hand that rested on his shoulder, clutched his tunic so tightly the knuckles went white. She hadn't forgotten, nor forgiven, the five years when she'd lived as no more than a shadow behind his grief but for now, Chandra had found her father and for now, that was enough.

"If I may presume, Your Highness," the lord chancellor stepped forward and bowed, his face respectfully expressionless, "my congratulations on returning The Stone."

Darvish inclined his head, a muscle in his jaw jumping.

"You didn't expect to see him again, did you?" Shahin asked, carefully watching the lord chancellor's face.

"No, my prince," he admitted, spreading plump hands, "I did not."

"Because of the way you had destroyed him."

"Because, my prince, he would be in opposition to a wizard and a king."

"And yet you supported my suggestion that he go."

"As I said before, my prince, I agreed with you that he was the only man for the task. And time, it seems, has proven us both correct."

Darvish looked from his brother's suspicious scowl to the lord chancellor's bland self-assurance. "Shahin," he said, reaching into the front of his vest with his good hand, "we didn't just return The Stone. We, that is, Aaron found a number of letters. . . ."

From the moment the wizards had begun to fall with him not yet called to safety, the lord chancellor had been walking a thin line. Almost tripping over Palaton's mutilated body when he finally forced himself out onto the royal platform to discover what was happening, pushed him closer to the edge. The mention of letters tipped him over and the veneer cracked.

Afterward, no one could figure out where he thought he was running to. Eyes wide, he darted across the platform, moving with a speed completely inconsistent with his age and size, and tripped over what was remained of Palaton's arms, stretched out where Darvish had left them. With a strange, gurgling cry, he slammed into the rail and began to fall.

Aaron threw himself sideways, grabbed for the lord chancellor's disappearing legs, and somehow managed to hang on.

"Too many deaths already," he said, after a frantic Darvish and three guards had dragged both of them back onto the platform. He touched Darvish gently on the cheek and sighed into darkness.

Aaron recognized the ceiling. Stucco. A good thief stayed away from stucco. The angle was wrong though and the breeze blowing in through the open shutters should be striking his other cheek. He stirred restlessly.

"Dar, he's awake."

Chandra's voice. She was all right, then. The volcano hadn't destroyed her. The edge of the bed sagged under someone's weight. He struggled to sit up. Large hands slipped behind his shoulders and gently lifted him, then just as gently eased him back on the piled pillows.

"Thank you, Oham." Darvish smiled up at his dresser. The big man nodded and moved away from the bed.

Aaron spent a moment just drinking in the sight of the prince. Bathed in sunlight, he had a bandage glowing a brilliant white wrapped about his chest and another around one of the fingers of his right hand. His damp hair shone with blue-black highlights and the plain gold earring he'd worn for so long had been replaced by a sapphire drop the same color as his. . . . "Your eyes are blue again."

"Yes." The long thick lashes swept down to cover them for a moment.

Aaron suddenly realized where he was and felt his face grow hot. "I'm in your bed." The words tumbled out of his mouth in an embarrassed cascade.

"Yes," Darvish said again, his smile broadening.

Feeling his breath catch in his throat, Aaron searched desperately for something to say. His mind felt vaguely disconnected, as though it were going to float off at any moment. "Uh, I heard Chandra."

"I'm right here, Aaron." She moved up to stand behind Darvish. Her eyes were rimmed with shadow and finely etched lines bracketed the corners of her mouth. "You've been asleep for two days," she blurted out. "How are you feeling?"

"Two days!" How could he have slept for two days.

"Shhh." Darvish laid a hand gently on his chest, resting it there until he calmed. "The healers gave you something to keep you asleep. But, now you're awake, how *are* you feeling?"

He hadn't actually thought about it, but now that it had been brought to mind he found he hurt all over. Given Darvish's sudden look of worry, he wasn't going to mention it. He raised a shoulder a hair's breadth and dropped it again. "I've been worse."

Darvish gave a shout of relieved laughter. "Not according to Karida, who was, by the way, rather angry about the mess you made of her earlier healing. She made me promise to keep you in bed for the next nineday at least." His eyes twinkled. "It wasn't a hard promise to make."

Which brought them right back to the subject Aaron had been trying to change. He tried again, fighting through the fuzziness that threatened to envelope him. "The Stone?"

"Still back where it belongs," Chandra told him. "None the worse for ever having been gone." A shadow slid across her face and she looked out at something the two men couldn't see. "We gave Palaton to the volcano," she added softly.

Darvish reached up and lightly gripped the hand that rested on his shoulder. Aaron's heart lurched as he remembered what had brought Chandra to Ischia in the first place and how things had changed. Quickly, he schooled his face to show nothing of what he felt.

"The lord chancellor confessed everthing," Darvish said, completely unaware of the near panic his sympathetic touch had caused. "Ischia, and, if possible, Father and Shahin were to be destroyed. Ytaili would step in—Ramdan has no interest in politics or power and wouldn't stand a chance—and the lord chancellor would be given what was left of Cisali to govern. He'd grown tired of being a powerful man with no power and approached King Harith at Shahin's wedding. You," he released Chandra and caught up Aaron's hand instead, "ruined their plan right at the start. Without you and your specialized knowledge, we'd have never discovered where The Stone was taken and then where it was sent. He tried to make up for that by sending me after it, sure I'd fail, but just to make certain, he let the king of Ytaili know we were coming. You and Chandra took care of that. And me. You'll never know how much I. . . ." His voice broke and he had to stop speaking to regain control.

Chandra cuffed him lightly on the back of the head. "Skip it," she suggested, her own voice a little hoarse. "We know."

Darvish smiled gratefully up at her and cleared his throat. "Anyway," he continued, including Aaron in the smile, "when we showed up with The Stone, he decided to bluff it out. After all, he was no worse off than he had been. He never supposed we'd bring that letter back with us as well." He took a deep breath and shook his head as though to clear it of an unpleasant memory. "There wasn't a lot of him left when the twins got through."

Out in the garden, a peacock screamed and all three of them jumped.

"Bugger the Nine!" Darvish swore. "I really wish they wouldn't do that. Oh, yes," he grinned, "speaking of the Most Blessed Yasimina, Shahin found out this morning she's expecting a most blessed event. He's beside himself and even Father seemed pleased, although," the grin broadened, "he never showed much interest in Ramdan's frequent additions to the family. Shahin and Father apparently had a bit of a falling out while we were gone but seem to have pretty much reconciled." Darvish shook his head. "Suddenly forced to recognize certain, uh, failings in our family upbringing, Shahin's even talking of reclaiming the twins from the Fourth.''

Aaron had to ask. Not knowing was worse than knowing. He hoped. ''And you?''

''Well, Shahin seems to think that Father will now clasp me to his breast and make a place for me at court.'' Darvish's mouth twisted and he gave a short, humorless laugh. ''Less than three ninedays ago that was all I wanted. Now. . . .'' He spread his hands. ''Now I realize that you can't be given a place, you have to make one for yourself.'' His expression grew a little sheepish. He cleared his throat and fixed his gaze on the wall above Aaron's head. ''Chandra and I have decided to go through with this marriage after all.''

All other pain receded before the pain of that and suddenly Aaron knew what it meant to truly want to die. The walls that had protected him for so long lay in ruins and it hurt too much to put up new ones; all he could do was lie there and listen and hope it would be over soon.

''We're friends and that's more than most treaty marriages have going for them,'' Darvish continued, beginning to look a little less embarrassed. ''It'll give me a place to start over—it'd be too easy to slip back into the old ways around here—and it'll get the traditionalists off Chandra's back. Married, she can continue as both her father's heir and a Wizard of the Nine. Maybe some day she'll realize she's so strong I don't have a hope without the Nine of fogging her focus.'' He grinned and winced as Chandra cuffed him again. ''But if that never happens, we'll either take a hand in raising her cousin's children or if we want one of our own, you can steal it for us. . . . Aaron, what is it?'' He leaned forward, startled by the sudden welling of tears in Aaron's eyes.

Aaron tried to gain control, tried to say something wry and witty but the tears rolling down his cheeks betrayed him. To his horror he heard a voice, barely recognizable as his own, say, ''I didn't think you wanted. . . .'' His throat closed on the rest and he turned his head away, eyes squeezed shut, unable to stop the wracking sobs that shook his entire body. Warm hands cupped his face and gently forced his head back around.

''Aaron, look at me.''

The sobs died to long shuddering breaths and Aaron opened his eyes, sure he'd see disgust, or worse, pity.

"You thought I didn't want you." Darvish's voice held hurt and anger about equally mixed. "You One abandoned idiot. I like Chandra well enough, but I love you."

The words fell into what remained of the void and filled it.

A moment later he was weeping into the curve of Darvish's shoulder. He couldn't stop. But strong arms wrapped around him and Darvish didn't seem to mind.

Chandra shook her head and laid one hand lightly on the black hair, the other on the copper. "If you think I was willing to take *him* without *you*," she said softly, "think again." Then, doubting very much that they'd even heard her, she slipped quietly out onto the balcony and smiled up into the warmth of the morning sun. Life was working out just fine.

She could feel the pull of The Stone, a faint pulsing along the channels now attuned to it, a teasing touch of its vast power and potential. *I may be a Wizard of the Nine,* she thought acerbically at it, *but that's no more all I am than this is all you are.*

From back in the room, she could hear quiet sounds of comfort and, chewing contentedly on the end of her braid, she eavesdropped shamelessly.

Down below, in the garden, a peacock arched his iridescent neck and spread the magnificent fan of his tail.

The palace blazed with light and rang with sound as the court celebrated a royal wedding. It spilled into the square outside the gate where the people seemed determined to show the nobility how to really party. Darvish was *their* prince after all.

Oblivious to the merriment below, a shadow slipped across the small room outside the king's bedchamber, footfalls making less sound than a heartbeat on the thick carpets. The lack of illumination didn't seem to matter for the shadow moved unerringly to the ornate brackets that held the royal staff.

At the ceremony a few hours before, the emerald crowning the staff had blazed, a beacon of brilliant green that almost seemed to have an inner light of its own.

With one hand steadying the wooden shaft, long fingers reached out and gripped the stone.

". . . and he told me he loved me, Faharra." Aaron leaned back against the wall of the mausoleum, the brass urn on his lap. Even in the cool of the night, he could feel his face flush. "I couldn't tell him how I felt, how I feel, not yet, but he understands." He'd been sitting there since moonrise, telling Faharra everything that had happened.

"He's taking all three dressers with him. Even the lord chancellor's man. Chandra insists he doesn't need all three, but Oham's been with him for years, it would break Fadi's heart to be left behind, and the lord chancellor's man has nowhere else to go."

He paused while the temple bells pealed, filling the necropolis with joyous sound. Throughout the night, as each of the Nine rose to the apex of their starry dance, the priests rang the Nine's blessing on the marriage.

Tugging a long green ribbon from inside his dark vest, he ran the silken length of it around and through his fingers. "This is off Chandra's wedding gown." The demon wings rose and he grinned. "She told me the green is fertility symbolism. Not particularly subtle when you think of it. I offered to kill them a chicken if they need to stain the sheets, but Chandra says she'll mange." A gold thread gleamed in the moonlight as he turned the ribbon in his hands. "The gold thread is for Dar. They've fought every day for the last week. Prince Shahin says that's normal, then he laughs and wishes me luck. He'll make a good king, Faharra, I wish you could be here to see." Running beside the gold, twined around it in places, burned a copper thread. "That copper thread's for me." He swallowed to clear a sudden tightness from his throat. "Chandra insisted they weave one into every ribbon." Remembering the looks on the seamstresses' faces, he shook his head. "And there were a lot of ribbons." Of course, Chandra could've asked them to make the additions in the dark, standing on their heads and they'd have done it. Nothing was too good for the three who'd saved Ischia.

He stopped for a moment, unsure of how to go on.

"I didn't forget my vow, Faharra. I had the emerald in my hand." It seemed that the entire necropolis waited for him to continue and behind him, in the dark of the mausoleum, he could feel the weight of Faharra's kin. He stroked the embossed curve of the urn.

"I couldn't do it." He draped the ribbon around the neck and knotted it. "I thought, maybe, you'd rather have this instead."

A heartbeat's worry that he'd feel like a fool disappeared. It felt right. He sat for a little longer, then he sighed, stood, and carried the urn back into the mausoleum.

At the edge of the boundary between light and dark he paused, then stepped over into shadow and settled Faharra back into the arms of the One Below. He ran his finger down the ribbon for the last time and raised one foot to turn and leave. As he had before, he put it down again.

"Take care of her," he told the goddess, his voice diamond bright in the realm of the dead. "She was the best gem cutter Ischia has ever known."

On the way out, he stole a small brass incense burner from its niche by the door; just to keep his hand in. While slipping it into the deep pocket of his trousers, he could almost hear Faharra's approving cackle.

As the door swung closed, a chance ray of moonlight swept across the altar. Caught by the metallic thread in the ribbon, it lightened the green, burnished the gold, and turned the copper to a red-gold flame.

DAW
Enter the Magical Worlds of

Tanya Huff

☐ **GATE OF DARKNESS, CIRCLE OF LIGHT** (UE2386—$3.95)

The Wild Magic was loose in Toronto, for an Adept of Darkness had broken through the barrier into the everyday mortal world. And in this age when only fools and innocents still believed in magic, who was there to fight against this invasion by evil? But Toronto did have its unexpected champions of the Light: a street musician, a "simple" young girl, a bag lady, an over-worked social worker, a streetwise cat, and Evan, Adept of Light, summoned to stand with these mortals in the ultimate war!

THE NOVELS OF CRYSTAL

☐ **CHILD OF THE GROVE: Book 1** (UE2432—$3.95)

Ardhan is a world slowly losing its magic. But one wizard still survives, a master of evil bent on world domination. No mere mortal can withstand him—and so the Elder Races must intervene. Their gift of hope to Ardhan is Crystal, the Child of the Grove, daughter of Power and the last-born wizard who will ever walk this world!

☐ **THE LAST WIZARD: Book 2** (UE2331—$3.95)

Kraydak, the evil sorcerer was dead, and Crystal's purpose for existing was gone. For in a world terrified of wizards, a land where only Lord Death was her friend, what future was there for Crystal, the last wizard ever to walk the world? Then she used her power to save a mortal's life and forged one final bond to humanity—a bond that would take her on a quest to destroy a long-dead wizard's stronghold of magic, a place which had lured many to their doom.